STAND UP
FOR BASTARDS

A NOVEL

CALEB MASON

First Edition   ISBN 13: 978-1-937484-98-9

AMIKA PRESS

466 Central AVE #23 Northfield IL 60093   847 920 8084
info@amikapress.com   Available for purchase on amikapress.com

Edited by Jay Amberg and Ann Wambach.

Cover photography by Caleb Mason and Florencia Chacón.

Author photography by Frances Iacuzzi. Chapter photography: 1 by gc1366, Pixabay; 7 by Vlada Karpovich, Pexels; 26 by Ryan Abbott; 30, 31, 33, 35, 36, 40, 41 by Caleb Mason; 51 by Caleb Fisher, Unsplash.

Book designed & typeset by Sarah Koz. Body in Miller, designed by Matthew Carter, Tobias Frere-Jones and Cyrus Highsmith in 1997–2000. Titles in Gill Sans, designed by Eric Gill in 1928–32; digitized by Monotype in 1989. Thanks to Nathan Matteson.

To Coleen, Meghan, and Luke

PRAISE FOR **STAND UP FOR BASTARDS**

"Starts with fists flying and never lets up. Mason has created a modern Marlowe—sharp as a tack, at odds with the world, and unrelenting to the last word. An uppercut of a yarn!"

—Nick Wootton, writer, *NYPD Blue;* showrunner, *Scorpion, Golden Boy*

"A brisk page-turner... Mason, a lawyer and former federal prosecutor, writes with authority and a distinctive voice; he clearly knows where all the bodies are buried in this fictional world, and his hard-boiled patois lands as solidly as Marcus' punches.... [A] solid tale.... Truly old-school detective fiction..."

—*Kirkus Reviews*

"A modern day, hardboiled crime novel. Caleb Mason intricately weaves together a compelling story with complex characters that ring true to life. From strong, well-heeled women that you want to root for to the street-savvy investigator with an unsavory past that you want to date, these characters will stay with you long after you finish the last page."

—Esther MyaPe, Detective-II, LAPD Robbery-Homicide Division

"Readers will find the tense action and cat-and-mouse games to be thoroughly engrossing and unpredictable to the end, as the intersection of crime and politics pushes the investigator to his limits. A detective novel that embraces the atmosphere and streets of West and East coasts alike and tells a powerful story about the 'informal side of law enforcement' with a compelling swagger. Highly recommended."

—Diane Donovan, Midwest Book Review

"Always intriguing, with just the right touches of gallows humor. This masterful novel features dirty cops, wily private investigators, and cunning prosecutors, using their wits to follow a trail from rural America to the lairs of the rich and powerful in New York, Los Angeles and Washington DC. Not only did this book remind me of some of the wild and exciting cases I've worked, it made me recall why crime fiction has always been my favorite genre. A captivating read from start to finish."

—Tom Cowley, Los Angeles private investigator and former FBI agent

Why brand they us with base?
With baseness? bastardy? base, base?
Who, in the lusty stealth of nature, take
More composition and fierce quality
Than doth, within a dull, stale, tired bed,
Go to the creating a whole tribe of fops,
Got 'tween asleep and wake? Well, then,
Legitimate Edgar, I must have your land:
Our father's love is to the bastard Edmund
As to the legitimate: fine word,—legitimate!
Well, my legitimate, if this letter speed,
And my invention thrive, Edmund the base
Shall top the legitimate. I grow; I prosper:
Now, gods, stand up for bastards!

—King Lear
Act I, scene 2

STAND UP FOR BASTARDS

Belvedere Castle, Central Park

One

When I play it back in my mind, the kid had it coming. He was a big kid, muscled up, with a sneer on his face. Came out the door of the bodega at Broadway and 137th, saw me, and didn't run. Didn't say a word. Just squared up at me and threw a jab and a hook like we were at the gym fighting fair. Maybe he even landed one. If I lean on the memory a little, I can almost feel a glancing blow above my ear, enough to send a pulse of pain through my head. It would have hurt his hand a lot more. The skull's no place to land a hook, not if you're planning on throwing another punch with that hand.

The kid was planning on it, but I didn't give him a chance. It was a right, the hook, and it pulled him forward, off balance. I stepped back with my left foot, pivoted, and got his wrist in my left hand as his fist glanced off my head. I finished the turn, spinning him the rest of the way around. I brought my right hand straight up, the heel of my hand connecting under his chin. Then I put my forearm into his throat and stepped forward, driving him back into the brick wall. I put some weight into it, and the impact knocked the wind out of him. I helped it along with a straight left under the sternum. Just one. Then I stepped back and let him collect himself to take another shot at me. When he did—

No, that wasn't it. Not really. The memories all blur together now, but every so often, more often than I like, they come back clear and sharp, and I know that the kid—it doesn't matter which kid—didn't take that second shot at me. Probably didn't even square up to begin with. They didn't back then, not much. But I beat the shit out of them anyway, because that was my job.

So nowadays I try not to play those memories back.

When I got the call on the Hausman case, I was in Central Park, up on Belvedere Castle, looking out over the Great Lawn, playing my clarinet. I was playing the clarinet to erase some memories. It doesn't matter which ones. I know you can't erase memories. But sometimes you can push them aside for a while. The clarinet does it for me, most of the time.

I play outside, the way Sonny Rollins did in those years when he was depressed over not being Coltrane. Sonny favored the Manhattan Bridge, and he had to play loud so he could hear himself over the traffic. He could, because he played tenor sax, which is a powerful instrument. The clarinet is about grace, not power. It was the king of swing but never made the transition to rock. Two of the biggest pop stars of the first half of the twentieth century played clarinet. But nowadays? A lot of people don't even recognize it. People confuse it with the soprano sax, the one with the straight bell, the one Kenny G plays.

Soprano sax is what you hear when you're flipping stations in the car and you land on the smooth jazz station. Soprano sax is not a macho instrument. Neither is the clarinet. You might say I play the clarinet to express the more delicate and sensitive side of my personality, the feminine side, almost. You might. But no one ever does.

I don't play outside because I'm trying to be Sonny Rollins. I'll never be Sonny. I have no illusions. I'm a corrupt ex-cop and a thug and a bagman and a fixer. But not when I'm playing my instrument.

I play outside because it's hard to find an indoor space in New York to play a loud instrument. You can't mute a woodwind. The sound comes out through all the holes, not just the bell. Best you can do is put the instrument, your hands and all, in a bag. There are actually some bags sold for that purpose. Supposedly you can cut the sound by half. But

I could never bring myself to play a horn in a bag. Some things aren't meant to stay quiet.

When I was in uniform I used to keep my horn in my patrol car and play whenever I got some downtime. There can be a lot of downtime in cop work. A lot of waiting around. A lot of time to practice.

I don't think it would go over well with most commanders nowadays to pull out your instrument at a crime scene, but this was a long time ago, and my boss played things loose. Especially with me, because I made him a lot of money. I appreciated that, because crime-scene aesthetics are perfect for jazz. Have you ever played your horn leaning up against a dripping brick wall at three in the morning watching the yellow tape flutter over a fresh homicide victim lying where he fell, waiting for the medical examiner to cart him away? I have. I played "Harlem Nocturne" and I think the stiff appreciated it.

I stayed in the habit of carrying a horn with me on the job the whole time I was on the force. You walk into a station house carrying a clarinet case and people think you just bought a fancy new handgun. I kept it in the car with me even when I was doing thug and bagman work. When the job involved violence, I always felt a little bad for the instrument, like it had been offended somehow, even though it had stayed safely in its case.

This particular beating I was remembering was run-of-the-mill. Why it was in my head that day I don't know. They just pop up. I used to think it was a visual cue, like maybe I was near the place where it happened, but that's not it. Maybe it was triggered by the song I was playing. Not the melody, just a phrase. Just a little run of notes, maybe an arpeggio sketching out a chord, then a little alteration. C-F-G, up to C, then down to A-flat. The opening phrase of "'Round Midnight": 1, 4, 5, 8, flat-6. That's all it takes, sometimes. A little run of notes. Maybe something I improvised and forgot, just sitting there waiting for the moment when the rhythm and the chord changes are right. People say that smell and taste are the most powerful memory triggers, but not for me. For me it's music.

It was debt collection, which was what they usually were. The debtor was a dealer in Washington Heights, and the creditor was my precinct captain. The debt was incurred as part of the standard protection agreement, according to which we'd let the dealer work and he'd pay the captain a monthly fee. The fee was a reasonable one and usually the dealers made out okay, but sometimes they'd come up short. Some guys had bigger crews to pay, some had bad business models, some just got unlucky.

My precinct captain at the time was Michael Settentio. "Big Mike." You probably read about him a few years ago when he went to prison. He was very strict about payment. We never, for any reason, tolerated delinquency. If a dealer missed a payment we'd roll on him and re-possess his assets. The problem for the dealers was when their assets couldn't cover the debt. Some guys would take a vehicle, but the captain deemed it too risky. There was department protocol for seized vehicles, and it definitely didn't include just taking the keys and rolling. Bling we could take, but it wasn't much good to us. We didn't wear it, and we weren't about to go wandering around the diamond district looking for buyers.

As for the product itself, it was worthless to the captain. He was in the extortion business, not the drug business. He wanted a revenue stream, not a trunk full of shrink-wrapped bricks of coke. Not that there was usually much product to seize—if the dealer had the product, he could move it and make his payments. It was mostly when he lost a load and didn't have a rainy day fund that we had to pay him a visit. And then we'd take our payment in flesh.

We'd time our visits for maximum viewership, because we needed to do more than just collect the debt. We needed some theater, so that the rules of the game were firmly instilled into every neighborhood entrepreneur, every customer, every mope on the corner.

The crew was pretty small then, mostly the captain, me and another detective, and four or five young uniforms who saw where the money and violence was and wanted some of it. No one else was around that day, so when the captain said jump, I went out to handle it solo.

You'd think it would be scary, walking up on a group of armed drug dealers working their corner. But it never was. They knew I could pull my gun and kill them and I'd get a medal and grief counseling, but if they raised a hand to me they'd be going to the hospital shackled to the gurney guardrail. It wasn't a level playing field. The only time you want a level playing field in a fight is if it's in a ring and you're not betting on it.

And I wasn't worried about accidental violence from someone who didn't know me and thought I was a mope. I still have the cop look, but now I work pretty hard to tone it down. Back then I dressed cop, walked cop, and talked cop. Cowboy boots; fitted suit, usually navy with chalk pinstripes; thigh-length leather coat, three buttons, deep V-cut for an easy reach to the shoulder holster. I had three vests: one black, one tan, and one a dark red-brown marine cordovan that matched my boots. Black leather gloves whenever it was cold enough. And I rolled up in a burgundy Crown Vic that I would double-park down the block so they'd all see me walking up nice and slow, no secret what I was there for.

Sometimes the crew would run. That didn't help them. They would have been better off squaring up and throwing a couple. I'd like to think they did sometimes. I'd like to think a lot of things about the past. But the past doesn't give a shit about what we'd like.

So I answered my phone, and I went to work.

Two

The job was for Eleanor Hausman. If you think the name sounds familiar it's probably because you've seen it on a construction crane. Or an office building, or one of those glass condo boxes on the far West Side. Hausman's not shy when it comes to self-promotion. She was a client of the law firm I used to work for. It's called Montrose Bryant, and you've probably heard of it too, usually in the same sentence as "white-shoe" or "high-powered" or "administration-in-exile."

I was working for one partner in particular. Jennifer Curtis. Yes, that Jennifer Curtis. She's not at the firm anymore either, as you know if you watch the news. But that's at the end of the story. The beginning of the story is back in the Fall of 2008, when I started working on the Hausman job. It was an "administration-in-exile" period for J.C., but after the election everyone knew she'd be going back to DC. The country had voted for Hope and Change, and the smart money said that Hope and Change meant Jennifer Curtis at the Justice Department. She'd been a rising star there back at the end of the nineties and had stayed on for the first term of the outgoing administration. Then she'd left at the beginning of the second term, like a lot of others, and gone back to private practice to do what people like her do at firms like Montrose Bryant. Some of that you read about in the papers. Some of it you don't. I guess that's why I'm telling this story now.

I had been working on another Hausman matter for a few months already. One of her development companies had gotten sued by another development company over some mall project that had fallen through. Bread-and-butter business litigation. That was the practice group J.C. was in, though the label was a matter of administrative convenience more than description. J.C. was a practice group unto herself. She had a team of lawyers that took up half a floor. And she had me. But I'm not a guy you advertise on your firm website.

Hausman was J.C.'s client, and Hausman wanted the lawsuit to go away. That was the sort of thing J.C. was good at. She was famous, of course, in the DC-New York law-and-politics world, anyway, but she wasn't just one of those big names just sitting on the masthead waiting for a change in administration. A lot of firms had those people. Montrose Bryant had some. J.C. wasn't like that. She was a real lawyer. After the election, everyone knew she'd be back in DC soon enough, but while she was at the firm, she was there to work.

J.C. attracted big clients like a stripper on a pole. You don't like the metaphor? I do: powerful men in suits threw money at her to watch her dance. You want a better one? She attracted big clients like an STD clinic at a Catholic college: you come in with a problem, she'll make it go away, and everyone will be very discreet about it.

J.C. attracted legal talent, too. She had a team of Bright Young Things who did not like my metaphors at all, thank you very much. "For several reasons," they would have said, emulating J.C.'s way of talking in roman-numeraled subparagraphs. "First, because they aren't metaphors, they're similes."

J.C.'s boys and girls were variations on a theme: editor-in-chief of the law review, Order of the Coif, clerkship with a federal judge, and all now desperately eager to sacrifice what was left of their twenties for the chance to describe the law in earnest capital letters. J.C. had the Bright Young Things for 2,000 billable hours a year, and they were grateful for every moment of it. If "J.C." was short for Jesus Christ—and to them, it might have been—they were the monks in the cathedral.

To the Bright Young Things, the law was "the Law." They could tell you that "the Law is no less Real for being a Human Construct" and really sell it. The Bright Young Things loved the Law. They were there to learn Real Litigation, to handle Bet-the-Company Cases, to get Down in the Trenches. They were there at seven in the morning, and they were there at midnight, and they were damn happy about it. They lived for the days when they got to walk into court arrayed in a V around J.C. like a formation of black-suited geese or, if you like your similes more military, like a phalanx smashing through the Persian lines to send opposing counsel fleeing in terror on his chariot.

The Bright Young Things weren't into military imagery. They had no psychological need to imagine themselves as soldiers. Their only psychological weak spot was that they hadn't become doctors. But they were primed to rebut any insinuation that all the really smart kids had gone to medical school. They could explain that legal problems were just as real as medical problems and so were the solutions. They really meant it. And they were right: going to prison is plenty real. You take your average busy executive making a ton of money in a legally questionable manner. Does he see much difference between a diagnosis of "You're going to die in prison" versus "You're going to die of cancer"?

I'm not sure where I fit in that metaphor. If the Bright Young Things were the doctors, I was the guy mopping the blood off the operating room floor at the end of the shift. And maybe driving the bodies out to unmarked graves at the edge of town.

So I was on the Hausman lawsuit doing what I was there to do: looking for something that wasn't quite inside the boundaries of the Law, something you'd get to when you got Down in the Trenches and Really Litigated a Bet-the-Company Case, but that you wouldn't put in your brief. That was my specialty, I guess—most of the things I did as a cop were things you wouldn't put in your report.

The Hausman lawsuit was pretty straightforward. Hausman's company had partnered up with a Greenwich investment firm to buy up some decrepit shopping malls somewhere out in suburban America and redevelop them as luxury housing. The first project was a big success, so the Greenwich firm had put in $10 million for the next one. But the next one didn't come through. There were some holdups with the local regulatory agencies, one of the other investors had pulled out, and the project had stalled. The Greenwich firm wanted its money back, and Hausman told them to go pound sand. Business is about risk; sorry, pal.

So they did what companies do in Real Litigation, Down in the Trenches, and they sued Hausman's company. The Bright Young Things got most of the claims dismissed, because the contract—which they had drafted—was solidly on Hausman's side. But as any business litigator will tell you, if the contract's against you, sue for fraud. And their fraud claim made it through the Bright Young Things' legal gauntlet and on to the discovery phase. Discovery is where you get to investigate. It's where I come in. It's the domain of facts—the kind you put in your briefs, and the kind you don't.

The fraud claim was simple: they claimed that one of Hausman's guys, the head of the subsidiary doing the mall projects, had called the head of the Greenwich firm and told him not to worry about the contract because the $10 million wasn't really an "investment," the way the contract had it, but was actually a "loan." It was a clever argument: you could get around the papers you signed by saying you'd been "fraudulently induced" into signing them.

The Bright Young Things had fought back. If you're alleging fraud, they argued, you have to be specific about the who, what, where, when, and how. And the judge agreed. So the Greenwich firm had to file a new complaint and go on record saying when the call came in. Then the Bright Young Things subpoenaed the firm's phone records and the boss's cell records. The boss fought like hell, but he was stuck, because he'd alleged a call in his complaint. "Put up or shut up," said the judge.

Records in hand, the Bright Young Things scheduled the Greenwich boss's deposition. They were split on whether he'd go through with it. Most of them thought we'd get a nice pre-depo settlement offer. Which we did. The Bright Young Things had a pool going on the size of the offer and when it would come in. It came in the day before the depo. I don't know who got head on the bet. I hoped someone did. They weren't getting it anywhere else.

But J.C. wasn't having it. I was in her office when she made the call to tell opposing counsel that she was looking forward to seeing him at the deposition. It was just after sunrise. That was her favorite time of day, and if you were opposing counsel, you took the call. She had a white leather couch along the inside wall of her office, facing east out across Midtown. The couch was my favorite spot in the city early in the morning. It was long enough for four people to sit without invading each other's personal space, but I mostly had it to myself. The Bright Young Things were nervous about sitting in it, even if I wasn't there. J.C. liked them nervous.

"Anxiety's good for a lawyer, Marcus," she would say to me, if they were around. "If you're not wondering whether you fucked something up, then you probably did."

Opposing counsel sounded plenty nervous on the speaker. "But Jennifer," he said, "this is practically a walkaway."

"Practically a walkaway's not good enough, Jared. Your offer still contemplates money going from us to you, which I'm afraid we can't agree to."

"Well, look, we can discuss the figure. Fundamentally, this is a business dispute, right? And it should settle for a reasonable amount—"

"Ok, tell me what you're offering to pay."

"What *we're* offering to pay?"

"Yes."

"But we're not...I mean, my client is the plaintiff here.... We're certainly willing to entertain a lower counter. But we've come down significantly..."

"Jared, I'm sorry. You demanded $20 million. Now you want us to give you one hundred thousand if we settle today and take the depo off calendar. Twenty million to one hundred thousand is a good try. I appreciate that. But my client has already incurred more than that in legal fees, and it's the day before your client's depo. I've personally cleared the entire day."

"You...personally?"

"Of course. You'll be there as well, I'm sure? It'll be so good to see you again."

She hung up and looked at me. "Stay close, Marcus. We'll see how it goes. If we need you, we'll bring you in after lunch."

So there I was up at Belvedere Castle, when my phone rang.

Three

The deposition was in full swing when I walked into the conference room. It was on the floor below J.C.'s, on the southwest corner. You could see across the river all the way out past Newark to where New Jersey started to look green. J.C. was at the table with two of her Bright Young Things next to her. The Greenwich firm boss, Stanley Redmon, was across from her, with Jared Rosen next to him in chalk-striped Armani. The court reporter and videographer were at the head of the table.

J.C. liked videotaping her depos. "It fosters a healthy anxiety in the deponent," she told the Bright Young Things. I appreciated the irony. When I used to interrogate suspects, it was the absence of video that made them sweat.

The room was quiet. I took a seat along the wall and eyeballed Rosen. I'd seen him on the Sunday news shows J.C. was always on. He was a big enough name for cable, but that was as far as he was going to get. His eyes flickered to mine, and he looked back down at his notepad. Redmon was reading from a stack of papers in front of him. After a few moments he looked up.

"Okay," he said.

"This is your Amended Complaint, isn't it?" said J.C.

"Objection," said Rosen, "calls for a legal conclusion."

"I'm not a lawyer," said Redmon, taking the cue.

"No, you are not," said J.C., giving him the same smile she had offered to the Senate panel that had asked her whether she had authorized drone strikes against U.S. citizens in Yemen. "You are, however, accusing my client of fraud and demanding $20 million dollars. So Jared, let's have your client turn to Paragraph 96 of the Amended Complaint, which for the record does not appear in the original complaint. Mr. Redmon, would you read it for me, please?"

Redmon read in a monotone, like a kid ordered to read a Bible passage at his sister's First Communion. "'On or about September 14th, 2007, Defendant's Vice-President Emilio Garza called Plaintiff by phone. In that conversation, Garza told Plaintiff that the $10 million wire transfer would be denominated as an investment in the West-Bridge project, but was in fact a "loan" to Defendant that would be repayable at 10 percent interest per annum in the event that the West-Bridge escrow failed to close.'"

"As you sit here today, do you believe that statement to be true?"

"Yes," said Redmon.

"And did the call come in on your cell phone or your office phone?"

"Cell," he said sullenly. He knew we had his calendar and that he hadn't been in his office all that week.

J.C. set two stacks of paper on the table in front of her and slid one across to Redmon. "Mr. Redmon, these are the call logs for your cell phone from September 7th to September 21st, produced by QuestCom in response to our subpoena. Let's mark this as Exhibit 12, and then let's take a look. I'd like you to identify, if you can, the call in which Emilio Garza told you that your investment in WestBridge was actually a loan."

"I—" said Redmon, but Rosen cut him off.

"Take your time, Stan," he said.

"By all means," said J.C. She looked at her watch. "For the record, it's...2:17." Then she picked up her phone and began scrolling through her email.

Rosen and Redmon made a big show of scrutinizing the list. I watched their eyes. Redmon's lingered in the middle of the second page, and his jaw clenched. Rosen didn't notice.

J.C. waited until Redmon looked up. "Okay," she said, "for the record, it is now 2:24 and Mr. Redmon appears to have completed his review of the call list. Mr. Redmon, having reviewed the list, will you please identify the call?"

Redmon fidgeted. "There's a lot of numbers here."

"Oh, I don't think it's that many," said J.C. "Let me suggest a summary, and please correct me if I'm wrong in anything. There are 346 total calls, but only forty-seven different numbers. Of those forty-seven, twelve are associated with your office or your residences, and one, I believe, is your wife's cell phone. That leaves thirty-four numbers that are not your own. Would you agree with me, Mr. Redmon?"

"I don't know. I mean...that's still a lot of numbers."

"Not too many for my investigator to call them all. How long did it take, Marcus?" J.C. didn't turn to look at me. She kept her eyes fixed on Redmon.

"Couple hours," I said. "Some people were chattier than others."

Rosen wanted to tell me to shut up, but we both knew he wouldn't. He spoke to his client instead. "Just wait for a question, Stan."

"Mr. Redmon," said J.C., "I'll have to insist on an answer for the record. Are you, or are you not, able to locate the alleged call from my client?"

"I don't know where he called from!" Redmon said. "He could have called from anywhere. Maybe he—"

Rosen put a hand on Redmon's arm. "No, no, don't speculate."

J.C. leaned toward Redmon. "May I ask whether you read Paragraph 96 of your First Amended Complaint before it was filed?"

"Objection!" said Rosen. "Attorney-client."

"May I ask why, if you have a clear memory of the call, your original complaint made no mention of the date, time, or place of the call? Or did you not read that one either?"

"Objection. Attorney-client. Don't answer."

"Or has your memory improved over time? Like a fine wine?"

"Badgering! Don't answer."

"Mr. Redmon, isn't it true that there never was any such call?"

"Objection!"

But Redmon wanted to answer. "Yes, there was! He called me, he—"

Rosen spoke over him, grabbed his arm. "No, no, don't answer, don't answer."

J.C. let the room get quiet, then flipped the pages in her stack. "Let's turn our attention to September 9th, shall we? That was a big day for calls, but let's look specifically at one from 11:15 p.m, lasting fourteen minutes. Do you see that one?"

Redmon shifted in his seat. He wouldn't meet her eyes. Rosen looked puzzled. He had no idea, as we had thought.

"Is that the call from my client, Mr. Redmon?"

"I, uh, no. No, no, it's not."

"Hmm. And you're sure about that because you recognize the number?"

Redmon was silent. J.C. turned the screw: "Because I think I heard you testify that my client could have called from anywhere."

Redmon looked at Rosen. "I, uh…"

"While you're thinking," said J.C., "let me just read the number for the record, just so it's clear for the transcript." And she read the number, slowly, a digit at a time, her eyes locked on Redmon's.

Rosen leaned over and Redmon whispered in his ear. Then they angled their heads the other way and Rosen whispered in Redmon's ear.

Redmon looked across the table at J.C. "I, uh, I don't recall."

"You know what," said J.C., "we can make this easy. Let's call it now. Marcus, would you, please?"

I stood up and took my phone out of my pocket, pulled up the call log, and hit Call. I knew she'd pick up; she was waiting for the call. I had talked to her an hour ago. I stepped forward and set my phone on the table, and hit the Speaker button. The ringing echoed in the silence.

"What is this?" said Rosen. "This is totally improper!" He was right. But it was my phone and I was standing next to it, and there was no way Rosen was going to reach for it.

J.C. smiled. "Let's just see who answers."

The phone rang once more, then a woman's voice answered. "Hello?"

"Mr. Redmon?" said J.C.

The voice on the phone sounded surprised, even through the speaker on my phone. She sold it pretty well, I thought. "'Mr. Redmon'? *Stanley?*"

Redmon stared at the phone, then looked at J.C. "Hang it up," he croaked, "hang it *up!*"

The voice on the phone sounded anxious, wounded even. He'd paid for her acting classes, after all. "Stanley? Stanley, is that you? What's going on?"

J.C. nodded at me, and I hung up and pocketed the phone.

"Jared, how about I give you two a minute?" said J.C.

We all got up and walked out. The hallway outside the conference room had floor-to-ceiling windows, looking south over downtown and across the harbor. It was one of those architectural touches that was calculated to intimidate: you really want to challenge us, when we can waste fifty feet of window on a hallway?

The Bright Young Things and I followed J.C. around the corner to the east-facing side of the building, and up a steel spiral staircase. No windows on this hallway. Here they were all in the offices. J.C.'s was halfway down. She didn't care about having a corner. She liked the view straight east, into the sunrise. She did like her space, though. They had knocked down a wall and combined two offices for her when she came over from the Justice Department.

She stood by the window. I took the couch. The Bright Young Things perched in chairs.

"How was she last night?" J.C. asked me.

"Pissed," I said. "She's way too nice for Redmon. Told her he was going to marry her."

"It's touching how stupid they are," said J.C.

"She had no idea he still had a wife."

"Yes, they never tell the girlfriend about the wife," said J.C. "And they never tell the lawyer about the girlfriend." She turned to the Bright Young Things. "And that's the worse blunder, don't you think?"

The Bright Young Things pondered that one. Wives and girlfriends, husbands and boyfriends, were outside of their experience.

J.C. looked down at the printout of call records. "Which one is Garza's, again?"

"On the 16th," I said. "Eight p.m. He was in a cab. Paid the driver cash to let him use his cell. Maybe cautious, maybe his phone died."

"The 16th," she said, shaking her head. "The little weasel was close. But Rosen didn't trust him enough to be specific on the date." She looked at her Bright Young Things again. "Life lesson, kids. When you think your client is lying to you, you verify the fucking story *first*. Because they *always* lie. Jared didn't trust Redmon, so he went with 'on or about' to give himself some wiggle room on the dates. And we got two weeks of calls instead of one day. Including little Brianna in her secret Chelsea apartment." She grimaced. "Did you fuck her, Marcus?"

"No, ma'am," I said, which was true. I allowed myself a wink for the Bright Young Things. I had no idea how they'd interpret it.

"So is Rosen down there on the phone trying to get someone to run all these numbers?" asked one of the Bright Young Things.

I shrugged. "Maybe, but it wouldn't get them anything. The cab driver's a whole lot of nobody, and he's not taking any calls today."

"Why not?"

"Because we're friends," I said, resisting the temptation to give them another wink. They could think what they wanted. But I hadn't had to pay or threaten the cab driver. I just told him that he might be getting some calls from some obnoxious lawyers about some silly lawsuit, and he had a right not to talk to anyone about anything without a subpoena. And I gave him my number and told him to call me if he ever needed anything.

"But they could—" the Bright Young Thing persisted.

"Sure, they'd figure it out eventually. But not today."

"And today," said J.C., "all Redmon cares about is us not coming back down there and asking him questions about Brianna. And so Jared is going to propose a walkaway, with a protective order to keep all the transcripts confidential. Which we will be gracious enough to accept if he also throws in our attorney's fees."

She stood up. "Okay, you two, write up the agreement. Money in our account within three days of signing. And you, Mr. Heaton," she said to me, "why don't you go over and meet Eleanor Hausman. She has a little project you'd be perfect for."

Four

I'm not really Irish, not in any sense that I find meaningful. That's where the name is from, but there have been a hell of a lot of other ingredients thrown into the pot since then. At least that's what it looks like in the mirror. I have no professional interest in my own family history, so I've never looked harder than that. And if you're serious about it, you have to look hard.

I've never liked doing family history work. It seems pretty pointless to me, unless there's a specific question to answer, like who gets what in an estate settlement. I never got some people's obsession with genealogy. Maybe my great-great-grandmother was a princess, you say. Or the disgraced lady-in-waiting of a princess. Or the artist who did that mediocre portrait of the disgraced lady-in-waiting before she fell out of favor. Or whatever.

In your mind your ancestors are glamorous and heroic and will validate your obsessive pursuit of their stories. But they never measure up. They're just nobodies who for some unknowable reasons never bothered to fill in their kids on all the unimportant details of their boring genealogies. I know—the way family trees branch geometrically, if you look back far enough, you'll probably hit someone famous. But really, who gives a shit?

Which is what I would have told Eleanor Hausman when she offered me the job. But I didn't get to say, chin up and chest out, "Sorry, ma'am, I don't do genealogy work," the way Philip Marlowe did about divorce work. I didn't pick my cases; the firm did. But I think I had a better deal than Marlowe. I wasn't just out there on my own. No one in the business is anymore, at least no one I have any respect for. There are some "solo operators" out there, but they're mostly the one-step-from-cons-themselves military/cop rejects who hang around gun shows with laminated bail bondsman licenses in their wallets.

You've seen the guys I'm talking about. Remember Jeff Gillooly? The 1994 Winter Olympics? When his trailer park-to-Lillehammer figure-skater girlfriend hired him to whack her competition in the knee before the Olympic trials? He got himself a tan raincoat and thought he was the Continental Op. He and his partner went down after bragging about the hit in a bar. You can imagine the conversation: "Hey bartender, get me another, I'm celebrating. Today I snuck up on a ninety-five-pound girl and hit her from behind with a billy club."

Even assuming some minimal level of professionalism, why would you want to be solo? Philip Marlowe got beat up by the bad guys and hassled by the cops in every story. Me, I don't get hit on the head much, and nowadays I try not to get rough with anyone if I can help it.

So I could have had it worse. And there are worse things to do than go to meet Eleanor Hausman, for sure. I had heard of her, of course. She was the kind of developer who transformed entire neighborhoods. You never saw just one giant Hausman crane, only block-long packs of them. The buildings all said "Hausman," but she told me to call her Eleanor.

She had to say it twice. I was distracted by her office, so I didn't hear her. I know my league, and I know when I'm out of it.

But I also know better than to admit it. Obviously the effect was intended. People will give you money if you look like you're used to being given money. That's why banks have marble lobbies, insurance companies build giant skyscrapers, and five-star waiters sneer at you. And detectives talk in hard-bitten similes, so everyone will know they're detectives. You play the game; you play to type. I was like a porn starlet going in for a collagen injection.

Ms. Hausman and I played to type. "Call me Eleanor," she said.

"I prefer a certain level of formality in a professional relationship," I said.

"Do you?" she said.

"If we start calling each other by our first names, there's no telling what could happen. *Us Weekly* would run some photos; we'd be in floor seats at Fashion Week. I don't know if I'm up to that."

"I haven't taken a date to Fashion Week in ten years."

"Nor have I." Dig the grammar—it goes with the sport coat.

"I do try to *attend*, though, and I admit it would be inconvenient for me to be seen with you in that...what is that?"

"Tweed."

"Yes, I suppose it is. Well. Shall I call in a stylist to recommend something a little more P. Diddy, or shall we stick to titles?" And pretend we're not itching to adjourn to the red leather couch under the south window, with the Statue of Liberty sticking up behind it like a decorative bronze cherub. But she didn't say that. And only I had to pretend.

"I don't get along well with stylists," I said. "I can't tell taupe from salmon, and they're so rude about it."

"That's a pity," she said. "I know a few who might get along with you." Eleanor Hausman was, according to her press bio, only a few years older than me, but she obviously got along well with whichever regiment of her staff was tasked with keeping her beautiful.

She came around the desk and motioned me to the couch. We sat. The intimacy was stifling. She couldn't have been more than eight or nine feet away. About as close as Hoboken, sitting out there across the Hudson, which shone in the afternoon light. I watched a tugboat pushing a barge downstream. You could get used to that view.

"I have an interesting problem for you, Mr. Heaton," she said, "but perhaps we should discuss it over tea."

"Oh, by all means."

Tea arrived in a gold samovar, with china cups and a silver platter with alternating slices of strawberry and pineapple surrounding a spread of those triangular cucumber sandwiches you always imagine would be on a tray like that.

Neither of us touched the food. Hausman accepted a cup of tea from the black-clad young man who wheeled in the walnut-paneled tea service, but made no move toward the tray. I was damned if I was going to reach for it first. I assumed that the food was a test of some sort: how would I respond to abundance set before me, mine for the taking, no strings attached? I wasn't going to go for that sort of offer because there are always strings attached. If I don't see any, I attach some.

"I want you to find out who I am," she said, when her assistant had gone. When I made no reply she continued. "I want to know more about my family history. Specifically about my parents."

"May I ask why? And what sort of information you have in mind?"

"You may. You have a reputation for discretion, I believe."

"I can't talk about that, I'm afraid." I've always liked that line, but most people don't get it. She did, though. Or at least she gave me a polite laugh for the effort, which was good enough for me. She had a lovely laugh, like Audrey Hepburn in *Breakfast at Tiffany's*.

"My reasons are simple enough. My parents are dead, I'm no longer young and carefree, and I'm curious about where I come from."

"Forgive me, Ms. Hausman, but don't you know where you come from?"

"Actually, no. Not with any specificity. I started boarding school in New England when I was twelve. From that point on, I saw my parents only on holidays. Before that, we lived in various places. Here in the city, Vermont, South Florida. They were in Europe a lot. The point is I just didn't *know* them. They were too rich and too *old*. They had servants to take care of me most of the time."

"Is there money at stake here, Ms. Hausman?" Montrose Bryant had a big trusts and estates practice group. J.C. didn't do that kind of work, but it was possible that she was loaning me out for another partner's case. I can't say that inheritance cases are my favorite kind, but in general they beat divorces.

"Oh, my goodness, no. They left me money, of course, but they've been dead for fifteen years. I'm sure there are no loose ends there. I'd just like to know the story of their lives."

"Just in case maybe you're really Anastasia Romanov's granddaughter?"

She didn't like my tone. "I'll give you what information I have. I'd like a report within the week."

"I'm sorry, Ms. Hausman, but really, doesn't this seem a little silly to you?"

"Not a bit."

"Look," I said, "I've been working the WestBridge case; I have a pretty good sense of your business acumen." I hoped she'd be impressed—ex-cop talk *real* good. "And I see pretty much two reasons why a person like you hires a person like me. There's something you want to find out, or there's something you don't want other people to find out. General curiosity? Doesn't make the list."

"It's my dime, as they say, Mr. Heaton."

"Yes it is. But you didn't scrape together all your dimes by throwing them away on vanity projects."

"I didn't. But now I can, and as vanity projects go, you're about as cheap as they come."

It was true, so I wasn't insulted. I'm sure I wouldn't have wanted to be one of her more expensive vanity projects. Not for more than an hour or two, anyway.

"Just a little genealogical research for fun, then," I said for the record, which was not being kept.

"You got it."

I didn't believe her. Would you believe her? Who would hire a private detective for this sort of thing? But the very rich hire people for everything, and she was right—I billed less than her masseuse. And anyway, she wasn't, strictly speaking, hiring *me:* she was J.C.'s client and had been for years. J.C. might not even be billing her for this.

In the lobby, another assistant—a young woman this time, dressed as the male assistant had been in sleek black, and ready, as he had been, to leap at a moment's notice onto a catwalk—handed me a handsome calfskin briefcase. It was a gorgeous deep red-brown and felt like it had been made from the hide of one of those Japanese steak cows you read about, who get a rubdown with sake every day to keep their meat tender. Best of all, it was big. Big enough, I thought, to close cleanly around a clarinet case. Which is what you look for in a good briefcase, right? When I touched it I had to resist the urge to hold it up next to my face and nuzzle it with my cheek.

"Can I keep this?" I said. "I've been thinking about replacing the cushions on my couch."

"My card's in there," she replied, declining to acknowledge that I was being funny. "Please let me know if you need anything else."

I held up the calfskin case and nuzzled it, just once. "Well, maybe a couple more of these, if this one works with my window dressings."

Five

The Montrose Bryant offices are in midtown, but I have my own space down on 27th Street, in an old warehouse building by the river. The firm has a floor there, for storage and back-office work. I'm not insulted. I prefer the quiet. The space had been leased by a tech start-up during one of the bubbles. The startup went under and Montrose Bryant took over the lease, furnishings and all, for practically nothing.

It's a nice building, architecturally. It's prewar, and I think it has some city landmark designation, which is why it's not a glass condo yet. You could walk by it a hundred times and not really notice it. But you start to notice the details when you look. Gargoyle drain spouts, for instance. I love those.

When J.C. brought me on, the space was mostly empty, just an acre of metal shelving holding all those paper files that accumulate in legal work. She told me to take whatever office I wanted, so I picked out a big room in the back. It had a long window, and under the window was an eight-foot-long, glass-and-steel desk that must have been too heavy for the tech startup boys to take with them when they slunk out of the building. The desk was rounded and asymmetrical, like a cartoon whale, with a wide head on one end and a narrow curling tail on the other. The tail was supposed to curl partway around you, so you could swivel back and forth peering at your multiple Bloomberg screens flashing market reports and a live news feed. I didn't have any Bloomberg screens, but I could swivel like a boss.

The window was big and single pane, so it was a little iffy as an insulator, but I could kick my feet up on the sill and see a triangle of gray river if I angled my chair just right. The whale didn't have a sightline from where his eye would have been.

I opened the calfskin briefcase and spread the contents on the whale's back. The briefcase contained surprisingly little, mostly snapshots with old newspaper articles clipped to them. Hausman was Eleanor's married name, I learned; she had been married briefly to a forgettable-looking man named George Hausman, with whom she'd run the development company until she divorced him. Eleanor and George posed before their wedding cake; on a boat somewhere, looking tan; and on the Sheep Meadow, with Central Park South in the background.

Eleanor's maiden name was Brideshead. Eleanor and George divorced in 1996, the year Eleanor's mother, Samantha Brideshead, died. Harlan Brideshead had died the year before. Harlan had been an old-school Captain of Industry. He owned lumber mills and paper mills from Georgia to Maine. Softwoods, pulped into paper and fiberboard. A local news clipping showed him shaking hands with another suit in front of a giant pile of shorn pine logs.

By the mid-1980s, Harlan had sold most of the mills and put the proceeds into New York real estate. He brought his daughter into the real estate business while she was still in college and set about teaching her everything he knew, as the *New York Post* put it in a fawning profile. By the time she was twenty-five, she was running the day-to-day operations. Eleanor got the rest of the Brideshead money after Samantha's death, plowed it all back into the development company, and became the quasi-public figure we know and love today. Eleanor and George had no children.

That was it. There was Eleanor's birth certificate from a hospital in Charleston, South Carolina, dated February 12, 1968. And there were some childhood photos of Eleanor.

I arranged the photos on the desk. Some had dates written on the back; I managed a rough chronological ranking of the others. At one end of the line of photos, Eleanor smiled broadly in a sports uniform (field hockey? softball?) on a manicured prep-school playing field. On the other end, she gazed solemnly into the camera from the cradle of Samantha's lap. The photo was dated August 1973. Harlan stood next to Samantha, as the two of them displayed for posterity their best Kennedy impressions.

Eleanor hadn't bothered to include newspaper obituaries for her parents, but they were archived electronically, along with everything else the *Times* had ever published, and a minute's search revealed what was obvious anyway from the photos: Samantha Brideshead was too old to have borne a child in 1968. At her death in 1996 she was seventy-eight years old. That made her fifty at the time she would have been giving birth. And that, I was pretty sure, didn't happen before the advent of our modern reproductive medical miracles. No super-ovulation drugs and in vitro fertilization in the Johnson Administration years. An hour's perusal of medical journals confirmed my suspicions. If Samantha Brideshead had given birth in February of 1968, it would have been front-page news across the country. And it wasn't. Not even in Charleston.

Forty years is a long time, but it's not forever. There would be plenty of people still living who would remember February 1968, and I doubted that they'd be hard to find. Which made me wonder why it was me who was going to find them. And why now?

Six

Two weeks later I was back in Hausman's office. Hausman wanted to know what I'd learned. Her assistant showed me into the office. Hausman wasn't there, but a moonlighting Calvin Klein model brought in a tea service again. There were no little sandwiches this time. I didn't complain. I'm used to disappointment.

I settled in to wait. After five minutes of staring out the window at the skyline, I got bored and did some pushups. Hausman came in at thirty-five.

"Why are you doing pushups on my floor?" she said.

I stood up. "I would have used the desk, but I didn't want to mess up your stuff." I like doing pushups on edges—curbs, railings, chairs, desks, whatever's around. Hausman's desk was spotless: completely empty, with only a closed laptop in the center. I had noted its pushup potential on my first visit.

She sat down behind the desk and opened the laptop. I poured myself some tea and sat on the red leather couch.

"I think you're adopted," I said.

"Oh, you think?" she said. "Congratulations, Sherlock Holmes."

"So you want to find your birth parents," I said. "No shame in that, you could have just said so."

"Oh, Mr. Heaton," she said, "I could have done a lot of things, couldn't I?"

I could think of a few, but I didn't mention them. I should have had a snappy comeback ready, but I didn't, so I settled for a cool, professional silence. She sighed, as if she'd been expecting something better.

"Here's the thing," I said, "database searching gets easier every year, and Montrose Bryant pays for the good databases. So I'm pretty sure I've got what there is to find. What we did was—"

"Please, Mr. Heaton, if I have to listen to a detective story, at least I want a dark alley and a man coming around the corner with a .45."

"Well, if you're free tonight, I know a few pretty close by."

"Just skip to the results, if you would."

"Right. What I was getting to. See, databases are only as good as the information in them, and when you go back more than a decade or two, there's a lot of information that never got entered in any database. I mean, you must run into that in real estate, right?"

"Certainly. Your point?"

"Like in the Department," I said, "with all the data coming in every day with CompStat, they can barely keep up with the new cases. Going back and filling in the entire past? Like summer interns going through file cabinets page by page and coding arrest reports? Forget about it."

"Yes, well, if I could have employed a summer intern for this project, I imagine I would have done so."

I shrugged. "Harlan Brideshead was a big-shot executive. Probably meant about the same then as it does today. Big-shot executive today can't keep a lot of secrets from a guy like me. Give me a couple hours and I can fill in more details of his life than he can probably remember. But back a generation? It gets harder."

"So if you could condense your labors down to a single paragraph?"

"Okay, say I was curious where Captain of Industry Harlan Brideshead was on February 12, 1968, the day baby Eleanor Brideshead was officially born, according to your birth certificate. But by hypothesis your birth certificate's a phony, because it listed Samantha Brideshead as your birth mother, and you can count as well as I can. Also, according to Wikipedia, February 12th isn't your birthday."

"We always celebrated it in October. They told me the date on the birth certificate was just a clerical error, but they kept it for sentimental value."

"Right. So let's assume February 12th was *someone's* birthday. We can start with it and see if it was yours. Hospital was in Charleston, South Carolina. That's good, because the Brideshead family had a big mansion there going back to before the Civil War. Sold and demolished, now it's a hotel. Hospital too. Gone since 1985. Last piece of information on the birth certificate is the attending physician. Someone did a good job filling it in illegibly by hand, and my best guess is it says 'Smith' anyway. So we're left with the date."

"So? If the rest is, as you say, 'phony,' why not the date too?"

"I don't know. Maybe it is, maybe it isn't. As *you* say, it appears to have meant something to your parents. But if you were adopted, it wasn't in 1968. Unless you have some baby pictures you didn't give me, the earliest picture you have, you're about four, maybe five. So whether the date's real or made up, whatever date they used, they couldn't go back in time and retroactively change the facts about what they were doing on that day. See the point?"

She nodded.

"Now a guy like Harlan Brideshead lives most of his life in public, right? He has a busy schedule, and there are a lot of records of where he was and what he was doing. Finding them is a little harder than just Googling a name and date, but they're out there."

"Where, specifically?" she said.

"Corporate records are the best," I said. "Harlan was on the boards of three publicly traded corporations. Public companies have to make all sorts of reports to the SEC, including reports of their quarterly board meetings. And the SEC keeps everything. Anyway, one of Harlan's companies was a lumber company with its headquarters in Fayetteville, Arkansas."

"Southern Mill & Pulp," she said. "I know, I liquidated it."

"In 1995," I said. "It was losing money. But it used to be pretty profitable, back in the day. Point is...Southern Mill had its 1968 winter shareholders' meetings in Fayetteville. A whole week of meetings, starting on Monday, February 12th.

"All right, so maybe Harlan just sent Samantha off to Charleston to give birth? Maybe, except that small-town papers back then still ran society columns. And the *Northwest Arkansas Times* ran a nice column on February 13th about a reception hosted by the Bridesheads the night before at the historic Carnall Hall Inn on the campus of the University of Arkansas."

She looked at me silently for a moment and then nodded.

"Did you try October, too?"

"October 5th, per Wikipedia, yes I did. They were here in New York, at the opening-week gala for the Met."

She nodded again. "Is there more to find?" she asked.

"There's always more to find. I'll need a little more material to work with, though."

"What do you need?" she said.

"The usual. Your parents' tax returns and medical histories, for a start. Then dinner."

What the hell, why not? She was about my age, and gorgeous, and worth a hundred million dollars.

Central Park, looking up at the Dakota and the San Remo from the Lake

Seven

Eleanor Hausman would be delighted to take me to dinner, I learned the next day, when I got a call from one of her fashion-forward gazelles. It was the female one, the one who had given me the calfskin briefcase. I could hear the disdain in her voice at the idea that anyone would be delighted to have dinner with me. She curtly informed me that a car would pick me up.

I tried for a cutting witticism, but she didn't bite. "Wardrobe suggestion?" I said. "Nothing too specific, just give me a couple looks to play with and I'll make them my own."

There was a brief pause while my phone started to freeze. I thawed it under my armpit.

"That won't be necessary," she said. "Goodbye, Mr. Heaton."

I went formal anyway, going with a nice trial-testimony suit, blue pinstripes, with a blue fedora. I've been a fan of the fedora for twenty years, and I was thankful the kids in Williamsburg were bringing them back.

The gazelle was partly right; I didn't need to worry about a dress code because dinner was in Hausman's apartment. But I was glad I'd primped; her apartment was nicer than any restaurant I'd ever been to, and there were plenty of staff around to get snooty if I'd been underdressed.

Not to mention that Hausman herself emerged to greet me in a dress that was probably already back-ordered for starlets all the way through awards season. I didn't ask, "Who are you wearing?" because I was being polite. And it would only have revealed that I didn't already know, which I sensed most of her dates would have.

Her apartment was on Central Park West. You know the building if you ever hang out by the Lake and watch the swans and the young couples in love. It wasn't quite a penthouse, but it had about an acre of floor space and a wraparound terrace on the southeast corner.

Dinner was more or less what you'd expect. I probably should have taken pictures of the dishes, so I could study them later and learn what to look for in a really elevated plating. Or I could have focused on the view, a view that Saudi princes would trade tanker ships of oil for.

But I couldn't take my eyes off of Hausman.

She asked a few polite questions about police work. Nothing too specific—nothing about the 30th Precinct or the state corruption probe. It had dominated the papers just a couple years back, but my name had never come up. And J.C. must have warned her off of "so why'd you leave the force?"

I returned the favor by not asking her about real-estate development. I tried: "So how did you meet J.C.?"

She laughed. "Oh, you call her that too? I always thought that was such a freshman-year, Women's Studies 101 thing."

"It's kind of universal now," I said. "With the lawyers, anyway."

She nodded. "She always said it was for practical reasons. Too many Jennifers. She showed me a *New Yorker* cartoon of an elementary school class picture where every child was named Scott or Jennifer. She was never a 'Jennifer' to me, though. She's always been Jenny."

I tried to imagine someone calling J.C. "Jenny." I couldn't do it.

"Have you known her a long time?"

"Our parents moved in the same circles. I went to Choate before they sent me up to Groton. Jenny went to Brearley. Then we both went to Wellesley. She was two years ahead of me. I got to know her my freshman year. We road-tripped out to LA that summer. Feels like we've been together ever since. When we were kids, I was on the Upper East Side, and she was over here, just across the park. Now we're just trading places." She made an elegant circle in the air with her finger.

"Were you friends, as kids?"

"Not so much. I imagine I got dragged over to the Curtises' a few times a year for some event or other. That was basically it."

"How about other childhood friends?"

"Ah, the interrogation!" She stood abruptly and went to the sideboard bar. "I really need a cigarette, but this will do, I guess. Whiskey sour?" She poured two.

She selected a leather divan by the window and draped herself over it. "I know what you're after. But early childhood? Mostly a blank. I was an only child with rich, absent parents. I probably wiped the memories out of boredom. My earliest memory is right down there."

She pointed down at the darkness of the park. "I was on the grass bank by the Lake, and one of the swans came swimming by. Probably it was a goose or a duck, but in my memory it's always one of the swans. It turned its head and looked at me, and I just wanted to be in the water with it, so I ran down the hill, across the path, and straight into the water."

She swirled the ice in her glass and took a sip. "I have no memory of being scared. I don't even have a memory of going under. I don't remember learning to swim, but I guess I must have."

"How old were you?"

"I'm not sure. Six? Five, maybe? I remember a nanny pulled me out, but I don't remember which one."

"How about your parents? What's your earliest memory of them?"

"Oh, God, hardly anything before maybe sixth grade, really. Which I know is probably just proof that they were never around, not that I was adopted. But...I don't know, what about you? What are your earliest memories of your parents?"

I shrugged. "My mom, she's in pretty much all of them. My dad? Who knows. I never knew my dad."

She stood and reached out her glass to clink with mine. "Then we

33

are two peas in a pod, Marcus Heaton. To absent fathers." She tossed back her drink. "Excuse me a moment." And she disappeared into the labyrinthine recesses of the apartment.

She reemerged a minute or so later. She'd let her hair down and had a fresh highball glass in each hand. My keen detective's eye marked them both as positive signs.

"I was just seeing the cook out," she said. "I told him I could fend for myself."

"I'm sure that's true," I said.

"So we're done, then, are we? With the interrogation?" She still held both glasses, as though whether she'd offer me one depended on my answer.

What the hell, then. If she wanted to fulfill her fantasy of fucking a cop, I wasn't going to stand in the way. Not that I was a cop anymore. I wasn't sure how that played with the standard fantasies. Or if her fantasies were the standard fantasies. They probably weren't.

I tried for a half-decent line. "With the questions? Yes, we're done. I may need, uh, a little more from you, though, at, uh…"

I couldn't pull it off. But she didn't care. "Oh, undoubtedly." She handed me a glass. I clinked her glass and took a sip. Some kind of whiskey cocktail. Not a sour. More of an old-fashioned, but missing the orange and cherry.

She looked at me over the rim of the glass. "Like, for example, a DNA sample?"

I held her gaze. I wanted to get at least one of the lines right. "Yes," I said, "I may need that."

"I thought you might," she said. She opened a drawer on the credenza and pulled out a package of cotton balls and an envelope. She took out a cotton ball, held it up to her mouth, and looked at me over it as she worked it over with her tongue. She dropped it in the envelope. "Is that the technique?"

"Uh, usually you put it, uh—"

"Put it in? Of course." She pulled out a fresh cotton ball, held it between two fingers and her thumb, and put it in her mouth. No quick cheek swab, either. She sucked on her fingers like a White House intern.

Then she delicately deposited the cotton ball in the envelope and sealed it. She reached out and took my hand, put the envelope in it, and closed my fingers around it. She leaned forward. I could feel her breath on my neck.

"The thing is, detective," she said, "to really analyze your sample, I think you need it absolutely fresh." She reached up, put her free hand around my neck, and filled my mouth with her tongue.

She tasted like whiskey and smelled like money. You don't have to know perfumes to pick the expensive ones. Hers probably came from the pollen of a flower that only blooms once a decade on a remote Himalayan peak.

She stepped back and looked at me critically. "I think you might need some more, just to be sure," she said. Then she grabbed my tie and pulled me into the bedroom.

Eight

Llewellyn Trask, MD, was old-school patrician. He hadn't missed a detail, from his Park Avenue address to his French cuffs to his shimmering white mane, which thrust up from his forehead and cascaded back down to his collar (white, on a blue shirt). His mane was layered and tapered to factory specifications and probably required professional fine-tuning once a week, but it was worth it, if your goal was to get people to stare at your head. I had to keep reminding myself to lower my gaze.

He had the posture, handshake, and perfectly maintained eye contact of a man who was used to other people feeling anxious around him. I wondered if this was typical of psychiatrists. The only one I'd met was right at the end of my NYPD career. Maybe it was a great session. I don't know. I was too drunk to remember much of it.

Trask settled himself in a leather armchair the color of an expensive Scotch. "So Eleanor Hausman has sent a detective to ask me questions about her. I shall chalk that up to the unavailability of the hour rather than the tedium of the conversation."

"I bet she could find an hour, Doctor, but I think she doesn't want to hear what you're going to say. Easier to filter it through me."

"And what ugly truth do you believe Ms. Hausman wishes to be filtered?"

"I think she's adopted, and I think she's known, or suspected, for a long time. Now she wants to find her birth parents, but she's not sure she wants them to know about her. That's my guess, anyway. She didn't tell me straight out."

"What did she ask you to find out?"

"She said to find out about her parents. She said she never really knew them."

"And you took that locution as evidence of a displaced fear of having been adopted?"

"Her unwillingness to say the word? Yeah, I did. I told her that was a strange thing to spend money on a PI for, without any concrete purpose. She said my time is cheap."

"Is it?"

"For her it is."

He sighed. "It's a great pity, this obsession people have with biological origin. I recall a study in which the paternity of a random group of subjects was tested. Fully 10 percent, if memory serves, turned out not to be the biological children of the men they thought were their fathers. A fortuitous discovery, I believe; the researchers were looking for something else. But the subjects, needless to say, were not made happier by that knowledge."

He spoke in the measured cadences of a man whose workdays were spent in a cool, dim room speaking to edgy, unstable people. He could have told you that you had terminal cancer or that you'd won the lottery, and either way you'd just nod and feel kind of sleepy.

"Eleanor Hausman recently turned forty, with no children of her own," he said. "Searching for her family roots is a perfectly normal emotional response. She has no biological connection to the future, and an uncertain connection to the past. She has buildings that bear her name, but no people. That dichotomy can be profoundly distressing."

"You have a lot of patients with their names on buildings?"

He smiled indulgently. "I can assure you, she's getting her money's worth if you succeed."

"So she is adopted?"

"That is for you to determine, Mr. Heaton. I was never explicitly told so by the Bridesheads."

"But you suspected?"

"More in the way of a hunch than a firm conclusion."

"Did you ever mention this hunch to Eleanor? You were her doctor."

"She was a child, and that was a different era. The notion that a patient has a right to be told everything her doctor suspects—that's a very recent invention. I was trained to keep to myself facts that might disrupt a patient's emotional stability. In the seventies, it would have been the height of medical irresponsibility to suggest to a troubled young girl that the people she thought of as her parents were in fact not."

"You mean you'd just sit on this information and leave your patient in the dark?"

"In the dark, Mr. Heaton, is where many of us prefer to stay. Self-knowledge is not an unalloyed good. I assume in your line of work you have had occasion to apply that particular maxim?" He raised his eyebrows and gazed at me under them.

"So did you tell her or not?"

"I did not. The Bridesheads brought Eleanor to me because she was having difficulty sleeping. She had nightmares. She was anxious and prone to panic attacks. Nowadays, I suppose, a five-minute consultation and a bottle of pills would be the standard of care. But things were different then. I was retained to talk to the girl, get to know her. I had the distinct impression that her parents did not."

"Didn't know her?"

"Precisely. Let me give you an example. When I asked her her name, the girl responded 'Lynn.' This seemed to me to be possibly a diminutive of 'Eleanor,' albeit one I had never heard before. But her parents called her 'Eleanor' exclusively, indeed, I may say, with a subtle emphasis, as if they were trying to impress that name upon her."

"What about the nightmares?"

"Oh, the usual nonspecific symptoms. She woke up crying, was difficult to console, feared being left in her room alone. Unfortunately, children can rarely report details of their dreams."

"But you concluded—"

"I concluded that the Bridesheads were more than capable of providing the child with an adequate home and education, and that whatever early trauma she had suffered would fade with time. Adoption is not, in itself, an evil fate for a child, Mr. Heaton. Children are put up for adoption because their birth parents are unable to care for them. The child was fine. My role was essentially one of reassurance for the parents."

"Did you treat the parents, too?"

"I did. I saw Samantha for many years. Harlan somewhat less. He was resistant to medical advice in any of its forms."

"So you knew them when they adopted Eleanor?"

"Careful with the cross-examination, counselor. I did not say they adopted Eleanor, and no, I did not know them before they brought Eleanor to see me."

"So you don't have a theory on where she was born, assuming she was, in fact, adopted?"

He smiled. "Mr. Heaton, I don't believe I said one way or the other, did I?"

"Do you?"

"I'm afraid I'm not in the business of theorizing."

"Well, if you decide to get into the business, give me a call. At the moment, I'm down to you and Harlan's tax returns."

Nine

Harlan's tax returns were actually pretty interesting, at least if you were looking for what I was looking for: something around 1973 or 1974 that just didn't fit. Something that might be connected to the sudden appearance of a little girl.

According to his tax returns, 1973 and 1974 were good years for Harlan. The whole decade was good for Harlan. The rest of the country might have been heading for stagflation and malaise and an energy crisis, but Harlan's income didn't suffer any. And then 1980 was a downright bonanza for him when he sold off most of his interest in the paper empire to a big multinational conglomerate.

On Harlan's tax returns, that bonanza meant that he had to declare a whole heap of capital gains. Capital gains are what you get when you sell something that has increased in value since you bought it. That something is usually stock. I'd never owned any stock. I could understand the concept of a thing increasing in value over time, but nothing I owned ever had. My possessions went the opposite direction.

The thing about capital gains is that you have to report them to the IRS, and in 1980, when he sold most of his shares, they were taxed at 36.5 percent. So Harlan owed quite a bit. As in twenty million or so. And so, being a fiscally prudent guy, he listed some capital losses as well, to offset the gains and take the edge off the tax bite.

Most of the losses looked like accounting mumbo jumbo of the sort I saw all the time when the firm rooted through financial records in J.C.'s cases. She had accounting experts, of course, but I liked to tag along to get the lay of the land. And one of the declared losses jumped out at me. Harlan had declared a million-dollar capital loss in 1980 from a December 1973 investment in a company called Talley Oil and Gas, in Mandanoches, Texas.

I thought J.C.'s accounting pros would find that a little fishy. Fishy because Harlan had never been in the oil business, before or since. Fishy because Mandanoches, Texas, was a dot on the map on the Louisiana border a hundred miles from nowhere, and as far as I could tell Harlan had no property or business dealings there.

Fishy because a capital loss is a write-off, a lost investment, a bad deal, money that disappeared after you paid it out. But Talley Oil didn't disappear. According to the Texas Secretary of State's office, Talley Oil and Gas was still a going concern.

Fishy because Talley Oil and Gas was incorporated, according to the same Texas Secretary of State web page, in November 1973, only a month before Harlan put a million dollars into it.

And fishy because when Harlan made his investment in Talley Oil, crude oil was selling for twenty dollars a barrel. In 1980? It was at a hundred dollars a barrel. And Talley Oil was selling a lot of crude. So by my high-school-graduate math, just looking at the price of oil, you'd think Harlan's investment in Talley Oil was a four-million-dollar capital gain, not a million-dollar capital loss. J.C.'s accountants might have had a lot more to say about it. But one thing seemed clear enough to me: Harlan didn't get his million dollars back.

So I went to the airport and bought a ticket for Shreveport, Louisiana, which was as close as you could fly to Mandanoches, Texas.

I drove west from the Shreveport airport, toward the Texas line. Mandanoches— "Your Friendly Destination City!" according to the sign at the town line—was the first town on the Texas side of the border. The sign also said the population was 35,756, which struck me, like the slogan, as a bit optimistic. There had been oil here in the '50s, I knew, but the wells were mostly tapped out now. And the remaining industries—pine trees and chickens, as far as I could tell—weren't enough to stem the migration to Houston and Dallas.

There were 118 births at the Mandanoches hospital in 1968, helpfully filed by month in a steel filing cabinet in a narrow hallway in the records room, to which a pleasant young woman at the front desk was happy to direct me. "You just take your time, now, and if you find what you're looking for, why I can make you copies," she said. "Ten cents a page."

I wondered if the Bridesheads had put Eleanor's real birth date on the fake birth certificate. Regardless, the girl in the 1973 photo couldn't have been more than four, or five at the outside. I decided to start with 1968, on the chance that the Bridesheads had kept the right birth year, and see if I could find any Lynns.

I started in December and worked backward. There were sixty girls, and it took less than a minute to flip through the files. There was a Sue-Lynn Hempersett, born on February 12. Nice of the Bridesheads to use her real birthday. Continuity and all that. I wondered idly whether Eleanor Hausmann would be a real estate magnate today if all else in her life were unchanged but she had had to live it as Sue-Lynn Hempersett. Then I imagined myself the victim of the same compound-naming ritual from which Eleanor had escaped. Billy Ray Heaton. Jimmy Joe Heaton. And I wondered whether, if I'd been born down here, looking like I did and with the mix of DNA that animated my cells, I would have grown up white or black. It was something I'd never wondered in New York.

I handed the woman a dollar and got my copies, then drove in a lap around the downtown, thinking over my options. Talley Oil's drilling operations were registered with the Texas Secretary of State's office. There were a lot of them, spread out from East Texas up through northern Louisiana, but the closest one was about ten minutes outside of town. I hadn't thought there was much drilling left in East Texas, but I figured now would be the time to find out. At least then I'd have an answer, you know, if someone asked about it at a cocktail party or something.

I found my answer ten minutes later. A big gate on the side of the two-lane blacktop read: "Talley Oil. Private Property—Keep Out." Beyond the gate was a gravel road leading into the middle of a field of some low crop—soybeans, maybe?—where a big skeletal metal tower stood, splayed out at the base into a mangrove forest of piping. A couple of mobile office trailers sat at the base of the tower, on the edge of a dirt parking lot occupied by three pickups and an empty flatbed.

The gate was open, so I turned in and parked on the gravel road leading to the tower. I walked up to the dirt lot and looked around. I didn't see any activity or hear any voices, so I walked on past the office trailers toward the tangle of pipes at the base of the tower. It was big, close up. A hundred feet? One-fifty? It didn't seem to be operating, though. I was about to turn back when I heard the crunch of boots on the gravel behind me.

"Get the fuck away from the rig, boy," said a Texas voice. Not a nice voice, either. It was a voice carefully calculated to project maximum toughness. It didn't impress me. Real tough guys tend to be polite. A tough-guy voice is usually a mask for deeper insecurities.

I turned around. There were two of them. "Afternoon," I said. "Anything I can do for you gentlemen?"

"Like I said. Get the fuck away from the well. Then get the fuck out of town and stay out." The speaker was the smaller of the two. He was about forty, with a sunburned face, wiry arms, and stringy brown hair brushed straight back from his forehead. He had on cowboy boots, jeans secured by a giant oval belt buckle with a map of Texas on it, and a white T-shirt depicting a skeleton riding a motorcycle and waving a Confederate flag. He had his T-shirt tucked under the belt buckle, so that Texas was being besieged from the north by the slowly encroaching glacier of his gut, like in the last Ice Age. Real Texas had survived the last one. Belt-buckle Texas didn't look like it was going to be so lucky.

"No, that's not quite it," I said. "It's more like 'Tell us what the fuck you're doing down here,' right?"

They looked blank. The bigger one adjusted his posture. The older guy was average-sized, but next to his hulking buddy he looked tiny. The young guy was barely out of his teens and didn't look like he'd fully grown into his huge body. He was a head taller than the older guy and could have been twice his weight. He had a similar outfit, except that his belt buckle was a monster truck crushing a line of cars, his Confederate flag was on the bandana tied around his head, and instead of a T-shirt he wore a flannel work shirt with the sleeves cut off. His arms were big but soft. I could see at a glance he wasn't a fighter.

I tried again. "I mean, don't you want to ask me what I'm doing here before you dive right into 'Get the fuck out'?"

They still looked blank, but the older guy thought of something to say. "Gonna fuck you up anyway," he said, stepping toward me with his chest thrust out. They definitely were in the mood for a beating. They were naive. I had been in the beating business for as long as the younger one had been alive.

I looked at the older one. "Well," I said, "what can I tell you? The boss sent me out to find you guys. Says you've got to stop sucking this guy's cock on company time."

I jerked my thumb at the young guy, and the older guy's eyes followed reflexively. I stepped to my left, putting the older one between me and the younger one, and hit the older one with a short right above the belt buckle. It was a good punch, and I felt the wind go out of him instantly. He bent over, clutching his stomach and gasping. I took hold of him under both his arms and crow-hopped back a step, getting him moving forward. Then I planted my back foot and swung him around me counterclockwise, letting his momentum do the work.

I brought him around 270 degrees and released him right into the knees of the big guy, who had stood there gaping at the punch, as I knew he would. The older guy rolled into him like a fullback throwing an illegal block on a defensive end. The big guy staggered and clutched at the little guy to keep his balance. His face was wide open for a right cross to the nose, but I didn't want to hurt him too badly. He was really just a kid. I took one quick step and got behind him, crooking my right arm up and under his chin.

He was taller than me, so I had to reach up to get my arm around his neck. That made the hold more effective when I grabbed my right wrist with my left hand and cranked back on his neck, jerking his head back and squeezing his carotids with my bicep and forearm. I leaned away from him and took a step back, pulling him back with me. I stretched him out into the position Ali adopted when Foreman pushed him back against the ropes in Kinshasa in 1974, when Norman Mailer said he looked like a man leaning back from a ladder to reach up and clean out his gutters. Except that the big guy didn't have any ropes to hold him up. Just me, with my arm wrapped around his neck. I lowered his head to the level of my chest, so I was holding up most of his body weight. I cranked my hold tighter. You get a fat guy off balance, it's easy to keep him there.

I saw the little guy picking himself up from the ground, taking a deep breath, and girding himself to come at me again, so I dropped the big guy. He fell flat on his back with a thud. I gave him ten seconds at least to get himself back in the game.

The little guy had recovered enough to take a wild swing at me with his right. It was a wet noodle of a punch—telegraphed, off-target, and way too circular. I blocked it with my left and broke his nose with a straight right, just a little jab, as gentle as possible. The nose is a much better place to land a punch than the jaw or the chin. It will crumple and absorb the impact like a Volvo, and I had no desire to break a hand hitting the hard parts of the guy's head. He dropped to one knee, clutching his hands to his face.

The big guy was now back up and decided to bull-rush me, which was a really terrible plan. I sidestepped him like a matador fighting in a warm-up round against a slow and predictable animal, and caught him with a hook to the kidney as he went past. He twisted sideways and almost fell again, and his momentum slammed him against the wall of the nearest trailer.

With one step I was in front of him with my feet set. The kid couldn't even get his guard up. It didn't seem fair to hit him in the face. So I aimed a straight front kick at his sternum, driving him back into the wall. The wall was made of cheap plastic siding, and it dented nicely around his body in a snow angel pattern. He slid down the wall and slumped over.

I turned back to the older guy. He had stood up again and taken his hands off his nose. Blood streamed down his face, but it wasn't that bad. He glared at me. "I'm a fuckin' kill you!" he bellowed, spitting out the blood that had run into the corners of his mouth. I saw him looking around on the ground for something to grab to hit me with. There were some lengths of pipe lying nearby, but they would be too heavy to swing effectively.

He went for one anyway. It was rusted brown and at least three feet long. It was an absurd choice of weapon. He had to use two hands to lift it, and his backswing would take so long we'd need an intermission before the blow landed.

"Oh, give me a break," I said. He couldn't have seriously thought he was going to be able to hit me with the pipe. But he wasn't thinking clearly, and I was not in the mood to escalate. I was on a genealogical research trip, and those were supposed to be nonviolent. So I reached in my pocket and got out my spray canister. I hadn't bothered to bring a gun along on the trip, but in my line of work you don't just walk around defenseless. I had a little can of pepper spray in my jacket pocket, with a breath freshener label on it. I caught him flush in the face with a burst of it as he was hefting the pipe. It put him on the ground instantly, the way it does. His screams were loud and dissonant. The pepper spray must have stung worse with his broken nose.

I turned to the big guy, who was still sitting against the wall, but showing signs of stirring. "Stay," I said and pointed a finger at him. He slumped back down. I turned and walked down the gravel path and through the gate to my car at a quick walk.

I pulled out onto the blacktop and went about a mile back toward town, then turned on the first side street I saw and parked behind one of those three-ton, eight-foot-bed, double-rear-wheel, six-miles-a-gallon behemoths that lumbered like hippos through the streets of Mandanoches. This one sprawled ponderously on the curb, at an uncomfortable angle. The truck was good cover. I adjusted my mirror and watched the road coming from the oil field.

They drove past me, about five minutes later, in another version of the truck I was parked behind. I followed, discreetly. The older guy drove slowly, no doubt still bleary-eyed from the pepper spray. They weren't watching for a tail, and it was apparent where they were heading anyway: the pickup was emblazoned with big yellow letters, reading "Talley Oil and Gas", and it headed back into Mandanoches and turned into a parking lot bearing the same emblem, a block off the town square.

So there went my introduction to Talley Oil management. No time like the present, then. I pulled over on the next block, between a Dairy Queen and a Jiffy Lube. The two buildings were oddly identical, so that if you were drunk and illiterate it might not be obvious which was which. I took out my phone and got the Talley Oil number, and then I got a receptionist who assured me that Mr. Talley was in the office and was extremely busy, but since I was in from New York, if I cared to come in and wait, she thought he might could see me. I liked the sound of the "might could." Maybe I'd try it out on Hausman's assistant.

I put on a tie and walked down the driveway to the office. It was a low brick building surrounded by pine trees and a green lawn. The landscaping was subdued: no lawn jockeys or plastic deer. The lobby featured framed prints of oil derricks and pumpjacks at sunset. The pumpjacks looked like birds pecking at the desiccated soil. The land-scapes didn't look local, though—more like West Texas, where the desert was. East Texas got plenty of rain, from the looks of the foliage around Mandanoches.

I gave my name to the young receptionist at the desk in the corner. She looked about twenty and wore a necklace with inch-high gold Greek capitals, which dangled just above her cleavage.

"Phi Beta Kappa?" I asked.

"Oh, no, *Sigma* Kappa," she said brightly, pointing to the letters in turn. "Kappa's right, though. You know it's just K."

"Timeo Hellenes," I said, to prove that I too could plumb the depths of an ancient tongue.

"We didn't have that one at A&M," the girl would have said, if she'd allowed me to play out my script. But she didn't say her line. She just smiled and said that I could just go right back.

Right back meant down a cedar-paneled hallway lined with more framed photos, mostly of men shaking hands or patting each other on the back. I guessed that the recurring figure was Talley—"Pops" as he was apparently known, judging from the inscriptions. I didn't recognize any of Talley's pals. At the end of the hallway was an anteroom with another secretary, this time a gray-haired woman in her early sixties. You could see at a glance how beautiful she had once been.

"Well now, what can we do for you today?" she asked. "Tea?"

Which meant iced, I'd learned at the hotel, so I accepted.

"I'm Linda Waters." She smiled warmly at me. "And you must be...?"

"Marcus Heaton, ma'am."

"From New *York*. Yes, of course. Well, go right on in. He's not doing anything."

I carried my tea through the open doorway behind the secretary's desk and into Talley's inner sanctum. I compared it, as I always do, with my own. Pops Talley's office was a dark, wood-paneled room with a large bay window with inset French doors behind the desk that looked out onto a riot of bright-colored flowers whose names I did not know. Whites, pinks, and yellows predominated. East Texas foliage was luxuriant. The thick hothouse atmosphere, so oppressive to large northern mammals, was delicious to the flowers. East Texas mammals—chiefly possum and armadillo, if the flattened corpses on the highway were a fair sample—prowled at night.

Talley was at least seventy, paunchy in a yellow golf shirt and Houston Oilers baseball cap. Under the hat his hair was thick and white. His arms were huge, hairy, and mottled. He was leaning back in an enormous red leather chair, smoking a cigar. The smoke curled up and was wafted around the room by cold gusts of air pouring in from the ceiling vents.

"Have a seat, Mr. Heaton," he said companionably, gesturing to a smaller version of his own chair in front of the desk.

"I see you're a nostalgic man, Mr. Talley," I said, pointing to the cap.

"Ah, hell, I cain't pretend to have any oil left; I might as well pretend to have a god damn football team." His "cain't" was precisely pronounced, exactly as I would have said it were I trying to imitate the thick, genteel accent he shared with the older secretary, and his "god damn" was distinctly two words, like Hemingway's. "Oil" sounded to me like "oral."

"Funny thing about football teams," he continued, "seems like they can just up and move anywhere they please. Alla those teams, come to think on it. The Rangers ain't nothin' but the old Senators. And hell, they're playing *hockey* up in Dallas, for Chrissake, team's called the Stars, but you know they just lopped the 'North' offa the 'Stars' and gave us a damn team from Minnesota."

"Well, in New York, both our football teams play in Jersey, and we lost two baseball teams to California," I offered. Maybe we'd bond over universal human suffering.

"Ain't that a shame? What a pity you cain't just up and follow them."

"I'm kind of rooted in New York. Anyway, it was a long time ago."

"What difference does that make? How're you gonna forget a betrayal like that? Someone cuts your heart out, it don't heal, son."

"I guess I just didn't take it that hard."

"No, but I did." He looked at me for a long moment, which turned into a silence, during which he stared at me under the brim of his hat and puffed on his cigar. When he blew out the smoke he leaned back in his chair, so that the smoke went up and then was buffeted by a gale of air conditioning back down toward the desk.

"Well," he said finally, "let's talk turkey." He gazed contemplatively at me under the brim of his hat. "Tryin' to sell god damn natural gas, who'm I kidding? I know damn well there ain't no money left in it, I ain't stupid, Mr. Heaton. Maybe if you'd just asked I mighta sold."

I raised my eyebrows inquisitively. "To be perfectly honest, Mr. Talley—"

He leaned forward suddenly and stabbed his cigar into a big glass ashtray on his desk. "Maybe I'm just stubborn. Tryin' to sell god damn natural gas when your tanks get blown up is a bitch, ain't it? Or when your lines keep gettin' cut? Or your pumps just happen to break down every big rain? Shit. I got nothin' left but land, son, and I got a lot of it, but you know what, I wouldn't sell you a god damn, swampy, no-good acre to buy a headstone for my dead mother, God rest her soul. Which is what I've told you god damn bullying thieves before, and when I find out who you're fronting for there'll be some hogs' asses on the coals, I assure you. I've spent my life building this business, and I'm sure as shit not going to knuckle under now, just 'cause somebody's seen too many god damn Al Pacino movies and thinks there's such a thing as an

49

offer you cain't refuse. Let me tell you..." He paused, calmly relit the cigar, leaned back again, and continued. "Did I mention that I'm an attorney? Haven't practiced for some time, but I am quite familiar with Louisiana property law. There just ain't a snowball's chance in hell that you or your coward bosses are gonna be taking title to my land." He stopped again and examined the cigar critically, then glanced over my shoulder at the doorway.

The encounter with the goons at the drill site made a bit more sense.

"Mr. Talley," I said, "I really am afraid that there's a misunderstanding here. I haven't come to make an offer on your land. I—"

He cut me off with a snort. "God damn right you haven't. You've come to tell me who you're working for and who's sabotaging my wells, violating numerous sections of the Louisiana and Texas criminal codes and subjecting themselves to vigorous local prosecution and a lengthy stretch of truly unpleasant confinement." He smiled warmly. "I suppose we'll start with aggravated assault." He looked again at the doorway. This time I turned, and of course the two goons were filling it. The older guy had donned mirror sunglasses. They hid his eyes, but couldn't cover his rapidly swelling nose, which he had plugged with a wad of tissue. He grinned at me.

I turned back to Talley and he had the phone to his ear. "Yes, why don't you come down here? We'll just wait here with him." He hung up and looked at me. "That's our local police chief. He's an old friend. He's kindly offered to come down and chat with you informally. Make yourself comfortable, Mr. Heaton; finish your tea. I'll be back shortly." He exited between the goons, and there I was.

I nodded back at the goon whose nose I had broken. "Love the shades," I said, "but they don't work with the outfit. You've got this Greg Allman meets Depeche Mode thing..."

I stopped mid-fashion critique. What was the point? The goons just stood there, and I had blown the line anyway. The obvious reference for '80s pop culture and mirror sunglasses was *Top Gun*. It should have been easy to land a decent line—"Hey Mav, looks like you lost that fight with Iceman." Something like that. But the moment was past. I felt like apologizing for screwing up the witty banter.

Ten

The wait wasn't long. The town was small, and the police chief was indeed on his way; inside of two minutes later, the goon wall parted and he came in with Talley. The two men were cut from the same mold, but the chief was in a better mood. He looked at me, then over his shoulder at the goons, and chuckled. "I hear you boys shed a few tears down at the rig." He turned back to me. "They should have known better, and they would have, too, if they'd ever been outside the county. Bobby Tarwood, pleased to meetcha. You a cop?"

"Ex."

"Uh-huh." Cops like to think they can always spot other cops, even off the job, kind of a blue gaydar. Some of them are pretty good at it. But Tarwood's ID didn't impress me. He had a lot of circumstantial evidence to work with. "And now?"

"Private. Am I under arrest? Mutt and Jeff here forgot their *Miranda* cards."

Tarwood laughed. "Oh, you're free to leave at any time, Mr. Heaton. I can't imagine why you'd feel otherwise." He glanced at Talley, who had returned to his throne, and Talley jerked his head sideways. The goons disappeared.

Tarwood settled in on a low couch against the wall upholstered in a pattern that approximated a black-and-white cowhide. Maybe it was a real cowhide. I was about to ask, but Tarwood spoke first. "The reason Pops here gave me a call is we've both been awful worried about this recent spate of, ah, *van*dalism, and, you know, any chance to get a little *in*sight into that problem?" He shrugged and raised his palms, asking for my understanding. "We thought you might could help us out."

"I'm not sure how. I've never been here until today, and I'm not in the vandalism business."

"Of course not," said Tarwood. Talley remained silent. "But you'll understand if I am just a bit curious about what business you're in."

"I told you. I'm a private investigator."

"Yes, and that fact kinda *adds* to my difficulty, wouldn't you say?"

"How's that?"

He smiled. "Well, you see, we've been experiencing a bit of a *crime* wave centering on certain Talley Oil properties. Mr. Talley has been given grounds to suspect that these acts are calculated to induce him to *sell* these properties, something he has expressed his reluctance to do. The acts of vandalism have *es*calated recently, so as to more or less shut down productive work on the land. Nonetheless, Mr. Talley has not parted with it. You understand, then, how I might in*ter*pret your showing up here? A tough guy coming in to make the offer *per*sonally, that sort of thing?"

"Well, I can put your mind at ease, then. I have no interest in Mr. Talley's property, and my business here has nothing to do with it."

"And what is your business here, Mr. Heaton, if I may ask?"

"I'm here on a case."

"Yes, I'm sure." He looked over at Talley. "Would you mind telling us who your client is?"

"Sorry," I said. "You gentlemen know the drill. I'll tell you this much, though: I am employed by a law firm, and all of my investigatory work is done under an attorney-client relationship. So I don't talk without my employer's permission, and if she doesn't want to give it, it can be hard to get." I hoped it would impress them.

They weren't impressed. "Okay, then," said Tarwood. "We'll just bring some lil' ol' battery charges, and then see how Pops's wells hold up while you're safely inside. That'll maybe put my mind to rest a bit.

Or—" he looked at Talley again, "on the other hand, why don't we just get your employer on the phone?"

Which was obviously what Talley wanted, and I would have had to call her anyway from the jail, so I nodded and pulled out my phone.

"Why not just tell us the firm, and we'll look it up?" suggested Tarwood. Smart old boy.

"Sure," I said. "Montrose Bryant & Wolfe, in New York."

Talley wrote down the name and glanced at the doorway. "Linda?" he said, raising his voice slightly, and in a moment Linda Waters's face appeared in the doorway. "Already got 'em for you," she said when he started to speak. "On your line."

Tarwood chuckled. "Girl's got good ears," he said. He walked behind Talley's desk and looked down at the phone. "May I?" he said, and picked up the receiver. "Yes, hello, ma'am, this is Chief Bobby Tarwood, of the Mandanoches Police Department down here in the Lone Star State. And what might your name be?" He paused and then continued. "Well, Patrice, I'd be right obliged if you'd patch me through to…" He paused and looked at me.

"Jennifer Curtis," I said. He hesitated a moment, then raised his eyebrows and repeated the name into the phone.

He listened a moment, covered the receiver, and looked at Talley. "This call is regarding what exactly, would you say?"

"This is where you drop my name so they'll put you through," I said.

Tarwood did, then he waited a minute, introduced himself again, allowed as he was sitting here with me, one Marcus Heaton, and that I had mentioned her name. He paused again, briefly, and then said, "Oh, no, ma'am, nothing as I'd call serious. A couple young fellers with some bumps and bruises. Not a scratch on Mr. Heaton that I can see. No, I'm quite certain they won't. Bruised egos, is all."

I imagined J.C.'s side of the conversation. This was not the first such call she had received, and I had listened to them from both sides. Was the altercation serious? Was anyone badly injured? Were the police called? Was there any property damage? Would anyone be pressing charges? And, always, delicately, was there anything she could do to help resolve the matter?

And as it so happened, there was, Tarwood told her. Mr. Heaton had led him to believe that she might could fill everybody in a little bit on what he was doing in Mandanoches. Then he listened for the space of maybe a minute, said thank you again, and hung up the phone.

"Well?" said Talley, as Tarwood returned to the couch.

"Well," said Tarwood, looking at me, "the client's name is Eleanor Hausman. You don't suppose, do you, Pops—"

But Talley was already out of his chair, coming around the desk with the aim of looming over me threateningly. "Hausman?" he shouted. "Hausman Development?"

Right at the "Development" was where he was planning to grab me by my lapels and shake me, but I was out of the chair by the time he got to me. I squared my shoulders at him so he could reach for my lapels if he still wanted them, and he looked at me and decided it could wait. Tarwood had a slight grin on his face, like he'd been hoping for some action.

I waited a beat, too, and said, quietly, "Yes, Hausman Development. But as I'm sure Mr. Tarwood there can tell you, I am here investigating a purely personal matter."

Talley glanced over at Tarwood, then took a step back toward his desk. "Yeah, purely personal," he said. "I got a purely personal matter in mind we could investigate." He shook his head, as if scolding himself for not hitting me when he'd had the chance.

"Apparently," said Tarwood, "he's been hired to fill in some details about Ms. Hausman's early life."

"The fuck does that mean?" said Talley, glowering at Tarwood.

"It means she was adopted and she wants to know about her birth parents," I said. "It's PI bread and butter, nothing more. Rich people don't like not knowing things. Especially about themselves. It scares them. So they hire people to find out. That's all."

Talley wasn't satisfied. "Well, ain't that just a nice little coincidence?" he said. "Biggest fucking golf-resort builder in the country just happens to hire Dick Tracy here to tell her all about her sweet loving birth parents, right at the time someone's buying up marsh property for a golf resort and I'm getting friendly offers to get the hell off my land and get out of the way?"

I had to admit it was quite a coincidence. "Is Hausman building the resort down on the river?" I asked. "I saw the signs on the way in."

"How the hell should I know?" said Talley. "They don't exactly put their names on the sign, do they?"

This was true. Big development companies tended to operate through an impenetrable thicket of fronts and intermediaries, particularly when a project faced local opposition or legal problems. Hausman's name was on plenty of signs, all right—but only when she wanted it there.

"Have you talked to anyone personally about selling?"

"No. Just these anonymous calls, then the well fires and cut pipes. Softening me up first, I guess, case I was thinking of holdin' out 'til the front nine got built."

"So no one has actually made you any sort of an offer for the land?"

"Not 'til you got here today."

I let it pass. Talley had let the violence cool for the moment, it looked like, but he was still pacing in front of his desk. My questions didn't exactly exonerate me, and my story, I had to agree with Talley, was pretty implausible. The fact that my employer had told them what I was doing there made me nervous, too. J.C. doesn't just hand over client information to anyone who asks. Maybe Hausman just wasn't all that worried about secrecy in this case, which was, she had told me, just a vanity project. Or maybe she wanted Talley to know who I was working for. But how would Hausman have known that I would be coming to Mandanoches? The thought made me uneasy.

Tarwood went back to the couch, which I was pretty sure now was real cowhide, and sat down again. He crossed his legs and looked at me. "Are you saying Eleanor Hausman is from Mandanoches?"

"No. I'm just following a lead. But there is a possibility that she was born around here. I'm just looking into birth records." I turned to Talley. "Which is what I was doing when I met your associates."

Talley gave a snort. "Birth records, huh? At my *drill* rig?" But he seemed to have calmed down a little. He sat down on the edge of his desk, wondering, I guessed, whether by some strange coincidence I might actually not be a hired thug sent here to threaten him.

I threw in some detail to reassure him. "Her adopted name was Brideshead," I said, "assuming she was adopted. If she was, it was done quietly. There are no adoption papers and both of the Bridesheads are dead. But Harlan Brideshead loaned you the money for your first wells in 1978. I thought you might remember the girl." Tarwood cleared his throat, and I turned to look at him. "I have reason to believe that her name at birth was S—"

But before I could finish the sentence I was knocked back against the chair with such force that it fell backward, too, and I was left sprawling awkwardly in the corner of the room with my feet in the air, looking up at Talley. He had leaped from the desk so fast that I had not had time to sidestep or brace for the blow. Now I saw him over me, his eyes wide and wild, and I cocked my leg, thinking I might be able to get him in the neck or head before he was on me.

But he didn't come. His arm swept club-like over my legs and his thick hand grasped the edge of the door, slamming it shut with a bang that echoed in the hallway outside. As the door swung past my face I caught a glimpse of Linda Waters, the secretary, sitting erect at her desk, staring at me.

Eleven

As the echo died away, the room was deathly quiet for a moment. Talley turned and leaned his back against the door, seeming to sag under the weight of his head, which tilted downward toward his chest. I could hear him breathing heavily. His eyes were unfocused. I took advantage of the lull to extricate myself from the fallen chair and get to my feet. I looked over at Tarwood, who sat impassively.

Talley abruptly raised his head and looked at me. "Bobby," he said heavily, "I'd be obliged if you'd take this man to the airport and see that he makes his plane. Whatever he wants here, he isn't going to find it."

I looked at Tarwood. Was this really how things worked in small Southern towns? Could the local squire really just order the constable to show me the door? I thought of Boss Hogg and Sheriff Coltrane from *The Dukes of Hazzard*, but I kept my mouth shut. My bargaining position was weak.

Tarwood shrugged. "Okay, Mr. Heaton. You heard the man. He's invited you to leave his property."

"My flight's out of Shreveport," I said. "You going to take me the whole way?"

He smiled. "Oh, we'll see that you get there."

He crossed the room and opened the door, holding it for me. Talley stayed where he was, staring out the window, and didn't turn his head or speak. I walked out and nodded at Linda Waters.

"Goodbye, Mr. Heaton," she said, standing to take my hand. "And good luck."

"Thank you for the tea," I said.

Tarwood and I went through the outer office and outside into the heat. "You serious about coming the whole way with me?" I asked.

"Oh, I believe so," he said. "Pops and I go back a ways. Seems like a small enough favor."

"I've got a rental," I said, indicating my car.

"Oh, you can ride with me. We'll bring yours along with us." He waved a hand at his cruiser, which was idling in the driveway, and a shaven-headed boy of no more than twenty leaped out, holding his spotless white cowboy hat in both hands.

"Roy, why don't you follow us in Mr. Heaton's car," said Tarwood. I tossed the boy my keys and sat down in the passenger seat of the cruiser. Tarwood got in behind the wheel.

"I hope you don't mind," I said, "but I think it'd be a bit presumptuous to ask me to get in the back."

He laughed. "Oh, help yourself. I have nothing against you, Mr. Heaton, even if you are down here trying to strong-arm Pops out of some marshland. Can't say as I wouldn't mind having a nice little golf course down there myself. Do you play?"

"No, I don't. But more to the point, I don't know anything about any land deals. Believe it or not, there are a lot of people willing to pay for genealogical research."

"Yeah," said Tarwood, "I bet there are." He pulled out of the lot and looked over at me. "I would say that story of yours is about the most bullshit thing I ever heard, but the thing is, I remember the Hempersett case."

"Case?" I said.

"You said Sue-Lynn Hempersett, right? And 1973, that's about right, I guess. It was my first year in the department here."

"You've been a cop here that whole time?"

"Thirty-five years. I guess that accounts for my laid-back demeanor, you think? I know in New York you all cut and run at twenty."

"Fifteen in my case," I said. "Five years of service credit."

"Army?" he asked.

"Yeah. You too?"

"My son."

"Overseas?"

"Eighteen months, then they hit him with another tour. Stop-loss, you know?"

"I know."

"When were you in?"

"After high school. Five years active, then the ready reserve. So I got a sabbatical from the PD when they doubled up in Iraq."

"They sent you back?"

"Yeah. A full tour. I was way too old for it, but what the hell, right?" I changed the subject back to the adoption. "What about the Hempersett case?"

"If that girl grew up to be Eleanor Hausman, she's pretty damn lucky." He shook his head. "Thing is, though, she didn't, 'cause the way I remember the story, she's dead. Died that same month, in the state hospital in Shreveport. Filthy goddamn place."

"That same month as what?"

"As the trial. How much you know about it?"

"Not much, so far. I don't even know if Hempersett was her name. It's a hunch, mostly, but it fits with what I do know."

"Shit." Tarwood shook his head again, as if disturbed by the memory. "Weren't nothing, really, more'n what I guess you'd expect to find down here in the swamps. It was across the river on the Louisiana side. Drunken white trash husband molests little girl. Wife calls him on it, gets the DA to bring charges. Then at the trial husband lets on that she used to be a whore—maybe still is, he says. Judge dismisses the charge on condition the husband leaves town. I guess his lawyer worked out a deal. But then the judge revokes the wife's custody on account of her lewd and immoral behavior. Little girl ends up a ward of the state, next thing you know, she's dead in the goddamn state hospital."

"Did you know any of the parties?"

"You mean the husband and wife? No, not personally. We just heard about it over here when it happened."

"What about the DA or the judge?"

"Well, the judge would've been Touissant. I'm sure he's long dead. And I don't remember the DA, if I ever knew at all." He looked over at me. "Hotshot New York City private eye like you, though, you'll be able to dig it all up."

"What happened to the wife?"

He shrugged. "No idea. Dead in a ditch? Down in New Orleans? Forty years is a long time to turn tricks, but there's a market for everything these days."

"The husband?"

"Who knows? I suppose when it is suggested to a man that he leave town, he generally does."

"Well, that would depend on the persuasiveness of the suggestion, wouldn't it?"

"Oh, those suggestions can be very persuasive, Mr. Heaton. Nowadays, maybe it's not so common. But in 1973, in north Louisiana? I believe the suggestion would have been followed."

"Even after the charges were dismissed?"

He laughed. "Oh yes, indeed. There's the formal side of the law and then there's the informal side, as I expect you are aware."

I nodded. I was aware of the informal side of the law. The informal side of the law was why I had finally turned in my badge and walked away. Not that I'd walked far.

I turned to look out the window. I stared at the landscape, pine trees over red dirt, long thin chicken houses, fields of soy. I replayed the scene in Talley's office in my head. Human memory is fallible, as a few years interviewing crime witnesses will teach you. But the closer in time, the better it is, and this scene was only ten minutes old. I saw Talley sitting on the edge of his desk, Tarwood on the couch, legs stretched in front of him. I saw myself explaining what I was doing in Mandanoches, telling them the baby's name. I saw the room whirl above me, saw Talley's fist swing over my head. And I knew, with a certainty that I didn't want to trust but knew that I would, that I had never said "Hempersett."

Twelve

So naturally I waited while the deputy returned my rental, walked with Tarwood into the terminal, changed my return flight to the next one out, shook his hand, and walked out to the gate. Then I read the newspaper for an hour, walked back into the terminal, rented another car, and drove back to Mandanoches.

It was dark when I arrived, and I pulled into the deserted, nineteenth-century town square to think. How could Tarwood possibly have known the name of the girl I'd picked out of the birth records? Could the goons have gone to the hospital and asked the clerk which birth certificate I'd pulled? No, I'd followed them straight to Talley's office. And how would they have known I'd been at the hospital before going to the oil field?

That left two big questions. Why had Talley attacked me when I'd mentioned the girl's name in his office? And how had it happened that my "vanity project" on behalf of the country's largest golf resort developer had, by chance, taken me straight into a land dispute between an oilman and an unnamed out-of-town golf resort developer? Or maybe it was the same question.

Either way, I felt like the hired fist I used to be, and it didn't feel good. You can't get much dirtier than shoveling someone else's shit, and I had done too much of that. At first, I didn't know what I was doing, and later, when I did, there was too much of it on me to say anything. I didn't join the force to be the beatdown guy, the bagman, the bodyguard standing outside the precinct fuck pad. But there I was, day after day, year after year, dishing out violence wherever the man pointed.

If Eleanor Hausman had strung me along to put the heat on Talley, well fuck her and fuck this job. I was going to march into Talley's office and apologize. For being stupid. For being a sucker. And then I was going to go back to New York and tell Hausman to find herself another hard guy. It wouldn't take her long.

I pulled up on the street opposite the Talley Oil building, where I could see Talley's office with its bay window and French doors. The light was on, and I got out of the car and started across the street. When I was halfway across, the light went out, and I stopped. I didn't want him to run into me standing on the darkened lawn outside his office, a posture that would undercut my claim to be something other than a hired thug. So I hustled back to the car and waited. Talley came out and walked across the lawn to the parking lot, getting into the only car there, a big Town Car. He pulled out and headed down the strip. I followed without much of a plan. I certainly didn't want to tail him home.

But Talley wasn't going home. He pulled into the gravel parking lot of a bar a few blocks down the strip. The bar was a nondescript place called the Piney Woods Tavern, on a side street a few blocks off the old town square. I drove past as Talley parked and went inside. This would be better. I could have a casual conversation with a guy in a bar without being a menacing extortionist, couldn't I?

I gave him five minutes, then walked in and spotted him at the bar. He had a shot of something dark in front of him. The bar wasn't full, but there were enough people inside for a few of them to notice me come in.

I sat down next to Talley. "Evening," I said.

He jerked backward on the stool and lost his balance for a second, then grabbed the bar to recover. He turned toward me and I saw surprise and anger on his face.

"What the fuck are you doing back here?"

I lifted my hands, palms up, a nonthreatening gesture, I hoped.

"Mr. Talley, I want to apologize for the misunderstanding. I'm not here on an extortion job."

"Yeah, you're here doing genealogical research. You told me that. That's about the dumbest god damn story I've ever heard."

"Which maybe should suggest to you that it might be true?"

"Oh, don't give me that 'it's-so-crazy-that-it-must-be-true' shit. In my experience people come up with cockamamie stories because they're too damn stupid to think of anything better."

"But I'm not stupid, Mr. Talley."

"You ain't no Einstein. But this ain't your story, is it?"

"It's Eleanor Hausman's story. And she isn't stupid."

"No, I reckon not."

"And I've done extortion. Plenty of it. It works best when you just come right out and threaten people."

"And you're saying you haven't done that?"

"I don't believe I have, sir."

"Well then, god damn, you haven't looked in a mirror lately, son. 'Cause you're nothing but a threat walking around on two legs and if you don't know that then you are waist deep in denial about your life. You are a guy people hire to send a message, not research their damn genealogy."

He spoke loudly enough that we definitely had an audience. I didn't turn, but I could feel the bartender watching from behind me. I kept both my hands in sight, up on the bar.

"Well, here's my message, then," I said. "If there's any extortion here, I'm out of it. I'll fly straight back there and tell them that. I'll quit my job if I have to. But I won't have to. I work for a *law firm*, Mr. Talley. I've knocked a lot of heads, but I don't do that anymore. I just want you to know that."

He stared at me for a moment. Then he tipped back his drink, slammed the glass down, and said, "You are a god damned patsy. Someone thinks they're god damned cute, well they can kiss my ass. You want to blackmail me? It was forty god damned years ago and I didn't do anything wrong."

"Mr. Talley, you've lost me."

His face was flushed and his eyes were bloodshot. "Is that son of a bitch even still alive?"

I spread my hands. "I don't know who you're talking about."

"Oh, really? Because you're just the stupid hired gun? Well, someone put it into your head to come barging into my office asking about the Hempersett case. So you can tell that someone to kiss my ass."

"You know," I said, "Chief Tarwood said the same thing, more or less. 'The Hempersett case.' Said he remembered it too."

"Well, of course he remembers it. And I suppose he told you about it while he was driving you to the *airport?* To get on a god damned *plane?* Which it appears you did not do."

I shrugged. "Free country and all that." I did not add: *because we kicked your asses in 1865.*

"Free country to get locked up for assault, sure it is."

"I came back to make it right with you," I said, hearing the edge in my voice contradict the words. "You think I'm threatening you, well I'm not. I came to see if it's possible that the girl—"

"The girl died!" he said, pounding a thick fist on the bar. "As I am sure Bobby told you. The girl died, and I did nothing wrong."

They told us in the Academy that when a subject volunteers that he did nothing wrong when you didn't ask, he probably did. It's a good bullet point for an exam, I guess. But over the years I found that in my more informal interviews, at night with no witnesses, my subjects often led off with it, and a lot of them were probably telling the truth. Talley was on his own turf, though, and he wasn't scared.

"Tarwood told me that the girl was abused by her father," I said. "Then the father told the court that the mother was a prostitute, and the court took custody of the girl. The father got some sort of plea bargain and left town, and the girl died in a state hospital."

Talley didn't answer. I turned toward him. "So what does that have to do with you?"

He stared at me for a moment. "I'm the lawyer, you damn fool. Are you telling me you didn't know that?"

I didn't answer. But Talley didn't want an answer. His blood was up.

"The man came to me and hired me and signed a retainer to pay me for my services. He pledged lawful collateral, and then he didn't pay."

Talley lifted his hand off the bar and wagged his finger at me. "The man made a *promise*. He made a *deal*. And *I* delivered! And *he* didn't pay. And do you know the first and last rule in this life, Mr. Heaton?"

I had a pretty good idea what it was going to be, but I let him tell me.

"You always have to pay."

"That's very profound, Mr. Talley," I said. "I'll be sure and tell that to my client."

"Yes, you do that. And you tell your *client* to read god damn *Kirchberg v. Feenstra* before sending any god damn lawyers down here to take a shot at my title."

"I'm not a lawyer, Mr. Talley."

"*Kirchberg v. Feenstra.* 1981!" He punctuated the date with staccato finger taps on the bar. "And I'm..." Talley stopped, stared at me for a moment, then looked down at his hands, nodding to himself. "No, don't bother. They know. They know. That's why they sent the PI and not the lawyer." He looked back at me. "So you can go back to New York and tell your *client* to forget about going after my title. It's bulletproof. I will not be bullied, threatened, or *sued*. When the United States Supreme Court tells me I am entitled to my legally held property, obtained by my honest labor, well, sir, I believe I am entitled to it."

I stood up. "Okay. Thanks for your time."

Talley was staring at his hands again. I put a bill on the bar and turned to go, but he put a hand on my arm.

"Wait," he said, in a different voice. I looked back at him. His hand was trembling, and he suddenly looked old. I wondered if he was drunker than he had seemed.

He started to speak, but his voice caught in his throat. I looked at his face. The light in the bar was dim, and his eyes were in the shadow of his Oilers cap, but I thought I saw a tear start in the corner of his eye. He cleared his throat and tried again. "Tell her..." His voice caught again.

I waited.

"The kid. Is she...?" He paused, looked down at his hand, which was still on my arm. He saw it shake, and his expression turned to disgust as he stared at it. He pulled his hand off my arm and made a fist.

"No, god damn it all. I did right by her. God damn it, I did. You can all go to hell." He stood abruptly, knocking over his stool and holding onto the bar for support. Then he pushed past me and walked unsteadily toward the door and out into the parking lot.

I sat back down. The last thing I needed was a bar full of witnesses to me chasing him out into the parking lot after a loud and very public argument. I gave him fifteen minutes and then went out to my car.

Thirteen

I pulled back onto the strip and drove back toward the center of town. When I passed the Talley Oil building, I saw his Town Car in the lot out front and the lights on in his office, spilling out through the bay window onto the flower garden.

I stopped the car and thought about it. The smart thing to do would have been to keep going, out to the highway, back to the airport, back to New York. But I don't get paid to do the smart thing. Talley wanted to tell me something, and I wanted to hear it. I parked across the street and walked through the hedges and across the wide lawn toward the door.

The lawn and the brick walk were dark, but as I neared the door it opened and Linda Waters stepped out in a pool of light. She stepped briskly down the walk, not seeing me in the dark.

"Good evening, Ms. Waters," I said.

She started as if I had slapped her, and I thought she was going to scream. But she regained her composure immediately and stared at me. I wondered if she recognized me in the dark.

"I'm sorry if I startled you," I said. "I'm Marcus Heaton, I was here earlier today. I've come back to apologize to Mr. Talley for causing any inconvenience."

She looked at me for a long moment. Then she smiled, a forced smile

I thought, and said, "Oh, that's quite all right, I'm sure, Mr. Heaton." She stood and looked at me for a moment. "May I ask why you're here? I don't mean to pry, of course, but I had the distinct impression that Pops was glad to see you go."

"You mean because I was escorted off the premises by the police?"

"Oh, I wouldn't be so dramatic about it. Bobby liked you, I could tell. He likes tough men."

"What about Talley? He didn't seem to like me too much."

"No, you scared the heck out of him, if you want to know the truth."

"I'm not sure I agree, Ms. Waters. He seems pretty well in control of things."

"Maybe, on the surface anyway. But everyone's got vulnerabilities. Pops has his."

"The land, huh? He seemed to think I was a heavy in some sort of extortion scheme."

"Well, aren't you?" She laughed. "I was given to understand, Mr. Heaton, that you are employed by a golf course developer who might have an eye on Pops's properties."

"I admit it looks that way. In fact, that's why I came back. I wanted to reassure him that whatever's going on with his land, I have no part in it."

"Are you so sure about that?"

"No," I said, "to be honest, I'm not. But if I do, it's going to stop. Violence isn't in my contract."

"It's not?" She sounded genuinely surprised, and I wondered if there were tough-guy pheromones, or something. I had worked hard to break free from the thug archetype. I could even use words like "archetype." But one glance, and people like Linda Waters saw me as I was, just as if they'd been there all those nights a decade past.

She waved a hand. "That's fine. Doesn't matter anyway. Not now." She was looking at me intently now, and I had an idea where the conversation might be heading.

"I'm not freelancing at the moment, either, I'm afraid," I said.

She shrugged. "All the same," she said, "come and have a cup of coffee. We might be able to help each other out."

"I'd like to talk to Talley," I said, indicating the door.

69

"Oh, he'll be there all night, most likely," she replied, "and into the morning. He does that. Besides, I doubt it would look good, you being found lurking around here at night. Bobby might decide to prove his manhood. He does that every once in awhile."

I nodded. "Okay." I could talk to Talley tomorrow, and Linda Waters might have something useful to tell me. She'd probably been with Talley for decades and might know even more about the business than he did.

"My car's in the lot," she said, gesturing to the parking area at the side of the building. "Would you like a ride?"

"Why not?" I said and followed her around the building. Her car was an old Taurus, parked in the back corner of the lot, away from the lights.

The diner was two blocks away, on the old deserted town square. Like the square, it was small and tawdry and sad. A country station was playing on a portable radio sitting on the counter. A few customers sat on the stools, old and tired-looking like the diner. We sat in a booth by the plateglass street window and ordered coffee.

She stared out the window at the empty square. "Do you think this is a nice town, Mr. Heaton?"

"I don't know. I haven't seen much of it. But I suppose I've seen worse."

"I guess you've traveled a lot?'

"A bit. You?"

"No. Hardly at all. The Gulf. Florida a couple times. San Antonio"— she pronounced it San An-ton-yuh. "I've never really been north to speak of. St. Louis once, is all." Which wasn't the north, in my opinion, Missouri being a slave state and all. I wondered why she was telling me this.

"You've seen nicer, though, I expect?" she continued.

"I'm from New York City. I don't like to leave when I can help it. No place measures up. It's not just Texas. I don't even like to go to New Jersey."

"So I guess you have a hard time understanding why anyone would want this land."

There was some truth to this. I certainly couldn't imagine myself

70

on a golf course out in the swamp. But I understood wanting things. That was my work: people wanted things, and sometimes they went too far trying to get them.

I said, "I understand not wanting to be pushed around."

"Do you?"

"Probably better than I understand anything else."

"Have you ever been pushed around?"

"Yes. And I didn't like it."

"What did you do about it?"

I broke an NYPD captain's nose on my forehead and lost my job and my pension. But I didn't say that. "Something that had consequences," I said. "Consequences I never wanted to face."

She nodded. I had no idea what she thought I was talking about.

"But you did, though," she said. "Face them, I mean."

"Yep." And in the end it hadn't been all that terrible. Cop vengeance is implacable if you testify against a fellow officer. But if you just put one in the hospital, well, maybe he had it coming. That sort of nuance was more common when the guy was not well liked. I was lucky on both counts. The captain was a renowned prick, and Internal Affairs never asked me to testify. And then I was conveniently shipped off to Iraq.

"I've been pushed around, too, Mr. Heaton," she said. "And I didn't like it either."

"I sympathize, Ms. Waters, but I'm really not available for hire."

She raised a hand, gracefully. "I just want to tell you about it, that's all. So you'll understand."

I exhaled sharply, my favorite signal of impending impatience. I wasn't impatient, really, but I was not in the mood to be solicited for a contract murder.

"I am not in the business of killing people, Ms. Waters," I said as forcefully as I could without attracting attention. Though isn't it a claim that anyone ought to have a right to make?

She threw her head back and laughed. "Well, you shouldn't be, anyway, not when you let Bobby Tarwood run you out of town like a pissant drunk. I mean, I *am* gratified that you came back. But I am *certainly* not offering you money."

That was fine with me, because I wasn't interested in whatever she might have wanted to pay me for.

"Okay," I said, "that sounds great. You can pay for the coffee."

She nodded, then picked up her cup and took a sip. "Did you ever own land, Mr. Heaton? A house, anything like that?"

"No," I said. "I rent."

"I did," she said. "I owned land. My family did, for generations. I inherited it when my parents died. I was the only child. I was nineteen years old, and I had a house and twenty acres, cultivated. It used to be a lot more, you know, a hundred years ago? But it was twenty acres when it came to me."

I guess I didn't look impressed enough, because she continued quickly, her voice rising slightly. "I know twenty acres isn't a lot, but it's the *owning* part that matters. We were one step away from being shit-kicking, white trash—pardon the expression—but we *weren't*, as long as we had the land."

I sipped my coffee. Maybe she was going to tell me that Eleanor Hausman had taken her family farm and turned it into a golf course.

"Then I got pregnant, and then I got married. And no, Mr. Heaton, you didn't see any ring on my hand because not only am I no longer married, the worthless son of a bitch never gave me a ring in the first place. Not a ring, not a goddamn thing."

This was a lot of swearing for Ms. Waters, I thought. Maybe her workplace demeanor was not her only one.

"He drank," she continued, "and he gambled. And that's pretty much it. He was worthless as a father and a husband and a provider, and he gambled away the farm and he just lit out. Disappeared. And then..."

She paused slightly, and, given the subject matter of her story, I figured this for the point at which she would break into sobs. But Linda Waters wasn't a sobber, and the expression on her face was rage, not sadness. I had seen enough of both to tell the difference. She wasn't going to sob. She was just remembering.

I said nothing. This wasn't the kind of story you listened to and then said "uh-huh" or "well!" This was the kind of story you just listened to. I had listened to plenty of them. I never liked it.

72

"I never recovered, Mr. Heaton, I admit it. I just lay down and died. Oh, I went on and lived out the rest of my life, but you just never forget. And you especially never forgive. I don't know why we tell children that. I won't forgive—" She paused, as if considering the possibility. "Maybe now I can; I don't know."

"Ms. Waters," I said, "I've found that forgiveness can be a very good thing, for everyone concerned."

"Oh, what do you know?" she practically spat at me.

"Quite a bit, actually," I said, pointedly looking at my watch. This conversation was neither enjoyable nor, it was turning out, particularly illuminating. I wanted to know if Eleanor Hausman was trying to dispossess Talley of his land now, not whether Linda Waters had been dispossessed of her farm forty years earlier. "And tracking down your ex-husband so that you can forgive him sounds like a really good idea, and I wish you all the best in doing it." I patted the table consolingly, in lieu of her arm, and slid out of the booth. "And when I get back to New York, I'll send you the names of some good national firms you can contact. People are usually easier to find than you'd think. I bet—"

She cut me off with a humorless laugh. "You think? I'm sorry Mr. Heaton; you think the next job is to find my ex-*hus*band so I can for*give* him? That's..." She shook her head and laughed, but there was no humor in it.

Fourteen

I said goodnight to Linda Waters and walked up the sidewalk to the side lawn of the Talley Oil building. The street was dark and utterly deserted. There were no cars or pedestrians, just the comforting sound of crickets. I started across the lawn on my way back to my car, and when I came around the hedge, I saw Talley's Town Car still in the lot. The light was still on in Talley's office, spilling out through the French doors onto his flower garden and the lawn beyond. I looked at my watch. It was almost ten thirty. I considered my options. I needed to try again with Talley. If I went in now, I could say my piece, head straight back to the airport, and maybe get back to New York by mid-morning. That sounded a lot better to me than hanging around Mandanoches another day, trying to get in to see Talley before Bobby Tarwood came looking for me to prove his manhood.

"What the hell," I said to myself. I turned and crossed the lawn toward Talley's patio. I went around the flower beds and stepped up to the French doors with my hand raised to knock, politely.

But I didn't knock. Talley wouldn't have heard me. He was slumped over in his chair with his head on the desk. It was the sort of position that would leave a kink in your neck when you got up. But Talley wasn't getting up. The desktop was covered in blood.

I tried the knob, but the doors were locked. I stepped back and slammed my shoulder into the inside edge, where the doors came together. There was no center column dividing them, and I felt the wood splinter around the latch. The doors flew open, and I reached Talley in one step and cradled his head in my arms to check for breathing and a pulse. When I moved his head I could see that I might as well have sat down at his computer to check my email before looking at him. He was thoroughly dead, with a small-caliber entry wound right between his eyes. That was the source of the blood; otherwise he was undamaged. His head was intact, which meant the bullet had stayed in his brain. From outside on the patio, he'd looked okay, except for the blood. The shot hadn't even knocked off his Houston Oilers cap.

The office looked okay, too. No sign of a break-in or robbery. I checked the inner door that led to the hallway. It was closed, and I opened it quickly and looked out. Linda Waters's desk sat quietly and in perfect order. The hall was empty. I tried the knob on the hall side of the door. It was locked.

I went back to the desk. The desktop was completely empty, except for the phone and computer monitor...and the blood. I looked under the desk and chair, but the floor was clear as well. The desk drawers were closed, and the monitor was dark. I stood for maybe ten seconds and thought. Opening the drawers was probably a bad idea. But then breaking the door down and barging in had been an even worse idea, indeed a spectacularly bad idea, one that was going to cost me. But that's the thing about detectives: we don't mind the cost because we want to *know*. A moment ago I had wanted to know if Talley was dead; now I wanted to know *why* Talley was dead.

I gave myself a little credit: I had also wanted to save him if I could. I would have to emphasize that motive when I informed the authorities, which I would also have to do, and soon. I picked up Talley's phone and dialed 911. A young woman answered on the first ring: "911, what is your emergency, please?"

"I'm at the Talley Oil building," I began, but I got no further, because the unmistakable sound of a shotgun pump and the unambiguous suggestion to "Freeze, motherfucker!" came simultaneously from behind me. I lifted the phone slowly from my ear and placed my hands on the back of my head. I held onto the phone. I didn't want it to fall and make a noise that could credibly be described as sounding, in the heat of the moment, like a gunshot. I moved very slowly. That's always best in such situations, and I recognized the voice behind the shotgun. It was Chief of Police Bobby Tarwood, and I had to admit, I had been warned.

Fifteen

Bobby Tarwood was not alone. He had with him the young deputy who had driven my car to the airport. I wondered whether the presence of a witness would make Tarwood more likely or less likely to try to prove his manhood.

It was an interesting question, in the abstract, so I pondered it for a second or two before he hit me in the right kidney with what felt like the shotgun stock. The blow dropped me to my knees, and the next blow—a good professional choice, it occurred to me—was a straight bootheel to the middle of my back, which put me down on my face. I prudently kept my hands on the back of my head, turning my head to take the fall on one cheek. A quick motion of the hands to the front of the body is a legitimate predicate for application of deadly force in most department protocols. The fact that the subject moved his hands to break his fall can only be inferred after the fact, when a search of the body fails to yield a weapon, and is therefore not likely to prompt board-of-inquiry second-guessing.

I still had the phone in my hand, pressed against the back of my head. Tarwood reached down and took it, then said quietly into it, "Yes, we're already here. But do have the coroner come on down to Talley Oil." Then he hung up and patted me down. "Roy," he said, "take this cold-blooded son of a bitch down to the station. I believe I'll wait here with Pops for a few minutes."

The young deputy handcuffed me and hauled me to my feet.

"Don't even think about it, Tarwood," I said. "I didn't shoot him and you know it. If you were following me you know exactly where I've been, and you saw me break down the door ten seconds before you came in. He's obviously been dead longer than that, and there's no murder weapon in sight. You can drop a throw-down gun if you want, if you happen to have a .22 with you, but you know damn well it won't stick. Why don't you at least search the office, see what's here?"

Tarwood let me talk. He held the shotgun in the crook of his arm, his fingertips drumming on the barrel. He looked at me for a moment, and I couldn't read his gaze. Suddenly he swung the shotgun like a baseball bat, holding it by the barrel and hitting me in the stomach with the stock. It was a solid strike, but I was ready because he'd already done it once, and I tensed enough that it didn't double me over. He was on target, which was comforting. Shotgun-stock-to-the-midsection can be dicey: too high and you break the subject's ribs; too low and you break his pelvis. Those injuries tend to produce medical documentation and are hard to attribute to the subject's own resistance.

I concentrated on maintaining eye contact and not altering my expression. I don't know why I'm like that. I made a mental note to ask Dr. Trask if I saw him again. Acting impervious to the first blow just buys you the second one. In the standard progression of nonlethal application of force with a shotgun, the next element would be the use of the barrel, held crosswise, to apply pressure to the subject's carotid arteries. Out of policy, sure, but oh so effective. For this technique, the subject should ideally be positioned with his back against a wall, and Tarwood stepped forward and pushed me in the chest, forcing me back to the wall. Then the gun barrel came up crosswise, and I began to choke as Tarwood leaned in, pushing the barrel up under my chin with both hands. You didn't want to crush the windpipe. That'll kill your subject, and be obvious on even the most cursory examination. But just above the windpipe, on either side of the neck under the subject's jawline, are the carotid arteries, just sitting there ripe for some compression.

I gave myself twenty seconds or so until I started to black out, and I concentrated on counting them, backward, enunciating each one in my head. At twelve the pressure eased up, and Tarwood grabbed my shirt and pulled me forward across the room onto Talley's desk. My face took the fall again as I doubled over, and I felt the sticky red-black pool of blood smear over my cheek and into my hair. "You've got to be more careful with your crime scene," I said, standing up and turning to face the next blow.

"You smart-aleck piece of shit," said Tarwood, holding the shotgun by the barrel again but making no move toward me. "That's my friend of thirty years dead there on the desk, and you may have noticed that he died the day you arrived in town."

"Come on, Chief," I said, "you can see I didn't kill him. I assume you followed me tonight, so you know what I did. I came back to tell Talley I didn't want to be part of an extortion scheme, if there was one, and I was going to find out if my client was the one threatening him. I talked to him in the bar down the street. He was drunk and yelled at me and stormed out. I waited awhile, then left. I saw the light on in his office and decided to give it one more try. I looked in the window. When I saw him, I broke down the door. You came in thirty seconds later."

I wondered if that would be enough to keep Tarwood from helping his crime scene along a little. It wouldn't be that hard to do. I was already covered in Talley's blood, and my fingerprints were probably on his head and neck and on anything I'd touched in the office. I put myself in Tarwood's place and thought the matter over.

You could come out either way, I decided. I pegged Tarwood as smart enough to spot the obvious problem, which was the murder weapon. He could pin a throw-down gun on me easily enough, but the bullet in Talley's head wouldn't be a match to it. If a bullet bounces around enough, matching is pretty useless for anything beyond caliber, but since this one had stayed in Talley's brain, it would probably be intact enough for some decent forensics. And Talley didn't even know the caliber. Just eyeballing the entrance wound, he'd think .22 or 9 mm, but he wouldn't be sure until the autopsy. And this was small-town Texas, not the 30th Precinct, so I doubted he carried around throw-down guns at all, let alone in multiple calibers. He'd have to wait until after the autopsy and then swap out the murder bullet with one fired from the throw-down gun. This was a riskier play and would involve more people and more of a paper trail.

And he had to assume that I'd have an aggressive defense, because I was working for a high-profile firm. He could still pull it off, but it would depend on how well he could control multiple independent actors, and from the way he'd talked about the good old days, he must have known it was harder to do that now.

Tarwood stood looking at me for maybe thirty seconds, while I assumed he was running those odds. Then he turned and paced the room, slowly, his gaze on the floor. At the end of his circuit he stopped, grabbed my arm, and walked me outside. The young deputy followed us outside. "Close the door and stay put," said Tarwood, and he gave me a push toward his patrol car.

The ride to the station didn't take more than five minutes. Tarwood didn't say anything in the car. When he opened the door to get me out I said, "What'll it be? B&E?"

"Sure," he said, "plus murder."

Sixteen

They took me into the station and put me in a sweat room. I didn't know if they called them that in Texas, but the principle was the same as in New York: a tiny gray room with just enough space for a metal table with a chair on either side. This one had no windows and didn't have a camera that I could see. They left my cuffs on and locked the chain into an eyebolt on the top of the table. I could sit forward with my elbows on the table, in a nice attentive posture like an eager applicant at a job interview. I could not kick back like a boss.

They let me sit for an hour or so, and then Chief Tarwood came in. He sat down in the chair opposite me and ran his fingers through his hair. Then he sighed, placed both hands carefully on the table in front of him, and said, "Help me out here, Mr. Heaton. Man to man. Cop to cop. Help me understand why my friend of thirty years is dead."

I thought about my first trainings in interrogation, back in the Academy, trainings I'd ignored during my career as a cop. One of the first things they taught us about was *Miranda v. Arizona*. You know *Miranda*—it's the case that gave us the post-arrest warnings you always see the perp get on TV, right before the detective politely but firmly shoves his head down into the back of the squad car.

They showed us some statistics in the trainings that have always stuck with me. Back in 1966, when the decision came out, all the talking heads predicted that the new rule would push confession rates down to zero. Why would anyone ever talk once you told him he didn't have to? Crime would explode and the police would be helpless to stop it.

Thing is, it didn't happen that way. For one thing, the police didn't really need confessions as much as the talking heads thought they did. If you can prove the guy did it, like if you found the murder weapon on him, you don't need his confession. And we've gotten a hell of a lot better with forensics since 1966. But what I remembered best was the statistics they showed us on confession rates. Turns out they *didn't* drop to zero, not in 1967, not in 1980, not ever. Sure, they went down a little, but not nearly as much as the talking heads predicted. For the jurisdictions that kept statistics, you mostly saw drops from a 50 percent confession rate before *Miranda* to a 30 percent rate after. Some jurisdictions saw no drop at all.

You might think, why would you ever want talk to a cop who's accusing you of a crime and wants you to admit doing it? You might think that if you'd never spent time sitting in sweat rooms with scared arrestees. But if you have, you'll know that people want to talk for lots of reasons, and it takes a lot more to get them to shut up than just telling them they have the right to. After twenty years as a cop, that seems obvious to me in hindsight. The basic human urge to talk is too strong.

We're social apes, hardwired to justify ourselves to the guy across the table. We're hardwired to care what that guy across the table thinks of us, and we want him to *understand*. And at some subconscious level burned into our evolutionary forebears around their hunter-gatherer campfires in the savanna, we think we can talk our way out of trouble. Nine out of ten perps in the sweat room think, at some point, that they can talk themselves out of the rap. Some part of their brain is yelling, "Explain! Explain!" And for most people the urge is too strong to resist.

So plenty of perps will listen to the *Miranda* warning and then just start chattering away. They're happy to trade away their rights for the prospect of a friendly audience. I've used all the lines:

"This is your chance to tell me your side of the story."

"I can help you, but only if you tell me right now what happened."

"The DA is really on my back here. I can promise you I'll take your story to him, but I can't promise you he'll be listening tomorrow. This is your choice, right now. I can't make it for you."

I learned over the years that for a lot of guys, the post-arrest interview was the first time in their lives that they'd gotten to just sit in a quiet room and talk about their problems with a polite, interested listener. Someone who *cared.* For a guy who's never had that, it's the high he's been craving but never knew it until he feels it. And when it hits him he's going to mainline it and milk that rush from his head down to his toes, every sweet tingle of it.

I've had guys confess in the sweat room, and then when I put them in the car to take them down for booking, they'd pipe up from the backseat and start all over again, just to get in a few more details. The whole sad story of their lives—their loves and losses, their hopes and dreams, their disappointments and frustrations. And their redemption fantasies. I had one cocaine smuggler who spent a twenty-minute post-confession ride making a pitch for what a great DEA agent he'd be, if they'd sign him up to spot trap cars. "You could just set me up at them checkpoints, man. I'd pop them sons of bitches like *bam!* Like them tires? You just whomp them things with a tire iron, you know what I'm saying? Just *whomp* 'em, and you listen for that ping? You know? You can just *hear* when it ain't right."

What did all the talking heads fail to understand in 1966? That for a lot of perps, that post-arrest interview, the one where they talked themselves straight into prison, would be the best talk of their lives.

None of that applied to me. I wasn't a mope with a lifetime of emotional baggage to unload. I knew the drill and the process and the tricks, and I knew that the "benefits of cooperation" were the purest bullshit and that nothing I said would ever, by any stretch of the imagination, in any possible universe, be of any help to me.

But I still felt the urge. I felt it strongly enough that my fists clenched to resist it. I felt the urge to help Bobby Tarwood understand why his friend of thirty years was dead. I felt the urge to make Bobby Tarwood understand that I, Marcus Heaton, was wrongly accused, that I was a good guy who wound up in the wrong place at the wrong time. That I was not a murderer.

The urge was strong. But I was stronger. I sat up in the chair like an eager job applicant and I said: "I want a lawyer."

Seventeen

THE COURT: All right. In the matter of the People of the State of Texas versus Marcus Alvaro Heaton, set for preliminary hearing this morning. May we have the appearances of counsel, please.

MS. LUTZ: Good morning, Your Honor. Anne-Marie Lutz on behalf of the People.

MR. NGUYEN: Lawrence Nguyen, Montrose Bryant & Wolfe, representing Marcus Heaton, the defendant in this matter. He is present in court, in custody.

THE COURT: Thank you. Ready to proceed?

MS. LUTZ: Your Honor, the People are ready to proceed. The People would like to have Chief Robert Tarwood of the Mandanoches Police Department designated as my investigating officer for purposes of the preliminary hearing.

THE COURT: Any objection?

MR. NGUYEN: No, Your Honor. On that point, Your Honor, the People and I have previously spoken. And I would add that, having conferred with Ms. Lutz, I believe the People have no objection to the Court issuing an order under excluding witnesses and ordering witnesses not to speak with each other during the pendency of the proceedings. I would request such an order.

THE COURT: Ms. Lutz?

MS. LUTZ: No objection.

THE COURT: All right. That will be the order. Ms. Lutz, call your first witness.

MS. LUTZ: The People call Chief Robert Tarwood.

THE CLERK: If you would come forward, sir, please. You do solemnly state the evidence you shall give in the matter now pending before this court shall be the truth, the whole truth and nothing but the truth, so help you God?

THE WITNESS: I do.

THE CLERK: Would you please state your full name and spell it for the record.

THE WITNESS: Chief of Police Robert Tarwood. Like it sounds, T-a-r-w-o-o-d.

THE COURT: You may proceed.

MS. LUTZ: Thank you. Mr. Tarwood, you work for the City of Mandanoches, correct?

THE WITNESS: That's correct.

MS. LUTZ: Can you tell us your occupation?

THE WITNESS: Sure. I'm the Chief of Police.

MS. LUTZ: How long have you worked for the police department in Mandanoches?

THE WITNESS: For approximately thirty-four years.

MS. LUTZ: Okay. How long have you been Chief?

THE WITNESS: For approximately twenty-three years.

MS. LUTZ: Did there come a time when you were called upon to perform investigative duties with respect to the case of People v. Marcus Heaton?

THE WITNESS: Yes, ma'am.

MS. LUTZ: When was that?

THE WITNESS: It have would have been in the late evening of January 9th, 2009.

MS. LUTZ: January 9th, 2009?

THE WITNESS: That's correct.

MS. LUTZ: When you entered the offices of Talley Oil and found the defendant standing over the dead body of James Talley?

THE WITNESS: Yes.

MR. NGUYEN: Objection. Leading.

THE COURT: Overruled. Answer will stand. Counsel, is there really any dispute that Mr. Tarwood found your client standing over Mr. Talley's body? Because if there is not, I would just as soon cut to the chase.

MS. LUTZ: Thank you, Your Honor. Now, Chief, did you in fact enter the premises of the Talley Oil building and find the defendant standing over the dead body of James Talley?

THE WITNESS: Yes.

MS. LUTZ: On that date, January 9th?

THE WITNESS: Yes.

Lutz's narrative, drawn out through Tarwood's laconic testimony, was vivid. The chief first saw me earlier that afternoon when he responded to a call from Talley's office, reporting that an out-of-town tough guy had shown up in Talley's oil fields and beaten up two employees who'd asked him to leave, and then barged into Talley's office and scared the poor man half to death. Tarwood had escorted the obvious mercenary to the Shreveport airport, then returned to town, only to respond to another call from Talley's office and find this same man back in town in defiance of Tarwood's orders, standing over Talley's dead body. Witnesses in the Piney Woods Bar reported a heated argument between Talley and the stranger just an hour earlier. What about? Hard to say. Sounded like money. Hearsay, Your Honor? Overruled.

The testimony sounded pretty good for murder. Especially when you knew that in a preliminary hearing, all the prosecution has to do is convince the judge that there is sufficient evidence to hold a full trial. Sufficient evidence meaning probable cause. And probable cause meaning (every cop knew this) a reasonable basis for believing that the guy did it, even if (every cop knew this as well) the evidence showed that it was more likely than not that he *didn't* do it. "Probable cause is your best friend," our instructor at the Academy had said. "It's a lower bar than preponderance of the evidence. That means you can have probable cause when the odds are that the guy *didn't do it*. Awesome."

This was an important lesson for us. Prosecutors use probable cause for indictments and preliminary hearings, but cops use it for *every-thing*—for arrests, for car searches, for warrant applications, for use of force, you name it. Our instructor explained it like this: Say you've got three possible perps for some crime, call it grand theft auto. Each perp owns a storage shed big enough to hold the stolen car. So you've got a one in three chance, for each perp, that he's your guy. That means— smart cop do math—that there's a two out of three chance, for each perp, that he's *not* your guy. So here's your question, boys and girls: on a probable cause standard, can you get a warrant for all three garages? First time we heard that hypo, we looked at each other and shrugged. The instructor laughed at us: "Hell, *yes*, you get your fucking warrant. One chance out of three? Probable *cause*, baby."

I later learned that every judge in America was apparently too gut-less to put a number on where exactly the lower bound for probable cause lay, in that zone below 50 percent. And I never had a case with three identical GTA perps, each equally good for the theft and each equally in possession of a car-sized storage shed, so I never got to push the statistical envelope. ("Hey, Sarge, how about *four* perps? Could you get your warrant then?") But I learned enough to appreciate the adage that a prosecutor could indict a ham sandwich. Although the cop tag to that line was: "Yeah, if the ham sandwich fucking *did* it."

From my seat at the defense table, though, in my orange jumpsuit and state-issued paper slippers, my training in probable cause was a little less comforting.

But Larry Nguyen was one of J.C.'s Bright Young Things, and he had the police report. Nguyen looked downright eager when Ms. Lutz took her seat. He stood up and went to the lectern, holding the report out in front of him like a vampire hunter brandishing a crucifix.

MR. NGUYEN: Chief Tarwood, you testified that at approximately 11:08 p.m, you "responded to a 911 call from Talley Oil," correct?

THE WITNESS: That's correct.

MR. NGUYEN: Who made that call?

THE WITNESS: I was advised of the call by our dispatch operator.

MR. NGUYEN: Yes, but who *made* that call?

MS. LUTZ: Objection, asked and answered.

THE COURT: Overruled.

MS. LUTZ: Foundation, Your Honor.

THE COURT: Overruled. Chief Tarwood, you may answer.

THE WITNESS: I did not receive the 911 call. I was advised of the call by dispatch.

MR. NGUYEN: Would it refresh your recollection to listen to the call?

MS. LUTZ: Same objection.

THE COURT: Same ruling. You may answer.

MR. NGUYEN: Let me try it this way. Chief Tarwood, during your investigation of this incident, did you at any time *listen* to the 911 call of which you were advised by dispatch, at approximately 11:08 p.m?

THE WITNESS: Yes.

MR. NGUYEN: Thank you. And you previously testified that you conversed with the defendant at the Talley Oil offices on the afternoon of January the 9th, correct?

THE WITNESS: Correct.

MR. NGUYEN: And you testified that after conversing with the defendant at the Talley Oil offices on the afternoon of January the 9th, you personally *drove* the defendant from the Talley Oil offices to the Shreveport airport, correct?

THE WITNESS: Correct.

MR. NGUYEN: And that drive took approximately how long, would you say? An hour?

THE WITNESS: Give or take.

MR. NGUYEN: And you conversed with the defendant during that drive, did you not?

THE WITNESS: I did.

MR. NGUYEN: In fact, the defendant was seated in the front passenger seat of your vehicle, wasn't he?

THE WITNESS: He was.

MR. NGUYEN: Not in cuffs, right?

THE WITNESS: Correct.

MR. NGUYEN: May I ask why?

THE WITNESS: He hadn't shot anyone yet.

MR. NGUYEN: Thank you. So you conversed with him throughout the trip to the airport, correct?

THE WITNESS: Correct.

MR. NGUYEN: And you conversed with him again in the Talley Oil offices on the night of January 9th, correct?

THE WITNESS: Yes.

MR. NGUYEN: And later that evening and then into the morning of January the 10th, when you interviewed him at the police station?

THE WITNESS: Yes.

MR. NGUYEN: And you see the defendant here in the courtroom, do you not?

THE WITNESS: I do.

MR. NGUYEN: This gentleman to my left, at the defense table?

THE WITNESS: Yes, that's him.

MR. NGUYEN: Okay. So you are quite familiar with his voice?

THE WITNESS: I spoke with the man.

MR. NGUYEN: Thank you. Let's play Defense A, then. This is the 911 call from Talley Oil, produced by the People in discovery.

[Defense Exhibit A was played.]

And there I was on the courtroom speakers, calling in Talley's murder. A computer voice on the tape gave an audio time-stamp: 11:08 p.m. Larry Nguyen stopped the tape and asked if Tarwood recognized my voice; he did. Then Nguyen wondered whether, in Tarwood's long experience in law enforcement, murderers typically called 911 to report their crimes. "Can't say," said Tarwood, "never been a murderer."

Nguyen smiled. But had Tarwood ever had a case in which the murderer had done so? Tarwood had not. "We don't get a lot of murders in this town, son," he said, "and I thank God for it."

"Let's play the rest of the tape," said Nguyen. And I heard myself again, then a pause, then the thwack of the shotgun pump, then Tarwood's voice saying "Freeze, motherfucker!"

MR. NGUYEN: Now, Chief, that is your voice we just heard, is it not?

THE WITNESS: It is.

MR. NGUYEN: So in fact you entered Mr. Talley's office while Mr. Heaton was still on the phone, didn't you?

THE WITNESS: That is correct.

MR. NGUYEN: Let's play the last bit of tape.

[Defense Exhibit A was played.]

MR. NGUYEN: And that is your voice again, is it not, saying "yes, we're already here"?

THE WITNESS: Yes.

MR. NGUYEN: So in fact you entered the office *before* dispatch put out the call for assistance, didn't you?

THE WITNESS: Yes, I believe so.

MR. NGUYEN: How is it that you were able to get to the scene before dispatch put out the call?

MS. LUTZ: Objection, vague, calls for speculation.

THE COURT: Overruled.

THE WITNESS: I don't believe I understand your question.

MR. NGUYEN: I'm just trying to understand your report, because you wrote—as I believe you testified a moment ago as well—that you "responded to a call for service at the Talley Oil Company." But as we just heard, you were already at the location, weren't you?

THE WITNESS: Yes, I was.

MR. NGUYEN: Sitting outside the Talley Oil building in your car, weren't you?

THE WITNESS: Correct.

MR. NGUYEN: With a deputy, right? It was...Deputy Goodwin, I believe?

THE WITNESS: Roy Goodwin, good kid.

MR. NGUYEN: Yes, we'll call him next. Now, when you and Deputy Goodwin entered the office, there had been no call for service yet, correct?

THE WITNESS: Well, I don't know about that. The man was on the phone, making the call.

MR. NGUYEN: But dispatch hadn't put out the call to you yet.

THE WITNESS: Correct.

MR. NGUYEN: And in fact, you got on the phone and told dispatch, "We're already here."

THE WITNESS: Correct.

MR. NGUYEN: So you were not, in fact, responding to the call.

THE WITNESS: We were... What do you mean?

MR. NGUYEN: I mean that you were not, in fact, responding to a call for service when you entered the Talley Oil building, isn't that true?

THE WITNESS: Yes.

MR. NGUYEN: Yes, that's true?

THE WITNESS: Yes.

MR. NGUYEN: So what were you doing outside the Talley Oil building?

THE WITNESS: What do you mean?

MR. NGUYEN: I mean what I asked. Let's take it one step at a time. You just heard the 911 call introduced as Defense Exhibit A. Do you recall that the time stamp on the tape was 11:08 p.m?

THE WITNESS: Yes.

MR. NGUYEN: Now in fact, you witnessed my client enter the outer office door approximately thirty seconds prior to the 11:08 call, correct?

THE WITNESS: I don't recall the precise time.

MR. NGUYEN: But you recall seeing him enter the outside door from the patio, correct?

THE WITNESS: Yes.

MR. NGUYEN: Because you were parked on the street watching the Talley Oil building?

THE WITNESS: Correct.

Things started to look up for me after that. Nguyen had the dispatch tapes of Tarwood's radio calls. He played a snippet of dispatch tape, time-stamped 11:07. It was Tarwood, on the radio: "Is he still at the diner? Say again? No, hang on, I see him. He's walking to his car. Wait. The fucking guy is walking up on the patio. He's looking... Shit—" and the tape ends with the sound of a slamming door.

Nguyen rolled: "Wasn't that you, sitting in your car at 11:07? And you knew that my client was at the diner? You knew that because you had another officer following him, didn't you? Following him since he left the bar, correct? And that other officer watched him walk back up the street from the diner until you acquired a visual, correct? You watched my client walk across the lawn and onto the patio and look in through the window of Talley's office? Then you saw him shoulder the door open? And you got out of your car and ran to the door the moment you saw Mr. Heaton force open the French doors, didn't you? How much time to run from your car to the doors? Twenty seconds? Less? Ten seconds? So you entered the office maybe ten to fifteen seconds after Mr. Heaton did?"

Tarwood answered each question with a clipped "Correct." Nguyen flipped the pages of the report, making check marks in the margins as he extracted each detail from Tarwood.

MR. NGUYEN: We'll get to time of death shortly, Chief, when we call the coroner. But I would like to ask you about the murder weapon. What was it?"

THE WITNESS: A .22.

MR. NGUYEN: And that's based on an examination of the bullet?

THE WITNESS: Yes.

MR. NGUYEN: The weapon was a handgun? Rifle? What?

THE WITNESS: Handgun.

MR. NGUYEN: And did my client have a handgun on him when you arrested him?

THE WITNESS: No.

MR. NGUYEN: Did you find any handguns in the office?

THE WITNESS: We did.

MR. NGUYEN: You found Mr. Talley's .45, correct?

THE WITNESS: Yes.

MR. NGUYEN: In his locked desk drawer.

THE WITNESS: Correct.

MR. NGUYEN: That drawer was closed.

THE WITNESS: Correct.

MR. NGUYEN: The lock had not been forced.

THE WITNESS: Correct.

MR. NGUYEN: And you had to break the lock of the drawer to open it, right?

THE WITNESS: Correct.

MR. NGUYEN: The gun was in its case?

THE WITNESS: Correct.

93

MR. NGUYEN: And the case was locked?

THE WITNESS: Correct.

MR. NGUYEN: In fact, you had to break the lock of the case to open it, didn't you?

THE WITNESS: Correct.

MR. NGUYEN: And when you had done all that, you examined the .45 to see if it had been recently fired.

THE WITNESS: Yes.

MR. NGUYEN: And you determined it had not been.

THE WITNESS: That is correct.

MR. NGUYEN: And just so we're clear, Mr. Talley was not shot with a .45, was he?

THE WITNESS: No, he was not.

MR. NGUYEN: Okay, and there were no other guns in that office?

THE WITNESS: No.

MR. NGUYEN: No other guns anywhere else in the Talley Oil building, right?

THE WITNESS: None that we recovered.

MR. NGUYEN: And you searched, didn't you?

THE WITNESS: We did.

I threw Bobby Tarwood a mental salute. Nguyen had assured me that there wouldn't be any surprise .22s pulled out at the hearing. "The law doesn't work that way," he had said. I told him he was naive. Now I wondered if I was.

Nguyen paused, took a step back from the lectern, and paced three steps to the right and then back, like the captain on the quarterdeck of a tiny ship. He put his hands behind his back, turned, and paced his quarterdeck again. Then he turned back to Tarwood.

"All right, Chief, I think that's almost all I have for now, though Your Honor, I would reserve the right to recall the Chief for the defense case. Let me just see, now—and then I'll be finished—if I have this right. Mr. Talley was shot with a .22; my client had no gun on him; there was no gun in the office other than a .45 in a locked drawer that had not been fired; and there was no gun anywhere else in the building. And you had my client followed since his meeting with Talley at the Piney Woods Bar, then personally witnessed my client enter the office at 11:07, and immediately ran in and followed him, entering the building maybe ten to twenty seconds after him. Do I have all that correct?"

Lutz fired a volley of "compound!" and "asked and answered!" but the judge deflected it with a raised hand.

"It's a prelim, Ms. Lutz, there's no jury here. You can answer, Chief. Is that all true?"

"All true," said Tarwood.

"So where is the .22 that fired the fatal shot?"

Tarwood shook his head. "I don't know."

Lutz wrapped up her case a few minutes later. I'd sat through enough prelims to know that I'd get held for trial. The standard was just probable cause, after all, and while the absence of the murder weapon might be enough for reasonable doubt at trial, I didn't think it would negate probable cause at a prelim.

Nguyen was more optimistic. We still had our defense case to put on, and he was going to call the coroner as a witness; the coroner's report put the most likely time of death at 10 to 10:30, long before I'd entered the office. "And that's stuff you can't fake and you can't plant, Heaton," he had said in my cell that morning. "Body temperature, blood coagulation. You can't turn a guy who's been dead an hour into a guy who's been dead five minutes."

I wasn't so confident. Lutz would put Tarwood back on for rebuttal, and I knew all he'd have to do would be to pick a ten-minute window and testify that he and his boys had lost sight of me. Then you sell it to the jury with me arguing with Talley in the bar, then going after him to his office, shooting him with a .22 I brought with me, slipping away and ditching the .22, and then coming back a half hour later for some reason. What reason? Who cares? Murderers revisit the scene of the crime all the time, on TV. If a jury wanted to pin it on me, they could.

When the defense case started in the afternoon, though, Nguyen's first witness wasn't the coroner. It was Linda Waters. Nguyen wanted to put me in the coffee shop with Linda to close off any possible time windows when I could have been in the office killing Talley.

They brought me out of the holding cell at 1:30 to wait for the judge to come out. I sat. Then Nguyen came in, and Lutz. Then the bailiff opened the hallway doors to the public, and the benches filled up fast.

The judge came in and we all stood up and everyone said, "Good afternoon, Your Honor." Then he looked at Nguyen and said, "Counsel, your witness?"

Nguyen nodded to the bailiff, who went back behind the judge's bench and opened the same door the judge had come through. Linda Waters followed him in. She was wearing a blue dress and clutching a leather purse. She looked around the courtroom, seeing for the first time how packed it was. The bailiff directed her to the witness box at the side of the bench, and the clerk swore her in. Then Nguyen stood up.

He ran quickly through her background. She was sixty-two years old and had worked for Talley Oil for more than thirty years. Lived right here in Mandanoches. Had she seen the defendant before?

"Oh, yes."

"When did you first see him?"

"He came to the office on January 9th, to see Mr. Talley."

She recalled my "amicable" greeting, after which I had gone into Talley's office for a meeting, joined shortly by Chief Tarwood. Then I had departed with Tarwood and another deputy.

"Ever see the defendant again after that?"

"Yes." And she described meeting me in front of the office at around 10:30 p.m.

"What were you doing at the office that late?"

"Oh, I often come in at night to take care of a few things. I only live a few minutes away."

She recalled inviting me to get a cup of coffee. "I was headed over there anyway, you know, and it's not often you get to meet a private detective from New York. I'd always imagined my... Well, I always wanted to go there, and I never have. I figured talking to Mr. Heaton was about the closest I would come to going there myself." She smiled sadly.

Nguyen asked if she had paid for the coffee. She had. "I also had a piece of pie," she added. Had she kept the receipt? She had.

Nguyen opened his exhibit binder and directed her attention to Defense Exhibit D. Was that the receipt? It was. Two coffees and a slice of pie. And the time printed at the bottom of the receipt? 11:05 p.m.

Nguyen sat down. "Nothing further. Reserve redirect."

Lutz stood up. She reached down and popped her exhibit binder open, extracted her copy of Defense Exhibit D, and held it in front of her, looking down at it like it was a bag full of dog shit someone had thrown at her door on Halloween.

She went to the lectern, still looking down at the paper.

"Ms. Waters, you said you paid, correct?"

"For the coffee and the pie? Yes, I did."

"And then you went home?"

"Yes."

"In your car."

"Yes."

"The defendant didn't come home with you?" That was unnecessarily nasty, I thought.

"Certainly not," said Waters, her tone indicating that she shared my assessment of the question.

"So you don't know where the defendant went after he left the coffee shop."

"That's correct."

"Now let me ask you this: did you exit the coffee shop at the same time, or did he leave before you did?"

"He left before I did."

"How long before?"

"Oh, I couldn't say precisely. A few minutes, maybe."

"'A few minutes,'" Lutz repeated. "'A few minutes, maybe.' And the coffee shop is how far from the Talley Oil building?"

"Not far. Down the block, around the corner."

"One more question," said Lutz, speaking slowly, as if pondering the question herself. "If the defendant left the coffee shop 'a few minutes' before 11:05, he would have had plenty of time to walk around the corner to the back of the Talley building, break in the door, and kill James Talley before 11:08. Isn't that true?"

97

Nguyen shot up. "Objection!"

Lutz jumped in before the judge ruled. That was bad form, but she didn't care. She'd already made her point. "Your Honor, the witness has personal knowledge of the locations and the distances. She can answer."

The judge thought about it. "Overruled as to the time necessary for the walk. You may answer."

Linda Waters looked up at the judge. "I can answer," she said. "That walk don't take but a minute, but Mr. Heaton didn't kill Pops Talley. Pops was already dead."

The gallery buzzed, as a hundred people turned to whoever was sitting next to them to ask if they'd heard that right. Lutz had turned away from the lectern and was looking down at a stack of papers on the table, probably thinking about the next witness already. She looked up, but she was momentarily speechless. She looked over at Nguyen, then stepped back toward the lectern, but it was too late. Linda Waters leaned into the microphone and spoke loudly and clearly.

"Pops Talley took from me everything I had in the world. I should have done it then and died with her. But I did it at last, and I'm at peace with the Lord. I shot him in the head with this gun, right here." And she reached into her purse, pulled out a .22 revolver, raised it to her temple, and pulled the trigger.

Eighteen

How do you get a gun into a courthouse? In the movies, that would be a technical problem, requiring some techno-wizardry from the wisecracking fat guy waiting out in the van hunched over his laptop. Maybe you use a custom-designed, all-plastic, single-shot pistol that comes apart in pieces so it looks like a cigarette lighter and key fob in the security tray. Or maybe you use a prosthetic limb with a lead-lined compartment. Or your tech guy out in the van flies one to you with a quadcopter and drops it in an open bathroom window. None of those are impossible—hell, there are open-source codes out there for 3D printing yourself a gun out of carbon fiber. It won't set off any metal detectors and you can disguise the shape cosmetically a hundred different ways. Your bullets still need to be metal, pretty much, but bullets are small and easily concealed. You could work a couple into your standard Texas belt buckle or steel-toed boot. Or just shove them up your ass. That's the time-tested, smuggler's go-to for any small piece of contraband.

It's just not that hard, if you really want to do it. The TSA ran a drill a couple years ago where they had plainclothes agents try to smuggle weapons through airport security checkpoints. The bust rate was 17 percent. Fully eighty-three out of a hundred waltzed straight through.

The left-wing talking heads love the phrase "security theater." For them it means that all our heavy-handed security protocols are just an act designed to fool the public into thinking the government's protecting them, or, depending on the talking head, to keep our fear level amped up. I happen to think your average left-wing talking head is full of shit, but it's still theater. Not because the security guys are acting—they're not—but because they might as well be. They're about as effective as Alec Guinness standing there with his light saber. For all the good your standard security protocol does, we might as well be using stage props, as far as a dedicated smuggler is concerned. And that's just weapons—if we're talking drugs, the numbers are much worse. Five percent bust rates or worse, for your typical checkpoint.

So Linda Waters could have MacGyvered herself a way to sneak in her .22. But she didn't need to. The best way to get a gun into a courthouse is to put it in your purse and ask your old friend the police chief to escort you in through the back entrance. Which is what she did.

When she pulled the gun out of her purse the whole courtroom froze. Even the bailiff, who was only ten feet away from her, just sat there gaping, even though he was in theory supposed to be prepared for this sort of thing.

I was on my feet, around the defense table, and halfway to the witness box before she slumped over. She fell forward out of the box, and I caught her and kneeled down on the floor, cradling her head in my lap. There wasn't that much blood, at first, but then I saw it soaking the front of my shirt and pooling on the carpet. She didn't speak or breathe or look up at me. She was dead, her eyes empty. She'd said her last words and done what she came there to do. So I just sat there on the floor and held her.

Nineteen

Larry Nguyen looked glum on the drive back from court, and I told him so.

"Glum? You think? Well, shouldn't I be?"

"You just saved an innocent man from lethal injection, so there's that."

"Okay, yes, that is a positive result. But forgive me for pointing out that in *my* world, this is not exactly the sort of thing you train for."

I took the implication to be that in *my* world, whatever Nguyen thought that was, little old ladies blew their brains out on the witness stand all the time. I didn't answer. Nguyen turned toward me, looking younger than the thirty he'd claimed. "Look, Marcus, I don't know the newly deceased murderer. I do know that we can now add two names to the list of totally unnecessary victims of gun violence."

"Yeah," I said, "and one name to the list of guys who aren't going to do life for murder for hire. Whatever their fucked-up history was, I didn't cause it and neither did you."

He drove in silence for another minute. Then he hit the steering wheel and started in again.

"Damn it, it was unnecessary. I didn't need to call her. I had them with the coroner. I fucking *had* them. A three-minute window? That's fuck-all, and it's after the time of death. I didn't need her."

I tried to reassure him. "This is not your fault," I said.

"I should have just gone with the coroner. Goddamn it. The judge would have kicked it."

"He wouldn't have," I said. "Believe me, he wouldn't have. And they would have gone to trial on that three-minute window."

"Well, we'll never know now," he said bitterly. "So yes, Marcus, I do feel just a tiny bit responsible. In a perfect world, that lady is still alive, and you walk on time of death."

"You think she killed herself because you called her as a witness?" I said.

Nguyen wasn't listening. He was still thinking about his perfect world. "And I'm the guy who got a Texas murder complaint kicked on the prelim," he said. "Goddamn it, I was *there*."

I stared at him. Was he upset that he wasn't going to get the credit for getting the charges dismissed?

He must have seen the accusation in my eyes. "It's not just about me," he said. "It's about you too. They dismissed, but jeopardy hasn't attached yet, so they could come after you again if they come up with some evidence. And so..." He looked at me.

"And so what?"

"Is there anything that I should be aware of or not aware of with regard to this case?"

He spoke hesitantly, as if it was the first time he'd ever asked a client that question. Maybe it was. I knew what he wanted to ask me, but he was a Bright Young Thing, and he needed to learn to say what he meant.

"Are you asking me if J.C. sent me down here for an execution?"

He didn't answer. I wondered what sorts of stories the lawyers in the firm told about me. As to whether J.C. herself was capable of ordering hits, I knew for a fact that she was. Along with whoever else had tuned into C-SPAN for the hearings, I'd watched her testify about the previous administration's "targeted killing" program. She'd been responsible for making the final recommendations to the President. Angel or devil. Innocent or guilty. Live or die. And she refused to say how many, or why they were chosen, or who they were. Or where.

"Does the targeted killing program extend to the territory of the United States?" a senator had thundered.

And she had answered: "The program is designed to provide responsive and adaptable protection from imminent threats."

Which, as the news hosts all pointed out, doesn't sound a lot like "no."

"Just what do you think J.C. does?" I said.

He didn't answer for a spell. We rode in silence, looking out at the soy fields and strip malls that lined Highway 59. Then he turned abruptly and said, "Can I tell you a story?"

I didn't say anything. They ask you that, they're going to tell you.

He did. "My first real job after law school, after I clerked? Public defender's office. No pay, too many cases. 'Live on your idealism, kid.' None of us knew any better.

"One of my first cases, they hand me this file. Kid's nineteen. First arrest, no record. I mean nothing, not even school discipline. Stupid little weapons charge, constructive possession. Gun was on a table by the couch the kid was sitting on. DA calls it a 'gang case' and they set his bail at two hundred grand. Ridiculous.

"I go up to the jail to see him, and he lays it out. No father, living with mom who's holding the family together, oldest of five, tough neighborhood, gangs everywhere, everyone's connected one way or another. He keeps his head down, nose clean, stays out of it. Says he was at this party. Not drinking, not doing drugs. Just playing video games."

"Like every other gangbanger that ever got busted at a party," I said.

"Yeah. But this kid was clean. I took a good look—no tats, not muscled up, got an Obama cut. Just a thin little kid. And he says to me, 'Mr. Nguyen, you've gotta get me out of here. I don't belong in here. They'll kill me.'

"And I'm like, 'Yeah, okay, I'm working on your bail, yadda yadda.'

"And the kid's like, 'No, you don't understand, they'll *kill* me.' And he leans close and he says, real quiet, 'Mr. Nguyen...I'm *gay.* They're gonna find out and they're gonna kill me.' Now, I was out at that point. I've been out since college. But there's no way that kid could have known that. I bet you didn't even know..." He looked over at me, accusingly.

"I did not," I said, which was true. But with J.C.'s Bright Young Things, you didn't really think of them as having any sexuality in particular. They were just her shiny toys.

"So I drive home," he said. "I'm working myself up about all the injustice in the world, how someone's gonna fucking Matthew Shepard this poor kid and the blood'll be on my hands if I don't get him out. I run into the office—which is a fucking liberal-guilt *echo* chamber, man —and I'm working plans to take a writ on the bond, find some big left-wing donor to put up a property. I'm thinking I'll put up *my* car, which was a nice one, I'm thinking I'll ask my *par*ents....

"So I run around for a week like that, put everything else off, you know, this is my goddamn crus*ade*. I call this girl I knew from law school, she's working at Lamba Legal. *Sweet* gig, those rainbow advocacy jobs, you know? This was back, like, around *Lawrence*, remember? When gay marriage was like the fucking Apollo Project? They had these lists, you know?

"So she gets me a name and I get my surety and a property bond. And I go in and I set a bond hearing. I bring in the whole family in their church clothes. I find some ringers to fill up the row, I mean I totally fucking Johnnie Cochraned this thing, right?"

He looked over at me. I knew where the story was going. But he wanted to tell it. Wanted me to hear him tell it. Probably the first time he'd told it to anyone. Client confidentiality was a bitch that way. But the one thing I knew the Bright Young Things knew about me was that I was a guy you could tell things to. Because they knew J.C. did.

"So we all get there at 8:15. I put the family in a motel so they'd be on time. I check in with the bailiff, go back to the holding cell to see the kid, get him ready. And I'm thinking, this is my moment. I'm doing *justice*. I'm saving this kid, this poor, helpless little there-but-for-the-grace-of-God-go-I kid.

"And he's sitting in there with this little smirk on his face. And I just knew. Right then I knew. Because he was totally different. Posture, voice, everything.

"He says, 'Man, I can't let you go through with this. You a good lawyer, you know how it is.'

"And I just said, 'What? What are you talking about?'

"He says, 'Look, man, I *am* a gang member. What did you *think* I was doing at that party? When you came up to see me after the arraignment, I thought I needed to get out. I had some shit on the street needed taking care of. And they send me a faggot PD, so I figure what the hell, give it a shot.

"'But now, we good. Shit got done, on the street. All taken *care* of. *Now* I need to do this time, get my propers inside. So you get me a plea, okay? I'm thinking they'll take eighteen months. They got nothing but circumstantial shit, and ain't no one gonna testify against me, you can be sure of that. So go make it happen.'

"And then he stands up. This kid, same little kid as before, right? Only all of a sudden he gets fucking *scary,* and he leans over and says, 'Ain't nobody here for you to save today.' Then he shakes his head and laughs at me."

He waited a moment, then said, "You with me on the metaphor here, Marcus?"

"I hate metaphors. Too hard to follow. I do better with similes."

"Who did I just save," he said, "the puppy dog or the fucking pit bull?"

"Neither," I said.

He didn't answer. "Come on, kid," I said, "Don't second-guess yourself. I didn't shoot Talley, and you came in there and proved it. Pat yourself on the back, and stop worrying about all the other terrible things I've done."

He shot me a quick, horrified look, and I winked at him. It was a stupid habit, but I couldn't help myself with the Bright Young Things. It was just too easy to mess with them.

Nguyen was silent the rest of the ride, but when we pulled up at the motel, he put the car in park, pulled his hands back off the wheel, clenched his fists, and exhaled sharply.

"All right," he said. "I have something for you, and I was trying to decide whether or not to give it to you, but I think I should."

"Okay," I said, "what is it?"

He opened his briefcase and took out a thick stack of papers held together with a clip. "Well, this, for starters. It's the rest of the state's discovery. I have a copy to put on the system, but in case you want a paper copy?"

He sounded hesitant. "Sure, kid, that's just what I want to read on the plane," I said. But I took the papers to be polite.

"Yeah, well, that's not all," he said. He reached into his jacket pocket and pulled out an envelope. "This," he said. "Linda Waters came to see me, night before last. I talked to her last week, after I saw you. Told her we'd need her as a witness. At the very least put you in the coffee shop at 11 p.m. She said sure, no problem. Took the subpoena, and that was that.

"Then, like I said, two nights ago, she tracks me down at my hotel. Probably wasn't that hard."

That seemed plausible. There was only one hotel in Mandanoches that a Montrose Bryant attorney would be likely to stay in. And it wasn't mine.

"She gives me this," he continued. "Says, 'Just give it to him for me, when this is over.' I say, 'Who?' She says, 'Mr. Heaton. Give it to him. He'll understand.'"

Nguyen looked at me carefully. "So that's the context for my little narrative about my gangbanger client. I haven't opened this. I don't know what it is. I just want to make sure that—"

"That it's not the next target on my hit list? Yeah, kid, I get it," I said. I sympathized. The Bright Young Things knew, at some level, that the coin of High-Stakes Litigation had a shiny side and a tarnished side. They thought, in the bright sunshine of their offices in the morning, that they were intellectually tough enough to see the line between them. But sitting there in a car with me in the dark night of East Texas, they weren't so sure. And that scared them.

"Not a hit list," I said. "Scout's honor. My guess? I'm the last sympathetic person she spoke with before she killed herself, and she wanted to thank me."

He nodded, slowly, and handed me the envelope. "All right, then," he said, "I guess we're all set. I'll go down in the morning and make sure we're all good on the bond exoneration. Then I'm flying back to the city. Call me if you need anything, okay?"

"Sure," I said. "Just stash the gun in the bathroom stall behind the toilet. We probably should do three restaurants, just to be safe."

His look was halfway between incomprehension and horror. "Easy,

Larry," I said, "it's a joke. *The Godfather*? Al Pacino? The young Robert Duvall? You guys really need some culture."

I expected a polite chuckle at least. I got silence. He stared out the window, then turned toward me. "Look at the discovery packet, Marcus," he said. "She called the firm."

I didn't follow at first. He tried again, and this time his voice quavered. "In October," he said. He repeated it in a hiss: "In *October*. The DA pulled the company phone records. There's a thousand calls and they probably never even looked at them, but..." He stared at me hard. "Someone from Talley Oil called Montrose Bryant in *October*. A *month before* you ever met with Hausman."

A chill ran down my spine. That's a cliché until you feel it. I didn't answer.

"I'm your lawyer, Marcus. I have to keep your secrets until I die. Unless—"

I opened the door and cut him off. "Yeah, I know the unless. There's no unless here. I haven't seen any phone logs and I have no idea what you're talking about. Now I'm tired and I'm going to bed." I went for a cop snarl to cover the chill. It was half-assed but it was all I could muster.

I got out of the car and walked up the stairs to the creaking exterior balcony that fronted the motel. The chill froze my legs and I barely made the top step. I knew the "unless." The "unless" was the exception to attorney-client confidentiality. Confidentiality covered past crimes, but not future ones. Larry Nguyen was afraid that there actually was a hit list, and I was checking off names. He was right to be afraid. So was I.

But the chill wasn't strong enough to crowd out exhaustion. I opened the door to my room and lay down on the bed in my clothes. I fell instantly asleep.

Twenty

had barely closed my eyes, it seemed, when someone knocked on the motel room door. I opened my eyes and sat up. The knocking repeated itself insistently. I took the pepper spray out of the plastic property bag from the jail, put it in my right coat pocket, and put my right hand in there with it. I opened the door three inches on its brass security chain. Two clean-shaven faces looked in at me. Mid-thirties, almost identical in appearance, framed by well-groomed, short-but-not-too-short hair-cuts, and propped up by charcoal Men's-Wearhouse-caliber suits. They weren't Jehovah's Witnesses. They were holding out their credentials, the little passport-sized leather wallets the Feds use, with photo and name on one side and the big gold badge on the other.

"FBI, Mr. Heaton," said one. "May we come in?"

"No," I said. "I'm tired. Call my office."

"Someone wants to talk to you," said the other.

"Yeah?" I said. "Someone wants a pony too, but you have to write Santa. Did you boys write Santa?"

"Let's talk," said the first one, putting his foot in the door opening so I couldn't slam the door. The other reached into his pocket, pulled out a small black wire cutter, and clipped the security chain.

"Not very good security here," he said, eyeballing me.

I wasn't going to win a shoving match against both of them to force the door closed, so I didn't try. I stepped back and let them enter. They did, politely. Their eyes moved around the room. "Nothing for you boys to find in here," I said. "As you probably know, I've been in jail for two weeks. You could have searched it while I was locked up."

"Let's take a ride," said the one who had clipped the security chain. He had a red tie. The other one had a blue tie. I figured maybe they had rules that agents had to coordinate different tie colors so they could tell each other apart. Red Tie's suit was a slightly darker charcoal than Blue Tie's suit, which went just a bit toward the gray side of charcoal. They were astonishingly clean-shaven, I thought, for their age and the time of day. "Do you guys shave twice a day?" I asked. "And isn't that rough on the skin in this climate?"

"Someone wants to talk to you, Mr. Heaton," said Red Tie, still extremely polite. They were not exactly in fighting stances. They stood on either side of the door, watching me. I stood facing them with my back to the bed. I took my hand out of my coat pocket. I was not about to go for a friendly ride with two Feds.

"You said that, and I made a cute remark about Santa, remember? You got a warrant, arrest me. Otherwise beat it. I'm tired and I'm taking a nap."

Blue Tie spoke up. "You haven't even asked why we're here."

"Maybe I don't care. Or maybe I know why you're here and I know it's bullshit."

"Try us," said Red Tie.

"You're here because you think Eleanor Hausman was extorting Talley Oil, and you think I was point man for said extortion. Which bullshit theory was conclusively refuted when Talley's secretary showed up with the murder weapon and confessed to killing him. Or weren't you in court today?"

They looked at me and said nothing. I didn't get a cop vibe from them. The FBI doesn't recruit out of police departments. I only knew a couple guys who'd made the jump from the NYPD and they were special-skills cases. These guys were practicing their silent stares on me, but they were out of their league. I was a champion silent starer in the department that invented silent staring. Slight raise of the eyebrows, slight widening of the eyes, lock in eye contact and hold it. You threw that on a perp and you waited for the surge of fight-or-flight, and then he'd make whatever move he'd make that would trigger the takedown.

"Ain't gonna work, boys," I said. "I'm gonna win the staring contest, and I'm not throwing down on two Feds. And you know I'm not even carrying."

"Let's take a ride," said Red Tie, one more time.

"Go fuck yourself."

Blue Tie hit me, cobra-quick, with a right to the upper stomach. It was a good punch. Right on target to put pressure on the diaphragm and knock the wind out of me, and no body language cue at all. I was impressed. If he shifted his feet even an inch, I didn't see it. Just great hip torque, all the power coming from the obliques.

So I did what you do. I went with the punch, which doubles you over, and I twisted sideways to avoid the next blow, which is usually a knee to the face. That's what I always used, anyway, when I was starting off with the sucker punch to the stomach. The combination of stomach punch and knee to the face saved your hands and was pretty much a guaranteed broken nose for the other guy. Of course, sometimes you didn't want him to have an obvious broken nose; you just wanted a quick takedown. That's how I figured these guys. And in that case, you went for an arm.

Which is what Blue Tie did, stepping quickly forward and locking his elbow around my right bicep. When I tried to straighten up from the punch, he would pull back, lever my right arm behind me, and lock onto my left. That was pretty standard.

So I didn't straighten up. When I felt Blue Tie's elbow lock onto my bicep, I grabbed my right wrist with my left and squeezed my arms tight to my sides. Now I had Blue Tie's arm pinned, and the more I leaned forward, the more I pulled him off balance. I dropped to my right knee and dipped my shoulder down to the floor, like Tim Tebow praying for another chance to be a quarterback. Blue Tie was stuck. He came up smoothly over my shoulder and slammed into the floor in front of me on his back. I still had his arm, but now I had it pulled up and back, just right for some joint pressure. I straightened up, locked one leg over his arm. and leaned very gently on the elbow joint. Blue Tie made no sound.

I wasn't particularly interested in breaking his arm, so I didn't lean hard. Red Tie had his gun out, anyway, and was sitting on the edge of the bed pointing it at me. "Okay, Heaton," he said. "Let my partner go. He's so stoical down there that you might hurt him by mistake." It was true. You usually got some screams just from light pressure with this hold. Even with those seriously tough guys you see in mixed martial arts fights on TV. You've probably seen it; they're not acting.

I relaxed the hold. Blue Tie stood up and brushed off his suit.

"What'd he have?" said Red Tie.

"This," said Blue Tie, opening his hand to reveal the pepper spray that I'd had in my jacket pocket.

I gave Blue Tie a polite nod. I am not ungracious, and they had made their play after all.

"See, Heaton," said Red Tie, "we could arrest you and charge you with a number of crimes. But we'd have to drive all the way to Houston—"

"And none of them would stick," I said.

"Well, you don't have all the facts, I'm afraid," he said. "More to the point, there's someone here in town who can explain a whole lot of things to you. Why don't we take that ride?"

Twenty-One

The ride ended at a nondescript, low-slung building about twenty minutes north of town, on Highway 59. It looked like it might have once been a warehouse, or maybe a factory of some sort. I wondered what sort of industries there were around here, besides grinding up chickens and pulping pine trees. The building had no signs, and the parking lot was in back, shielded from view from the street.

They walked me inside, through a little waiting area with some chairs and a coffee maker, and Red Tie knocked on a gray metal door and pushed it open.

Inside was a big empty room with an Ikea conference table in the middle. Long fluorescent lights hung down from the ceiling, and a bunch of whiteboards were set over on one wall. The floor was concrete. I wondered what the place had been used for. It didn't have the lingering smell of rot you'd expect from meat processing.

At one end of the conference table a man sat typing on a laptop. His suit jacket was hung over the back of his chair, and he had his top button undone and his sleeves rolled up. He looked up as we approached, pushed back from the table, and stood up. I pegged him as military. White guy, late forties, thin like a runner, light-brown hair with a cut I recognized as clipper-guard #4 on top, #2 on the sides. And the posture that came from a full twenty in a uniform, which the FBI

Mormon twins couldn't match. He came around the table, smiled, and extended a hand.

"John Scofield," he said. "Pleased to meet you."

"The jazz guitarist?" I said, not shaking his hand. "Big fan. Loved your work with Miles. I have the Montreux record at home."

His smile broadened. "So do I," he said. "Gotta root for your namesake."

"I bet your goons have no idea what we're talking about," I said.

He shrugged. "Depends on the agency. FBI, yeah, you don't really see too many jazz aficionados. DEA, we do a little better." He turned to Red Tie and Blue Tie, who were standing in some civilian approximation of parade rest. "What do you say, guys? You have any Miles Davis records?"

"No, sir," said Red Tie.

"That's because you're a soulless piece of shit," I said, giving him my best come-on-and-hit-me-again grin. He said nothing. Maybe someone had told them to use their inside voices around the adults.

"Tell you what," Scofield said to them, "why don't you guys wait out in the lobby for a couple minutes?"

They turned and left. I watched them go and then sat in one of the cheap fold-up chairs. I left a chair between Scofield and me as a buffer zone.

Scofield sat and leaned forward on his elbows. He was wearing a big Naval Academy ring, which he tapped twice on the table, as if calling our little meeting to order. "All right, then," he said, "I'm a trial attorney with the Department of Justice," he said. "Thanks for coming by."

"DOJ cutting back on the furniture budget?" I said.

"Oh, quite the contrary. We put this place together just for you."

"Really? Well, you did a bang-up job of it. Where's the waterboard?"

His smile flickered, but held. He wasn't going to let me needle him.

I tried again. "Thing is, I'm not that great with the district boundaries, but I think we're in the Eastern District of Texas here."

"We are."

"And that office is in...?" I didn't know the answer to that one. You had Houston and Dallas, I knew, for the Southern and Northern Districts. But Eastern? Why was there even a separate federal district for East Texas?

"It's in Tyler," he said. "Just down the road. But I'm from Main Justice. I go where the cases take me."

"Well, I'm flattered you came all this way," I said, "but I think we both know this is kind of pointless."

"And why is that?"

"Because you know who I work for. And I'll bet my boss is playing golf this weekend with someone who'd be very concerned about your Mormon goons running around kidnapping people and bringing them to your little Reservoir Dogs hideout."

He held his smile. "I don't know anything about that. As far as I'm concerned you came here of your own accord because you're concerned that you're being used as a pawn in a criminal enterprise." He peered at me closely, as if inspecting me for damage. "You certainly don't appear injured. And you're free to leave, of course."

"Great," I said, turning for the door.

"But I don't think you will."

"Ten seconds," I said. "I've used that line enough times myself. Usually when I'm bluffing."

He nodded, looked at his watch, and pushed a key on the laptop. And I heard my own voice from the speakers.

—*Mr. Talley, I want to apologize for the misunderstanding. I'm not here on an extortion job.*

—*Yeah, you're here doing genealogical research. You told me that. That's about the dumbest god damn story I've ever heard.*

—*Which maybe should suggest to you that it might be true?*

—*Don't give me that 'it's-so-crazy-it-must-be-true' shit. In my experience people come up with cockamamie stories because they're too damn stupid to think of anything better.*

—*But I'm not stupid, Mr. Talley.*

—*You ain't no Einstein. But this ain't your story, is it?*

—*It's Eleanor Hausman's story. And she isn't stupid.*

—*No, I reckon not.*

—*And I've done extortion. Plenty of it. It works best when you just come right out and threaten people.*

—*And you're saying you haven't done that?*

—*I don't believe I have, sir.*

—*Well then, god damn, you haven't looked in a mirror lately, son. 'Cause you're nothing but a threat walking around on two legs and if you don't know that then you are waist deep in denial about your life. You are a guy people hire to send a message, not research their damn genealogy.*

—*Well, here's my message, then. If there's an extortion here, I'm out of it. I'll fly straight back there and tell them that. I'll quit my job if I have to. But I won't have to. I work for a* law firm, *Mr. Talley. I've knocked a lot of heads, but I don't do that anymore. I just want you to know that.*

"I like it," said Scofield. "Indignant, self-righteous, and just a soupçon of snarl—that's good work."

"I know what a soupçon is, if you were wondering."

"Oh, I don't doubt it. And you know what RICO is."

"I worked RICO cases with the US Attorney's Office back when I was a cop," I said.

"That's nice," he said. "How would you like to be in a RICO indictment?"

"That'd be fantastic," I said. "I'll put it in a frame and hang it on the wall next to this murder charge that just got dismissed."

"Oh, they don't let you have frames in prison," he said. "Too easy to make shivs out of them."

"You have anything else you want to play for me?"

"Sure," he said. "You want to hear your client on the phone engaged in a racketeering conspiracy? Let's see…" He made a show of scrolling through folders on his laptop. "I have them organized by predicate criminal act. You're on a couple. Your *boss* is on a bunch of them."

"You're recording attorney-client conversations?"

He spread his hands. "I'm recording what my warrant allows me to record. I'm not going to use it all in court. There are other uses."

"Like twisting my arm to sign me up as a cooperator? Forget it." I stood up.

"Oh, come on, Marcus. You actually come off pretty well on the tapes. A little too deferential with the attorneys, if you ask me, but on the whole, yeah, maybe you could convince a jury that you're not a thug."

"Yeah, maybe I could. And maybe you're just a bullshitter."

"Did you wear tweed to Fashion Week and sit with P. Diddy?"

I stopped and turned halfway around. He wasn't bullshitting. He had actually bugged Eleanor Hausman's office.

"So," said Scofield, "do you know how she made her money?"

"The old-fashioned way," I said. "I dunno. Building things, I would guess."

"Yeah. Sometimes. And sometimes there's more money in not building them."

I didn't answer. Scofield stood and began pacing. Three slow steps, stop, military turn, three steps back. "Say you have some project you want to build, some mall or whatever. You draw up some nice pictures, think of a fancy name. Then what do you do?"

"Build it?" I said.

"No! You know how many pretty malls with fancy names never get built? Most of 'em. Somewhere along the development line they just peter out. Land, zoning, tenants, whatever. There are a bunch of hoops and most of them get hung up on one of them."

I let him talk. What did I care? My flight wasn't until tomorrow.

"But you need the investment up front. People put money into a project before it gets built. Obviously."

"Obviously," I said.

"So what happens when it doesn't get built?"

"You tell me."

"Okay. Say a developer draws up plans for a big mixed-use development—residential, retail, commercial. *Awesome* plans. Growth projections off the charts! Barnstorms around lining up investors. Put your money in now, big returns. Talks a great game. Get in on this joint venture with my limited liability company. Sign up for your funding commitment, we're all gonna make the big *green*. But then..."

"But then?"

"But then the deal falls through. The project stalls, But not before the developer's LLC spends all the invested money. There were a whole lot of contractors and a whole lot of nonrefundable deposits to all of 'em. Black fucking *hole*. The money's gone. Sorry, investors. Risky business, real estate."

"And then what? The investors sue the developer?"

"No, that's the best part. The developer sues *them*. Says they didn't meet their funding commitments, and that's why the joint venture failed. *Big* damages claim, there."

"So?"

"So then everyone goes back and looks at the joint venture contract agreement and figures out that they're fucked. See, the contract says the LLC manager—that's your developer—has sole authority to conduct business below a threshold amount. Which those nonrefundable deposits conveniently were. And those big funding commitments—we're talking seven, eight figures here—well, the developer says they're due and payable, or the LLC is entitled to them as damages. You don't want to pay? Then we'll tie your ass up in litigation for the next two years. Or you settle. Most of them settle."

"The investors actually pay?"

"A lot of them do. See, these are mostly institutional investors. Hedge funds, pension funds. They can write off a few million, but not the publicity. So they all settle with nondisclosure agreements, the joint venture folds up, and the money that went into the black hole stays there.

"So you can guess where I'm going with this," he said, doing a light drumroll on the table with his index fingers. "The developer is Eleanor Hausman, and her attorney is Jennifer Curtis, of Montrose Bryant & Wolfe."

"So what?" I said. "So she was smart about making her contracts. Last I checked that wasn't illegal. You play in the big-kid sandbox, you lawyer up, you cover your ass. Sounds like business to me."

"It's fraud, Heaton!" he said forcefully. "It's fraud if you don't intend to actually build the thing. It's fraud if you sign people on to a funding commitment whose sole purpose is to sue them for it later."

"Says you, I guess. Me, I wouldn't know. You know so much, you must also know I never even finished college."

"I do know that. And I know you've been plugging away at night classes at CUNY for the past ten years. You're getting close, Heaton. Too bad you missed your sergeant's exam."

"Don't patronize me, asshole," I said. "You don't need a degree to take the fucking sergeant's exam. I just didn't have a congressman to write me a letter to the Naval Academy." Fucking officers.

"Well, I suppose that was the Navy's loss, then," he said, "but I admire your commitment. That's one reason I decided to talk to you. You're smart enough to think about this."

"Think about what? Being your rat? To make a case you clearly haven't made, unless you're keeping all the good stuff for yourself?"

He was silent for a moment. Then he said, "I am, Marcus. I am. But I have it. And you're smart enough to wonder what it is."

"So what?" I said. " I'm doing the work she hired me to do, which is perfectly legal. You're a lawyer. I bet you've given a speech to some junior-high civics class about *Gideon v. Wainright.*"

"I have indeed," he said. "It's a good speech. But *Gideon,* now, that's about the rights of criminal defendants. And correct me if I misunderstood, but you're doing genealogical research here, right? You're not defending a criminal case, are you?"

"You tell me," I said. "From the fact that I just got kidnapped by a couple of Mormon hard-boys to get lectured by a Fed in an unmarked warehouse, I'd say yeah, maybe I am."

"Is that what you were hired to do?"

"Go pound sand."

"I appreciate your politeness, Heaton. So I'm going to leave you with a final question. Do you have any idea what Talley's land is worth? Do you have any idea what's *under* it?"

"Screw you, Jack," I said, standing and turning toward the door. "Free to go, right?"

"I *know* you, goddamn it. I know everything about you. And I know you're not a fraudster. I know your role in the 30th and I know why you did it."

"You don't know shit," I said. I walked to the door. "I'm calling your bluff, *John.* File your indictment, do what you gotta do. I'm not a criminal."

Now he showed some temper for the first time, slamming the table with his fist. "You were the enforcer in the 30th precinct for ten years! You were a fucking *bagman* for the most thoroughly corrupt police captain the NYPD has ever *seen.* You don't just take a shower and wash that shit *off!*"

"I can try," I said.

"Well, you're using the wrong soap," he said. "It was nice meeting you." He sat back down and turned to his computer.

I walked out into the dingy warehouse lobby, where Red Tie and Blue Tie were drinking coffee.

"Who wants to take me home?" I said.

The twins dropped me at my hotel. We didn't talk on the ride, which was fine with me. I was thinking about how Scofield had gotten the audio recording from the bar. The sound quality was pretty good, but that didn't mean much nowadays. It could have been a directional mic from across the room. You could enhance just about anything with the right software, and the right software was easy to get. But if he had had someone in there recording, then he had had someone following me… or following Talley. If he had been trying to get me to wonder what else he had, he'd succeeded.

And I wondered something else, too. I wondered why he hadn't shared whatever he had with Tarwood and the Angelina County DA.

Twenty-Two

We got back to the motel a little after ten. I watched the Fed sled drive away, then went inside, showered, and packed for my flight. Packing was tricky. I had to decide whether to fold my extra shirt or just shove it into my roller bag. I folded it. Old habits and all that. Then I lay down on the bed to get some sleep. The night air was just the right temperature, so I opened the windows and let the highway noise lull me to sleep.

I woke to knocking on the door. I looked at the clock: 1:30 a.m. I sat up and looked at the door. The knocking was polite, but insistent. "For Christ's sake, just kick the damn thing in!" I said.

Scofield's voice answered. "You had three hours. That's plenty."

I rolled off the bed and walked to the open window. Scofield was standing on the walkway that ran along the second floor of the motel. He was in the same suit and tie. "It's just me," he said. "I apologize for the hour."

"Oh, *now* you apologize?" I wasn't going to get any more sleep anyway, so I opened the door and waved him in.

"For the hour," he said, looking around the room for a place to sit. "For the occasion of our meeting. For the United States of America wiretapping attorney-client communications, sure, you name it. What

I do not apologize for is believing you are an honest man and giving you the chance to prove me right." His voice was slurred, just a touch, but he didn't wobble an inch.

"Go home and sleep it off," I said. "Or wherever you go. I don't give a fuck what you believe."

"Did you notice," he said, "that I didn't ask you whether you killed that old man?"

"Linda Waters killed him," I said. "Remember?"

"But you almost went away for it, Heaton," he said accusingly, jabbing a finger at me. "And *you* need to think about *that*. Only reason you didn't is because it was an honest crime."

"I don't know what it was," I said, "and I'm tired."

"Yeah," he said. "Stop me if you've heard this one. A couple decades ago Congress was debating a sentencing bill. Gonna be enhancements for 'crimes involving dishonesty.' Some people said, hey, *all* criminals are dishonest; they're *all* willing to break the law, right?

"A representative from Texas named Lamar Smith stood up and said, 'Boy, y'all ain't got the first clue about crime. Hell, *yes*, there are honest criminals. A man puts a gun in your face and says, "Give me your money or you're dead." Why there's nothing dishonest about that whatsoever. Least not if he's serious about it.'"

Scofield delivered the speech in a broad Texas accent.

"You like that one?" I asked.

"Sure. I use it all the time. Your average perp can distinguish between honest and dishonest crime. I find the distinction useful. It appeals to a certain moral sensibility I find in many of the people I deal with."

"You think fraud is worse than violence?" I asked. I knew he was trying to bait me, but this view genuinely surprised me.

"No," he said. "No I don't. We bump sentences up for violence too. What I'm saying is that fraud begets dishonest violence. Violence to hide the fraud. Violence that isn't your style, Marcus."

"Are you through?" I said.

"No, I'm not through. Not with Hausman, and not with you."

"Oh, you're through with me, all right," I said. "You have fun with

Hausman. I'll tell her to give you a call. Now I'm going to get some sleep."

"Oh, sure," he said. "By all means. I just want you to have a sense of where this is headed."

I waved it away. "I don't need a sense of where this is headed," I said. "I know where it's headed. You're looking for a scalp. Or someone above you is and you're getting it for them. You're no better than a schmuck state trooper setting a speed trap to make his quota."

"And you're down here doing genealogical research. Come on, Heaton, who's the naive one here?"

"I make an honest living," I said, doing my best Jack Nicholson.

"Yeah, I've seen *Chinatown*," he replied. "And I like the analogy, come to think of it."

"Yeah?" I said. "Well, I'd love to hear about it, some other time."

"Now's a great time," he said. "Now's a really great time." He sat down on the faded faux-leather easy chair by the window.

"Fine," I said. "Tell me all about it. I'm not getting back to sleep anyway."

"Okay," he said. "Let's start with you. You're Jake Gittes. Beginning of the movie. He gets hired by a beautiful woman to do run-of-the-mill matrimonial investigation."

"All right."

"And he does. And he thinks he's making an honest living. The poor woman's husband was cheating on her. So he sleuths around, gets the goods. But then he finds out that it wasn't what he thought—it was a setup. He was just a patsy being used to dirty up the City Engineer so the developers could build the big dam he didn't want to build. And Gittes figures that out and he doesn't like it. He gets mad. Decides to get to the bottom of it himself, so he goes to look for the engineer and... uh-oh, the guy's dead. And then John Huston buttonholes him and says, 'Find the girl.' Man, I love that scene."

Scofield did a bad Huston impersonation: "'Of course I'm respectable; I'm *old*.'"

"You're a real film critic," I said.

"And you don't like being a patsy. I *know* you don't like being a patsy. I know it because I heard you say it on the goddamned *tape*."

"So?" I couldn't summon anything worthy of Gittes on three hours' sleep.

"So here's what I want you to think about. Remember those joint venture development deals we were talking about?"

"Your bush-league fraud theory? Sure. Not interested."

"That's *one* theory. But let's stick with *Chinatown*. So first it's adultery, right? Then you think it's a land grab. And then you find out it's this crazy incest shit, and they pull Jake away, 'cause it's Chinatown."

"Right. And then the movie ends, and we go back to real life."

"The development deals, Heaton. I've looked at a lot of them. I've been working my way back to the very first one. And that one's different. The ones I told you about? Companies invest, deal falls through, the investment's gone, they write it off. Okay, that's a pattern. I understand that. Some of them even got into litigation, so I can look at the joint venture agreements, see the logic in settling. Like you said, you play in the big-kid sandbox, you take some risk, that's capitalism. Okay. But the *first* one? That one's different."

I didn't say anything. He knew I'd listen. He was right about me, as far as that went.

"You know how it's different, Marcus?"

"No, John. How is it different?"

"Because the other deals in my file, I know who the investors were. I know who their lawyers were. And I know why they invested—Hausman had a good track record. As you pointed out, she did actually build a lot of things. And the plans were all legit. But this *first* one? She hadn't built *anything* yet. And the land was complete shit. Fucking desert scrubland north of Los Angeles. It's still shit, ten years later. No one should have invested a dime in it. But someone *did*. Someone put in ten million dollars. And then, when the project died, that someone just walked away. No lawsuit, nothing. Never said boo. Just vanished."

I didn't say anything. Let him have his dramatic pause.

He took the pause, then pointed a finger at me. "So who was that someone? That someone who gave Eleanor Hausman her seed money? That's what I've been wondering. And I don't know."

I let him have another dramatic pause. I was too tired to interject anything clever.

He leaned forward. "Who, Marcus? *Who?*"

"How the fuck should I know?"

"Because I can only think of two reasons why someone would do that, Marcus. And I've been kind of mulling them over, see? Why would you give someone ten million dollars and then just let them walk off with it?"

"Stop with the bullshit," I said. "Laundering or extortion, I get it."

"Laundering or extortion. Yes, my point exactly."

He shrugged expansively. If we were in a noir movie he would have taken a dramatic drag on his cigarette. But he didn't have a cigarette. The Feds don't smoke anymore, even in cheap motel rooms off noisy exit ramps.

"So I had a case a few years ago," he said. "You probably heard about it. Big-shot politician. Law-and-order guy. Real old-school, solid, middle American. Candidate for President once even. Didn't make it much past New Hampshire, though. Retired to be an elder statesman, do a little consulting. Then a few years pass, and we get a call from some banking regulators. The Financial Crimes Enforcement Network. It's in the Treasury Department. They tell us that our elder statesman has been making some big cash withdrawals. Fifty grand a pop. Banks have to report those."

"Yeah, yeah, I know, anything over ten grand," I said.

"They call up the Public Integrity Section because that's our baili-wick. Public officials. And we look into it a little. Turns out the bank called him up to ask about the withdrawals and what happens next? He stops with the $50k. Starts taking out $9,500 at a time. Starts really hustling on the consulting gigs, too. Bringing in a lot of money, pulling it out just as fast. Old retired lion of the party, should be enjoying his golden years, right? Or at least putting his money into a foundation or even a goddamn boat or something. But he's not. He's just pulling it out as cash.

"So we send a couple agents out to talk to him, and you know what he says? Says he's putting the cash in a safe somewhere because he doesn't trust the banking system. Former chair of the fucking Finance Committee, the guy that ran the committee hearings on the Federal Reserve, and he doesn't trust the *banking* system? It's a stupid answer anyway, because if the zombie apocalypse comes, all that cash isn't going to help you much, right? Anyway, you know the rest."

I knew the rest. Mr. Elder Statesman had been paying off a couple of former Congressional pages who he'd been especially close to, when they were spending their junior year of high school on the Hill learning about the nuances of democracy.

"Just clumsy, Marcus. Dumb. Dumb on all sides."

Scofield was right about that. The Senator ended up pleading to money laundering and obstruction charges, and then he swallowed a bottle of pain pills a week before sentencing. No one came to his funeral, and they sandblasted his name off of a post office and an elementary school. And the pages got busted for extortion.

"And it struck me at the time," Scofield continued, "that if you wanted to do it right—if, you know, you had good *legal* advice—you could come up with a lot of better ways to move the money. Like, for instance, put it into an LLC, channel it into a joint venture, and then just let it vanish."

Scofield looked out the window. I listened to the truck traffic. Then he turned back to me. "Let me give you a hypothetical. Let's say you were moving money through an LLC. Let's say it was 1998. And let's say you called your LLC 'Antelope Palms.'"

I didn't answer. He locked eyes with me, held the stare. "That's a good hypo, Marcus. That's a hypo we could work with."

We sat there and silent-stared at each other. Scofield's stare was better than his Mormon twins'. He still wasn't in my league, though. Or maybe he let me win. He broke it off after a second or two, stood up, and started in on his naval-officer, three-step pacing, back and forth in front of the window.

"So here's the thing," he said. "You start off with DOJ, you get hired as a rookie Assistant US Attorney in one of the high-volume districts, one of the ones with open slots, right? Say the Southern District of Texas, like me. And now you're a federal prosecutor, and you've hit the goddamn jackpot because now you're going to be a real live crime-fighting trial lawyer. And then you go in and grind out the same damn case over and over. Ten thousand different federal crimes, or whatever the count is, and you're gonna do about three of them. You got your illegal aliens reentering after being deported. You got your border-bust drug cases—your coke loads coming in in hidden vehicle compartments and whatnot. And you got your run-of-the-mill gun cases. Felon-in-possession, mostly, referred from some dipshit traffic stop.

"And you look around in your office and you got fifty files a month cycling through, and you know how much there is to *try* in those cases, Marcus? *Inves*tigate? *Lit*igate? *Fact*-find? Pour through the crucible of the great American adversarial trial process? *Fuck*-all. Because your perp is just sitting there, with all the elements of the offense in his stupid pocket.

"And there *we* are, the best and the brightest from the best law schools in the country, doing these goddamn cookie-cutter cases, one after another, feeling brain death setting in, and you know *why* we're doing it?"

Scofield stopped his pacing. "You know why?"

I sighed. "No, John, I don't know why."

"Because we all know that *after* that, if we just push through and don't jump ship and go off and do *bus*iness litigation, if we stick with it, then waiting up there"—he gestured toward the ceiling—"up there is major frauds, public corruption...the real cases, the real trials. You know what they say? 'We pay you in prestige'?"

"No," I said, "no one's ever said that to me."

"Well, they say it. And for a long time I thought it meant that you knew you'd be a legit candidate for a judgeship or you could run for Congress or you could be that guy on cable news looking serious with 'Former Federal Prosecutor' on the screen under his face.... But that's not it, Marcus. It means if you put in your time, one day you can be the guy who gets to go after people no one else ever goes after. You can be Elliot Fucking Ness. You can be the guy with *one case* on your shelf, one case you take where it leads you, and where your target is going to have the most money and the best lawyers and the fanciest club memberships, and you *still* get to go after him."

He turned on his heel and opened the door. Steady on his feet. Navy guys hold their liquor. He stepped out onto the walkway and looked back over his shoulder.

"I put in my time, Marcus. And now I have one case on my shelf."

"Yeah?" I said. "Well, you better be damn sure it's the right case."

The effect on Scofield took me by surprise. He took a step back toward me like he was thinking about raising a fist.

"What did you say?"

I liked the guy: he could talk jazz and detective movies. I had no desire to knock him out. I spread my hands placatingly.

"Hey," I said, "cool your jets, Top Gun. I'm just saying...if I only had one case, I'd want to be good and sure it wasn't a dog."

He stared at me for a moment, then nodded. "Go to LA, Heaton," he said. "Prove me wrong." Then he turned and walked down the stairs.

I closed the door and lay down on the bed, but I couldn't sleep. I gave up on it and turned on the light. I had two hours until I had to leave, and I had plenty of reading material to kill the time. I had the discovery packet Larry Nguyen had given me, with its incident reports and crime scene photos and the phone log that Nguyen thought was evidence that I was at the center of a murder-for-hire plot. And I had Linda Waters's letter, which was, in a way, the last words of a desperate woman I'd walked out on when she was trying to ask for my help. I weighed my options and took the letter out of my pocket and opened the envelope.

I looked at the letter. It was handwritten, carefully, the letters neat and the rows straight.

Mr. Heaton,

Please give this to her. You know her. I think you know her well enough to understand, and I hope you can help her understand too.

Do that for me, please. I have a clear conscience and I only regret I didn't do it sooner. It had to be me, and only me. You have to believe me, I thought she was dead. He told me she was dead. You can only imagine what that was like. That's the day I died, Mr. Heaton, and I only came back to life for a little while when I learned that she was out there. I came back to life to do what had to be done, and now I'm just back where I've been for the last thirty-five years.

You have to understand why I can't go and try to see her. I can't face the thought that she won't want to know me. Or that she'll hate me. She'd be right to. I let her go, and I didn't fight for her. I can't undo that, and I'm not going to lie about what I've done. All I can do is go to Jesus with my head held high. It's been a long time. You lie down for long enough, you forget what it feels like to stand up. She stands up for herself now. I know it. I've seen her. Now it's my turn.

It was all my fault from the beginning, Mr. Heaton. I got in bed with the Devil, and you know what happens when you do that.

Just let her know this. She was my whole life, and even though she's gone and grown up without me, I know that I'm still with her. I want to tell myself that I never really believed she was dead. I think for a while I didn't. I saved my pictures. They're in her bedroom at the old house. I hid them. He destroyed everything else. Maybe she'll want them.

You tell her I never forgot her. Some of me was there with her. Every time she laughed. Every time she ran after a butterfly. I don't know if she played a sport, if she was in musicals, if she was a dancer. I imagined her doing all of it. For years I would go and watch girls her age, just to look at them and see her face. I saw my little girl pitch a softball. I saw her play the violin. I saw her walk down the sidewalk coming home from school. I saw her trying on every new teenage fashion. I saw her in a car with her friends singing along to something with the volume all the way up. I saw her at the prom with her boyfriend. I saw her cry and laugh and swim in the Pacific Ocean. It was all in my head. But now I know that she did all those things I imagined. And more. And I was with her a little bit of the way for every one. Don't ask her if she remembers me, Mr. Heaton. I can't bear to hear it, and I won't be there anyway. But I want her to know, if there was any good in me, then a little bit of it is there with her always. Talk to Bobby. I can't put it all down here. He's a good person, underneath.

That was it. She'd signed it in her neat cursive. The W in "Waters" was slightly smeared. Maybe from a tear hitting the page, maybe just from folding the paper. Hard to say. I didn't cry reading it. If I were a better man, I would have.

Twenty-Three

My flight back to the city landed at LaGuardia at noon, and I took a cab to my apartment. I was living that year way out on the far West Side, past 11th Avenue, almost to the river. I was tired, and anyway at Montrose Bryant you just turned in your cab receipts every month and got reimbursed. I still wasn't used to that. Cops tended to just drive, even in Manhattan. Me, I had a take-home vehicle, so I could park anywhere, anytime, any way I wanted. But guys would use their personal vehicles, too, and put a PBA placard on the dash. Or a dress uniform hat. Or a shirt on a hanger in the window. It didn't really matter. Flag the car as "cop" and the parking guys wouldn't ticket it. I hear they're tightening up now. But hey, I'm in a cab.

I dozed in the cab and sleepwalked up to my apartment. I wanted to sleep, but I had one thing to do first. I pulled out my phone and called Mohammed Faizalla. Mo had been a forensics tech with the Department, did a lot of DNA analysis. Now he had his own lab across the river in Jersey City. Last I talked to him, he said was doing contract work for a dozen departments and had tripled his income. I'd helped him out a few times on the job. One of the benefits of being a dirty cop—I'd earned myself a lot of favors, and no one ever forgot to repay them.

So could Mo turn around a simple maternity test in a couple days?

No problem, Marcus, you got it. Overnight it, and I'll have your results tomorrow. I unzipped my bag and dumped the contents on the floor. Two identical light-blue dress shirts looked back at me, both smeared with blood across the front. I wanted Linda Waters's blood. You wouldn't think it would be hard to tell two-week-old blood from two-day-old blood. But it wasn't obvious to me which was which. Neither was wet to the touch, but one looked fresher than the other, I thought.

Well, Mo could straighten it out. One of them would be male and one would be female. I took scissors and cut three two-inch squares out of each shirt. I put the squares in envelopes and put one of each in a paper bag and the others in my freezer. I took one of the envelopes with Eleanor Hausman's cotton balls out of the freezer and put it in the paper bag with the shirt swatches. I sealed the bag in a manila envelope and wrote "Heaton" on it, and then I walked over to the post office to send it off for next-morning delivery in Jersey City. The post office was two and a half blocks away, crosstown. It nearly killed me, I was so tired. I nodded off on my feet on the way back, but I made it.

No clean-cut Feds came to roust me out of bed, so I slept the rest of the day and through the night. I dreamed of the old days, like I always did when I didn't drink enough to fog the mirror.

Twenty-Four

Captain Michael "Big Mike" Settentio had a small crew when I started with him, but he was ambitious. He had come up two decades earlier, when crack first hit the 30th and you had turf shootouts just about every night. By the time I got there it was a little calmer, and Settentio was the boss, better placed for some real earning. As long as his weekly stats were good, the downtown brass left him alone. And his stats were good: stops, frisks, searches, seizures, guns and drugs and perps, logged in and counted and filed away on a spreadsheet. The Captain rewarded the guys who could reliably go out on a shift and come back with a gun or some dope.

The CompStat system the Department was bringing online to track crime statistics in real time created a beautiful synergy just waiting to be tapped by a smart guy who read business-leadership books, like Settentio did. You had products: guns, dope, and arrests. You had consumers: the Department brass downtown with their stat sheets. And if you took a look at that economy you'd notice that the best way to maintain a good supply of products for the consumers was to manage your relationship with the *producers*—all those perps guys like me went out and rousted every day.

Settentio noticed. All cops did, at some level. You managed your relationships. We didn't call it a business synergy, but we got the concept of mutual benefit. They teach you from the first days on patrol to cultivate snitches. And the way you cultivate a snitch is to show him that he can either *be* another arrest for the CompStat board, or he can be a *producer* of arrests for the CompStat board. Somebody's going in, because we are going to make our numbers. So it's going to be you, or someone else. If you don't want it to be you, then tell us who the someone else is. Your call. And that's how it starts. Every law enforcement agency in the world does it that way.

A guy like Settentio sees right away that the price points are screwed up. You think the dollar value that mope puts on *not* getting busted is equal to the dollar value *we* put on one more lousy arrest that we're going to get anyway? *Hell* no. You really try to put a number on it, he probably values it a hundred times higher than we do. A thousand, maybe, depending on how badly another arrest would fuck up his life. Bottom line, we're selling him a product—his freedom—for *way* less than he would be willing to pay for it.

Simple economics, Settentio said. Think about sneakers, he told us. Why would you sell them for what it costs you to make them, when people will pay a hundred times that? I heard that from Settentio a dozen times. It was his favorite illustration of the basic economics of street-level police corruption. We're sitting on a stock of Air Jordans and selling them like bargain-basement Keds knockoffs.

Settentio saw the potential in the price instability in the market for local police corruption. Consumer confusion meant a lot of transactions unconsummated, a lot of money left on the table. What do you do if you're a smart, statistically minded guy, the kind of guy who was rising in the new NYPD? Simple. You figure out the price point.

You didn't do it for every arrest, obviously. There was risk and what Settentio called transaction costs. Putting the right price on not getting arrested is not something most people have any experience with. And most people run their mouths. You do a traffic stop and say, "Hey, buddy, this is a $400 ticket, but you can skate for $100 cash", and you're going to be reading about it in the papers and then you'll get shitcanned and indicted. The modern, professionalized American police Department doesn't work that way anymore. That's third-world shit.

Tijuana. Russia. Or those rent-a-cop companies that get contracts to run juvie centers, immigration detention, stuff like that. They don't pay their guys shit, and they'll hire anyone. So you get the guy driving the van of deportees to the border who just pulls over and announces: "Anyone got five grand? Family who can pay? Tell me the address."

But the big-city Departments figured out if you make being a cop the best goddamn municipal job there is, if you pay us double what teachers get, with unlimited overtime and retirement after twenty years, that will cut down on the penny-ante graft. And it did. A guy who knows if he sticks it out he'll get up over a hundred grand and retire at forty-five with a better pension than anyone else on the rolls, that guy will play ball when you tell him not to hold up Joe Citizen on traffic ticket shakedowns.

But he also *damn* well won't say anything when he sees his captain running an extortion racket with the precinct drug crews. And he won't say anything when he's out on a call and a colleague lets the violence get out of control and has a baton party on some schmuck's face. What's the single biggest motivator for a cop? Keeping his job. So you think *hard* before you rock any boats.

Nick Becker transferred into the 30th in my last year in the Department. He was a mid-career bruiser who'd never get promoted out of patrol. I could see what he was the minute he showed up to his first roll call. Stocky, puffed-out face like a juicer, strong but you knew he'd waddle when he ran, blondish hair in an Ivan Drago flattop, a little smirk on his face, talking a little too loud, stroking his baton like he was jerking it off.

I didn't like the guy. I knew that I was corrupt and violent. But my violence was *directed*. I did legit cop work 90 percent of the time, and I could be trusted to do it professionally. This guy, you could see how badly he was itching to put his hands on someone. You could practically smell it in his sweat.

Becker never got in with Settentio's crew. Settentio wanted his guys smart and discreet, and Becker was neither. He loved bragging about his collars, especially when he sent people to the hospital. "And then the motherfucker tries to stand up and I just Bruce Lee him right in the ribs. Bam!" He and his buddies would laugh like they were the first cops to kick someone in the ribs. He was like your obnoxious cousin who you tolerated because he was family.

I pretty much ignored him. He tried to impress me a few times with hard-guy talk, the way a lot of the young guys did, but I blew him off. Then one night Becker ran into Bradley Farmington.

Bradley was a Wall Street banker. You could sense that the minute you saw him, the way you could smell the thug in Becker. Bradley was Wall Street even in his casual attire, which on this night was a pair of Nantucket Red slacks, polo shirt, and penny loafers. He drove his BMW up into the 30th, and Becker saw him and just started salivating.

I had to piece together what happened from a lot of different sources, but the outline was something like this. Farmington parked on Broadway near 137th and went into a bodega and asked, in prep-school Spanish, for some dulce de leche. This attracted the attention of a dealer hanging out by the bodega door. The proprietor, assuming that Bradley was looking to score, just shook his head and turned away.

That much I saw on the surveillance video from the store. It didn't have sound, but Bradley enunciated so clearly, with a big smile on his face, that you could read his lips.

The dealer stepped into the store as Bradley was turning to go. "C'mon man, they got it next door," he said, or something like that. Bradley gave a little shrug and followed the guy out like a puppy.

They walked out onto the sidewalk and took about two steps when Becker and his partner rolled up and hit the lights. Becker's partner was a former Division I lineman named Rory McAvoy. He was a 6'4" farm boy from Kansas, a herd animal through and through. He'd come east and played at Rutgers. That was back before Rutgers football was much to brag about, but it was close enough to big-time college football to get him drafted in one of the late rounds.

He never played a down in the NFL, got cut in his first preseason. But he had graduated with a criminal-justice degree, and the Department still likes size. McAvoy had big forearms and did what he was told. Becker told him he was getting a great education in policing, and McAvoy probably believed it.

As far as anyone was ever able to tell—and we looked hard—Bradley was actually trying to buy some dulce de leche. Creamy, sweet condensed milk that comes in a little can. We found out that he was on his way up to Rye, where a friend of his had a house. The friend had a yacht in Port Chester Harbor, and he was having a little party on it. He'd invited some girls, one of whom Bradley had met before and wanted to impress. "She was Mexican or something, and Bradley liked those little gestures," the friend said. "He thought he'd show up with something ethnic, I guess."

Even this turned out to be true, to some extent. I talked to the girl: she was Puerto Rican and hated dulce de leche, but she liked Bradley. She told me he was cute and sweet.

Bradley stopped being either of those things that night. When he made it to the hospital, he was in a coma with his face smashed beyond recognition.

The bodega's camera only showed the sidewalk right outside the front entrance, so the last we see of Bradley is him walking out with the dealer, a silly half smile on his face, like he's thinking maybe his Spanish isn't half bad after all. Then you see the lights from Becker's cruiser, and the dealer takes a couple steps like he's thinking about running. He leaves the frame and then for an instant, a single screenshot in jerky ten-frames-a-second low def, we see Bradley's face turn in surprise, like someone has just yelled "Up against the wall, motherfucker!"—which is what the witness I found recalled Becker yelling—and he just can't believe that *he's* the motherfucker.

I got the video in that first hour, after the Captain called me down to the St. Vincent's emergency room at three in the morning. He was sitting outside, by the ambulance dock, smoking a cigarette.

Three in the morning and he was wearing a suit. Silk tie, pocket square. Always the dresser. He nodded at the bench next to him and I sat.

"I sent the fucking gorillas home," he said. "Told 'em to disappear and call in tomorrow. Buy us a couple days. And schmucko's in surgery, be a few hours. They notified family, but no one's local. So get on it."

"Have they written anything?" I asked.

"No, and they're not fucking going to. You are. Now go find out what the fuck happened. I can hold the lid on it as long as that jomo doesn't die."

Twenty-Five

I woke up to the orange-gray light before dawn, got dressed, and walked down to the river. It was bitterly cold, and I had to run to stay warm. I tried heading downtown, but the wind was coming up off the harbor, so I turned and let it blow me uptown to 57th. Then I turned east and got to the Montrose Bryant building by six.

I caught J.C. in her office. That was our normal time to meet. J.C. was a compulsive pre-dawn exerciser, 5 a.m. on whatever new machines the gym in her building had just invested in, and 6 a.m. at her desk. Out across midtown and over Queens, you could see the sun coming up over Long island, the reflections shimmering pink in a million sheets of glass as the sky lightened. I liked that time of day. And I liked the quiet in the office. J.C. didn't make her team of Bright Young Things match her hours. The new ones tried, sometimes, showing up at 5:30 hoping to get seen, but it didn't help them. J.C. didn't *want* her Bright Young Things around her at six in the morning.

"So," she said.

"So, did you send me down there to put a bullet in Pops Talley's head?"

"Why? Did you?"

"As far as I know, Linda Waters did, but it sure as hell could have ended up on me, if she hadn't conveniently committed suicide with the murder weapon."

"Hmm. So I see three possibilities. Make it four, actually. One: the purpose of your trip was to scare Talley and get him to sell. Two: the purpose of your trip was to kill Talley and get away with it. Three: the purpose of your trip was to kill Talley and get caught. Four: the purpose of your trip was to get caught for killing Talley while Linda Waters got away with it."

That was how she talked. It came from twenty years of not getting interrupted, I guessed. Maybe she used shorter sentences with the President.

"That assumes we're discarding genealogical research," I said.

"Yes," she said. "We're assuming—*you* are assuming, anyway—that you are either a thug or a patsy and not a genealogical researcher."

"That's pretty much Talley's last words to me," I said.

"Oh?"

"That I'm an idiot if I thought anyone would hire me for a family background job. That sending me down there was a threat one way or another."

"Hmm," she said again and pursed her lips. "But it was your idea, wasn't it? Going down there? As I recall, your brief from the client was simply to find some details about her childhood and family history. Which you interpreted, quite astutely, I should say, as reflecting the client's suspicions that she was adopted.

"And then you visited the doctor she saw as a child. Your idea again, yes? Which is where you learned that she'd gone by 'Lynn.' And you researched her father's tax records, leading you to Mandanoches. I do read your reports, Marcus."

"You mean if she'd just wanted me to show up down there, there were a lot of easier ways to go about it."

"Easier, yes, and more certain."

"Yeah." This was true, and it nagged at me.

"Okay," I said. "Just tell me, is she trying to get Talley's land? I mean, she hires me to find out where she's really from, and I do and the minute I get there it turns out the town oil boss is scared shitless about some out-of-town developer that he thinks must be our client. And then he gets shot by his secretary, who's been sitting outside his goddamn office every day for thirty years not saying boo 'til I show up and utter the sacred name of Sue-Lynn Hempersett. Who, according to the police chief, died thirty-five years ago."

J.C. looked at me with an expression I couldn't read. Not that I normally could read her expressions.

"You'd like to know whether Eleanor Hausman is trying to acquire the Talley Oil properties."

"Yes," I said. "I would."

She didn't answer the question. "Let's reconvene in a week, shall we?" she said. "You can use the time to finish your report on her parentage."

I wondered if she had read Larry Nguyen's discovery file, if she knew that the Mandanoches police had pulled the Talley Oil phone records. I wondered if she knew that I knew that Linda Waters had called the firm. Nguyen might have told her that he told me that. I gave it decent odds. He would have been scared to tell her, but more scared not to.

But he might not have mentioned that he'd given me a copy. To Nguyen, the only scary part of that log was Waters's call to the firm. Because Nguyen didn't know what else to look for. But I did. And I had seen something else in the log, when I paged through it on my flight back to the city, something that had made me get up and stagger down the aisle and lock myself in the bathroom on the edge of vomiting.

Nguyen didn't spot it because he didn't know the number. And he didn't know the number because there were only about ten people in the world who did, and it changed every six months, always an innocuous, Midwestern area code, prepaid. J.C.'s private cell. For conversations that never happened, that couldn't happen face-to-face.

And Linda Waters had called it. Three times, the week after she called the firm.

If J.C. wasn't going to answer my questions, then fuck it, I'd go see whatever John Scofield thought there was to see in LA. But I had one more person to see first.

Mobile home park, Leon County, Florida

Twenty-Six

I found Duane Hempersett in North Florida, in a little piece of nowhere on the way from Tallahassee to Crystal River.

He was living in a trailer in a sweaty patch of red dirt next to a sugar plantation. You could say it was the Gulf Coast if you stretched "coast" to fifty miles inland. He paid $150 a month for the ground lease and owned the trailer outright, so he told me. Won it in a card game.

Duane would have been a Carl Hiaasen character, except Hiaasen's hillbilly trash always turned out to have good hearts underneath. Duane didn't make the cut. He was sixty-eight and bitter about how it had all turned out. The first thing he said was that he'd been hoping for more Social Security.

"Ain't my damn fault I always had to work for cash," he said.

The second thing he said was to ask me, when I told him why I was there, whether he had anything coming to him from Linda's death.

"There oughta be," he said. "Married to a goddamn whore, I oughta get something."

I had found Duane the old-fashioned way. A man like him wasn't likely to be on social media, but he owned his trailer outright—won it in a card game—and when the game had broken up, it was morning, and Duane had marched right down to the DMV to change the registration. The other guy had signed over the pink slip right there at the table. Duane had intimated to me the consequences if he hadn't, and stroked the pistol in his waistband for emphasis.

I wasn't impressed. It was a cheap .22, old and filthy. But it had been enough to get him the trailer.

So there he was in the DMV records. Florida hadn't been my first try, but I knew Duane wouldn't have gone far. My only real worry was that he'd be dead.

I knocked on his door in the late afternoon. He opened up and looked me over. He appeared sober and had probably slept most of the day, so he was in reasonably good humor. He was barefoot, in camo shorts and a Skynyrd T-shirt. He was not fat and still had his hair. Not bad for a half-century of wasted life.

We sat in two lawn chairs in the red dirt by the side of the trailer. He had to hunt for the second chair, but he found one folded up in the back. I came prepared with a cold six-pack. I handed him one and pulled one off for myself.

He opened the beer and looked at me suspiciously. "So you come down here to tell me that whore's dead and you ain't from the government and I don't get no money," he said.

"Let's call her Linda, Duane," I said. "Show some respect." He looked at me quickly to see if I was being funny. I wasn't.

He shrugged companionably. "Whatever you say."

I held his gaze for a second so he got the point.

He shrugged again. "Hey, maybe she changed. I ain't seen her for thirty years. What do I care?"

"Did you ever go back?"

"Did I ever go back? *Hell,* no, I never went back. They're goddamn psychopaths. I ain't going any closer than two states away."

I wasn't sure whether he meant two states from Texas or Louisiana, but I was more interested in the who.

"Who?" I said.

"Fucking Tarwood and Talley. You come from there, you musta met 'em. *They* ain't dead, I know that."

"What do you mean?"

"Threatened to kill me. Worse'n that, what they threatened. They done some of it, too. Beat me like a goddamned dog, 'fore they let me loose. Naw, I ain't been back." He looked at the ground, and his voice trailed off with the shame of having been beaten and threatened and taken it. I knew the face. I'd seen it enough times.

"I thought Talley was your lawyer," I said.

He laughed, a short, derisive snort. "My lawyer. Yeah. My lawyer."

"I thought he got you a deal. You could have gone away for a long time. Child molestation. Serious offense."

"Is that what they told you?" he said.

"Yeah."

"Yeah, well, it ain't true."

"Tell me what's true."

"No, I don't believe I'll say anything more. You got no idea."

"Of what? What Talley will do to you?"

He didn't say anything, just looked at the dirt.

"Talley won't do anything to you. Talley's dead."

His face brightened noticeably. "Yeah?"

"Yeah. Dead from a bullet between the eyes. Want to know who fired it, Duane?"

"Why, was it you?"

"Linda did, Duane. She walked into his office and shot him between the eyes. Why do you think she did that, Duane?"

He stared at the ground for a long minute. I stayed quiet and let it sink in. This was the point in the interview where your subject broke one way or another. You fed him a new piece of information, and you hoped it would open the floodgates. Sometimes it welded them shut.

Finally, Duane sat up and took a long drink of his beer.

"I wasn't a good father," he said. "I wasn't no father at all. But I never touched the kid. No one ever thought I did. Hell, if Tarwood thought that, he'd of just shot me and left me out in the swamp.

"What happened was my wife...Linda"—he looked at me sharply—"was a whore...was a...shit, man, she was getting paid for sex, what can I call it? And fucking Talley was her best customer. And I...I ain't going to deny that it was my fault. I couldn't keep a job, and I drank and gambled and we didn't have no money."

"So she was trying to put food on the table?"

"I'm not gonna defend what I done. I know when it started. At least I think I do. I went off on a bender, musta been a couple weeks, and I know there was no money in the house. 'Cause I fuckin' looked, man, before I left. And she was there with the baby, and..."

Duane paused for a moment. I recognized the look of self-loathing. I knew it well.

"So I come back, you know, and there's food and shit, and the gas and electric's still on and then..."

I let him tell it. I wondered if it was the first time he had told it.

"Then men would start showing up. Talley, yeah, some others. Not too many. Big shots, you know. Linda was *pretty*..."

He said this with what sounded almost like pride.

"What did you do?" I asked.

"Me? Nothing, man. I was the town *drunk*." He snorted derisively. "They were...shit, Talley, well, you knew him, I guess. *I* didn't wanna fuck with him, and then that fucking *cop*—"

"Which cop?"

"Which fucking cop do you *think*? His buddy, Bobby Tarwood. You think Talley wasn't going to *share*?"

"Why'd she accuse you of molesting Sue-Lynn?"

He stared at me. "Do you really wanna know?"

"I really do, Duane."

He spat in the dust. "You sure Talley's dead?"

"Just a second," I said. I walked to my car and got out my briefcase. I carried it back to the chair and pulled out my case file in its three-ring binder. I took out an eight-by-ten glossy of Talley with the bullet hole between his eyes and handed it to Duane.

"He can't hurt you," I said.

"And Linda done it?"

"Yes, she did."

He sighed. "All right. Here's what happened. Talley come to see me one day. I was working that month, some oilfield work. He come out

and offered me a ride home after my shift. Started talking about buying my farm. Said he'd pay good money, knew we needed it."

"Your farm?" I said, opening the binder to the docket from his criminal case. It was there for the asking at the De Soto Parish Clerk's Office,
if you were willing to spend most of a day rooting through dusty paper
files on sagging metal shelves in the basement. Nothing was digitized
earlier than 1990. De Soto Parish didn't have the money to have teams
of interns cataloguing their old criminal files. I finally found it in a
manila folder in an unlabeled cardboard box, underneath a hundred
other files from 1973 that no one else would ever come looking for.

I showed Duane the first page of the criminal complaint, with his
address listed in the arrest narrative. *"This* farm? I thought it belonged
to your wife."

"What I *told* him," Duane whined. "I *said* it wasn't mine to sell, it was
Linda's. She inherited it. And I knew *damn* sure she didn't want to sell."

"Linda wouldn't sell?"

"Hell, no, Linda wouldn't sell."

"Why not?"

"She said that farm had been in her family for three generations and
owning land was the only thing kept us from being white trash. I told
her Talley says we can keep living in the house if we want. She said it
weren't about *living* there, it was about *owning* it. And there wouldn't
be no *need* to sell if I could keep a job and stay sober and not gamble
away everything we made."

I didn't say anything. Duane had had forty years to see the truth in
those words. If he hadn't yet, nothing I said was going to show it to him.

Duane kept his reflections, whatever they were, to himself.

"So Talley comes to see me again, couple weeks later. Says, did you
think about it? I said, 'Yeah, I sure did, but Linda's dead set against
it, sorry.' He says he understands. Says he's seen the property deed, he
knows I can't sell without her approval. But then he says, 'Look, Duane,
you know that you're the head and master, right?'

"I said, 'Sure, yeah, the head and master. Tell *her* that.' Thought he
was telling me to man up and just make Linda sell. I told him that
wasn't the way it *worked* with Linda, and he said, 'No, Duane, it's a

legal term, head and master. You may be a spineless piece of shit, but the *law* says you're the head and master of your marital property.'

"I said, wait a minute. You just told me I couldn't sell it on my own. He said that's right, you can't, but you can 'encumber' it."

"He said 'encumber'?"

"*Course* that's what he said. You think I learned that kind of word on my own? I use it now, though. It's how I got my current abode. Motherfucker wanted to play another hand, he had to en*cum*ber his trailer."

"You mean he said you could borrow on it? Use it as collateral?"

"Yep. He said the law allowed me to do that without my wife's permission. Said he'd give me real good terms."

"What did you say?"

"I ain't stupid, mister. Least not *that* stupid. Man offers to buy your land, it's 'cause he wants your *land*. Man comes, back, offers to loan you *money* on it? Well, he ain't a goddamn bank, right? He *still* wants your land. I knew what would happen if I took the loan, same as he did."

"You told him no?"

"I told him I'd have to think about it. Guy like me, you don't just say no to a guy like him."

For a moment, I wondered where my life might have gone if I'd said no a little sooner. But I quickly banished the thought. I'd said it, finally. And that would have to be enough.

"Why did he want to buy the farm?" I asked.

Duane didn't answer. He stared into the distance at nothing, remembering.

"About a month later," he said, "they come and arrested me. Took me right out of the bar. Don't remember the name, but it was in Shreveport. One of my usuals. Don't know why they had to do that. I was *flush* that night. But Tarwood, he just walks right in, grabs me by the collar, throws me down off the stool onto the floor.

"Everyone turns, man, looking at me. You know how in the movies, it's like that, where the one guy's at the bar and the other guy comes in behind him, and he's like, 'Draw, you coward!' And the whole bar's watching, you know, from the corners of the screen? And then they have this kick-ass fist fight, and they bust through the windows into the street and then everyone starts shooting?"

He paused, and looked at me for confirmation.

"Yeah, Duane, I know those movies," I said.

"Well, it was just like that. 'Cept there wasn't no fight. He threw me down and just stood there over me, like he was waiting for me to get up. But I didn't get up."

He looked at me again, his eyes pleading for understanding.

"It was Bobby *Tarwood*, man! What was I gonna do? *Fight* him? He would've fucking *horsewhipped* me and then dragged me out into the street by my fucking *balls*. So I just lay there. But he picks me up and beats on me anyway. Ain't right. Then he drags me out to his car, and takes me in, and that was that."

I knew the date Duane was remembering. He'd been arrested on September 29, 1973. It was the first event on the docket. The next event was his arraignment, two days later, and his bail hearing a week after that, when he was denied bail. And the docket told me the name of the lawyer who had represented him at the bail hearing: Joseph Andrew Talley.

"Why did you call Talley?" I asked.

"I *didn't* fucking call Talley!" he said. "Fucking Talley showed *up*, day after I was arraigned. Strolls in like he owns the place, sits me down, says he heard I was in trouble, says he could make it go away. I said I didn't *do* nothin' like they was sayin', he said he understood. Said he knew the judge, said we could plead it down, I'd only do a year.

"I said man I didn't *do* nothin', how do you plead down from nothin'? And he looked at me and he said…thirty years, man, and I can still hear him saying it… 'Sometimes you just gotta take what you're offered. Sometimes if you fight it, it only gets worse.'"

"But you had to pay him."

Duane sighed, and looked around at the red dirt and the line of scraggly palms behind his trailer. "Yes, I had to pay. Lotta coin to plead guilty when you didn't do nothin'. Shit, man, I couldn't do no hard time. And they was talking hard time. Ten years, they was talking. And I didn't have no money."

I finished the story for him. "But he was willing to take a note."

Duane nodded.

"Secured by a lien on the farm," I said.

Duane nodded again. "I would've repaid it, goddamn it. I *would* have. I tried, but...shit, they made me leave the state, and where was I gonna find work? I just..." He paused. "I never saw them again," he said, finally. "I heard Talley foreclosed a couple months later."

"How? Did you talk to Linda?"

"No," he said. "I got a *letter.*"

"From Talley?"

"No," he said, looking down involuntarily at his lap, at the photo of Talley with the bullet hole between his eyes. "No, it was from a *oil* company."

"What'd it say?"

Duane drained his beer and tossed the bottle in the direction of a cardboard box full of empties next to his front steps. He missed, and the bottle hit the red clay with a soft thump. He looked down at the six-pack. I pulled off another and handed it to him. He popped the cap and took a deep sip.

"Shit," he said. "I still *got* the motherfucker." He stood and entered the trailer, emerging ten seconds later holding what looked like a drugstore diploma frame. There behind the glass was a letter, yellowed with age. He handed me the frame and I read the letter.

It was one page, single-spaced, dated December 21, 1973, and addressed to "Mr. Duane Hempersett," at a Louisiana State Penitentiary address, from a company called South Central Oil & Gas Exploration Services.

Mr. Hempersett,

As you know, it is in the vital national interest to expand domestic production of petroleum resources. Over the past six months, our firm has been conducting subsurface reserve surveys on behalf of a major oil company. Our geological analyses suggest that the strata under your property may contain a substantial reservoir of recoverable oil. We wish to begin immediate discussions with you regarding further exploration and more definitive testing. If our projections are borne out, we will be prepared to offer you very substantial royalties for drilling rights. As head and master of the property, you have the authority to conduct these transactions.

We wrote to you and your wife in September. Unfortunately, we did not receive a response. Time is of the essence on this project, and your present incarceration may have interfered with your receipt of mail, so we are contacting you directly to invite you to phone us at our offices, at our expense, to discuss terms on a mineral-rights lease.

The letter was signed in spiky blue ink by a company vice-president, and below his name was a phone number, bold and underlined.

Duane watched me read, and when I looked up I saw a hint of tears in his eyes.

"All these years, I kept it on the damn wall," he said.

"Why?" I asked.

He tried a shrug. "Ain't got nothin' else from back then." But that wasn't it, and he knew it. He looked down at his beer bottle. "To remind me, you know?"

"Of what?"

"Of how I coulda been rich. Of how some people get everything, and it ain't fair."

I didn't argue with him. Nothing was fair.

Duane shook his head sadly. "Plus, it was the only piece of mail I got in prison. 'Cept for the divorce papers. I didn't keep them."

"Did you call the number?"

"Didn't have no phone privileges. I asked, but I didn't have no pull with the guards to get shit like that. So I did my year, and every day I thought about my oil money. Then I get out, I find me a phone, and I make my call. Gave 'em the address, they said hang on, we'll pull the file. That's how I found out Talley foreclosed. This lady comes on, says did I execute a deed of trust? To a James Talley? I said I guess so. She says, well, he foreclosed on the farm while you were in prison. I said you mean he went and *took* it? She says I can get a copy of the papers if I want. They keep records of all that shit in some county office. Then she says, 'Have a nice day.' I don't know why she had to go and say that."

I wanted to get up and walk away and leave him with the beers and his memories. But I wasn't finished. There was one more entry on the docket from Duane's criminal case. I let him take a pull on the bottle. Then I showed him the page.

"Duane," I said, "the last entry on the docket is your sentencing hearing. You remember that?"

He set the bottle down on the arm of his chair. "Why I had to leave the goddamn state. Judge *said*."

"Yeah," I said, "but there's another order here. It says: 'The Court finds that in light of evidence of lewd and immoral conduct on the part of Linda Hempersett, Mrs. Hempersett is unfit to maintain custody of her minor child, and it is therefore ordered that said minor child shall forthwith be remanded to the custody of the State.'"

Duane stared at the ground.

"You remember that, Duane?"

Duane stood abruptly, knocking his beer into the dirt. It poured out, pooling at his feet. He turned toward me, balling his fists, unsteady on his feet. He reached for the arm of his chair for balance, but the lawn chair in the mud made a slippery support, and he fell awkwardly on his elbow, taking the chair with him. I stood, picked up the chair, and grabbed him by both arms. I picked him up and pushed him back into the chair, hard. The chair rocked back and Duane's head dented the stained siding of his trailer.

"What was the evidence, Duane?"

"Whaddayou mean?" he whined, then heard himself whining and tried for a tough-guy growl. "You ain't got no call to be puttin' your hands on me." He sat forward, gripped the arms of his chair, and planted his feet.

I could see the dueling homunculi in his brain—the id telling him to stand up and fight, the ego reminding him of all the times he'd been whipped by guys like me. I decided to let them argue it out. I gave him my mean-cop smile and said, "Oh, but I do, Duane. So I'll tell you what. I'm going to step back and give you a minute to make the call.

Heads, you tell me what I want to know. Tails, you stand up and make me leave you alone."

I reached in my pocket and pulled out a quarter. Flipped it, let it thunk onto the clay, stepped on it. "Up to you," I said. "Heads or tails?" I waited. I could hear my own homunculi having their argument.

Id: Wouldn't it feel good to give this son of a bitch a beating?

Ego: Yeah, but his only crime was being weak.

Id: And isn't that the worst crime of all?

Ego: Maybe you're right...

They weren't helping. I cut the debate short. "Duane," I said, as quietly as I could, "what did you say to the judge?"

Duane heard the violence in my voice the way an antelope hears a twig snap under a lion's paw. He twitched once, then his shoulders slumped. He relaxed his grip on the chair arms and let his hands flop onto his lap. "I told him...I mean, Talley said..."

"Talley said what, Duane?"

"He said it would help me. Said if I told the judge, he'd go easier on me."

"If you told the judge what?"

"Told him she was a whore."

My fists balled. I looked down at them, forced them open, took a breath. They balled again. I stepped forward with my left foot, felt my weight shift, felt the torque in my obliques, felt the power coming from my legs, the rotational velocity rolling like an ocean wave out into my right shoulder, down through my arm into my fist, driving forward into the outer three knuckles. I had just enough control to channel the wave past Duane's head into the side of the trailer. The plastic siding crumpled like cardboard, and I heard the rotten fiberboard inside shatter and spray into the trailer.

I exhaled. My arm was sunk to the wrist in the crumpled siding. I extracted it and stepped back. My knuckles were bleeding a little, but nothing was broken.

Duane was looking up at me, his mouth open a little. He started to say something, but I held up my hand. He flinched.

"Jesus, Duane, be a man. I'm not going to hit you." I opened my brief-case and took out a pack of Q-tips and an envelope. "Saliva," I said.

"What?"

"Swab the Q-tip on your cheek and drop it in. Or I take a sample of blood from your fucking nose." I handed him the Q-tip. Duane hesi-tated a moment, then obeyed. I got three from him, just to be on the safe side. No telling when I'd be seeing him again.

I stowed the envelope in the briefcase. I put Duane's framed oil com-pany letter in as well. Duane didn't need it anymore. He didn't need any more reminders that life wasn't fair.

"Thank you, Duane," I said. "Keep the beers." Then I turned and walked to my car.

Twenty-Seven

I was sitting in the terminal at the Tallahassee airport when Mo Faizalla called to tell me the results of his analysis of my samples: nothing. "You've got two females here and one male, and no one's anyone's parent or child," he said. "Good news or bad news for someone, I guess."

Talley, Hausman, and Waters: nothing. No parent and no child, just two dead bodies. It was bad news for someone, all right: bad news for me. Two people were dead because of my questions about what became of Sue-Lynn Hempersett, and, if the magic of DNA identification could be trusted, Eleanor Hausman was not little Sue-Lynn Hempersett. Linda Waters's lost daughter was not rich and famous and beautiful and happy in New York, and Linda Waters had killed Talley and gone to Jesus for nothing.

Or maybe for something else entirely. Maybe something that neither Hausman nor J.C. had seen fit to share with me, but that had almost landed me on death row in the state prison in Huntsville. Larry Nguyen, J.C.'s Bright Young Thing, had hinted he was afraid that J.C. might have engineered Talley's death. He'd spotted the call from Talley Oil to Montrose Bryant. That call might, conceivably, have been innocent. But the three late-night calls to J.C.'s private burner were definitely not innocent, because no calls to that ever-changing number were ever innocent.

J.C. was not telling me the whole truth, or maybe any of it. I was not interested in being a fall guy, which meant it was time for me to keep some secrets of my own. I had a good collection going already: John Scofield, this "Antelope Palms" company out in LA, Duane Hempersett. And I had Linda Waters's letter. Larry Nguyen hadn't opened it, so even if he told J.C. about it, no one knew what was in it but me. "I saved my pictures," Linda had said. "They're in her bedroom in the old house." Which meant that I had one more trip to make before flying to LA. Waiting for me in a bedroom in an old abandoned farmhouse in north Louisiana was some evidence that only I knew about. If I could find it.

I knew the address. It was in Duane's criminal file. Longstreet, Louisiana, southwest of Shreveport, most of the way to the Texas line. It looked to be a ten-hour drive from Tallahassee to Shreveport. Too much, unless I was a retiree doing a tour of Civil War sites. I pushed my LA flight back a day and booked a morning commuter flight to Shreveport. It was only twenty miles from Shreveport to Longstreet, to little Sue-Lynn's childhood home and whatever clues it held about what happened to her and why people were dying all these years later.

Twenty-Eight

I never visited Bradley Farmington's childhood home, but I found out what happened to him. I put his life together like one of those late-night TV landscape painters who do an entire oil painting in the course of a ten-minute infomercial. I hit the sky, the trees, the snow, the lake, the flock of birds, the log cabin, even the kid in the red hat with the goddamn toboggan. It took me longer than an infomercial, but when I was done, the painting was ready to hang. In a diner or an insurance office, if you're still with me on the metaphor. Not a gallery. But ready to hang.

The Force Investigation detectives' file was ten pages of nothing. I knew because I saw a copy of everything they wrote, saw their logs the moment they filed them. Settentio wasn't taking any chances on those guys getting anything he didn't want them to have.

He didn't have much to worry about. No one talked to Force Investigation. Cops saw them as Internal Affairs without the teeth, which is what they were. The Department was still trying to wrap its head around how using force was supposed to be a bad thing. And the civilian witnesses, the drug dealers and bodega owners in the neighborhood, they could tell the difference between the lions who made the kills and the jackals who came and sniffed around the carcasses. They weren't going to say boo about the precinct cops to any suits from downtown. The suits would fold up their investigation in a week, but the precinct cops would be kicking in their doors for the rest of their lives.

Talking to me was another matter. I was a guy you talked to. Because I was not Force Investigation. Because what you told me wasn't going to get written down anywhere. But it would be remembered. And back then, it was worth a lot, to some people, for me to remember that they'd come through when I asked.

And what I wanted to know was what the hell Bradley Farmington was doing at 137th and Broadway that night. What Becker and McAvoy were doing there I knew. They were on their regular patrol, coming south down Broadway, and they saw Bradley's Beamer stop at the bodega. Becker saw a white guy with Greenwich hair and Nantucket Red pants get out and he saw Bust/Shakedown. It didn't really matter which. He was too incompetent to get either one right. That was why he was never tapped for detective, or for Settentio's crew.

I found Becker and McAvoy at the precinct, working out their story. Department protocol was that officers involved in a serious use of force were supposed to be separated immediately by the first supervisor on the scene. Once they were separated, they would each be assigned a monitor, a sergeant or above, who would physically stay with them until they gave their statements to Force Investigation. That way they couldn't collaborate on the story.

But protocol was, as the lawyers say, honored in the breach. Unless it was a shooting or the suspect was dead at the scene, the supervisors waited for the ER report from the hospital before deciding whether to classify the incident as "categorical." That meant the officers involved would have time to ride back to the precinct together, or even write out their reports together, before being separated.

Since Bradley wasn't dead and no one had shot him, that's what happened. No classification until the ER report came back. Settentio was the precinct captain, so the classification was his call. And he hustled down to the hospital to make sure he saw the report first and to give me time to get to Becker and McAvoy.

They'd been together for an hour by the time I got there, but I wanted their stories separately anyway. I didn't trust Becker, and I didn't trust McAvoy with Becker in the room. McAvoy was as guileless as a puppy. So when I got to the precinct and found them sitting in the break room hunched over with their heads together like two junior high kids surfing for porn in the school library, I walked over and put my hand on Becker's shoulder, like I was offering him some sage advice. Which I was.

"Two minutes," I said. "McAvoy takes a bathroom break, goes down to the locker room. He comes back; two minutes later it's your turn. Got it?"

McAvoy turned halfway in his chair to look at me. Becker started to say something, but I tightened my grip on the back of his shoulder, and then slapped him lightly across the head. One cop reassuring another. "You'll be fine," I said. "You did good." I gave them a good-cop grin and walked out.

When McAvoy found me in the locker room, he was practically shaking with fear. I knew what he was afraid of—that he and Becker had just tuned up the wrong guy. There were a lot of potential wrong guys: politicians, donors, organized crime players, and connected relatives and friends thereof. Farmington could have been any of those. Becker and McAvoy were too stupid to have thought of it at the time, but the thought probably occurred to them both when they saw me come through the door.

The locker room was empty and dark, just the lights from the bathroom spilling out. I was standing in the back corner, at the door to the weight room.

"Hey," he said hesitantly.

"Shut up," I said and pushed him around the doorjamb into the weight room. It's easy to push a 240-pound slab of meat, if it's scared. "Did you write anything?"

"Huh? Oh, like, the report? No, the Captain said—"

"The Captain told you to go home. Right?"

"Right, but we—"

"But you came back here...?"

"Uh, just to change."

"You're not changed, dipshit. You're sitting up there in the fucking break room. Who did you talk to upstairs?"

"No one! I mean...not to talk to. I mean...just like to say hi to, is all."

"Get your clothes. Bring them here. Change while you talk."

McAvoy hurried to his locker and was back with his clothes in thirty seconds. He started changing, fumbling in the dark.

"Listen to me good," I said, "and don't answer until I tell you. And when you do answer, don't hold back, or you will be in a deeper pile of shit than you're already in. Am I clear?"

"Yeah," he said. Then, because he couldn't help himself: "Who was he? Was he—"

"What the fuck did I just say?" I said, laying it on a little thick, but I was in a hurry. "We have ten minutes, if we're lucky, to get your idiot asses out the door before this is classified categorical. Now...the *name* of the mope in the pink fucking pants."

"Bradley Farmington," he said.

"Which you got from?"

"His license. Plus he told us."

"Told you where?"

"In the car. Guy wouldn't shut up."

"Wouldn't shut up about what?"

"About what a big shot he was. Investment banker, whatever. MBA, went to Harvard. Played ball in high school."

"He told you he played football in high school?"

"Yeah. Asked me if I played. I said a little. He said I look like I should have played pro ball. I said I did, a little. You know."

"Was this little chat before or after you beat him into a coma?"

"Before."

"That was a rhetorical question, Rory. Where were you taking him? Here?"

"No, man, the motel."

I waited for a moment to see if he would elaborate. He didn't.

"What motel?"

"The Hamilton Heights Motel at 140th and St. Nicholas."

I knew the place. The clientele were prostitutes, IV junkies, and new parolees from Rikers spending their first-night-housing vouchers.

"Why were you taking him there, Rory?"

"He *asked* us to."

"He asked you to take him to the Hamilton Heights Motel?"

"Yeah."

"By name?"

"What?"

"By *name*. He asked for that motel specifically?"

"Well, not *exactly*. I mean, we gave him some options, right?"

"You gave him 'options'?"

"Yeah. He was like, maybe I should just go to a motel, right, and then we were like, okay, well, there's a couple near here."

"We, meaning you and Officer Becker?"

"Well, I was mostly doing the vehicle search, so..."

"So...?"

"So I was..."

"So you did or did not hear Bradley Farmington request a transport to the Hamilton Heights Motel?"

"Well, I didn't *hear* it, exactly, but once we were in the car, you know, I was driving, the guy knew where we were going. I mean, Becker walked in with him, he went up to the desk..."

"So that's a 'no,' then? As in, 'No, Your Honor, I did not hear him request transport to the Hamilton Heights fucking drug-den, semen-on-the-walls Motel'?"

"Um...right."

"You're going to do great on the stand, Rory. What's Becker going to say?"

"What?"

"Is Becker going to say that Farmington requested the transport?"

"Yeah! I mean, sure, I guess. He was talking to him. While he was doing the field sobriety test. While I was searching the vehicle."

"Why were you searching the vehicle?"

"My partner..."

"Okay, your partner directed you to search the vehicle. Why?"

"We busted him trying to score in front of that bodega at 137th."

"Trying to score what?"

"I dunno, he—"

"What did he have on him?"

"Contraband, you mean?"

"Drugs, numbnuts. What drugs did he have on him?"

"Nothing."

"What did the dealer have?"

"Uh, the, uh, dealer, uh...absconded."

"Who was it? The dealer?" That would help. I knew the crew that worked that block.

"I don't know. Male Hispanic, late teens, 5'6". Fled the scene..."

"Forget it. What about cash?"

McAvoy hesitated. "Yeah. He, uh, had some currency on him."

"How much?"

"We, uh, didn't do a full count. He had a lot on him. More in the car."

"And while you were searching the car, Officer Becker had a conversation with him that culminated in a request to be driven to the Hamilton Heights Motel."

"Um, yeah."

"A conversation you didn't hear."

McAvoy hung his head.

"Go home, Rory," I said. "Call in sick and disappear."

"What should I—"

"You do nothing. You keep your stupid mouth shut. Me, I'm going to fix your story."

The Becker-McAvoy narrative started out okay. Ordinary street bust, the dealer fled, they nailed the buyer. Rich guy, nice clothes. Talking nonstop, jittery, maybe showing signs of amphetamine use. The report couldn't be too specific, because we didn't have a tox screen on Farmington yet. We couldn't write it up with him showing stimulant and then find out his blood was full of oxy.

The subject consents to the vehicle search. No contraband, just some prescription stuff, and lots of cash. He's saying what you'd expect from a white banker busted on 137th Street—hey, whoa, fellas, just a misunderstanding, you know, I'm really a respectable guy, really a smart guy, look, hey, I don't want any trouble.

It all would have been fine if the story ended with them arresting his ass and bringing him back to booking. But they didn't arrest him. Somewhere between the field sobriety test and the conclusion of the vehicle search, the officers agreed to "do the guy a favor" and "drive him to a motel to rest." They were "concerned for his well-being" because his behavior was "erratic," and he stated that he was "unhappy" and "didn't want to go home." They told him the Hamilton Heights Motel was close by, and he said that it "sounded nice." So he voluntarily, with a smile on his cherubic banker face, hopped into the back of their car—in handcuffs, for his safety—and rode the half mile to the motel. Whereupon Becker walked him in and watched him check in, pay his $57, and go to his room.

Ten minutes later, there they are, back on their patrol a few blocks away, and there's Bradley running down the middle of St. Nicholas Avenue, shouting at the top of his lungs, and "pulling on door handles of parked cars." They stop, get out, try to calm him down, and all of a sudden he "comes at us with, like, these lobster claws, like snarling and swiping." McAvoy, who approached first, was "in fear for my life," and took out his baton and hit Farmington with "just like maybe a half power stroke to, uh, approximately the lower half of his body." Then Becker jumped in and the two of them "used reasonable force" to "subdue" Farmington, who had "superhuman strength" and "kept trying to head-butt us and bite us."

Straightforward, sure. It was the biggest bunch of bullshit I'd heard in years.

I knew the story wouldn't hold up to even the lightest scrutiny. I was a connoisseur of the fictionalized Use-of-Force Report. I'd done dozens of them. Guys brought them to me for editing. This one I would have sent back for a rewrite. Except this time I was going to have to do all the rewriting.

Twenty-Nine

At the Shreveport airport, I rented a car and headed south on State Route 171. I stopped at the first gas station I saw and paid cash for a donut and coffee and a pair of those cheap yellow gardening gloves that gas station markets have on the rack next to the trucker hats and jumper cables. There were no interstates near Longstreet. The drive down from Shreveport was mostly two-lane roads running through pine forest and farms. I couldn't tell soy from cotton, but there was a lot of green. I passed plenty of old houses that were slumping over and disappearing into walls of kudzu vines. Some were completely covered in kudzu, rectangular green mounds slowly losing their hard angles. I imagined myself walking out into one of those abandoned fields and standing still. How long before I was a green scarecrow and then how long until I was just another bush that looked vaguely human-shaped out of the corner of your eye at twilight? How many Sue Lynn Hempersetts were out there, swallowed by the kudzu, their outlines blurred beyond recall?

The town of Longstreet was the intersection of Route 171 and Route 3015. It consisted of a church and a water tower. Not even a gas station, though you could see the remains of one, along with five or six buildings on both sides of the intersection that used to be something—diner, drug store, hardware store, maybe—back when there was a town here.

Now it looked like half the houses were abandoned, slowly returning to nature. I hoped the Waters farmhouse hadn't been swallowed up by vegetation like the rest.

It hadn't. About five miles past the water tower I found a gate with a faded metal address sign dangling from one corner, ready to fall with the next storm. Beyond the gate was a dirt driveway leading up an incline. Pine trees lined the road, but I could see open fields up the hill. The gate wasn't locked. It was barely even upright. A rusty chain that might have once held a padlock was wrapped around the gate and a metal post. I got out, unwrapped the chain, and pushed open the gate. It sagged on its hinges. A good kick would have knocked it off. I drove partway up the driveway and parked. All around me were overgrown green fields, thick with knee-high grass and dotted with wildflowers in whites and yellows.

I climbed the hill until I could see the whole property. It was twenty acres, Linda had said. I vaguely recalled that an acre was about a football field, and I did a slow turn, filling the space around me with football fields, down to the road on one side, the encroaching pine forest in the back, and a distant fence line off to my right.

I wondered what crops the Waters family had grown here. I hadn't asked Linda. There were no crops now. Instead, there were a dozen rusting oil pumpjacks, their angular bodies poised like birds pecking at the ground. There were three spindly-looking derricks, too, tapering metal towers that looked like erector-set projects. They were all succumbing to the kudzu, which had engulfed their bases in puffy green cumulus clouds of leaves, and was now climbing up the sides. There were tendrils near the top of the pumpjacks now. A botanist could have measured the growth and told me how long it had been since those pumps were in use. I didn't have a botanist with me, but it had to have been years.

The house itself wasn't as overgrown. It looked to be at least a hundred years old, not that I was an expert on either architecture or the speed of decay in this climate. It was two stories, wood-framed over a brick foundation, with a giant live oak in front shading most of the house from the noon sun with its huge overhanging canopy. The wooden siding had once been a bright yellow, I guessed. Now it was a dull tan. There were two windows on the first floor, on either side of the front door. Four panes of glass in each, none broken. The second floor had a steeply pitched roof with two dormer windows protruding. The roof shingles were falling off in patches, and a branch from the live oak was pushing its way up under the eaves. The weeds and grass grew all around the house, right up to the walls, but they were all much smaller and younger. And you could see the stumps of roots and vines, where someone had hacked them down with a machete or a Weedwacker or whatever you used on hyper-aggressive kudzu.

I put on the gloves and tried the front door. Locked. I went around to the side of the house, where what looked like a kitchen door opened onto a crumbling brick patio with an ancient set of metal patio furniture with a thick coat of orange-red rust. There was a broom and a plastic bucket leaning against the wall, maybe left there from the last time someone had cleaned the place. I wondered when that was.

The kitchen door was locked, but it rattled in its frame and looked about as sturdy as a popsicle-stick school project. I leaned my shoulder into it and the rotten wood of the inner frame crumbled and gave way around the latch. I stepped in and looked around.

Someone had kept the kudzu from swallowing the house, but no one had done anything for the inside. The house clearly had not been lived in for decades. There was a sink and a stove and an ancient refrigerator with the door hanging open, and a thick coating of dust on every surface. The dust coated the floor as well, which meant I'd leave museum-quality footprints as I walked through. I gave that problem a moment's thought, grabbed the broom from the patio, and took a test swipe on the floor. Then I crossed the kitchen and went through the open doorway into the front room, which would have been the parlor or sitting room or whatever they had called it.

The stairs leading up to the bedrooms were in the front room, opposite a little entryway by the front door. There was no furniture left, but there was a built-in bench in the entryway, with hooks on the wall opposite. I imagined Sue-Lynn Hempersett coming inside on a winter day, hanging up her coat, sitting on the bench to take off her shoes.

Then I imagined her hungry and cold and wondering why the heat was off and there wasn't any dinner. Or maybe Linda had hidden their poverty from her. Maybe Sue-Lynn had had happy memories in this house.

I turned and started up the stairs. The bannister was a massive slab of some heavy dark wood. Someone had carved intricate patterns into it, abstract swirls, leaves, flowers. You could probably rip the bannister out and sell it on one of those TV shows where guys travel the country looking for antiques to polish up and resell. I didn't know what the market was like for bannisters, though, and there were no chandeliers or stained glass anywhere in the house that I could see.

At the top of the stairs was a landing, with what looked like a bedroom on either side of the house. The stairs were offset from the house's midline, so the right-hand bedroom was larger than the left-hand one. I went into the smaller one. It was brightly lit by the dormer window and was definitely the right room. The walls were faded and dusty, but they had once been painted bright yellow, and the top half of one wall had a light-blue sky with puffy white clouds, with the pattern stretching whimsically up onto the ceiling. Had Linda done that? I didn't see Duane up here with a brush, making his daughter's room cheery.

There was no furniture in the room and no closet, but I thought I could see faint scuff marks through the dust, maybe marking where a crib or a chair had been. There was a short wire dangling from the ceiling above the scuff marks, as if something had once hung there. A light? A mobile, maybe, hanging above a crib? I tried to picture the mobile: Butterflies? Trains? Flowers? Maybe little bells for baby Sue-Lynn to reach up and bat?

I stood in the center of the room and did a slow 360, scanning for hiding places. Nothing jumped out at me, so I started with the floorboards. They were coated in dust, but I swept a patch clean with the broom to get a look at the material. Some kind of hardwood, in pretty good shape for its age. I turned the broom upside down and made a circuit of the room, pushing on the end of each board where it adjoined the one next to it longitudinally. Floorboards are often laid over a grid of planks or two-by-fours, spaced so that each plank supports

165

the ends of two floorboards. If you wanted to use the space under the floorboards to make a hiding place, you could cut one so that its end came in between two planks. Then you could get a knife under it and pry it up. If Linda had done that, then one of the floorboards in the room would have an unsupported end, and it would bend when I pushed on it.

It was a good theory, and I spent a dusty half hour proving it wrong. I moved on to the next option, the walls. The same thing went for dry-wall as for floorboards—you hung it on a frame that left a space underneath. And by hypothesis Linda had hidden whatever she'd hidden after the walls had been built, plastered, and painted, so if there was a hiding place, there'd be a way to get at it short of ripping out the walls.

If there was anything there, I didn't see it. The plaster was smooth and uninterrupted. I went back to the middle of the room and did another 360. What was I missing? It took me about ten seconds to realize that I was an idiot. The hiding place was right in front of me. I stood under the dangling wire, lifted the broom over my head, and tapped at the plaster where the wire entered the ceiling. Sure enough, it was loose. I prodded gently around the wire and the plaster cracked in a Frisbee-sized circle around the wire. I worked the broom handle around the edge of the circle until I'd broken all the plaster. Then I peered up, squinting against the dust and plaster flakes raining down on my head. There was a circular hole in the ceiling, about a foot in diameter. Someone had covered it with a piece of plywood, then plastered and painted over it. The wire ran through a drill hole in the center. I poked at the plywood with the broom handle. One edge lifted and as the board tilted up I heard something sliding on the top.

I put down the broom and went back down the stairs and through the kitchen to the patio. I looked around. The property was still and empty, and there was no sound but the faint background hum of a million insects. My car was parked where I'd left it on the grass at the edge of the dirt driveway. There was no one around, no thugs or deputy sheriffs or FBI agents or ghosts. Just me. I picked up one of the rusted metal chairs and carried it into the house. It was heavy, and the rust flaked off it like a sugar crust on a wedding cake. I tried to hold it away from my body, but I still got plenty of rust on my pants.

Back in the bedroom, I set the chair under the hole and stood on it. I didn't get quite enough height standing on the seat, so I had to balance on the armrests. I reached up slowly and slid the plywood board over about six inches, enough to get my right hand through the gap. I got my hand in and felt around in the opening. My fingers brushed something at the limit of my reach. I had to get up on my tiptoes to grip it, trusting my balance and the rusted-out armrests. It felt like a shoebox. It was. I slowly worked it out of the opening and then carefully stepped down from the chair.

I set the shoebox down, then climbed back up and slid the plywood back over the hole. Then I moved the chair and the shoebox out to the hall and swept the floor, pushing all the dust and plaster flakes into the corner. I carried the chair and the shoebox back down the stairs and set them in the kitchen. Then I went back up and walked slowly backward from the bedroom to the hall and down the stairs, sweeping the path behind me with the broom. I swept my way back to the kitchen door, put the chair and the broom back on the patio, and closed the door behind me. With the wood of the doorjamb splintered around the latch, it wouldn't stay closed, so I wedged a twig at the bottom of the door to hold it in place. If anyone looked closely, it would be obvious someone had been inside, but from a distance you'd never know. And who was going to look closely? The people who had lived here—Linda, Duane, and Sue-Lynn—were long gone. Pops Talley had pumped oil here once, but not for years from the look of the pumpjacks in the field. And now he was dead, too. The house might sit and fill up with dust for another decade before someone came back to it.

I carried the box back to my car and backed out the driveway. I stopped at the street and pulled the gate closed behind me, wrapping the chain back around the post to hold it closed. Then I drove north, back toward Shreveport.

Twenty miles north of Longstreet I saw a gas station and pulled into the parking lot to look in the box. It was small for a shoebox. Then I realized it had held a child's shoes, and a wave of sadness hit me. I was holding a dead woman's memories of her dead daughter taken from a dead house.

I put my gloves back on to open the box. It was sealed with a thin strip of masking tape, brittle with age. It snapped when I opened the lid. Inside were two plastic bags. The first held photos. I counted thirty-two, mostly instant Polaroids, small and square with their white borders, but also a dozen taken with some other camera and developed in a drugstore, probably in what had once been the town of Longstreet.

The photos were clear and sharp and had held their color perfectly, sitting all those years sealed away from light and humidity. They were all pictures of a girl, and Linda had left them in chronological order. I thumbed through them. The girl aged from a baby to a toddler to what I inexpertly guessed was four or five. Most of them looked like they had been taken at the farmhouse, in the fields in front or on the front porch. The earliest ones had been taken in the bedroom I'd just left. The sky-and-clouds painting was fresh on the wall. It looked like a happy place.

I looked at a photo of the four-year-old Sue-Lynn, compared it in my mind's eye to the earliest of the childhood photos Eleanor Hausman had given me. Was it the same girl? Mo Faizalla's DNA results had already established that Hausman wasn't Sue-Lynn. Hausman's photos were in my briefcase back in my hotel room in Tallahassee, but I didn't need to analyze them. I had a detective's memory for faces, and I had spent plenty of time with those pictures. Sue-Lynn wasn't the girl in Hausman's photos.

The last photo was different, and I stared at it for a solid minute. The girl was smiling at the camera, holding an ice-cream cone. Behind her was what looked like a Ferris wheel and the garish hues of red and yellow lights reflected off the background. State fair, maybe? But what drew my attention were the two other people in the photo, the man and woman standing behind the girl with their arms around her shoulders. The woman was a young Linda Waters, stunningly beautiful, as I knew she must have been then, with no hint of pain or bitterness pulling at the edges of her smile. The man was not Duane Hemper-sett. But I knew him instantly. It was Mandanoches Chief of Police Bobby Tarwood.

I exhaled slowly, sealed the photos back in their plastic bag, and placed them back in the box. Then I pulled out the second plastic bag. It held a lock of brown-blonde hair and a slip of paper with a hand-written date, 8/15/73. Sue-Lynn's hair. A piece of her that no one could lie to me about and that no one knew I had. I didn't put it back in the box. I put it in my jacket pocket and thought about safe storage places in LA.

Century City, Avenue of the Stars

Thirty

Eighteen hours later I was in Los Angeles, blinking at the morning sun and the palm trees at LAX. There was an investigations firm in LA we used sometimes, CenterPoint Solutions. It was a big firm, with a mix of ex-FBI agents, ex-cops, and computer techies.

I had a friend in the NYPD who had moved out to the West Coast when he retired from the force. His name was Francis Muller, but he was born in Colombia and his mother was Mexican. Lot of Germans in Colombia, he said, you'd be surprised. We got along because we were both hard to pigeonhole racially. At least Frankie *knew* what he was.

He wasn't in the Reserves like I was, so he just put in his straight twenty on the job and bailed. And luckily for our friendship, he spent most of that twenty way out in the outer boroughs, so he no doubt heard I was a corrupt thug, but he didn't have to see it for himself. Frankie was not dirty.

Maybe that's why CenterPoint picked him up. And why I'd never gotten the call. FBI guys sniff dirty cops the way coyotes sniff rabbit shit. Perks their ears up. They have the luxury of being honest, I guess, with unlimited budgets and their pick of cases and no general peace officer mandate. An FBI agent—sorry, *"Special* Agent"—can walk right past a fight or a shithead domestic violence call on his way to his wiretap appointment or his white-collar securities case debrief. That's why you don't see cell-phone videos of a gang of Feds choking out some dirtbag on a two-bit DUI arrest. It's not because they're above choking guys out. It's because they're above even responding to street crime.

Anyway, most investigations firms are either ex-Fed or ex-cop, and they split up the work accordingly. The ex-Feds get the corporate work —background investigations before big deals, opposition research for litigation firms, that sort of thing. The sort of thing that generates a nice pdf report with attachments. Database work.

The ex-cops get the legwork. Walking a neighborhood canvassing for witnesses. Surveillance on workers' comp scams. Domestic stuff, regular snooping. And security. There's always work standing around looking tough. Lord knows I had done enough of it. We all did. It was just free, beautiful money. My theory of private security is that it's mostly just another version of the suit or car or Rolex. Just another way to shout that you can pay for something shiny and expensive and useless. And there were plenty of celebrities who picked their security staff for sex. Which was fine, too, if you were into that sort of stuff.

Frankie did a little bit of all of it at CenterPoint. The office was in Century City, in west LA, on a street they actually called Avenue of the Stars, I guess because CAA, the big talent agency, had its headquarters there. Frankie did a lot of work with them, he told me. Backgrounds on actors, mostly. Like whether you could really write an insurance policy for some movie star that would be voided if he tested positive for coke or was arrested for a sex crime. *Very* specific, some of these policies. It wasn't bad behavior that spooked the studios, it was surprises.

I hadn't seen Frankie in a couple years, and he offered to pick me up at the airport, but I decided to rent a car. Whenever I come out to LA I rent a convertible. Sort of a "New Yorker in paradise" kind of a thing. And then I drive up to Santa Monica and walk out on the boardwalk and just look at the perfect sand and the perfect water and the perfect sky and the perfect grass, which to the East Coast eye looks like it must be synthetic until you actually reach down and touch it.

Frankie was doing pretty well. He had his NYPD pension and his CenterPoint gig, and his divorce settlement hadn't hit him as hard as a lot of guys. He hadn't quit drinking exactly, but I guess he had it under control, because CenterPoint didn't hire drunks. He told me he was living on his sailboat, like Don Johnson in *Miami Vice*. The boat was out in an unincorporated slice of LA County called Marina Del Rey, north of LAX and south of Venice. They had carved a huge channel stretching inland a couple miles, a giant artificial harbor with marinas on both sides. Thousands and thousands of boats. The streets were all named after Polynesian islands—Mindanao, Palawan, Fiji, Bora Bora, Marquesas.

I drove a couple laps around the marinas, gawking at the boats. Finally I found Frankie's marina, out near the main channel, next to a park where he said sea lions came up to bask on the docks. I could see why they'd want to. You had perfect blue sky, perfect blue water, perfect green grass, and perfect white boats.

I found Frankie's boat, a thirty-foot sailboat out toward the end of the dock. I didn't see any name painted on the side. Maybe Frankie hadn't thought of a good one yet. I didn't see any sea lions basking, either, but I was tired and I thought a little basking might do me some good. Lucky for me, Frankie had left a dock key at the marina office, with a note saying there were beers in the fridge and he'd be there by late afternoon.

I went out to the boat and found a plastic deck chair. I unfolded it, tipped back against the rail, and closed my eyes.

Boats at Marina Del Rey

Thirty-One

"I heard a rumor about you once," said Frankie, taking a sip of his beer. The sun was setting over the Pacific, down at the end of the channel past the breakwater. The water was rippling softly under the deck, the moon was rising, and the sea lions were barking somewhere out in the twilight. We were in California, all right.

"Yeah?" I said. "Probably true, then."

"This one's about how you made detective."

I said nothing.

"Story was," said Frankie, "that your promotion started out as a Board of Rights investigation."

"Who'd you hear this from?" I said, hearing the edge in my voice.

"Andy Naeman, back when he retired. Came out to Rockaway for a party. He was your union rep when you were in uniform, right?"

"Yep."

"So Andy tells this story, you get referred on an excessive force complaint. Probably a righteous use of force, but there were a lot of wits, and you had a history. They were just setting up the Civilian Review Board back then, and so they have this lawyer from the Mayor's office, hot young thing, in the precinct to liaise with command on the review process.

"You and Naeman go in for your meet with Captain Settentio, he's gonna advise you about the process, ask questions, yadda yadda. So you're sitting there waiting outside Settentio's office, Naeman's telling you about this lawyer, how she's hot, how his theory is that Settentio is fucking her.

"You know that Naeman's always hated Settentio, so you don't think anything of it. Then you go in for your meeting and Settentio tells you to get ready for desk duty, you're gonna be on leave and then probably shit-canned. Official word soon, tough luck, son.

"So you walk out of there and Naeman turns to you and says, 'You wanna keep your job?'"

Frankie turned to me. "Am I right so far, or was Naeman bullshitting?"

"Who all was there when he told that story?"

"Just me and him. It was late. So it is true?"

"Frankie, are you asking me is that when I first got dirty?"

Frankie heard the tone in my voice and raised his hand, palm up. "No, man, I don't judge. I stopped that a long time ago. And I'm floating in fucking Santa Monica Bay in my fucking *sail*boat, so no, I don't judge."

"Goddamn right you don't," I said, tasting the bile in my throat, "because last I looked you have a full-fucking-100-percent pension on top of your PI check, and you have it because *you* didn't get shit-canned for fucking vehicular *hom*icide—"

I broke off. Ten years, and neither of us had talked about it. At least I hadn't, and I was pretty damn sure Frankie hadn't, unless he was stupid enough to go to a therapist or AA or something.

We were halfway through our twenty. Frankie was still patrol, and smart enough to figure out that he was never going to get a gold shield. I don't know if it was bitterness over that, or what, but he started hitting the sauce hard—hitting it with both fists like it was the heavy bag in the gym. Frankie had not been a big drinker when we started out, but he caught up quick. Maybe ten years of patrol in Far Rockaway will do it to anyone.

I got the call at 3 a.m. I was up. And I was sober. Drunken cop calls dirty cop. Yeah, buddy, how are you, you gotta get out here.

Frankie had been bombing in on the Cross Bay Boulevard after a hard couple hours at a bar after his shift. Must have been doing seventy or eighty when he hit the guy, from the looks of the body. Almost cut in two. Frankie was practically catatonic when I got there, but he had retained enough cop instincts to make sure there were no witnesses —not likely, on a causeway over Jamaica Bay—and to shove the body down onto the embankment.

It was his personal car, too. Lucky for him he never made sergeant and got a take-home vehicle. And lucky for him he had the number of a guy who could clean it all up for him.

I chilled it all. I showed up with a shovel, a big duffel and some concrete blocks, and one of the young eager thugs from Settentio's crew who had been looking for a chance to earn some points with me. I put the kid on the road in my car with the flashers on in case a patrol car came by. I put Frankie in the back of his car and told him to shut up, and I sank the body in the bay. I couldn't get it deep, because I had to drag it out into the water on foot, but I left the bag open enough for the crabs to get in. Couple days, there'd be nothing left.

I poured two cans of bleach on the stains. Lucky for Frankie, the guy had been a good three feet on the shoulder when Frankie hit him —he had probably passed out at the wheel, and if he hadn't hit the guy he would have driven straight off into the bay.

Homeless guy, definitely. And old. No one to worry, no one to file a missing persons report.

I cleaned off the bumper and windshield and drove Frankie home. Had the kid lead the way in my car. I followed close so the damage wouldn't be obvious to any other drivers we passed. You know: "Uh, I don't know if it's important, but I just thought I should call it in. I saw this car with, you know, a broken headlight, dented fender, cracked windshield, and...maybe it's nothing, you know, but I thought I saw, like, smears of *red*...."

I dropped him at his building, walked him to the door. Told him to forget the whole thing. Don't talk about it. Never happened.

I took his car straight to a chop shop we had on our list. Not one we taxed directly—we were out of Settentio's territory, out here in Brooklyn—but one that got a lot of inventory from guys we did tax, so the operator had plenty of reasons to want to do me a favor. Had the car back to him in time for swing shift the next day. Frankie didn't even take a day off.

I sent some guys out a couple times over the next week to walk the area, roust any homeless guys they found, ask some pro forma questions about drug activity, robberies, that sort of thing. Nothing. The guy vanished without a trace.

And Frankie stayed on. Finished his time. His marriage fell apart, and he didn't stop drinking. But he finished and he got his pension.

And I lost mine, five years later, for breaking my captain's nose in a room full of cops. His nose, and then his jaw, and then his arm, until they pulled me off him.

None of which I said. I didn't have to. Frankie and I just stared at each other, under the moon, floating in the marina on his fucking *sail*boat.

And he said, "Okay. I'm sorry."

"No," I said. "No, don't be. You want to know, I'll tell you."

"Look, man," he said, "I'm—"

"No. It's okay. It's all in the past. Yes, that's when I first got dirty. I told Andy hell yeah, I want to keep my job. He said I know he's fucking that lawyer from the mayor's office. Let's follow him and nail their asses. You get your job, I get something over on that fucker, and it'll bring a smile to my face.

"So we tail Settentio that night. Sure enough, he heads for a motel in Fort Lee. They were discreet, at least. Crossed the river. She shows up an hour later. We give 'em ten minutes, badge our way in, knock the door down with the camera flashing. Naeman didn't say a word. He just pointed to the camera and said, '8 a.m, your office.'

"We get there the next morning and Settentio has a new report for me to sign. Has me breaking up a robbery, shielding civilians, and protecting my fucking partner. There's a commendation and a referral for a fucking gold shield, and he just says, 'Congratulations, Detective.'

"Settentio told me later he was going to recommend that I be fired. Would have started things off right with the Civilian Review Board, and he thought I was dumb and violent anyway. No use to him. Said the trick with Naeman, well that showed I was *smart* and violent. Which is what he wanted."

"So from that moment on…?" Frankie said.

"Yeah, from that moment on I've been a fraud," I said. "A self-hating fraud."

"You and me both."

"*No,*" I said. "*Not* you. You were a good cop, Frankie."

"What would you have done off the force?"

I thought about that for a moment. "You mean me, or you?"

"Both of us, I guess."

"I dunno, man, I don't want to talk about it. I got enough free therapy with that old shrink in New York."

"All right, fair enough, fair enough."

There was silence while we listened to the water slap the side of the boat. Then he said: "What was the UOF?"

"Fucker had a knife, didn't drop it. I power-stroked him to the head with my baton. No robbery, no civilians, no partner in peril. Not dirty, though. I could've shot the little prick."

"Okay."

There was a silence. "The head, though?" Baton head strikes were supposed to be off limits.

I said nothing.

"I guess you swung at his knife hand just when he was crouching to come at you? He brought his head down?"

That's what the report had said. That's what they all said.

I took a long puff on my cigar, let the smoke drift slowly up. "Fucking punk-ass bully, with a smart mouth," I said. It felt good to tell Frankie the truth.

"Marcus," he said, after another long silence, "I know I owe you. My pension. Shit. This boat."

There was another silence. He said, "The lawyer, you remember her name?"

"No." I said. Lying didn't feel so good. But if Frankie was trying to test my honesty, at least I was one for two. I remembered the lawyer's name. Back then she went by Jennifer.

Thirty-Two

The next time I saw J.C. was maybe a year after the Fort Lee motel roust got me my gold shield. I was in plainclothes, loafing around down by City Hall, waiting for the Captain, when she walked up.

"Remember me?" she said.

I nodded. Sure, I remembered her. I was still a kid, and when I looked at her closely I could see that she wasn't that much older than me. She was maybe thirty, probably not even. Which is a lot when you're twenty-four, but not too much that you don't start picturing her naked, *in flagrante*, the way I had last seen her.

"Yeah, I looked good, huh Marcus?" It was as if she'd read my mind. It probably wasn't that hard. "It's okay to admit it. I happen to think so myself. I'm fucking *great* in bed. Don't you think?"

I didn't know what to say. "You...still with the Captain?" I said. Stupid question, but I was actually curious. Because *I* was with the Captain a lot of the time, and I'd never seen her.

She threw back her head and laughed. It was a beautiful laugh, I thought. Not tentative like some women, or like me when one of the older guys made a joke and I didn't get it but I knew I was supposed to laugh.

"Sure," she said, "sometimes. But a girl has to move on. Onward and upward, right Marcus?"

I nodded. "Uh, so, what's up?"

"Let's take a walk," she said and took my arm, walking us down toward the Brooklyn Bridge. It was one of those early spring days where you get that combination of a cold breeze off the river and sunshine that's actually warm, not that thin winter shit that doesn't give you anything but a little light.

"You know what I am now, Marcus?"

"No," I said. "You used to be the Civilian Review Board lawyer, right?" I didn't even know her name.

"No, no, honey. I was the Mayor's liaison to the department. Big difference, Marcus. Means I was on *your* side. And I still am. Now I'm higher up the food chain, though. Bigger game. Bigger guns. Bigger trophies."

That was the thing about J.C. She always talked like that. Even back then. At least she did to me. You were never quite sure if she was offering you something or threatening you with something.

"I like your captain," she said. "He's a good guy. I like you too."

"Me? You don't even know me."

"Oh, I do. I know you pretty well. I've heard things about you. Good things."

"Yeah?"

"I know that you're willing to break into a motel room and blackmail a captain to keep your job. And I know that *you* know that I endorsed your bogus commendation and covered up a completely unjustified beating to save *mine*. So, two peas in a pod, huh, Marcus? We're in this together. Maybe we go down together, or maybe we rise together. That's how it works, right?"

I was quiet. For fifteen years, that's how it's been with J.C. You're never quite sure what she's telling you.

She took out a card, reached inside my jacket, and slid the card slowly into my shirt pocket, her fingers pressing on the muscle.

"I'm one of those people it can be real good to know," she said. "You and me, I think we're going to be friends."

Santa Monica Pier

Thirty-Three

I went in to the CenterPoint offices with Frankie the next day. He introduced me to Tom Jarron, the boss of the LA office. Jarron had been FBI, mostly in LA, but Frankie said he'd done a stint in New York, too, back in the day. If Jarron knew me, he was polite enough not to mention it. But he knew J.C., and that was enough to get me the keys to the kingdom, as Frankie had predicted.

Jarron had been one of the Bureau's white-collar guys, a Certified Public Accountant with a badge. He was two decades older than Frankie and me, and he'd moved over to CenterPoint when he cashed out of the Feds. Now he was the managing partner of the LA office. He still wore a suit every day, with a pocket square, and he brought in a lot of background investigation work from defense contractors, Frankie said. He knew where his bread was buttered, and he wanted to be on J.C.'s radar when the appointment came through.

"For these guys," Frankie had said, "personal connections, man, that's everything. Way we stay in business, in that fancy office, on that fancy street? Is some big shot says to some other big shot, 'Hey, man, I got this problem,' and the other big shot says, 'Yeah? I know this guy.' You gotta be *that guy.*"

J.C. was that guy, if you were in the national-security business. Or plenty of other businesses. Or else she was the big shot. The line between the two sort of blurred at the top. And the "that guy" property was powerfully transitive. Whatever I wanted, say the word. Was I thinking of moving out here? Did I want a job? CenterPoint could use a guy like me.

I told Jarron I was trying to run down the money trail on some real estate investments. Due diligence on a possible deal. Sure thing, he had just the person.

"Heather Cusamano," he said. "Just hired her out of the Bureau last year. Ten years in and they reassigned her to Omaha. Gave her two weeks to pack." The FBI was notorious for that, I knew. It was an ironclad condition of working there: they could reassign you anywhere, at any time. And you would shut your mouth and go. Or quit and double your salary with Jarron. "Their loss. Terrible policy, if you ask me. Especially for the folks with marketable skills."

"Heather's a CPA, too," Frankie put in.

"Like I said," said Jarron. He pulled out a card, wrote a number on the back. "Heather's out on something this morning, but she should be around in the afternoon. I'll tell her to expect your call. On the house, by the way. If anything comes up later, have Ms. Curtis give me a call."

"Great," I said, "I'll be at the beach."

I drove down Olympic to the Santa Monica Pier. I had my clarinet with me, in its case, in Hausman's calfskin briefcase. It was a beautiful thing, that briefcase: big enough to fit the clarinet case and still close at the top, like the virtuoso Italian designer who'd first sketched the thing had had that in mind. Maybe he did.

I walked out to the end of the pier and stared out into the ocean for a while. You could stand at the rail and look straight out and let your peripheral vision blur away until you saw nothing but ocean and sky and cloud. The waves rolled in from the west in swells that rose up as they approached the pier and then slid under, dark green with foam bubbling at the crest.

Pelicans surfed the wave fronts, gliding laterally along the angled green faces of the waves just inches from the surface, then rising up and wheeling around for another pass. I wondered if they were fishing or just having fun, like dolphins surfing the bow wave of a ship. I'd seen them do that in Iraq. It was a sight worth seeing, even if you had to go to the worst place on earth to see it. In the best place on earth, New York City, I'd stood at the rail on the Staten Island Ferry many times and looked down for dolphins, but I never saw any. I didn't see any out in the Pacific either, but I knew they were there. Frankie said he saw them from his boat every time he went out. If I stood here all day I'd see them.

I figured I might as well stay until I did, so I pulled out the card Jarron had given me and texted former Special Agent Heather Cusamano, CPA, and said I'd be on the pier. Then I sat down on a bench and took my clarinet case out of Hausman's briefcase.

A clarinet case is the same size and shape as the case for a high-end pistol. Your gun crowd and your clarinet crowd don't mix much, so this fact remains relatively unknown. And most people don't carry their handguns around in cases, anyway. A working gun stays on your body where it's needed. But cops know gun cases, and when I walked into the station with the clarinet case guys would sometimes ask if I'd just bought a new piece.

The clarinet rides disassembled in its case, like a fancy gun, so you have to put it together every time you play. That activity had some military echoes, too: you have a tube in several pieces that have to fit together precisely in order to work. You have to repeatedly break it down, clean it, and reassemble it, and grease and spit and your hands are your tools. And the last step was the same, too: when I had gotten the instrument together and slotted a reed into the ligature, I always held it by the bell and sighted down it, making sure that the reed was lined up with the octave key.

I closed the case and put it back in the briefcase. One thing I never did was play with an open case next to me on the bench. The last thing I wanted was some idiot coming up and tossing a dollar at me.

I started the way I always did, with some drawn-out slow arpeggios, twenty-four of them, major and minor in each key, two octaves each. Then I did Coltrane's "Mr. PC," which is just a minor blues, nice to warm up on, and "All of Me," which I learned when I was about fourteen and can never get out of my head. Then "Stella by Starlight" and

"All the Things You Are" and "'Round Midnight." Tunes where every step in the chord progression is a conscious choice, a fork in the road that you could take a hundred times, hear it a different way each time, and never wish it was anything else.

I opened my eyes and looked out at the water. Usually I played with traffic somewhere in the background, but there was no sound out here on the pier but the waves and a few kids' voices laughing. It was too damn pleasant for me. What the hell was I supposed to play? "O, What a Beautiful Morning"? What did I know that was even remotely appropriate for the setting?

I went with Ellington's "In a Sentimental Mood." I liked it down in the low register, the chalumeau, starting down on the low G and pushing up that first run, 1-2-3-5-6-8-9, and then diving back down. And that melody in the bridge—you could put a hundred composers in a room for a year, trying things out, and no one would hit on it again.

I ran through it a couple times, keeping my solos simple so I could still hear the melody underneath, then closed it out, running the last phrase up to the top of the clarion—trusting myself to hit a high C and D but not going for the F—then dropping back down to finish at the low G. I always loved the low notes on the clarinet. I used to think about buying a bass clarinet so I'd have more low notes, but I never did. The instrument's too big; you can't carry it around with you in a briefcase.

I opened my eyes and reached for my phone to see how much time had passed, whether I needed to hustle off to meet Tom Jarron's CPA. On the next bench over, a woman was watching me. She was straight-up Southern California gorgeous, was my first thought. Early thirties, with dirty blond hair that curled down to her shoulders. She was in business wear and had taken her jacket off and laid it on the bench back. She had a white sleeveless top on underneath, revealing the arms and shoulders of a runner who wasn't afraid of a few pull-ups either. She was leaning back on the bench with her legs crossed, legs that dared me to challenge her to a race at any distance. I wouldn't have taken the dare. These Santa Monica women, Frankie had said, when I announced my intention to hit the beach, you seriously won't believe how fit they are.

I nodded, politely, trying to keep my eyes to myself, and looked down at the clarinet in my hands. She smiled brightly. "That's beautiful," she said. "What was that?"

"Duke Ellington," I said. "'In a Sentimental Mood.' Thanks." Then, because she was still smiling at me, "You, uh, a musician?"

She laughed. "Oh, my God, no. I've been trying to get into jazz, though. It's on my list of things that'll make me a better person."

I nodded. I'd never heard that one before. "I dunno," I said, "you get in too deep, it's pretty dangerous. OD, pneumonia...take your pick. Charlie Parker died at thirty-seven."

She put on a serious face. "Well, hopefully I'll be all right if I just listen."

"Yeah, that ought to be safe enough."

She looked up and down the pier. "Are you done, or were you still playing? I'd love to hear another. I'm meeting someone, I think, but I guess I'm early." She took out her phone and thumbed out a text, then put it back in her purse and settled back on the bench.

I didn't need to be asked twice. I started right in on "Stardust."

I played with my eyes closed. I always have. Most musicians do, especially when they're just playing for themselves and the music. After the first chorus, I forgot she was there. I lost myself in the song, seeing the chord changes roll past in my head as I reached for the perfect line, knowing I'd never find it. I brought it back on the last A section of the third chorus, repeating that last descending melody—"the mem'ry of love's refrain"—dropping down to my bottom octave and then sliding up for the final D.

I held the last note, then opened my eyes. She was watching me, and her expression was nakedly sensual. I felt my face flush instantly. I looked down, fiddled with the ligature, took off the reed. I looked up. She caught herself, cleared her throat, and looked down at her purse.

"Uh, look," she said, "I have this work thing I'm supposed to do, but I'm...do you have, like, a card or something? I mean, you know, I'd like to come and see you play sometime. Do you, like, play around here?"

I almost laughed, but I stopped myself just in time. "Sure," I said, "whenever I can. I don't have a card, though." I had plenty of cards, but they said private detective, not clarinet player. And right now I was a clarinet player. "But I'm pretty free the rest of the day, if you'd like to get a drink. How long's your work thing? What is it, beach volleyball tournament or something?"

The line was so lame it barely limped out of my mouth. But she actually blushed. "Oh, God, no, I wish," she said. "I'm an *accountant*, if you can believe that. I'm supposed to meet some law firm guy to talk about a real estate investment. *So* exciting." She pulled her phone out of her purse.

I reached in my jacket and pulled out my phone. There was a new text from Heather Cusumano, CPA: "On the pier, by the clarinet player."

I texted back: "Likewise." Then I put my phone back in my pocket and extended a hand. "Marcus Heaton," I said. "Law firm guy."

She laughed. "Really? Tom said to look for the ex-cop from New York. I wasn't expecting a musician."

I felt a weight suddenly slide off my shoulders. I knew the feeling of dropping an eighty-pound rucksack in the sand after carrying it for twelve hours. This feeling was new. I tried to turn it around in my mind, get the taste of it burned into my memory, because I knew the weight would be back and I'd have to pick it up and carry it again. But just now, at this moment, it was gone. Because she'd sat there on the bench looking right at me for twenty minutes and she hadn't seen cop, hadn't seen thug, hadn't seen tough guy. She'd just seen the guy playing Duke Ellington and Hoagy Carmichael. I knew it wouldn't last, but I wanted to just sit here in the sun and be that guy for a little while longer.

"Well," I said. "How about that drink?"

Thirty-Four

It took Heather an hour to pull together the public-records story of the Antelope Palms Mall in Tarzana, out in the Valley. I told her it was a due diligence project for a deal Hausman was putting together. Investors demanding the usual corporate colonoscopy before they signed on. I pulled off a pretty good bored shrug: We're just the drones, you and I. Ours not to make reply/Ours not to reason why. Not that I quoted the poem (though I could have—check the ex-cop reciting Tennyson from high school English). I didn't need to. We'd both spent most of our careers finding things out without being told exactly why.

The Antelope Palms story wasn't much of a story. The mall had had a great life on paper, back in 1998, but had never quite cracked physical existence. If John Scofield was right, Eleanor Hausman had gotten a ten-million-dollar investment in it from a shell company, Antelope Palms Development, LLC. The money changed hands and then the project died and then...nothing. The plans went into a drawer somewhere, the building site went quiet, and the joint venture evaporated. And the unknown ten-million-dollar investor never made any effort to get its—or his or her—money back.

If Scofield knew any more than that, he hadn't said. But he knew I'd be curious. When a person gives someone ten million dollars, gets nothing for it, and then walks away from the money like a guy who drops a quarter in a puddle of piss under a bus-station urinal, there are three possible explanations. One is that he *did* get something for the money—just not the something he wrote down in the contract. Another is that he didn't really lose the money at all, and the transfer was just a paper transaction, designed to fool the government or whatever suckers actually got fleeced. The third is that he was afraid of something scarier than losing ten million dollars.

Scofield's message in my motel room in Texas was clear enough: somewhere in his office, or at least in his brain, was a draft prosecution memo putting a face to that scarier thing: me. And he was giving me a chance to make an edit. "Go to LA, Heaton," he had said. "Prove me wrong." Well, okay, then.

The thing was, you couldn't tell, from the public-records side of the story, whose ten million it was. A limited liability company was just a piece of paper in a drawer in the California Secretary of State's office.

"It's an elegant system, in a way," Heather said. She was drinking a Rob Roy. I had a gin gimlet, not because I liked gin but because we were in LA and that was Marlowe's drink in *The Long Goodbye.*

"A limited liability company comes into being when the Secretary of State gets a form in the mail with a $70 filing fee. Anonymous postal money order is the way to go there. The form's public but it doesn't say much. You need to name an organizer and specify a service-of-process address so you can be sued. But the only rule for that is that your agent can't be another LLC and the address can't be a PO box. Doesn't have to be a person, though. It can be a company if you want, and we have a whole industry of filing companies—corporate-services companies, you know? Pay a few hundred bucks, and they'll be your registered agent. Now you're legit. You don't have to file anything else —no articles of incorporation, no annual reports, nothing."

"And then," she continued, "if you're smart, you make your LLC a single-purpose entity. You set up your company for just a single transaction. Then you file another form to dissolve it—and that one's free, by the way. Sometimes people use a single-purpose LLC with a single-purpose services company as registered agent, and then when the deal's done they dissolve them both. Cute, huh?"

She finished her Rob Roy and fished out the cherry and inspected it critically. "You're not going to tie that in a knot with your tongue, are you?" I asked.

"Well, I need another first," she said. "In the Bureau they train us to do it with two of them." She got up and headed for the bar.

I swirled my gimlet and wondered whether John Scofield knew more than he was letting on. Had he run into a wall trying to trace the money and didn't have the juice to co-opt agents from the LA field office to chip away at it? Hell, it wouldn't even have to be the FBI. There were other agencies he could ask. And he could subpoena bank records, too. That's the first thing I would have done.

Maybe he was trying to keep his investigation off the radar. That would be the only reason to avoid subpoenaing a bank. Off whose radar, though? Hausman? Was he afraid of her? "Shoot at the king, you better not miss"—that sort of thing? Was he concerned that if he started subpoenaing records, she'd catch wind of the investigation? That was possible, but it didn't feel right. Hausman was rich and politically connected, but she wasn't at the level where you couldn't keep a bank subpoena secret from her.

So was Scofield trying to keep his investigation off the radar of his own department? Was he going off the reservation? Hunting out of season?

There was another possibility, though. Scofield might be trying to make sure that I was compromised with Hausman and J.C., so that when he made his move he could tell them I'd been cooperating. "Better make a deal—your friend Marcus has been so helpful, there's no point in fighting this."

Or was he trying to use me to do his legwork? He knew that I'd come out here after he put the bug in my ear. I'd *have* to know. "You're still a crook, Marcus, you're still working for dirty money." That was all it took, and he had known it.

So whose LLC was it that had transferred the ten million? That was the problem: a single transaction that took place ten years earlier between two long-dissolved corporate entities. Hausman's end of it was easy enough to follow. Her LLC was called EHH Management California, and the signatory on the creation and dissolution forms was a corporate flunky of hers. There was no mystery about where the money *went.*

The other company—Antelope Palms Development, LLC—was the problem. It had been formed less than two weeks before the transaction. Its registered agent was a corporate services company called U-File Services, which was dissolved six months later.

So who was behind Antelope Palms?

"Interesting problem," said Heather, when she came back with two more drinks. "You see it in any laundering operation. The whole point of laundering is that you don't want to use cash in a suitcase. But unless you're using cash in a suitcase, *someone* has to sign things. So if you're moving money through companies, there's always a name on a form somewhere. Your pros, they use a whole bunch of names. Keep the money moving continuously. *Matryoshkas,* we used to call them. You know, those little Russian dolls? Nested, one inside the other? Pull one up, there's another underneath? You nest your front companies like that, the more the better. The Russians are great at it."

"Inspired by their dolls?"

She gave me a grin. "Sure, maybe. Some smart people in the Bureau thought so. We had a seminar on it. 'Cross-Cultural Patterns in Organized Crime.'"

"Seriously?"

"Seriously. If I remember the PowerPoint, the idea was that you could see the same cultural signifiers in art and criminal methodologies."

"How'd you do on the exam?"

"Aced it. Your tax dollars at work, baby," she said with a light laugh. I laughed too, picturing Red Tie and Blue Tie dutifully filling a pad with notes on cultural signifiers.

She had a beautiful laugh. Not a derisive Fed laugh. It was a laugh that went with her hair, which was now grown out to a more-than-Bureau-standard fullness, and her outfit, which I knew without asking was an "I-just-left-the-government" purchase, the kind of girlish sundress you could wear when you didn't need a place to hide your gun. And when you had the time to go home and change after work.

I looked at her sundress and I knew the sense of freedom that had fueled its purchase, and the trip to the hair salon that went with it.

I saw it in Frankie's Hawaiian shirts and Tom Jarron's periwinkle chalk-striped suit with the huge pocket square, stuffed—*not* folded. I knew the feeling, but I'd never felt it. I wished I could see it in myself when I looked in the mirror, but I never could. Not quite. My exit from the force hadn't been voluntary. I had missed out on the moment of elation and freedom. I'd gone from anger to fear to resignation to depression, none of which had warranted an extravagant clothing transition. The closest I'd had to the real thing, the real feeling of liberation, had come with the first blow I'd landed on Settentio's jaw that day in the precinct break room. The feeling that I was *done*, that I could do what I wanted. But all I wanted, that day, was to keep landing punches, until my guys pulled me off him.

I realized I'd stopped laughing, and Heather was looking at me curiously.

"How'd you know Frankie, again?" she said. "NYPD, right?"

"Yeah," I said. "We were on patrol together for awhile."

She nodded, and I looked closely, but I couldn't see any reservation in her face, any subtext to the question. It occurred to me that for the first time in a long time, I might be talking to someone who didn't measure me against everything they knew about my past. Someone who saw me not as a fixer, not as a thug, not as a repository for dirty secrets, but as a guy who could play Duke Ellington on the clarinet. The guy I wanted to be.

"And now you work for a law firm?" she said. "Good move."

I shrugged. "Just until my screenplay gets picked up."

That got me another laugh. "Isn't it incredible?" she said. "I know some former Bureau guys who could barely write a coherent field report, then they get out and they think they're the next Tarantino." She frowned. "Not so many plotlines in forensic accounting, though."

"Come on," I said, "they're there. What about *The Untouchables*? The accountant on the team?" I did my best Connery: "'Carry a badge? Carry a gun.'"

"Yeah," she said, "and he was a nerd and he got his brains blown out all over the elevator. No way, Heaton." She took a sip of her drink and eyed me over the glass. "*My* accountant is going to be tough and sexy —and get laid."

193

Sea lion on the dock at Marina Del Rey

Thirty-Five

Heather lay back on the pillows with her hands behind her head. Lauren Bacall would have lit a cigarette. Lauren Bacall couldn't hold a candle to Heather. I got up and stood by the window, admiring her body in the moonlight. I was no Humphrey Bogart, but that was just as well. Heather would have knocked out Humphrey Bogart with one hand without breaking a sweat. And Humphrey Bogart didn't play the clarinet.

She looked at me and smiled. She said: "Okay. Who's behind an anonymous LLC and no bank subpoenas?"

"Impossible?"

"'Difficult—not impossible.' Damn, that's not quite it. *Godfather II*, remember? Can we get to Hyman Roth at the airport in Miami?"

"Close enough," I said. "I hope it's not that bad, though. The guy that got to Roth got shot like three seconds later."

"No, not that kind of difficult. Just shoe-leather difficult. But we can handle that."

She did most of it. I spent most of the next two days sitting in the sun at the beach and drinking beers on the back of Frankie's boat. I wasn't in a hurry. I was in California in February, and Heather didn't need me for her shoe-leather work. Shoe-leather work at CenterPoint was mostly keyboard work. If you had a name and access to the right databases, you could get your actual shoe leather down to one trip. That one trip, I'd handle.

She called mid-morning. I was sitting in a lawn chair on the dock next to the boat, watching a family of sea lions sunning themselves on the dock across the channel. A few big ones, a few little ones, lying there in the sun. No one else paid them any attention. They were just loafers, like me, hanging out at the marina in the middle of a workday.

Heather had what we needed. Enough to start with, anyway. She had requested the two public forms Antelope Palms had filed with the state of Delaware: the Articles of Organization form and the Certificate of Cancellation form. They were the only public records that existed on Antelope Palms LLC. But they had names on them. The Articles of Organization had the name and address of the "organizer," and the Certificate of Cancellation required the signature of "a majority of managers" of Antelope Palms. She hadn't been expecting to get much from them.

"But here's the thing," she said, "you can't just list any old rando on the cancellation. The manager of an LLC signs off on the LLC's transactions. Controls the banks accounts. If you're using the LLC for anonymity, you have to have someone you trust as the manager. Someone you trust with your money and who can keep their mouth shut. Which means you usually use your lawyer."

That was what they'd done in the FBI, she said, when they were trying to untangle the webs of LLCs that corporate fraudsters used to hide their transactions. You look at enough filings, and you're probably going to see a lawyer for one of the hidden principals.

"I mean, you can do layers of Russian nesting dolls there too, but for Antelope Palms? There was only one organizer listed on the Articles of Organization and only one manager listed on the Certificate of Cancellation. And it's the same name."

"What's the name?" I said

"Daniel Bergillius. Ring any bells?"

"No. What did Google have to say about him?"

I could hear her smile on the phone. "Quite a bit. Buy me a drink tonight and I'll tell you all about it."

I put my phone in my pocket and stood up. The sea lions were still just lying there, so I decided to show them I wasn't quite as lazy as they were. I went out to the end of the dock and did some pushups on the edge. Docks are great for pushups. Nice grip on the wooden planks, and you can look down into the water and imagine a shark coming up at you, gaping jaws ready to break the water and close around your head.

No sharks appeared, and the sea lions didn't follow my example. I walked back up the dock to the marina. Frankie's dock key let me into the "boater's lounge," a big room with some old furniture, a pool table, a TV, and a computer workstation. I sat down and Googled "Daniel Bergillius." I had to try a couple spellings, and then there he was. The guy even had a Wikipedia page devoted to him. He had been a big-shot Hollywood attorney, a dealmaker more than a trial guy it looked like.

Most of the Wikipedia page was about the Tony Palomaro scandal, which had almost destroyed his career. Somehow he'd skated though. He stayed out of prison and even kept his law license, while his firm crumbled around him and Palomaro and two of Bergillius's law partners went to federal prison.

Palomaro retired from the FBI in the early nineties and set his sights on cashing in as a Hollywood fixer. Those guys had been around as long as Hollywood and they mostly came from the same mold: big, tough guys with a law enforcement background and a penchant for fancy cars and nice suits. Palomaro fit the bill, but he had two advantages: the FBI had taught him all it knew about electronic surveillance and he had no moral scruples whatsoever. Wiretapping is illegal unless you're a cop with a warrant, which is a deterrent to most private investigators. Not Palomaro. He'd bug anyone for a fee, and he wormed his way into the cutthroat world of celebrity contract negotiations, high-dollar divorces, and tabloid lawsuits, where off-the-record knowledge of who was fucking who was the currency of the realm.

He peddled his skills to the agents and litigation firms who weren't concerned about the legality of his methods. There were enough of these clients to make him rich, but if you read any Shakespeare in high school, you know how the story ended: the character traits that made him a star burned his ass up, too. He couldn't keep a low profile. He decided he wanted to be a celebrity himself—bad idea for a private investigator, particularly when it's an open secret that your stock in trade is a federal crime. He did so many "wink-wink-nudge-nudge" interviews that you could have written his indictment by cutting and pasting the transcripts. That's pretty much what the Feds ended up doing.

Palomaro's bigger problem was that he double-crossed his own clients. Think about it: when you hire a blackmailer, you're putting your name down on his victims list. He started double-dipping his dirt, looking for payouts from both sides of every deal and both parties to every secret roll in the hay. Sooner or later that catches up to you.

Palomaro's run lasted about ten years. Whether that's sooner or later is a matter of perspective, I guess.

I felt a little "there but for the grace of God go I" as I read the story. Not too much, though. Palomaro's tragic flaws were obvious: he had to be the center of attention, he couldn't keep his mouth shut, and he had no loyalty to his clients. I was pretty sure I didn't have those problems. I had my own problems. But they weren't splashed all over a Wikipedia page.

There was one piece of good news, down at the bottom of the page, in a section titled "Current Practice." Bergillius's firm had folded up and two of his partners had gone to prison, but he had avoided prison and even kept his law license. By a hair, it looked like. He'd been suspended for a year. But he'd come back and had a solo practice with an office in Beverly Hills. Walking distance from CenterPoint.

I scrolled down the page looking for Bergillius's clients. It was quite a roster. And Wikipedia would only have the publicly known ones. But the name I wanted was probably on that list. Bergillius represented celebrities, not hedge-fund managers. And if he had used Antelope Palms to move money for someone, that someone would have had to have ten million dollars lying around in 1998. I looked at the names again. There were a dozen possibilities at least, just from the ones I recognized. Too many. And Bergillius wasn't likely to tell me. Not willingly, anyway.

I went back outside and down the ramp to the dock. Out at the end, by Frankie's boat, John Scofield was sitting in my lawn chair. He was dressed Fed-casual: he'd unbuttoned the top button on his shirt and loosened his tie an inch. He had on Navy sunglasses and was looking out across the channel at the sea lions.

He nodded at me when I approached. "I'm glad you came out here."

"Wish I could say the same to you," I said. I stepped up onto Frankie's boat, opened the locker, and pulled out his other chair. I opened it up, kicked my feet up on the rail, and pulled a beer from the cooler. The last thing I was going to do was ask him how he found me.

"I appreciate you not sending your goons after me, at least," I said. "Or don't you have a chicken warehouse handy out here?"

He waved a hand. "No need. It's nice here. And I knew you'd come."

"Yeah? Does your office even know you're here?"

He ignored the question. "My apologies for the theatrics. And I can enjoy a little LA vacation, same as you."

"Yeah. Except you're not on vacation."

"Neither are you. So tell me what you're going to do next."

"Sit on my ass, drink a beer, and then fly back to New York and get on with my life. You want one? Or maybe a cocktail? We're stocked." I liked offering booze to a Fed at 11 a.m. on a weekday.

Scofield surprised me. "Much appreciated," he said and picked up his chair and moved it down onto the boat next to mine.

I reached into the cooler and handed him a beer. "So you quit?" I said. "If you're looking for cheap rent, the slip fees here are great. You have to have a boat, though."

He ignored me, took a big sip of his beer, and looked out across the channel at the sea lions. "They really just sit there all day? Right on the dock? And no one messes with them?"

"Far as I can tell," I said. "They like the sun. Like me. And *un*like me, they have a moment's peace."

"Funny. A buddy of mine works down in the Southern District. San Diego. Says it's a real issue for the office there, the sea lions. 'Cause they have this beach they like to come up on. Nice beach. Little cove. La Jolla, you know? Real fancy town, north of San Diego."

"Yeah, I've heard of it," I said. "Where Raymond Chandler went to drink himself to death."

He raised his eyebrows. "Did not know that," he said. "Huh." He turned to me. "How the hell do *you* know that?"

"PIs, we like Chandler. Some of us. My copy of *The Long Goodbye* has some 'critical essays' in the back." I made air quotes for him, though he seemed like a guy who might know what a critical essay was.

He laughed. "Which you read?"

"Finished the book, didn't want it to end," I said. "Just kept reading."

He nodded. "Okay. Well, here's the thing about your sea lions there. They're federally protected. Law's called the Marine Mammal Protection Act. Says you can't fuck with marine mammals at all. Like at *all*. Can't kill 'em, catch 'em, throw things at 'em, run up and kick 'em in their fat little sides. And you sure as hell can't organize a posse of family-values soccer dads to run 'em off of your favorite beach with sticks and dogs. And you maybe really shouldn't videotape yourselves in action and post it online."

I shrugged. "So go bust 'em. You're the big swinging dick from Main Justice, right?"

He wagged a finger. "Ah, now *that* is the moral of our story. We don't. No one does." He took another sip. "I hope you understand, Marcus, that I am making a somewhat more general observation here."

"Yeah? Well, I wish you'd tell me what it is, so I can go back to sitting in the sun."

"The more general point is that the pressures from the bosses in DC can extend beyond the realm of marine mammal harassment cases."

The skin on the back of my neck tingled, but I was not about to bite. I said nothing.

"And those pressures need not push in the direction of refraining from pursuing a particular investigation."

This time I bit. "Are you telling me that some political bigwigs in DC are pushing DOJ to investigate Hausman?"

Scofield twirled his hand in a "go-on" gesture. "And/or..." he said.

"And J.C.?" I said. "Shit, John, the election's *over*. It's February. Hope and Change is in charge now."

"Indeed," he said. He smiled a tight smile, waved at the sea lions with his beer. "I've never seen them before. In the flesh, I mean. Big fuckers, huh?" He drained the beer, started to stand, then paused and sat down again. "But you know? I will share another interesting anecdote, because it has been on my mind lately, and I think you'll appreciate it."

He crumpled the can and raised his eyebrows at the cooler.

I handed him another. "Careful, counselor, you don't want to crash your G-ride on the way home."

"Oh, I'm in no rush."

"Well, maybe I have to be somewhere," I said.

"No, you don't. You're sitting here watching the sea lions. So you can listen to my damn story."

I shrugged, drained my beer, and reached for another.

Scofield leaned back in the lawn chair. "Maybe five years ago? Senator Steven Tedeo? From Hawaii? Remember?"

"Some corruption thing, right?"

"Right. Tedeo was basically the founder of the state. First the House, then the Senate. Pulled in military bases, fuel subsidies, protection for the fruit industry, you name it. Thirty years. Makes a lot of friends, makes a lot of enemies.

"Every so often, someone accuses him of something—the usual, you know? Nothing ever stuck. He wasn't Duke Cunningham-level stupid, for one thing."

I remembered Representative Duke Cunningham. J.C.'s Bright Young Things loved that case. The Bright Young Things talked about white-collar-criminal trials the way sports-radio callers talked about football games.

Cunningham was a former fighter pilot who claimed to be the model for Tom Cruise's character in *Top Gun*. He got himself elected to Congress, bulled his way onto the Armed Services Committee, and then got caught red-handed taking bribes from a defense contractor for funneling military appropriations to his company.

Cunningham's DC residence had been a yacht in the Washington Marina owned by the contractor and called, in an irony the press couldn't have dreamed up, the *Duke-Stir*. The trial had featured testimony about DC parties centering on coke, prostitutes, and briefcases full of cash.

The Bright Young Things would pull up the docket and analyze transcripts like TV commentators. For them, the case was all about Jason Forge, the young hot-shot prosecutor, versus Mark Geragos, the future hall-of-famer defense attorney. Geragos was good, but Forge was better, and the Duke crashed and burned.

Scofield knocked down half the can. "So a few years ago, DOJ opens an investigation into Senator Tedeo. He's the big prize, you know? The one your ambitious Deputy Chief looks at and sees 'nomination to the federal bench.'

"The ambitious Deputy Chief was a guy named Morris Branda, in the Public Integrity Section. He decided Tedeo was his ticket to a judgeship and he was going to punch it. So he puts some line prosecutors on it and says, make me a case."

"Line prosecutors meaning you?"

"No, not me. I was in Iraq. Young guy, real bright apple, named Nick Boggs. Georgetown Law, good clerkship, straight arrow. Nick gets the grunt work on the investigation. Spent a year in Hawaii."

"Not exactly grunt work," I said.

Scofield shrugged. "Good location, still grunt work. Limelight's in DC. Anyway, Nick gets a couple agents, works it for a year, but they don't find much. And Branda starts getting frustrated. Starts putting the heat on Boggs. 'Bring me the damn case, kid, unless you want your next evaluation to say 'Lacks initiative.' That sort of thing.

"So Boggs comes up with a possible crime. A hotel builder named Allen Persons had had one of his companies do the renovations for Tedeo's vacation house out on Kauai. Hundred grand or so of work. Boggs follows the paper trail; it looks like Tedeo only paid about fifty. So then they go and check his Senate financial disclosure forms. Senators have to report any 'thing of value' they received, which would include a fifty-grand-discount on the renovations. Tedeo didn't list it.

"So there's your crime: False Statements, in violation of Title 18, section 1001 of the United States Code. Open and shut, right? They write up their indictment, and Branda holds his press conference. Going to be a nice, clean paper case, and Branda's going to get his scalp.

"Except that Tedeo's not rolling over. He's spent fifty years in politics not rolling over, and he's not going to start now. He hires Williams & Connelly, and they've got more white-collar acquittals than twenty other firms combined. So they get an order for pretrial discovery and they get twenty boxes of paper from the government, and they find their ace in the hole. Turns out Persons had a whole folder of handwritten birthday and Christmas cards from Tedeo that he'd gotten over the years. Tedeo sends him one for his birthday, the first one after the renovations, and it says this: 'Thanks for all the work on the Kauai property! Your guys are true craftsmen and it's been a pleasure to watch them work. Now don't forget you owe me a bill for the rest of the work—those ethics rules are strict and I need to cross all the t's.'

"And then, six months later, at the bottom of the Senator's Christmas card? 'Al, don't forget, I'm still waiting on that bill for the renovations.'

"So the defense puts these up on the screen in their opening statement: 'Ladies and gentlemen, just look at the evidence! It just jumps off the page and grabs you by the throat—Steven Tedeo knows his obligations and he's trying to meet them. He knows he has to report and so he's asking for his bill. You cannot report a bill you haven't gotten yet!'

"Pretty good defense, right? Except that then the government calls Allen Persons, and you know what he says? Says he met with Tedeo in person, at his birthday party, and Tedeo says, 'Hey, Al, I gotta cover my ass, right, so I'm going to ask you for a bill. I'll send you a couple notes, make a paper trail. Just ignore it. It's for show.'

"Which is pretty damn good testimony for the government, right? Takes Defense Exhibit A and turns it into Government Exhibit A. Except here's the thing…the FBI interviewed Allen Persons during the investigation, showed him the Senator's notes, and asked him why he never sent a bill. And Persons never mentioned that 'cover-my-ass' conversation. You know what he actually said when they asked him? He said, 'I meant to, I just never got around to it.'

"That's what we call a prior inconsistent statement, and any juror would see that Persons just made up the 'cover-my-ass' story for trial, to give the government what it wanted. Except the defense didn't know about that interview because the government didn't turn over the notes. They straight up buried it."

I probably didn't look horrified enough, because Scofield wagged a finger at me. "What are you thinking? 'Oh, so they buried a statement, big deal.' I'm not even going to ask you if you've ever done it, because the difference between you and me is—for me? The only thing separating us from fucking Tajikistan is we don't do that shit."

I didn't say anything. I kept my thoughts to myself: *Oh, but we do, John. You're telling me a story about it right now, aren't you? You may not like it, but we do. And we're still not fucking Tajikistan.*

"Aren't you exaggerating a little?"

"Maybe. Let me finish and you tell me."

I sat back and let him finish.

"That wasn't the only interview they buried. There was another one. Seems Allen Persons liked the company of prostitutes. Young ones. He had one in particular he liked; she was fifteen. The FBI went and talked to her. She says, Oh, yeah, Allen, he told me if I ever get busted to lie and say we never had sex. He got worried lately with this Tedeo investigation, and he had his lawyer bring me an affidavit to sign saying that.

"You know what that is, Marcus? It's fucking subornation of perjury, not to mention statutory rape. It's impeachment evidence. Same as the inconsistent statement about the bills. The point is, of *course* Tedeo was dirty; everyone in DC knew he was dirty. But you don't fucking *convict* him dirty. You understand?"

I didn't say anything. I thought I understood. I still think so. But Scofield wouldn't have believed me if I said so.

"Who buried it?" I said.

Scofield shrugged. "Collective failure of memory on that point," he said. "But it came out, because it always comes out. You can't hide a fling with a fifteen-year-old prostitute forever. What happened was a few months after trial one of the FBI agents filed a complaint against another agent—I don't know what their beef was—and he throws in a charge that the other guy withheld evidence in the Tedeo case. So that goes up to the top of the flagpole at Main Justice. And they tell the judge, and he appoints an outside counsel to go over the files with a fine-tooth comb.

"And then the prosecution team, they see that shitstorm coming, and they make sure they shovel that shit downhill. So those cowardly, career-covering fucks point the finger at the junior member of the team, the kid five years out of law school—the kid who didn't and couldn't possibly have made any significant tactical decisions, but fuck him because it's all just musical chairs…." He trailed off.

"The senior guys threw the junior guy under the bus?" I knew that story too.

"Yes, they did. And they all got promoted, and Nick Boggs sat there for six months twisting in the wind, wondering whether he'd get fired, disbarred, or indicted first."

"Did he?"

"No, he didn't. Because he got tired of waiting. He hung himself in his basement on his thirty-second birthday."

I looked at my feet. I remembered leaving the force, the feeling a lot of cops have that they've lost part of their identity. Maybe it was harder when you really believed in it.

Scofield spoke again. "I knew Nick Boggs, Marcus. Not well, but I met him a couple times. And I believe I know what he was feeling when he hung himself. I didn't tell you this story because I like telling it. I'm telling you because I swear to God that's not going to be me next."

"What do you mean?"

"You know exactly what I mean."

"I wish I did. I get that you've got an analogy going here. I'm just not sure where I fit in it."

"Come on, Marcus, don't play stupid. The Tedeo case was pencil pushers looking for a scalp to put on their resumes. What I'm telling you is I think this one might be worse." He paused, took a breath. "You know what an October Surprise is? A big revelation comes out of left field right before an election, maybe swings it. Like the Reagan campaign made a deal with Iran in '80 to hang on to the hostages until after the election. Nowadays they're smear jobs, mostly. Or maybe a big indictment of some of Hope and Change's closest associates? That works great, if you control the indictments."

I didn't say anything. He looked down at his beer. "I have come to suspect that the outgoing administration initiated multiple criminal investigations as a last-ditch effort to swing the election. One of the targets was Jennifer Curtis. And I think I know what they did to get their star witness."

"Well, the election was three months ago, so whatever you're talking about didn't work."

"No, but you don't just stop these things in their tracks, and you can't fucking *hide* the tracks, either. So now *some*one is going to get fucked, and we're in musical chairs mode. And I think I know why I got invited to the game."

I thought about a line the Bright Young Things used. "Your name on the pleadings, your ass under the bus." Something like that. I said: "So what do you want from me?"

"I want confirmation that I'm right. And I'm not supposed to know what they did." He looked around, as if the sea lions might be eavesdropping. He finished the beer, crumpled the can, and clapped me on the shoulder. "We're in the same boat, buddy."

He stepped up on the gunwale, put one foot on the dock, and chuckled at his joke. "Cheap fucking pun," he said, shaking his head. "But you work with what you've got." He pointed a finger at me, thumb up to make a finger pistol. He sighted along it and then brought his thumb down, cocking it. Then he stepped up on the dock and walked away.

Beverly Hills, Rodeo and Dayton

Thirty-Six

I sat in the sun for half an hour after Scofield left, trying to look relaxed and carefree in case any telephoto lenses were zooming in on me from a surveillance van parked across the channel. I imagined myself as I'd look through the lens: jeans, black T-shirt, Yankees cap, gas station sunglasses. Then I ducked into the boat, threw a white dress shirt and gray suit pants into Hausman's giant briefcase, and walked up to my rental car in the marina parking lot. I looked around for lurking Feds waiting to tail me, but I didn't see any. I didn't expect to. Scofield had a much easier way to track me, and his appearance at the boat was pretty good evidence that he was using it. He was using cell-tower location data from my phone.

Your phone is constantly "pinging" all the cell towers in range. It sends out its pings every thirty seconds or so, whether or not you're using it. Little digital "Hello, I'm here!" radio signals that the cell towers dutifully transmit back to the phone company computers. With a court order, the Feds can get the records of those little "hello" signals in real time. And since there's usually more than one tower in range, they can use the difference in signal strength between the "hellos" at various towers to triangulate a phone's location. Nowadays they don't even have to triangulate, if your phone has its GPS turned on. They've got you down to the meter. Triangulation is more like down to a football field.

But triangulation is all Scofield would have needed. It would have put me at the marina, and I was plenty visible, sitting out there on the dock all morning. Which meant I was in the warrant application that put the bug in Hausman's office. Maybe I had my own numbered paragraph: my name, my connection to Hausman, and probable cause for pulling cell-tower locations.

TELEPHONE #26 is a New York-based cellular phone, registered to Marcus A. Heaton (Subject 12), a known associate of Subject 1 (J.C.) and Subject 2 (E.H.). Subject 12 has used Telephone #26 to contact Subjects 1 and 2 on multiple occasions. Based on my training and experience, I believe that probable cause exists that Subject 12 will travel for activities relevant to the Investigation and will keep Telephone #26 on his person and use it to communicate with Subjects 1 and 2 as well as other unknown associates and/or co-conspirators.

I'd seen plenty of those applications. Written some myself. It occurred to me that they were probably tapping my phone as well. Why not?

I wondered if that was what Scofield was trying to tell me, by coming out and sitting there: this is real, pal, and you're in it up to your neck. Snitch or go down hard—the usual cop threat. But it wasn't just that. Scofield was trying to tell me that *it wasn't just him.* "I'm not supposed to know what they did," he said. Was he trying to warn me? About what?

I was in no mood to ponder the philosophical distinction between a threat and a warning. When you're on the receiving end, there's not a whole lot of daylight between them.

I drove to the CenterPoint offices and parked in the garage. In the bathroom I changed into the dress pants and shirt, putting the T-shirt and jeans in the briefcase. I took my phone out of my pocket and put it in the briefcase too, in one of the little zippered inner pockets. Then I went upstairs to Frankie's office.

CenterPoint had three floors, and Frankie had a whole office to himself. I put in ten years as a detective in the NYPD and I never had an office to myself. Never even shared one. I had a desk in a cubicle. Frankie put in twenty on patrol and never even had a cubicle. He'd typed up his reports on a shared computer in a cramped, windowless "report-writing room" that smelled of sweat and stale coffee, and his only personal space had been his locker. Now he had an office with a window and a plant and books on a shelf behind him. Like a fucking college professor.

I took a minute to wander the office, admiring Frankie's digs. Frankie had a black ergonomic office chair, a big desk with two computer screens, a framed picture of his boat in the marina at sunset, an armchair across from his desk with plump cushions, and built-in floor-to-ceiling shelves along one wall. The shelves mostly held banker's boxes full of papers and big Redweld file folders. I shoved the briefcase in between two cardboard boxes on the bottom shelf, then sat down in the armchair and put my feet up on the edge of Frankie's desk next to a heavy-looking glass tray stuffed with Frankie's CenterPoint business cards, printed on thick, cream-colored stock with the CenterPoint logo in blue and gold.

"Busy day?"

Frankie was typing away at something on the computer. He was not a graceful typist. Still used mostly his two index fingers, though you could see him making an effort to get some work in for his other fingers. I'd learned to type pretty well under Captain Settentio. He hated sloppiness and inefficiency, and cop typing infuriated him. And I was used to getting my other fingers involved. You need them all for the clarinet.

"Not so bad," said Frankie. "The usual chaos, right?"

"Want to grab some lunch?"

He grimaced. "Man, I'd love to. Can you give me like an hour? I've got to run to this meeting in about thirty seconds, but then, you know, the afternoon's pretty clear." He stared intently at his screen. *"Print, motherfucker."* He banged the return key and raised his head, listening. I heard the whir of a printer out in the hall.

"There we go," he said. "These ex-Bureau guys, fuck, they want fucking

reports. Like they can't pull the rod out of their asses when they retire, you know? Like how about I just *tell* you what drugs the fucking guy came back positive for, you know? Which I read off the fucking *lab* report? But I'm supposed to write it up *again?"* He stood and hurried out into the hall to the printer.

"Take your time," I called through the door. "I'll catch you later on. Got a couple things to do myself."

Frankie came back in, frowning down at the paperwork in his hand.

"Can I borrow a tie?" I said. "You got one in here?"

"Help yourself," he said, putting his papers in a manila folder. "On the door there. Let me take care of this, and I'll call you in an hour or so."

"Can you do me one quick favor?" I said.

"How quick?" said Frankie. "Impatient people down the hall."

"Daniel Bergillius," I said. "Celebrity lawyer, used to be, anyway. What's he drive?"

"You mean do we have a DMV database?"

I shrugged. "Sure. Or something."

He spread his hands. "Let's say or something. Jarron says you get the red carpet, so..." He sat back down at his terminal. I averted my eyes politely. I didn't know what databases they had. Firms like this, they were secretive about that sort of thing. You'd get their reports, and every paragraph would start, "Research suggests that..." They'd never tell you *what* research exactly. I figured a guy's car would be child's play. It was. "Only one registered," said Frankie. "He on hard times, or what?"

"I dunno," I said. "Never met him. Office is in Beverly Hills, though."

"Nice ride, anyway," said Frankie. "BMW Z4. You know, the two-seater with the retractable hardtop?"

"Not off the top of my head, no."

"Easy to spot. Just look for the guy with the little dick."

"Okay," I said. "Can I use your motorcycle, too?"

"Whatever, man," said Frankie, halfway out the door. "Just be back for lunch. It's in the garage by the gate." He fished in his pocket and tossed me the keys.

"Hey, if you see Heather Cusamano, tell her I stopped by."

Frankie put a hand on the doorjamb, turned, and gave me the grin he'd had at twenty-one. Somehow he'd managed to keep it all these years. "Sure thing. Wondered where you were last night. Playa."

I closed the door behind him and looked at the hook on the back of the door. Frankie had a blazer and three ties hanging on the hook. I picked a dark red pattern and put it on. Then I sat down at Frankie's desk, picked up his phone, and called Daniel Bergillius's office. I got his receptionist. I raised the timbre of my voice half an octave, tough-guy baritone up to a reedy tenor.

"Yes, I'm calling from CenterPoint Solutions? We're wondering if Mr. Bergillius has a few minutes this afternoon. We've had a small situation come up, and Mr. Jarron thinks very highly of him."

I had no idea if CenterPoint had ever used Bergillius or what Jarron thought of him. But it didn't matter. She didn't even ask my name. Yes, the receptionist said, he was at lunch, but should be back soon. Would forty-five minutes work?

"Certainly," I said. "We'll send over our investigator."

I took the elevator down and stood around in the lobby until a group of ten guys dressed exactly like me—dress pants, white shirts, mostly red ties—came through, walking out for lunch. I walked out with them, just in case anyone was watching the entrance. I wasn't expecting foot surveillance. I didn't know if Scofield was even staffed for it, and if he was, he would probably just have them on call in case the phone went somewhere interesting. And my phone was going to be cooling its jets up in Frankie's office all afternoon.

The suits walked out onto Avenue of the Stars heading for lunch. So was the rest of the suit population of Century City. Lawyers and agents, all headed for Craft, Cuvée, Hinoki & the Bird, whatever. You could throw a rock in any direction and hit a young white guy in dress pants, white shirt, and a tie that was probably red. I tagged along for half a block, then cut across to the big mall between Avenue of the Stars and Century Park West.

The mall was like our East Coast malls, except it was open-air. Just another slap in the face of places with weather. I wandered for a few minutes, looking at the stores: high-end teas, high-end cheeses, high-end sneakers, high-end watches, high-end razors and hair oils, perfumes, and every variety of clothing boutique. It took me most of a lap to find a kiosk selling phones. I walked past it once. It was out in the center of the open-air esplanade, and I didn't see any security camera on the kiosk itself. I took another lap and went back, keeping my gaze low.

The young guy manning the kiosk was sitting on a stool and talking on his phone when I approached. I couldn't place the language. I did a once-over of the inventory, picked one that looked to be about the middle of the pack, and nodded at the kid on the stool. He said something to whoever he was talking to, set his phone down, and turned to me.

"You see something you like?"

I pointed. "That'll do. Good phone?" I kept my eyes down on the display.

He shrugged. "Yeah, man, all good phones." He opened the glass case under the counter, pulled out a phone in its cardboard and plastic box, and rang me up. I paid cash for the phone and a gray clamshell case.

"You want me to change out your SIM card?" he asked.

"No, thanks, it's cool, I can do it," I said, looking down at the box.

The kid nodded, picked up his own phone, and went back to his conversation. A week from now, if things went wrong and the FBI traced the phone back to the kiosk and braced the kid for details on who he'd sold it to, I'd be a complete blank.

I walked back down Constellation Avenue. The towers full of lawyers and agents and bankers glittered all around me. I went back into CenterPoint's building and took the elevator down to the garage. Frankie's bike was right by the gate in a row with three others, helmet with gloves in it hanging by the handlebars and jacket folded over the seat. I donned the gear and gunned it up the exit ramp, turned left on Century Park East, then right on Santa Monica, then took the two blocks into Beverly Hills in second gear. I turned right on Charleville, across from the Beverly Hilton, and then went the two blocks down the street to Bergillius's office. I stopped at the corner and parked the bike in front of a Starbucks across the street. Then I took out the phone and threw the box in a trash can.

Bergillius's office was in a pink three-story building he shared with a plastic surgeon who called himself a "body sculptor" on the brass nameplate in the lobby. I had twenty minutes until my appointment with Bergillius. I walked around the block and confirmed that the entrance to the building's underground garage was a ramp next to the lobby entrance. Then I went in the Starbucks and sat with a cup of coffee in a seat by the window. I powered up the phone and scrolled through its built-in applications, then adjusted the settings and tested it out to see if it would work the way I wanted it to. It did.

Bergillius's office was up on the third floor. The elevator opened onto a pink-and-green-tiled hallway leading to a reception area done up in pale wood and white leather. A young woman sat behind a chest-high circular desk made of green-tinged marble. Bergillius still had a furniture budget, at least. And a receptionist budget. She looked like she was between takes on the set of a soap opera. She'd be the young emergency room doctor with the heart of gold, maybe, or the naive prosecutor who still believed in justice. I believed in justice just looking at her.

I smiled my nicest smile. "Hi, I have a two o'clock with Mr. Bergillius? Marcus Heaton from CenterPoint?"

She smiled back. "Of course. Just a moment. Have a seat and he'll be right with you." She had the voice and the smile for a soap opera, too, though they were wasted on the mundanities of small talk with me. Or maybe not, I reflected: there were worse places for an aspiring actress to work than in a Hollywood fixer's office in Beverly Hills. She stood a better chance of getting spotted in Bergillius's office than she did waiting tables at Mastro's.

I sat and pulled out my new phone, as if going through my email. I opened the Voice Memo application and pressed Record. I had two hours of record time. I closed the clamshell case. I had set the screen to lock down after one minute, but the Voice Memo app would keep recording. At least it had at the Starbucks.

Bergillius only kept me waiting a minute. CenterPoint's reputation preceded me, as I knew it would. Bergillius's rent wasn't cheap, and his business must have taken a hit when his partners went off to federal prison. He came out to the reception area himself to shake hands. I stood up, putting the phone in my left front pants pocket.

He wasn't as old as I'd expected. Late fifties, probably. Impeccable suit that you could probably trade in for a sports car when you got tired of it. Salt-and-pepper hair, just the right touches of gray at the temples. And shoes so polished you wouldn't want to look down at them in direct sunlight. He led me back to his office. It matched the reception area, with pale wood paneling on the walls and white leather chairs across from his desk, which was the same green-flecked marble as the reception desk in the lobby. I wondered what the green was, and how it ended up in the marble. Just another item on the list of things I might have known if I'd gone to college instead of joining the Army. I made a mental note to ask Heather. Maybe the FBI had sent her to a geology seminar.

Bergillius closed the door and settled himself behind his desk. "So, tell me about this situation. How can I help?"

I kept my voice polite and neutral. No threat in it. "There may be a situation," I said, "or there may not be. I'm hoping there's not."

I let the silence hang for a moment, watching his face. The words were just ambiguous enough to spark a flicker of fear. Bergillius's eyes widened slightly, his neck muscles twitched, his knuckles gripped the armrests of his chair. He covered it well, and you never would have seen it if you weren't looking. But I was looking.

"I'm an investigator with Montrose Bryant & Wolfe," I said. "We use CenterPoint for most of our LA matters, but we may need local counsel on this one. There is a certain amount of urgency."

He leaned forward, put his elbows lightly on the desk, all brisk attention at the prospect of a big-firm retainer. "Okay. Why don't you tell me about it?"

"We represent a client," I said, "who I believe you did business with some time ago. Late nineties, thereabouts."

I let the silence hang again, let him run through a mental list of all the dangerous people he'd dealt with back then. I figured it for a pretty long list. I gave him a minute to work his way down it. He waited about ten seconds, then nodded and looked at me expectantly.

"Okay. And?"

"There is a particular transaction from that period. A sizeable transaction in which you were involved. The amount in question was ten million dollars."

I watched his face. That must have narrowed it down. Not all the way to one, probably, but I guessed to single digits. I locked in eye contact, and he held it without flinching. He'd dealt with tough guys before, and he knew the drill. Stay calm, don't show your fear. But I knew the fear was there. A lot of people in his orbit had gone to prison, and he hadn't. And most of those people were undoubtedly not happy about that.

He tried a thin smile. "I'm sorry, I'm not sure, off the top of my head—"

"My client is now involved in other transactions," I continued, cutting him off, "in which a certain amount of, ah, due *diligence* is required by other parties, and it's become important for us to make sure that everyone is clear on the extent of the, ah, *documentary* record on this particular transaction. Just a formality, really. Checking the paper trail and so forth."

I emphasized "diligence" and "documentary" to make sure he got the picture: someone's digging around, and I'm here to make sure they don't find anything. If I just asked him who was behind Antelope Palms, he'd never tell me. But if I told him I suspected him of blabbing about it, there was a chance he'd lead me right to the source of the money.

He nodded and seemed to relax slightly. "All right, well, anything I can do to help, of course…" He trailed off, waiting for me to continue. He'd probably played out this scene a dozen times since the Palomaro scandal blew up, and he knew what came next. I was going to give him a name, and he was going to confirm that a secret was safe.

I watched his face. "My client is Eleanor Hausman," I said, "and the transaction in question involved a company called Antelope Palms Development, LLC."

There was the flicker again, but longer this time. It travelled in a wave down his face. His eyes flicked away from mine, his jaw clenched, and his Adam's apple twitched. He covered it again, cleared his throat, and nodded in a lawyerly way. "Okay."

"You recall it?"

He spread his hands. "Well, no, not in any detail…"

"You were the manager of the company," I said, "if our records are correct. The issue for us is that our records are incomplete. It was some time ago, and Ms. Hausman has been asked, in this, ah, due *diligence* process, to provide additional information on Antelope Palms. The usual: operating agreement, ownership shares, list of investors."

He nodded slowly, getting what I hoped he thought was my drift.

"As far as Ms. Hausman is concerned," I said, "those records are just not available. It's entirely possible they've been lost. Or destroyed. She believes that they were never filed with any state agency."

He nodded again, back in control, definitely getting the drift now.

"Oh, certainly not," he said, with the confidence of a lawyer talking law. "Nothing like that is ever filed."

"And the sources of the funding?" I said. "Wire transfers, for example? Ms. Hausman is in the position in this...due diligence matter...of being unable to provide any information on the sources of Antelope Palm's funding..." I let it hang in the air.

"I see," he said.

"But before making a...firm commitment to that position, we need to be quite sure that we have...fully exhausted other possible sources."

"I understand."

"We need to confirm that the well is completely dry. We want to be as compliant as we can, obviously, but sometimes information is just..." I shrugged, "not available."

I watched him ponder this. Was I offering a fee, or a shallow grave in the desert? Or were both on the table? I knew my clothes didn't fool him. He'd looked hard at my hands when he'd greeted me out in the lobby. "Well, of course, I'd be happy to assist in the research," he said carefully. "I think that your client may be right, though. I very much doubt there's anything to find."

"Your own files, for example," I said. "I understand the standard practice is to maintain them for only five years?"

"That's correct. And if I recall, this particular LLC was dissolved ten years ago?"

"That's our understanding," I said. "And obviously we wouldn't have any access to bank records..."

He nodded. "Of course not. And anything of that sort, if it had been in my files, would have been destroyed with everything else."

I copied his lawyerly nod. "Though I suppose they might, in theory, be *subpoenaed?* Just out of curiosity?"

He stroked his chin, going from lawyerly to downright professorial. "Well, in *theory*, sure, that's that's always possible, but a subpoena to me would yield nothing, because I don't have those records. And—hypothetically—a transfer from a numbered account, very probably from an offshore institution, doesn't provide usable information in any event."

He sat back in his chair, satisfied that he'd given all the right answers. I nodded and shifted my weight in the chair, crossing my right leg over my left. I slid my left hand against the phone in my pants pocket, nudging it up and out onto the leather seat. It slid into the crack where the seat cushion met the armrest. Bergillius's desk was wide, and the chair had thick armrests. He had no line of sight down to the phone. I stood and offered him a handshake, pushing the chair away from me at an angle and in toward the edge of the desk.

"And I don't suppose there's anyone else I should be talking to?" I said. "It's important that we are as...*thorough*...as possible here. Anyone else I should see, in person?"

He stood as well and shook my hand across the desk. I squeezed hard. He didn't dare. "No," he said, "no one that I can think of."

"You're quite sure?"

He nodded. "Very sure."

"Okay," I said. "We'll be in touch with a local counsel agreement. I imagine your research might take some time, but I'm authorized to tell you that we have a sufficient budget to ensure that we get this one right."

"Thank you," he said, "I appreciate that."

I turned halfway, then stopped. "Ms. Curtis will especially appreciate your efforts," I said.

His mouth twitched, just a hair. "I'm sorry?"

"My employer," I said. "Jennifer Curtis. She'll be grateful that you're taking an interest in this."

He didn't answer.

"We'll be in touch," I said. "I'll look forward to seeing you again soon." I pushed my chair in another six inches, in under the edge of the desk, then turned and walked out.

I walked across the street to Frankie's bike. The helmet, gloves, and jacket were still there, at least. It had only been fifteen minutes, and if you were a potential impulse thief, would you take a jacket off a motorcycle sitting in front of a Starbucks? I put on the gear, fired it up, and repositioned it across Charleville, facing north on Spalding. I cut the engine and sat, watching the garage ramp for a midlife-crisis BMW roadster.

It wasn't a long wait. Inside of ten minutes, a two-seater Beamer came up the ramp. Bergillius even had the top down. I squeezed the clutch and thumbed the starter, watching him. He revved his engine and peeled out left onto Charleville. Traffic was perfect for a tail—not so heavy that I'd lose him, and not so light that he'd notice me.

I followed him down Charleville to Beverly, then left across Santa Monica Boulevard and up into the residential half of Beverly Hills. He stayed on Beverly past Sunset, then up into hills to where it jogged right and turned into Coldwater Canyon. Bergillius gunned the road-ster up the hill. We were most of the way up to Mulholland Drive, on the top of the ridge, when he hit the brakes and made an abrupt left into what looked like a gravel driveway.

I was back a hundred yards and I slowed and pulled over to the right. There was a lot of money tucked into the canyons below Mulholland. Up on the ridge you had the flashy ostentatious houses with their walls of glass, cantilevered out over the hillside, begging to be looked at, noticed, pop in the background of tourist photos of the hills. But there were dozens of canyons, twisting deep into the south side of the slope, thick with sycamores and eucalyptus and jacarandas, where your money made sure no one would look at you.

I waited two minutes, then drove slowly past the driveway, glancing over as I passed. All I could see was a heavy wrought-iron gate twenty yards down the gravel. It was closed. No sign of the roadster.

I made it back down the canyon and into Beverly Hills in ten minutes and parked the bike in the same spot in front of the Starbucks. I

219

took off the helmet, gloves, and jacket, and I was mild-mannered law firm guy again. I ran my fingers through my hair and went back up to Bergillius's office.

The receptionist was there, ready as ever for her audition. She smiled brightly. "I'm so sorry, Mr. Bergillius had to run out for just a few minutes, but he'll be back later this afternoon."

I smiled back. "Oh, that's no problem. I was just about to call, but then..." I made a comic show of patting my pockets. "Looks like I left my phone here?" I peered around the reception area, where the phone plainly was nowhere to be found.

She looked at me sympathetically.

"Funny," I said. "I was sure I had it... You know, it could have slipped out of my pocket. Could you by any chance check the chairs in his office? I was sitting in the one on the right, I think."

Of course she could. And she did, returning a moment later triumphant, phone in hand.

I returned the motorcycle to the garage in the CenterPoint building and went upstairs to Frankie's floor. I found an empty conference room down the hall from Frankie's office, went in, and closed the door. I opened the phone and thumbed the passcode. The Voice Memo app came up, still recording just as I'd left it. It was at just over an hour. I hit pause and ran it back to the beginning, heard myself making small talk with the receptionist, heard Bergillius come out and introduce himself.

I ran it forward, looking for the end of our conversation. There it was: "My employer. Jennifer Curtis. She'll be grateful that you're taking an interest in this."

I heard the scrape as I slid the chair forward toward his desk. I heard my footsteps leaving, heard the door close. And then I heard Bergillius swearing to himself, softly, under control, no temper tantrums the receptionist might overhear. Just a rhythmic, mezzo-piano "fuck, fuck, fuck, fuck, fuck, fuck..."

And then the sound I'd been waiting for, Bergillius's phone lifting off its cradle, his finger punching the buttons. A pause, then: "Silvio. It's Dan." Pause. "No, forget about that for a minute. I'm thinking you

220

maybe rethink this whole thing." Pause. "No, no, Silvio wait! *I* told you not to come in the first place! Now, listen to me, I think we might have a problem." Pause. "Yes. Yes, and *you* fucking agreed, remember?" Pause. "Yeah, well, of *course* I'm not dead, I'm fucking *calling* you—" Pause. "No, no, nothing like that, but I'm... No, I'm not being paranoid. I mean, *yes,* I'm being fucking paranoid, and maybe you should be too." Pause. "Come on, Silvio, forget about that—" Pause. "For what? I don't care who you invited. For what, a fucking party? No, no photo shoots." Pause. "No. No, it's a terrible idea. *Low* profile, in and out. *That* was what we said. You're not here to make a fucking movie, Silvio. You shouldn't be here at all. No—no, I don't *care* what they say, it's— Look, I'm coming out there, okay. I don't want to talk about it over the phone—no, don't leave yet, I'm driving up there. No, that can wait fifteen minutes. *Yes,* I'm fucking paranoid. You should be too."

The phone slammed down. "Fucking idiot," Bergillius said to the empty room. Then his chair squeaked, and his footsteps receded. And that was it.

There was a computer in the corner and I pulled up Bergillius's Wikipedia page and scrolled down to the list of his famous clients. It wasn't really necessary. I had read the list once already, in the lounge at Frankie's marina, and there was only one "Silvio" on it. And it wasn't a name you would forget: Silvio Angelides. It was a name I'd known all my life, and one I'd seen on plenty of other lists, usually lists of the best movies of the decade. Or the century.

I pocketed the phone and walked back to Frankie's office. He was at his desk, holding his phone to his ear with one hand and taking notes on a pad with the other. I sat down in his armchair and kicked my feet up on the edge of the desk.

Frankie signed off the call. "Okay, copy. Won't be a problem." Then he turned to me. "Perfect timing, brother. Late lunch, early happy hour? Your call."

"Early happy hour," I said. "But first, I need your help with one more thing. A little project for tomorrow."

Thirty-Seven

took Frankie's bike out again that night, just to reorient myself to the city. It had been a long time since I'd been in LA and I wanted to feel its rhythm. That was harder in LA than in New York, I've always thought, but maybe that's just the East Coast talking. I'll grant you the poetry of riding a motorcycle at night in the Hollywood Hills. You put some elevation under you, go north from Sunset, up and up through the canyons, all the way to Mulholland, then west to the fire roads. Get up on that ridge, ride west down to the ocean, then come back south along the Pacific Coast Highway toward Santa Monica. The sun was going down as I wound down Topanga Canyon to where it hit the PCH in Malibu. The ocean glowed orange when the canyon opened up, and so did the steep embankment for a few minutes, before fading to black.

Frankie's motorcycle was a mid-1980s Honda, 750 cc, with low handlebars, cafe-racer style. No windscreen, and Frankie's headgear was a half-helmet and a pair of untinted glasses. I could feel every molecule of air on my face, every bump in my feet, every lean of the bike in my core. I could feel the vibration in my hands as I twisted the throttle, feel the hum of the engine in my legs. If I sat up straight and looked out in front, I couldn't see the bike at all. Just me, floating down the road, disembodied, flying like in those dreams where you leap off a hill and coast, like you're hang gliding but without a glider. Just me and speed and the wind and the road, nothing separating us.

This was why I loved riding a motorcycle. But I knew it wasn't true, that feeling of being disembodied. I was embodied all right, embodied in a water balloon balanced on top of a blender, and if I lost focus or pushed too hard, I'd be a smear on the road in an instant—*that* was the real lesson of riding. Scofield had said we were in the same boat. It was a cheap pun, he'd said, but true. He might have said we were both riding motorcycles, fast, at night, on the Pacific Coast Highway with a fog rolling in.

I drove my rental car to the meet the next morning, wishing I was on the bike, still juiced from the night before. It was Frankie's idea to use the studio. I didn't want to brace Angelides too directly. I wasn't entirely sure what I wanted to ask him, or whether I wanted the answers. All I told Frankie was that I wanted to talk to the guy. Frankie didn't press me, but I knew he didn't like it. I was bringing bad-cop juju to his clean private-cop beat, dirty New York snow falling on the perfect Hollywood fescue.

He played along, though. He had the idea of using Phil Geronian, who had been a CenterPoint client for years, and lately one of Frankie's specials. Geronian was a producer with some hit shows on his bio. He had recurring drugs-and-hookers flare-ups that had to be tactfully chilled, and Frankie was good at that. Good enough to call in a favor or two. This one was simple. I needed to talk to Angelides, but I didn't want to spook him. Based on Bergillius's end of the phone call it sounded like Angelides didn't believe there was really a hit man after him, and he'd been asking around town trying to get work. So we'd have Geronian call Angelides and say he heard he was in town and would love to film some scenes at Angelides's house. In one of Angelides's early movies, a noirish cop movie, he'd used his own house as the femme fatale's faded mansion. The critics had loved it. Geronian would tell Angelides he was thinking of filming an homage scene for an upcoming episode of his show. It'd be a callback to the movie, just in time for the Oscars. He said Angelides would appreciate the flattery.

You've probably seen some of Geronian's shows. The one we picked was about a bitter ex-cop with a checkered past and a penchant for violence, working as a fixer for a high-end law firm. Frankie liked the irony.

Geronian apparently liked it too. He tried to sign me up on the spot as a consultant.

"Or a fucking *character,*" he said, offering us a drink at 10:30 in the morning. Frankie declined, but I accepted. I had whatever Geronian was having, which I'm pretty sure was a very expensive whiskey. I had no reason not to drink in the morning. I never killed a homeless guy while driving home drunk. I clinked my glass with Geronian and knocked it back.

"Yes—*Jesus,*" he said, "Just fucking *look* at you. Just have you walk in the frame and *say* something. *Hit* someone. You know what I'm saying? I mean, could you *do* that?"

"How 'bout right now?" I said in a cop voice, squaring up at him.

He flinched and took a step back, sloshing his drink. Frankie burst out laughing.

I felt bad immediately. This guy had had the shit scared out of him, more than once, and not long ago. I'd seen those eyes before, too many times. I felt a stab of self-loathing, and I wondered what Frankie had had to do for the guy.

I tried to take the edge off. "Well," I said, sitting down on his couch and crossing my legs in what I hoped was a more intellectual pose, "sure, but I really see myself more in a love scene."

It worked. Geronian laughed and relaxed a little. He took a chair. "So, kids," he said, "Silvio, huh? What a piece of work."

Silvio Angelides had written and directed two dozen movies, two of which were on every critic's top fifty list for the best movies of the twentieth century. But he'd been making them in Europe for the past twenty years, since he fled the country while awaiting sentencing on a rape charge. The extradition case had dragged on for a decade and then fizzled out, at least as far as I knew. Some procedural problem with the case that meant no retrial. But still he never came back. Then, over the winter, the story broke that Angelides was coming to LA for the Academy Awards. He'd missed out on a couple Oscars while he was a fugitive, and now the Academy was going to let him pick them up in prime time. The decision had led to some tension in the Academy. There was talk of a boycott by a bunch of female nominees. It was enough of a story that even I read about it.

The Academy Awards were still two weeks away, but Geronian said Angelides was back and had moved into his old house, up in the Hollywood Hills. Big old place, Geronian said. Most of an acre off Coldwater Canyon, way up under the ridge. Had sat vacant ever since he'd skipped town.

We had Geronian's assistant make the call, so Angelides would see the number, and could Google it and call back if he was suspicious. He wasn't, though. He sounded downright eager on the phone. His house? For a shoot? What a great idea. Sure, he'd meet us.

Frankie and I parked on the gravel in front of the wrought-iron gate and rang the bell. Angelides came out to meet us, walking down the gravel path with the posture of an alpha male, past his prime but damned if anyone was going to mention it. He was wearing a silk shirt, linen pants, and a baggy corduroy jacket that was too big for him. He'd probably filled it out nicely thirty years earlier. He had a full head of hair, but I was skeptical. Something about that generation, they'd take a wig over a nice shaved head. Maybe it was because when they were in their prime, big hair meant virility.

I didn't stare. It could have been real, after all. Reagan's was. So was Conway Twitty's.

And he was duly flattered by Phil Geronian's call. "Yes, of course, a great idea, a great idea," he said. "Television, I assume? Or has Phillip gotten the big promotion?"

Typical movie director snobbery. Frankie smiled. "It's TV, yeah. We're basically just looking at security issues, really, to start with. Got a couple big cameos, they're looking for a little seclusion."

"Yes," said Angelides, "well, we have that." He had the barest trace of an accent. Just a touch of European class, like the villain in a Bond movie. He gestured around the property, at the steep canyon walls,

225

thick with eucalyptus. You couldn't see any sign of human habitation, though we were only a mile or so from Sunset Boulevard. "Shall I show you around?"

The house was two stories, built into the slope of the hill, with big dormer windows on the second floor. Redwood shingles covered the walls, like the house Marlowe rented in *The Long Goodbye*. You could tell it was old. There was a wooden trellis wrapping around two sides of the house, and some sort of flowering vine, like ivy with giant purple flowers, had worked its way up the trellis and continued up the sides of the house all the way to the roof. At ground level, the vine was practically a tree, with big gnarled roots as thick as my arm.

"Beautiful house," I said. "Pretty old, huh?" Which was a stupid thing for a location scout to say. We would have had all the specs in our laptops. But we didn't have laptops. And Angelides was in a talkative mood.

"Old indeed, my friend," he said with an indulgent smile. "It was built in 1920. One of the first houses built in this canyon. I bought it in 1975, and my brokers advised me to tear it down and build from scratch. Can you imagine? But I liked the history. And of course my architects were able to do a lot with the interior. Will you be shooting interiors? The light in the afternoon is excellent this time of year." He looked up at the sky. "A little early yet, but..." He stopped and looked at us expectantly. I wondered if we were supposed to hold up our hands and frame imaginary shots, making little rectangles with our thumbs and index fingers. I looked at Frankie. Angelides gave us a half laugh, half sigh.

"Oh, but of course that is not your department, I suppose. Let me show you the garden."

The garden was in back. It was a half-acre paradise of grass, flowers, and terraces, roughly triangular in shape, hemmed in by the canyon walls on either side. The back of the house opened onto a huge patio of granite flagstones. On one side was a pool, empty, but tiled in an abstract Art Deco mosaic like the downtown subway stations on the 1 and 9 Lines. Or Grand Central. Except this was the bottom of the guy's pool.

The pool was rectangular and pointed away from the house. At its far end, like the cross of a T, was a pond, also rectangular and ringed with a white gravel path. The pond was surrounded by a dense curtain of bamboo and was full of water lilies and half a dozen big koi flashing white and orange patterns under the surface. Past the pond was an oval of grass, thick and green and manicured, surrounded by rose bushes that marched along the perimeter of the lawn to meet at a point where the canyon walls came together.

"Yeah," said Frankie, going for some location-scout enthusiasm, "this'll be perfect." He walked off down into the grass and started a slow circuit of the oval. Smart, discreet Frankie, giving me space to talk to Angelides.

I stood by the pond and framed a shot in my mind. You'd have the camera follow the detective out the back door onto the patio, pan around, take in the whole scene—pool, grass, flowers, eucalyptus trees rising behind them on the canyon slope. And then you'd track over to the femme fatale sunbathing in a lounge chair by the pool. She'd have a cocktail and a cigarette, and she wouldn't look up until the detective walked over and said something roguish. "I'm sorry to disturb you, Mrs. Easterbrook, I was looking for your husband. But I can see you're not hiding him anywhere." She'd respond in kind. "Well, don't look too hard, Mr. Marlowe. You're liable to find all *sorts* of things." Then she'd get up and throw on a silk robe, but leave it untied, and walk arm in arm with the detective on the gravel path, past the pond, and down to the lawn. She'd tell him about the dark family secret she needed him to unravel. He'd come back with some hard-boiled double entendre. She'd meet his gaze for just a second, you'd zoom in, hold the shot—

"You like the koi, Mr...ah...?"

"Heaton," I said. We'd introduced ourselves, but you can't expect the director to remember the security guys' names.

"I would like to be able to tell you that they are the original inhabitants," he said. "The pond is original to the house, of course. And koi can live a hundred years, so they say. But not here. I am afraid that we are surrounded by too many predators here. When I lived here before,

I tried every heroic measure I could think of to combat them, but to no avail. By day the herons, by night...the raccoons."

"Yeah, raccoons are tough," I said, thinking of nighttime encounters in Manhattan. You'd see them around the parks all the time. Smart, tough, not the least bit afraid.

"One year, I recall," said Angelides, "I had been away for months, on the Vietnam film. Weeks and weeks of night shoots, in the jungle. I don't know if you..."

"Yeah," I said. "I've seen it, I remember."

"Yes, well, I came home and found the pond decimated. Only a few remained. The wiliest, I suppose. The ones who learned to stay at the bottom. That is a hard thing for a koi to learn, you see, because we feed them on the surface. We tell them, all their lives, here, this is for you, come and get it. You've earned it. You are so beautiful. Come and eat. Lettuce, for instance. They love lettuce. The koi will rise to the surface to welcome you when you come to the pond with lettuce. But then we walk away and we do not protect them from the herons and the raccoons, eh, Mr. Heaton? We turn them into lambs for the slaughter, and then we come home and curse nature for being nature. I came home like Odysseus, winning my glorious little war and finding my household in shambles. I swore revenge on the raccoons. I restocked the pond, and I told myself I could protect them. I thought—silly, of course, I know—I thought that I would put my jungle training to use. I sat out here night after night with a shotgun, waiting. But..."

He gave an elegant little European shrug.

"No luck?"

"No luck, sorry to say, Mr. Heaton. It turned out that the raccoons were better at waiting than I was."

He was looking at me so intensely that I wanted to apologize for not catching all the metaphors. I could tell they were there but I couldn't decode them. It occurred to me I'd probably missed a lot of them in his movies, too.

I suddenly felt stupid standing there pretending to be a location scout. "Look, sir," I said, "let me be honest with you. I like your fish and all, but we're not here scouting for a TV location."

"I know," he said.

"You know? Then why'd you let us in?"

"Because I wanted to see you face-to-face," said Angelides. "Eye-to-eye. That is only fair. Even you must understand this."

"Mr. Angelides," I said, "I just need some information. I need to know what you remember about an investment you made in 1998. Antelope Palms, LLC. Ten million dollars. Where'd it go?"

He stared at me. A tear welled up in his eye and rolled down his cheek. "Two weeks," he said softly. "Two weeks until the ceremony. You could not even give me that?"

Then he reached into the front pocket of his coat and pulled out a .45.

Thirty-Eight

The gun looked heavy in his hand. He was a big man and still strong, but he was old. I looked out of the corner of my eye for Frankie, but the bamboo grove screened us from the yard. Angelides had chosen his spot well.

He looked at me with a half smile, half sneer.

"Antelope Palms? What do I *know* about it? You mean, who have I *told* about it? What have I *said?* Have I traded her for a golden trophy? That is what you want to know, yes? What I have said? Before you kill me to shut my mouth forever? Does she think I am stupid?"

He kept his voice low, but his gun arm swung back and forth as he gestured. The muzzle gaped at me with each pass. We were ten feet apart at most, with soft gravel between us. Too far to step and grab, but I could cover the distance with a dive roll. He'd pull the trigger, but the shot would be high. He had the .45 leveled at head height, and it would kick up viciously when he fired. I doubted that he'd fired it recently enough to remember the recoil. With any luck at all I'd get under the first shot and come up right under him. One hand on his gun arm and he was done. My best chance would be if he looked away for a moment. Which he would, sooner or later. Everyone did.

I decided to keep him talking. Talking was better than shooting. And

230

I still wanted my answers. "Antelope Palms," I said. "Why? Why'd you give Hausman the ten million?"

He looked at me with what appeared to be genuine surprise. "They do not tell you these things?"

"No," I said, "they don't. I don't know anything about it."

"Except to ask if I have talked about it."

"That's not what I—"

But Angelides wasn't listening. His expression grew dark. "Then you are a dog. Worse. A hired killer who does not even care about the 'why.'"

"I told you, I'm not—"

"I gave those girls what they wanted. All of them, from the first to the last. They know they did. Even the ones that went to the police, they know they wanted it. And every time, afterward, I wondered if someone would come to kill me. Fathers, brothers, lovers—I would have accepted that. For honor, yes. For vengeance, yes."

His sneer deepened. "But none of them ever did. Oh, they came. But they didn't come to kill. They came for money. To make *deals*. And I paid the money, and I put them on the screen and they went away. All of them. Some were more expensive than others. But price was no object. I was a wealthy man, and the heart wants what it wants."

"Ten million? Every time?"

He laughed an ugly laugh. "No. The average rape is much cheaper." He laid a little stress on the word "rape," as if to make sure I got the message that he wasn't protesting his innocence. I got the message. The .45 sent it loud and clear.

"They were different, those two," he said. "They were smart. I was a like a mouse, a plaything for a cat. They let me run, then they pounced. Antelope Palms was timed to hurt me. I didn't have ten million dollars, then. They gave me one month. They needed 'liquidity,' they said, and they knew about the extradition. I knew the Swiss government would never extradite me for one little case, but they had...they had *all* of them, somehow. Names, dates, places, statements—more than I remembered myself."

He stamped his foot like a child. "So I paid. I raised the money. I worked. I signed to make five pictures, payment up front, no 'back end,' in your disgusting parlance. And I paid. And they were good, my pictures. Good! I filmed *Quoth the Raven*—in Prague!—and then..."

He wiped a tear away with his free hand. If he'd used his gun hand I would have gone for him, but he held the gun steady. "I won," he said. "For the first time in twenty-five years, I won. And then she called me, the cat calling the mouse. 'Stay in your hole, little mouse. If you come to get the cheese, you die.'"

He raised his voice, a whine echoing the foot stamp: "It's not *fair!* I am *old.* It was so long ago. Why won't they just forget? She took the money, can I not have at least my honor? So her enemies want to use me against her, so what? Does she think I do not know who the cat is? I have said *nothing!* There is no paper, no tape; she *must* know that! They wanted me to testify before the grand jury, but I implored them to put it off until after the ceremony, and they agreed. Sympathy for an old man. They were bigger fools than I. I would have forgotten anything I ever knew. I thought she believed that. But apparently she did not. Now I am a loose end."

Angelides was pacing back and forth on the gravel. I'd seen the body language a hundred times. It was the same in millionaire's rose garden as it was on surveillance footage of gangbanger beefs, right before the bullets flew.

I raised both palms placatingly. "Look," I said, "I don't know what you're talking about, but we can work this out. Just put down the gun."

He didn't answer. Just stood there, turning the gun in his hand, examining the side of the barrel. Then he lifted his left hand and wagged his index finger back and forth, then extended it out to his side, like a one-armed Jesus on the cross. A shaft of sunlight pierced the bamboo curtain and lit up his head. He looked for all the world like that guy in one of his movies. You know the one I'm talking about. Right before he took about fifty bullets, as the crane shot pulled up and the Morricone score crescendoed?

Angelides seemed to notice the cinematic potential of the shot, because for just a moment he tilted his head back to catch the sun. That was my chance, and if I had been a hair quicker I would have rolled, come up under him, and taken the gun before he looked down. But just as he lifted his head, Frankie's boots crunched on the gravel to my right, and Frankie came around the bamboo, smiling at me. Angelides wasn't in his sightline yet.

"All right, then," he said, "you all set?" Then he saw Angelides and he froze.

Angelides swung his gun arm around and I leaped toward Frankie. I got my left arm across Frankie's chest and tackled him just as the .45 roared.

You look at a bullet, and it's a pretty small thing. Even a .45 is only about the size of the middle joint of your little finger. And most of that is the shell casing, which is just a hollow tube filled with gunpowder. The casing stays in the gun and gets ejected, like the first stage of a rocket. The bullet itself is just the little piece of lead at the top, the crew capsule, if you're still thinking about rockets. It's about the size of your fingernail. Not a big decorative nail either—a working fingernail, bitten down low. Even on a .45, the bullet's a pebble. Go ahead, throw one at my head, as hard as you can. I won't even blink.

Which is why I've never gotten used to the damage a bullet does to a body.

They taught us in Basic that most of the damage comes from the shockwave caused by the impact. That's why exit wounds are so much bigger than entrance wounds. The M16 shoots a .223 caliber bullet, which is half the diameter of a .45. Goddamn tiny, when you hold one in your hand. But accelerate one of those babies to 2,800 feet per second? Well, you'll understand Newton's second law then. If you have time before you die.

They told us that 2,800 feet per second was 1,900 miles per hour. Which didn't mean anything to us. I remember one of the instructors telling us that was like Houston to Seattle in one hour. Which also meant nothing to kids who'd never been on a plane and had only a vague idea of where Seattle was or how long it ought to take to get there.

It was pretty goddamn fast, though. And we got the idea: pump a bunch of those little guys into someone at that speed, and there's not much left on the other side.

A .45 pistol pushes the bullet out a lot slower. Only about 600 miles an hour. But that was enough. Frankie took one in the chest from a distance of eight feet. It splintered his sternum going in and his scapula going out and ripped out most of what was between them.

I was a half step too slow to tackle him out of the line of fire. The roar of the pistol deafened me, and I knew one of us was hit. A spray of blood and bits of skin and bone and lung hit the side of my face, hot and wet and sticky. Frankie dropped like a two-hundred-pound bag of tomatoes, if you hung it six feet up and cut the rope.

I landed next to Frankie and got up on one knee to look at the wound. If Angelides was going to shoot me next, he had plenty of time. Going for him now would just panic him into shooting again and wasn't going to save Frankie. I looked at the wound and doubted if anything would. It was hard to tell what the bullet had hit. Plenty, I figured. Lung and bone at least, because I had them on my shirt, and I recognized them from the war. Not the heart, though, judging from the rhythmic upwelling of bright red blood coming out of Frankie's chest. And he was still breathing. His chest was heaving and I could hear him gasping for air. The bullet had collapsed one lung, but maybe not both. I put my right hand over the entry wound and leaned down hard, putting my weight on it. The upwelling slowed. That wouldn't matter if he was bleeding out through the exit wound. But there was nothing I could do about that, and I couldn't roll him over to look without taking pressure off the chest wound.

"Frankie, hold on," I said. "It's gonna be all right." Though I knew it wasn't.

I kept my eyes on Angelides. He held the gun out to the side, away from his body. For maybe ten seconds, we just looked at each other. Neither of us said anything.

"What the hell did you *do?*" I said.

He swallowed, worked his lips. Then he spoke slowly. "I...I didn't mean to... Who was he?" His accent had thickened, as if shock and fear had sanded away fifty years of varnish.

"He's my *friend*. And you just fucking *shot* him."

"Your friend? But he must have known your purpose in coming here?

234

Because surely, you would have had to tell him? Before you did the deed?"

"What fucking *deed?*" I said. His lips curled into a slight smile.

I turned, panic hitting my brain like the nicotine in the first cigarette you've inhaled in a decade. Like the knock on your door at midnight with the badge held up to the peephole.

I craned my neck, did a 360 around the property, from the gate to the back door to the bamboo grove behind the koi pond. Back to the gate. Nothing. I couldn't hear a bird. Not even an insect.

"I...am...not...a goddamn executioner!" I had to force my hands to stay on Frankie's chest. "I told you, we didn't come here to kill you, for Christ's sake!"

He just shook his head. "I paid. I paid and paid until I had nothing *left*. I know I was not supposed to return. But the men, they told me... they told me they would let me come back and receive my award. An appeal to an old man's vanity. My vanity was stronger than my fear. That was my mistake. We feel fear for a reason, do we not? Like the fish? They know the heron is waiting, but they rise to the sunlight nonetheless."

"Drop the gun," I said, "the cops'll be here in three minutes." Though I knew it would be longer. And that was assuming there were any neighbors to hear the gunshot and call it in.

"I am a stupid old man," he said. "I thought we had a detente, she and I, gun-to-gun, mutual assured destruction. I am a fool. She had the only gun."

"No, buddy, you have the gun. Only gun here. I'm not carrying. We were just here to talk."

"No," he said, "I do not think so. It is too late to talk." He brought his left hand over his right to steady the gun. Then he leveled it at my head.

I went into a dive roll straight at him, leading with my right arm and tucking my head down as I rolled over my right shoulder. I heard the roar of the .45 as I hit the ground. It was a clean roll and I had calculated the distance right, and I'd been right about the recoil kicking his shot high, because when I came up under his extended arms I wasn't dead.

I was aiming to get a grip on both his wrists as I came up from the roll, but he stumbled backward and jerked his arms in toward his body, probably a combination of the recoil and surprise. His right hand was still gripping the pistol, his left still gripping his right wrist.

I came up from my roll a half step in front of him with my left arm up and reaching for his right wrist just below the gun butt. The gun barrel was at forty-five degrees, pushed up and back by the recoil.

I got my left hand to his right wrist as the momentum of my roll carried me into him, but I couldn't get a clean grip. He stumbled back a step and jerked his gun arm out to the side, and my fingers slid off the cuff of his thick corduroy jacket. He reached out for my throat with his left hand, but I got my right up in a solid block, knocking his arm up and to the side. Then I stepped forward onto my right foot and brought my right arm across my body, still going for his gun hand. I knew it was the wrong move as soon as I started it. Too gentle. I had an opening for a straight right hand to the chin and I should have taken it. One punch would have knocked him out or at least staggered him enough to let me take the gun from him. But something in me had hesitated at hitting an old man.

He didn't hesitate, though. He swung the .45 wildly at my face, like a tennis player hitting a forehand on a high-bouncing serve. If it had caught me in the temple I would have been out cold. But the .45 was heavier than a tennis racket and slower to swing. I saw it coming just in time to drop to a knee and duck under the barrel as it came around.

I only realized he had pulled the trigger when my hearing shut down instantly, replaced by a dull ringing. I felt the noise more than I heard it. I looked up at Angelides's chest as his torso twisted past my face, carried by the force of the swinging gun. I gathered myself to tackle him and take him down, when he jerked back twice, like a marionette pulled on a string. Two round holes appeared on his linen shirt, just under his collarbone.

Angelides staggered and collapsed backward into the koi pond. I couldn't hear the splash. I just watched him fall, his legs on the stone pavers bordering the pond, his left hand dangling in the water, and his right hand across his chest, still holding the .45. He floated there on the lily pads with the gun clutched in a death grip, and his dead eyes staring upward at the sun, like a Viking holding his sword on his chest as he sailed off on his funeral barge. The water ran red under the white flowers.

I turned and looked back at Frankie. He was still on his back, but his head was up and both arms were extended, holding a Glock automatic. I didn't even know he'd been carrying. His shirt and jacket were soaked red and his face was ashen and spattered with blood and dirt.

I ran to him and got my hand back on his wound. His eyes were open and his mouth was moving, but I couldn't hear anything but the ringing in my ears. Then his eyes closed, his arms flopped limply to the ground, and his head dropped back to the dirt. I could feel the blood pumping under my hand and wondered how long I had been away from him. Ten seconds? I hoped it hadn't been too long. An artery can pump out a lot of blood in ten seconds. I reached for my phone with my free hand and called 911. I could barely hear the 911 operator's voice. I gave the address, reported a shooting, said we needed an ambulance in a hurry. Then I hung up and called Tom Jarron. He picked up. I said Frankie and Angelides were down. Shot.

"I'm on my way," he said. His voice through the phone sounded like the neighbors' music through an apartment wall. "Stay put. Call it in. You can fill me in when I get there."

Smart guy, not asking for details on the phone. J.C. had the same habit.

Then I knelt there, leaning over Frankie, feeling his pulse weaken beneath my hands. The sun was warm, and I could smell the flowers underneath all the blood and sweat. And I knew that whatever detective caught the case would have some pointed questions for me. Like how I came to be sitting there on a famous old director's lawn on a beautiful sunny day, in between two dead bodies.

Thirty-Nine

But Frankie wasn't dead yet. I kept my hands on his chest until the ambulance arrived. It was five minutes, maybe less, and he was still breathing shallowly, but I had no idea how much blood he'd lost out the exit wound in his back. At least he wasn't pumping it straight out his chest.

My hearing started coming back, and I heard a siren, then the engine, then tires on gravel. Two paramedics came up the driveway at a run. Some departments didn't let paramedics approach a GSW victim until the police had cleared the scene, which was a stupid policy, in my opinion. I was glad to see that the LA Fire Department didn't have the rule, or at least didn't follow it at ten-million-dollar houses in the Hollywood Hills.

One of the paramedics knelt next to me and put his hand over mine, on the wound.

"Gunshot wound, .45 from up close," I said. "Exited through his back. I haven't moved him. Got pressure on it quick. Tell me when."

He didn't ask if I was the shooter. Just said, "Three, two, one," and I pulled my hand out and he took over. Definitely not their first gunshot case. LA was running around 250 murders a year, I remembered. Probably a thousand or so GSWs.

I stood up and flexed my fingers. The other paramedic had gone to Angelides. He knelt at the edge of the koi pond but didn't reach for the body.

"Hey!" I yelled at him. "How 'bout we save my partner!"

He looked at me, reading "cop" the way they all did, and seemed to agree. He turned away from the koi pond and with two quick steps was down on a knee next to Frankie. He put his head close to Frankie's face, pulled up one of Frankie's eyelids, and then put his head to the ground to try to get a look at the exit wound.

"You off-duty or what?" he asked.

"Yeah," I said. "What do you need?"

"Go get the gurney," he said, "and hurry." I could hear more sirens now, getting closer.

I ran to the ambulance, pulled the collapsible gurney out of the back, and jogged back up the path, holding it under my arm like a surfboard. The first paramedic still had his hand on the chest wound. The second paramedic had his hand under Frankie's back, and I saw a bunch of plastic packaging next to him on the ground, like he'd opened up all his gauze to pack the wound. I laid the gurney next to Frankie, and the first paramedic looked up at me.

"Take his legs," he said, "and slide him over." I slid Frankie by the ankles. Then the first paramedic reached around with his free hand and took hold of whatever the second paramedic had packed in the exit wound. The second paramedic pulled his hand out, took hold of Frankie's armpits, and slid his upper body onto the gurney. Then he moved to the front of the gurney and jerked his head at me.

I moved to the back of the gurney, and on his count, we lifted it and locked it into its upright position. Then we wheeled it across the lawn and down the driveway to the ambulance, just as two black-and-whites roared up the driveway. I helped the second paramedic lift the gurney into the back, and the first paramedic climbed in with it, keeping his hands locked on Frankie the whole time.

"Where are you going?" I said to the second paramedic as he got into the driver's seat.

"Cedars-Sinai," he said and slammed the door. He hit the lights and siren and I stepped back as the ambulance accelerated down the driveway, spraying gravel.

I turned and walked over to the cops on the driveway. There were three of them, all uniforms. Two young ones, a male and a female, and a sergeant. The sergeant was older than me, probably past his twenty. He was talking on his phone. The young ones just stood there.

I approached, nonthreateningly, and stood there with my hands in plain view. I didn't know what exactly they thought happened here. The sergeant finished his call and walked over to me.

"Mr. Heaton?" he said. Not friendly, but not overtly hostile either. Someone had just told him my name on the phone. I could tell he saw cop, but hadn't been told anything. Which was good, because I had no idea who Jarron had called or what he had said.

"Yeah," I said. "Scene's back there." I pointed to the back garden and the two uniforms started off around the house. I followed. No one told me to stay put or to get on the ground with my hands behind my head. We stood on the lawn looking at the scene. Frankie's Glock lay there on the grass next to the pile of bloody gauze and plastic wrappers. And Angelides's body floated in the koi pond, the .45 clutched to his chest. The sergeant came up behind me.

"So that's Silvio Angelides?"

"Far as I know," I said.

"How about the other victim?"

"Frank Muller."

"What happened?"

"What it looks like," I said. "My partner took a .45 in the chest from eight feet. Missed his heart, somehow. He drew from the ground, put the shooter down."

"I mean what were you doing here?"

"CenterPoint Solutions," I said.

He'd heard of CenterPoint, I could tell. He'd probably moonlighted for them a few times himself. I took the opening. "You got detectives coming? Reason I ask is, whoever you were on the phone with, who told you my name? They were probably just on the phone with our boss, Tom Jarron."

I could see him relax slightly, shifting me in his mental threat profile from perp to colleague. "Security, huh? Didn't really earn your money today, did you?"

I figured Jarron had gone with a story along those lines, with whoever he'd called at LAPD. There were several plausible scenarios you could work with here. The best one would be that a depressed, volatile movie director calls his agent, says something that sounds like suicidal ideation. Agent knows the director's a gun nut, gets nervous, calls Jarron. Jarron sends a couple guys to babysit, Angelides goes nuts. That would play.

I went with vague self-recrimination. "No," I said, looking down and trying to sell the line. "No, I fucking didn't."

He gave me the benefit of the doubt, a little half nod, and we stood in companionable cop silence for about thirty seconds until his phone buzzed again. He answered, listened for a moment, and said, "Copy that." Then he looked at me and said, "They'll be here in two minutes."

"They" was four detectives, in three cars. One from the Hollywood Division, a young guy with the body language of the junior partner on scene. Two from the Robbery-Homicide Division, gray-haired late-career males. The fourth was a black female, mid-forties, an investigator with the DA's office, she said. I thought that was a pretty quick callout for a DA investigator, and I wondered if that had been Jarron's doing.

They all introduced themselves, presented their cards, and stood in a semicircle facing me. The DA investigator took the lead. Pre-arranged, I assumed, because the gray-hairs from Robbery-Homicide didn't look too happy about it. LAPD detectives saw DA investigators as glorified process servers.

"Leticia Moss," she said. "Major Crimes."

"You're in the right place," I said.

She didn't ask what had happened on the lawn. She said, "Did you go inside the house?"

"No."

She nodded to the young detective from Hollywood Division, and he hustled up to the house.

"Why were you out here today?"

I hoped Jarron would show up soon. "CenterPoint Solutions. One-day thing. Helping out Frankie. I don't really know much beyond that. He's a friend, had a gig."

"And you weren't told what the 'gig' was?"

"No, ma'am, they're pretty tight-lipped."

The three of them looked at each other and raised their eyebrows in unison. Then they looked back at me. I waited. Moss pursed her lips, tried again.

"You're a CenterPoint employee, then?"

"NYPD, detective. Retired." Which would draw "move to strike as nonresponsive" from opposing counsel if we were in court. But we weren't in court, and there was no opposing counsel. And all three of my interrogators were a few years away from being retired themselves. And then maybe pulling CenterPoint gigs that they, too, would want to be tight-lipped about.

I held out my hands. "Tell you what," I said, "why don't you take some swabs from my hands, so you'll have them, and then let me clean up a little." I looked from Moss to the gray-haired LAPD guys. One of them spoke up. He looked a little older than his partner and had more hair, though the gray was going white.

"Okay," he said. "Leticia, you got your crime-scene kit?" Indicating by his tone that he doubted very much she did.

"Go ahead," she replied, her voice neutral.

The detective looked at his partner, who was closer to bald, though with a bit of brown left in the gray. The partner produced some cotton swabs and clear plastic collection tubes from his briefcase. He put on latex gloves and took two swabs from each of my hands.

"Maybe get my face a little, too," I said. "That'll be Frankie's lung and some bits from his sternum, probably."

He did, then nodded at me. "Got it."

"You want to use the hose, or what?" said the first detective.

"Sure," I said and began walking toward the side of the house.

The two detectives walked with me. Moss turned her back and got on her phone.

I washed my hands and face as best I could, then stood in the sun to dry off.

Out of earshot of Moss, the two detectives got downright chatty. "Joey Melendres," said the older one. "My partner, Kurt Allen."

"Marcus Heaton," I said. "Nice day."

"Yeah," he said. "You know why she's pissed, don't you?"

"No idea," I said.

"Because her fucking career case is closed now," he said. "That was her perp."

The Hall of Justice and the old Federal Building
facing each other across Spring Street

Forty

I got the full story from the head DA of the Major Crimes Division, in his office at the Hall of Justice. The building had just been reopened after a decade-long renovation, and it gleamed like a Greek temple. The county had closed it after the Northridge earthquake in 1994, and it had sat there empty ever since. It was right across from the federal courthouse, and so for ten years you could stand on the corner of Spring and Temple and look to your right at the Feds' Art Deco palace with its flower gardens and manicured lawns, and then to your left at the Hall of Justice with its scaffolding and boarded-up windows and soot-stained walls, just in case you needed a reminder of who the alpha dog was in the criminal-justice pack.

But now the tables were turned, architecturally, anyway. The Hall was back in business, in full neoclassical force, and the federal building across the street was showing its age. They were building a big glass tower a couple blocks over to replace it. Rumor had it that the old Spring Street building was going to become condos or something. And so the county had the Hall of Justice floodlit at night, like the goddamn Acropolis.

Alex Johnson was head of Major Crimes. I'd heard of him, even in New York. He'd just lost the race to be the next DA, and the campaign had turned ugly toward the end. In Manhattan, we'd had the same

DA for forty years, so we all followed the LA race, just to see what a prosecutor-versus-prosecutor campaign looked like.

Johnson was the go-to high-stakes trial guy in the DA's office. He was the courtroom king in a department with a thousand courtroom lawyers. In LA, high-profile criminal trials were televised, and Johnson had taken some big scalps, with highlights on the six o'clock news every time. I remembered him from when he put Phil Spector away.

There were four or five contenders in the DA race, but Johnson was at the top of the list for most of the campaign. The line prosecutors worshipped him, the police union liked him, and the media played him as the anointed successor. But with a month to go, the old retiring DA endorsed his top administrator instead. She was another office lifer, but she ran spreadsheets, not investigations.

And then suddenly she was the chosen one, and the business donors fell into line. And whoever she hired for campaign advice persuaded her to go negative. The campaign got ugly, and Johnson didn't have the money to match her ad for ad. Jarron told me that Johnson refused to go dirty, anyway. "He thought it was beneath his dignity," Jarron said. "That's why he's not the DA now."

Johnson's days in the office were numbered now, so the Angelides case was probably the end of the road for him. "Up or out, that's the way of it," Jarron said on the ride over. "She's up, he's out." I didn't ask whether "out" meant coming over to CenterPoint. And Jarron didn't say anything more. But they were evidently on good terms: we got the no-wait escort straight up to his office.

His office was on the tenth floor, with twenty feet of window looking out across Spring Street at the federal building. The tenth floor was double-height, with a line of marble columns all around the outside. Johnson's office windows looked south, over at the Federal Building. You could line up a dozen cops to flip the bird across Spring Street when the wrecking balls finally came.

We sat in dark-red leather furniture around a polished coffee table. Moss, Jarron, Johnson, and I took the couches. Melendres and Allen got straight-backed wooden chairs a couple feet outside the power circle. But they looked happy to be in the room.

"You probably don't know this, but Angelides was one of my first cases," Johnson said. This was addressed to me. Moss and Jarron knew it already.

I remembered the scandal. Anyone who went to the movies in the '80s had heard of it. Big movie-release party up in the hills, at one of those cantilevered palaces with a huge pool deck looking over the city. It was 1989, and everyone was having a good time doing coke off of each other's Academy Award trophies. Statuettes, I should say, since I'm in LA.

Sometime around dawn, when the party was emptying out, Angelides had raped a sixteen-year-old aspiring model in a downstairs bedroom. Allegedly raped, I guess. Everything about the party was pretty firmly allegedly and counter-allegedly. How the girl had ended up at the party, who else was there, and a lot of other details, had been, as the tabloids put it, "murky."

Angelides had been very publicly arrested, but six months later he was on a plane to Italy, where he stayed for the next twenty years. And in France and Switzerland and anywhere else that had ski chalets and film awards ceremonies.

The Feds tried to get him back a few times, but that only muddied the waters even more. The extradition request claimed that Angelides was a fugitive and that he should be sent back to the U.S. and sentenced to prison. But Angelides's lawyers mounted a ferocious defense in Switzerland, arguing that in that six-month period after his arrest, Angelides had pleaded guilty and served his sentence. Sentencing him again would be double jeopardy.

What happened, the lawyers said, was that Angelides's defense counsel had worked out a plea deal with the DA's office. Angelides would plead to a misdemeanor, do thirty days of psychiatric evaluation, and then three years of summary probation. And everyone agreed that Angelides had done the thirty days of psych eval. He'd gone to a state facility in Chino. That was a matter of public record.

Thing was, that was the only part of the case that actually *was* a matter of record. The rest of the record, the documents you'd ordinarily look at to figure out what happened in a criminal case, just weren't

247

there. There was no formal Judgment and Commitment paperwork. There was no probation report. There wasn't even a transcript of a plea hearing. Turns out the judge, Lucas Wittenband, had held the important proceedings in his chambers with only the lawyers present and no court reporter.

By the time the extradition fight hit the Swiss courts, Judge Wittenband was dead, and the lawyers had, to put it in a lawyerly way, inconsistent recollections of the terms of the plea. The lead DA swore up and down that the plea was "open," with no hard commitment on sentencing, and the thirty-day psych eval was for the purpose of getting a psychiatric report that the parties could use in determining how to proceed. The lead defense attorney swore up and down that the thirty days, with probation to follow, *was* the sentence.

And there wasn't anyone else to ask. Angelides had three other lawyers on his team, and so did the DA, but none of them were invited into chambers. The junior guys all had to sit in the courtroom while the senior guys went back and hashed it out. Johnson had been one of the junior guys.

"We sat there for a fucking hour," he said. "Nothing to do but pick our fucking asses and wait. Angelides's guys were probably billing at $500 each, so they didn't care. But I was fucking pissed. We fucking told Duplessis"—he was the lead prosecutor, I recalled—"to bring a court reporter. Told him those cocksuckers would ratfuck him the first chance they got, but he and Wittenband were poker buddies or something. He just patted my shoulder like I was a fucking puppy dog and said, 'A.J., you worry too much.' Goddamn right I worry too much. Twenty years later and I'm still worrying about this prick."

Melendres decided to try some humor. "Well, our worries are over now," he said.

Johnson didn't answer. He turned his head halfway around toward the two cops and held it there for about ten seconds. When he was sure Melendres had had a chance to read the "shut-the-fuck-up" thought bubble over his head, he turned to Jarron.

"So, Tom," he continued, "why'd he shoot your guy?"

Jarron and I had worked out the story on the way over. My job was

248

to nod and provide color commentary if asked. "Accidental, we think," he said. "My guys got there, he was on the lawn. Not very coherent. Freaked out, waving the gun around. They tried to calm him down, get the weapon from him."

Johnson looked at me. I met his gaze. I was waiting for him to ask how it was that two twenty-year NYPD veterans couldn't take a pistol from a seventy-year-old man, or at least stay out of the line of fire. But he didn't. All he said was, "I'm sorry about your partner."

I nodded.

"You never went in the house?"

"Correct," I said.

"And he didn't give any specific reason for becoming suicidal?"

"Correct."

"Didn't mention any threats?"

"Correct."

"Didn't mention any names?"

"Correct."

Johnson nodded at Moss, and she opened her briefcase and produced a large ziplock bag holding a manila envelope. "We found this inside," she said. "Opened."

Johnson nodded again. "Fill them in."

"The envelope contains photographs of seventeen young women," she said. "On the back of each is a DOB and a date, and a...a brief narrative."

She paused, then continued: "The final sheet had a single line: 'CC Alex Johnson, Los Angeles County District Attorney's Office.'"

I didn't ask the follow-up question, but she answered it anyway. "We did in fact receive the package. Got it a week ago in the mail. Same package, same narratives."

"You may not be aware," she continued, "that we reopened the Angelides file when he came back to the United States."

I remembered hearing about him coming back. It had made the news when the Academy of Motion Picture Arts and Sciences announced that he would be attending the next Oscars to accept the Best Director award he won in absentia five years earlier for that Edgar Allen Poe biopic. You remember the movie: *Quoth the Raven.* The sort of gritty, hyperrealist period drama that always wins Oscars. They filmed it in Prague or somewhere. That British guy who's always playing some anguished world-historical figure played Poe. He won Best Actor too, I think. But Angelides hadn't been there to get the trophy, so now the Academy was going to do a special presentation for him. Probably someone would throw him a big "So-You-Got-Away-with-Rape" afterparty, too.

I remembered going to see *Quoth the Raven*. It was pretty damn good. Angelides took Poe's short stories and filmed them as little movies-within-the-movie that sort of ran in Poe's head as he was writing them. The critics loved that shit. David Denby wrote in *The New Yorker* that the "Telltale Heart" sequence was like Angelides's confession. You remember how in the story, two cops come to investigate the disappearance of the old man, and the narrator has them come sit in the room, right over where he stashed the guy's body? And the dead man's heart starts beating louder and louder, only the cops can't hear it? Denby said the heart was the rape case, and the two cops were like the film elite, who were sitting right on top of it but refused to hear it.

One of the late-night TV guys said that Poe was the perfect subject for Angelides, because they were both into thirteen-year-old girls. I forget which guy. Not one of the network guys. And definitely none of the Academy big shots. *They* treated him like Jesus Christ—part martyr and part returning king. I remembered that a bunch of Hollywood A-listers had signed an amicus brief for Angelides during the extradition litigation.

"The original case was toast," said Moss. "Double jeopardy, end of story. Straight from the federal courts." She glanced at Johnson, waiting for him to scowl and say, "Spineless motherfuckers," or something like that. But he didn't. He just glanced sideways out the window for a second, at the federal building.

"But we reopened the file because—"

"Because it wasn't fucking over," Johnson said, bringing his gaze back to me. "It wasn't a single incident. You read that file, and the one fact that just jumps off the page at you is that it wasn't a single incident. It wasn't a single incident, it wasn't a single perpetrator, and it sure as hell wasn't a single victim. Silvio Angelides was an unrepentant rapist. And *Water and Power* wasn't even that good, no offense to the fucking Academy."

He looked over his shoulder at Melendres and Allen. "You guys aren't dumb enough to think you heard that, are you?" Allen gave a two-inch head shake, for both of them, I presumed.

Johnson nodded, then continued: "Because I'm going to give a press briefing in half an hour and express the People's sincere condolences for the tragic death of a great artist. And I might need a couple of respectable-looking detectives up there with me."

Figueroa and 6th, Los Angeles

Forty-One

Jarron and I took the back elevator down to the parking garage and walked to Jarron's Town Car. We were just getting in when a beige Crown Vic pulled up behind us. Leticia Moss was at the wheel.

"Mr. Heaton," she said, "can I offer you a ride?"

I looked at Jarron. He shrugged.

"Okay," I said, "How 'bout Disneyland?"

She favored me with a smile. "That's very sweet of you. But I'm working today."

I reached for the passenger door, but she nodded toward the back seat. The back windows were tinted full black, and there was a black glass divider between the front and back seats. I raised my eyebrows. "If I'm under arrest, let's drive by at least. I've never even seen it."

"Just get in the car," she said.

I opened the back door and got in. Alex Johnson was sitting in the back, behind Moss. There was a Redweld file folder on the seat beside him. I closed the door and Moss drove out onto Spring Street. Johnson gave me a nod.

"Where are we going?" I asked.

"We're going to drive in circles for a few minutes, and then I'm going to get out and do the damn press conference," he said. "They're writing up a statement in there now. The *boss*"—meaning the District Attorney, I assumed—"is in Sacramento, as it happens. Probably calling my assistant right now demanding that we hold all the media attention until she gets back." He laughed. "Too bad she couldn't reach me."

He knocked on the glass divider and I heard the muffled thump of bass as Moss turned on the radio.

"Privacy, Heaton," he said. "Don't worry, it's not bugged. And Leticia, who I would trust with my fucking *life*, is not listening in."

I didn't say anything. That kind of reassurance rang hollow, in the back of a police car.

"Just curious," he said, turning to eyeball me. "Did you guys whack that prick?"

I returned his gaze but didn't answer. In my mind's eye I saw Angelides's face six inches from mine, his eyes wild and his forearms straining to bring the gun barrel down.

He held the stare for a moment, then nodded. "Whatever. Professionally done, then, except for your partner taking one in the chest."

That got a response. "Did you get any word from the hospital?" I asked.

He waited a moment, nodded. "Still critical. He's not dead, though. Thanks to you, they're saying. He's in surgery now."

I exhaled. I hadn't realized I'd been holding my breath. It was three hours since the shooting. If Frankie wasn't dead yet, chances were he'd survive.

"Here's the thing," Johnson said. "If Muller is a material witness to a crime—like premeditated murder—then I'd want to keep him under guard at the hospital. Make sure no one talked to him. Get a clean statement as soon as he comes out of the OR."

He paused again and looked out the window. Moss made a left on Second Street and went down the hill past Main. Johnson's technique was good, I reflected. I recalled that he had been one of those DAs who interrogated his suspects himself.

Moss made another left and we drove under the pedestrian bridge connecting the main City Hall with City Hall East, the blocky office annex on Los Angeles Street.

"But on the other hand," he continued, still looking out the window, "if there's no crime here, then your partner has no need of a guard. We can get his statement in due course, when he's feeling up to it. And he just needs to rest and recover."

He waited another block, as Moss followed Los Angeles Street around the curve toward Union Station. "And a cop, recovering from a shooting...well, the best thing for him, when he wakes up, would be a friendly face there at his bedside." He turned toward me. "Like his partner."

We made a left on Cesar Chavez and headed up the hill toward Grand. Johnson tapped the Redweld. "This is for you. I want you to take a look. A nice, *quiet* look."

I reached for the Redweld. It was secured with a plain brown rubber band. Johnson shook his head. "Not now," he said. "At your leisure. With your customary discretion."

I put my hands in my lap.

"Tom Jarron's a good guy," he said. "A smart guy."

"Yes he is," I agreed.

"But so am I," said Johnson. "And so is Leticia." He nodded toward the front seat. Moss made a left on Grand, and we headed south, toward Disney Hall.

"And here's the thing. You don't work for CenterPoint."

"Contract gig," I said.

Johnson waved his hand. "Come on," he said. "Show me the contract."

"Verbal."

He snorted. "Yeah, I know it was. Look, you want proof we're talking privately? I'd be fucking *delighted* if one of those college girls from '89 decided to get some rough justice." He gestured around the backseat. "Whatever. Fuck it. You sit there, I'll talk."

That was fine with me. I sat there.

He nodded. "You know how I know you don't work for CenterPoint? Because I know who you do work for, and I know about your little vacation to East Texas, and I know how *that* one ended up."

I sat. He nodded again. "Ms. Moss is very thorough. Quick, too. And she's still got some friends at the Justice Department." He gave a snort.

"More than me, at the moment, probably. I was pretty worked up about the extradition shit. A little intemperate, maybe."

He shrugged. "But hey, that's our business, right? We ruffle a few feathers. Then maybe we smooth them."

I was pretty sure it wasn't my feathers he wanted to smooth.

"Thing is," he said, "circumstantial evidence is a bitch. It's a bitch in the courtroom. But it's an even worse bitch outside the courtroom."

Another pause. The Crown Vic slid past MOCA and headed south toward Staples Center.

"I'll tell you," he said, finally, "I spent twenty years thinking about bringing that son of a bitch to justice. It just nagged at me. Fucking nagged at me. I put away a dozen murderers in that time, and this one little case just nagged at me. Why?"

I cleared my throat to answer. He waved his hand again.

"That's rhetorical, Marcus. It doesn't matter. Point is it did. Thing is, *I* wasn't one of the victims. I was just the young guy without the balls to stand up to my supervisor about a stupid fucking chambers plea that ninety-nine times out a hundred wouldn't have gone sideways the way it did. And then, when I *had* the balls, and I *had* the power, I couldn't fix it. I got sandbagged. You read about the campaign, in New York?"

I nodded.

"Yeah, well, what you didn't read about was why it all turned *her* way at the end there. Why all the heavyweights suddenly came out for her."

"Why?" I said.

"You really have no fucking clue, do you? Don't answer, I don't care. Maybe you do, and you still think we're on tape and you want to hear me say it. Fuck it, I already told you, I *want* you to know."

"Know what?"

"That it was a *deal*, Heaton! Angelides coming back. Why the fuck do you think he came back?"

"To get his Oscar?"

"Yeah, but how did he get in?"

I thought about that for a moment. "The court decision. Double jeopardy..." I trailed off. The dumb cop talking law talk with the lawyers.

"The court decision means we can't charge him again. Means the extradition request was dead. Doesn't mean he gets permission to fucking move back, does it?"

I was reminded again of J.C. She told me her Socratic-method interrogations were intended as educational, but I always thought it was more that she enjoyed toying with me. Johnson looked like he truly wanted me to understand whatever he was about to tell me. Needed me to understand it. I had interviewed a hundred suspects who wanted the same thing, but this was different. I was the suspect here.

Johnson seemed to read my thoughts. Not that surprising, really. He'd probably interviewed a thousand perps.

"Marcus," he said, "this is not an interrogation, okay? Do you think I take my homicide suspects on scenic tours of LA?"

"All right," I said, "I get it. You're going to tell me something important about Angelides, and you're trying to take me through it step-by-step so I understand the details. I appreciate the respect. But I'm not a lawyer. I don't know the answer. What I was going to say is I didn't think French people needed any special permission. I was never in France, except for a stopover on the way back from Landstuhl one time, but in New York I got the impression that they just hopped on a plane. Your average rich French guy, that is. That's how they talked about it, anyway. Not that I was exactly part of those conversations."

Johnson looked at me for a long moment, then nodded. "So you can talk, after all," he said. "That's more than I've heard you say in the past three hours. Okay. Thank you for taking seriously my desire that you fully understand what I'm about to tell you."

"You're welcome," I said.

"All right. Then first thing: Angelides isn't French. He's Polish. I can see why you'd think he was French. He made enough movies there, anyway. Me, I thought he was Italian, back in the day. Doesn't make too much of a difference, in Europe. But it's a big fucking difference when it comes to visiting the U.S. Your French friends in New York don't need visas. But Polish citizens do."

"So he got a visa," I said. "So what?"

He nodded again, looked around the car. Moss was heading west on Olympic now. He exhaled sharply and looked down at his hands.

"Middle of August. I'm up ten points. Mayor, DA, police union, they're all neutral. *Good* neutral. Like 'all-the-major-candidates-are-highly-qualified' neutral. *Times,* same thing. Neutral on an endorsement, but giving me the right coverage, right? And I was getting the invitations, you know, to send the message? Fundraiser at the California Club—except they don't allow fundraisers there so it was a fucking "public policy lecture," but everyone in the room gave me their cell number, you know?"

I nodded. I had never heard of the California Club, but I'd been to enough functions like that in New York to get the idea. "Been to" was maybe a stretch. Driven there. Stood in the back of the room. Waited in the hall. But still.

"Then I get this call. Could I step across the street and go up to the U.S. Attorney's Office? Fourteenth floor? Some people wanted to see me.

"So of course, sure, I'll go over there. I go up to fourteen, and there in the room is the big boss and *her* fucking boss from DC—not the Attorney General, but some Assistant AG. And *he's* got the head of the Criminal Division with him. And some fucking flabby pinhead named Kyle Simpson. Said he was from the White House Counsel's Office. Arrogant little prick. Nasally voice. I can tell you he never a tried a case in his fucking life.

"So we shake hands, I sit down, and the guy from the Criminal Division says, 'Tell us about your office's interest in Silvio Angelides.' I say, you guys fucked yourselves royally on that one—words to that effect—but don't worry, we're not letting him slide. We've got him on other sexual assaults. I'm thinking, okay, they're as pissed as I am and they're there to assure me that if and when I bring new charges on new rapes, they'll put their smartest and best-dressed Feds on it and they won't embarrass themselves a second time.

"And they just stare at me. And then that little shit from the White House says, 'Mr. Johnson, we think it would be in the interest of the United States if the District Attorney's office closed out the file on Angelides.'" Johnson did Simpson in a Pee-wee Herman whine, the contempt dripping from his voice.

"I didn't even like to look at the guy. I didn't answer him. I turned to the actual prosecutors and said, you know, what the fuck. Words to that effect. And the head of the Criminal Division—he's at Baker Botts now, I think...left right after the election—he says," and Johnson switched to a pretentious white-shoe-Washington-lawyer drone, "'It appears that Angelides may be an important witness in a...more serious matter.'

"'More serious?' I said. 'As in what? Islamic terrorist serious, or what? Because from where I sit, drugging and raping young girls? That's pretty damn serious.'

"He says they're investigating some 'large-scale financial frauds.' I say, what kind of financial frauds? He says, real-estate development fraud. I say, oh, you mean like mortgage-backed securities, that kind of shit? I mean, you guys have fucking open-and-shut cases all over the damn country, and those are paper cases. What do you need Angelides for? He's been in fucking France for the last twenty years, and he left the country at least two bubbles ago.

"And then that little dipshit pipes up again, and he says, 'It's in the nature of the target, Mr. Johnson. Angelides can implicate a very big fish.' So I finally turn and look at the guy, and I say, who? And he says, 'The White House is very interested in this particular subject.' And then they all look at each other, like the fucking DOJ leadership is deferring to this pissant from the White House Counsel's office, and he says: 'Jennifer Curtis.'"

Johnson paused to let that sink in. I looked down at the Redweld.

He continued. "I guess I'm a politician now, right, Marcus? I mean, I was running for elected office. I don't mind a little shit on my shoes. You just hold your nose and get used to the smell, right? So I just sat there. I *didn't* say, 'Oh, you mean the Jennifer Curtis who's going to be the next AG if your party loses in November? Yeah, you better indict her on something right away—how can I help?' No, I just sat there. Kept my face blank.

"You know District Attorney is a non-partisan race here in LA, right? As in, there's no party affiliation on the ballot? As in, it is *supposed* to be about making a commitment to the people of Los Angeles County that you're going to bust people who victimize the citizens of Los Angeles County, right?"

I nodded.

"So I sit there. And no one says anything. And I say, 'The DA's office has always been open to cooperation with the DOJ, blah blah blah.'" I mean, I'm the head of Major Crimes, right? We cooperate with the Feds all the time, even though they don't tell us shit half the time and rat-fuck us the other half. I mean, this is the leadership of the fucking federal law-enforcement bureaucracy sitting there... Anyway. So the Deputy AG clears his throat, says thank you for your time, looks at his watch, and turns to the U.S. Attorney. Says 'We're late for that meeting downstairs,' some shit like that, and she gets up and walks out with him and the guy from the Criminal Division. Leaves me in the fucking room with that little shit Simpson.

"I start to get up too, but Simpson holds up his hand. 'One moment, please, Mr. Johnson.' Then he pulls out this little sheet of paper and slides it across the table to me. And he says, 'Mr. Angelides is going to be returning to the United States. And the White House is very interested in getting a commitment from the next District Attorney that Mr. Angelides will not be contacted, investigated, or prosecuted upon his return to the country.'

"I look down at the paper, and it's a handwritten list of names. Some people I knew. Some I'd heard of. Some that looked vaguely familiar. There were two columns. Simpson says: 'The column on the right is endorsements. The column on the left is donations. *Size*able donations.'"

Johnson paused. I looked out the window. We were at Highland Avenue. Moss made a right.

Johnson turned back to look at me. "I gather you've had your share of disagreements with supervisors, Marcus."

I didn't answer. I wondered what he knew or had heard. Whatever it was, it would be double filtered, if it came through Jarron by way of Frankie.

"Then you will appreciate it," he said, "if I told you that I took him by the throat and shoved his fucking paper into his puffy little mouth and made him eat it."

"Did you?" I said.

"I did not," he said. "I took the paper with me. Thanked him for coming out to meet with me. Asked him if I could call him."

I raised my eyebrows.

"No," he said, "he did not give me his number. Said he'd call me the next day. Said: 'This may be a very tight race.' Got up and walked out on me. Little prick. You want the rest of the story?"

I shrugged. "Rest of the story was in the papers."

"Goddamn straight it was. He called, right on schedule—anonymous U.S. Attorney number, came through our main office; yes, I fucking checked. I said that the District Attorney's office views serial sexual assault as a very serious crime and that our policy is and will continue to be to prosecute offenders to the fullest extent of the law. Hung up and went home. Opened the paper the next morning and saw that every fucking name on that list was coming out to endorse *her*. Turned on the TV that night and saw a new attack ad. Saw it three times. And a new one each week until the election. Guess I wasn't the only candidate up on the fourteenth floor that day."

We rode up Highland in silence. Moss made a left on Beverly.

Johnson spoke again, finally. "And you, for better or worse, are the only person who has heard that story. Because *you*, for better or worse, are the guy who needs to hear it right now. I'm asking you to remember what I told you. I'm asking you to make sure that it is *known*. By the *one* person who needs to know."

I looked down at the Redweld. "What's in there?" I asked.

"The past," he said. "And the past is the past. What I am interested in, Marcus, is the future."

We stopped at the light at Fairfax. He looked out the window. "The future. Some people have a very bright future at the moment. *Very* bright. And some people with a very bright future know that to get to that future, you have to let go of the past. Which I understand sometimes means making sure the past lets go of you." He tapped the Redweld again. "The past is in here, Marcus. A very specific past that, at the moment, exists only on paper. We didn't keep this on the system." He nodded again at the front seat. Moss was moving again, turning left on Olympic.

"We had plenty of cases. This was sort of an extracurricular for us. But you know how those extracurriculars go." He raised his eyebrows at me. "You get sort of attached. You can be thorough." He sighed. "But then? Well, a day comes when you realize that maybe it's best to just let it go."

He handed me the Redweld. "This is everything," he said, "and the last page in here? That was in the house. We didn't make copies." He knocked on the glass partition. Moss pulled over at La Cienega, across from Cedars-Sinai.

"Mr. Johnson," I said, "what exactly are you asking me to do?"

He leaned over me and pushed my door open. "Go in there and help your partner recover."

"What are you going to do?" I said.

He gave me a half smile. "Justice," he said.

Forty-Two

Bradley Farmington was in a coma for two weeks. During that time I pieced together his life story. It wasn't hard: most of it was in his official bank bio. Ivy League BA and MBA, hard-driving trader for ten years, groomed for management. Apartment in Gramercy Park. Not married, and not secretly gay as far as I could tell. If he was, he was careful. No history of late-night ATM withdrawals in Chelsea or weekend ferry tickets to Fire Island. He spent a lot on clothes, but the establishments were banker-straight. He had a golf membership at the Hampshire Country Club in Mamaroneck, and the last two years he'd rented a summer place in the Hamptons.

Settentio wanted a coke profile for Bradley. It would have been believable in theory. Coke was the Wall Street alpha-male drug of choice, then as now. Drug fads come and go, but coke and Wall Street are like hot dogs and mustard. Classic, traditional, perfect together. If no one asked too many questions, coke could put Bradley in Washington Heights, coke could gird his loins to take on two cops with his fists, and coke could give him superhuman strength and insensitivity to pain. It would be mostly bullshit, of course: bankers didn't buy their coke in Harlem; their dealers brought it to them downtown. And while insensitivity to pain was accurate enough, it only got you so far, and we'd all handled enough coked-up perps to know that the superhuman-strength claims were bogus.

Besides which, you could only put the physiological and psychological markers in your report if the guy actually had coke in his system. Which Bradley, unfortunately, did not. His blood was unhelpfully negative. Negative for coke and everything else on the tox screen. Cannabinoids, opiates, barbiturates, amphetamines, methamphetamine, PCP, LSD. Even alcohol.

Which didn't mean the guy didn't use. Of course the guy used. You didn't strut down Wall Street for ten years in thousand-dollar suits without taking the odd snort. Coke and speed were rites of passage at those firms, along with hookers and helicopter commutes to the Hamptons. But he didn't have anything in his system, and I couldn't get anyone to spill.

Two days in, Settentio was running out of ways to string the family along. He had been hoping it could play as an unsolved mugging, with Becker and McAvoy finding Bradley unconscious on the street. But there was no chance of that. We could lose the surveillance footage from the bodega and let the bodega manager figure out the virtue of silence, but that wouldn't be enough. Becker and MacAvoy had put Bradley in cuffs and sat him in the back of their cruiser for fifteen minutes while Becker ransacked Bradley's BMW. On Broadway, at a busy corner, at ten o'clock at night. Fifty people saw the whole thing, at least. They'd all remember it, and chances were at least one of them took some pictures. It's hard to remember sometimes, that back then, which wasn't all that long ago, you didn't have guaranteed cell-phone video of every use of force. Back then most phones couldn't take video. But a white guy in a hundred-thousand-dollar Beamer in custody on 137th Street? Chances were decent someone made a record.

And McAvoy's story about the motel? That turned out to be true, too, loony as it sounded. They really had driven the guy to the Hamilton Heights Motel and checked him in. Cleaning that up was item number one on Settentio's to-do list. Settentio had been taxing the motel owner for years, taking a percentage of the nightly commerce and keeping the place free from unannounced raids. On any given night half the clientele was probably engaged in drug transactions or prostitution.

I went discreetly and inquired. There was Bradley's signature on the register. And there he was on the goddamned lobby security camera video, with Becker hovering behind him with that creepy smirk on his face. Bradley looked scared out of his mind. He fumbled his wallet, dropped it on the floor, looked around constantly. Probably for help, I figured. But there was no help. Whatever Becker told him, he must have believed it.

I watched the video ten times through, frame by frame, in the little windowless manager's office, which smelled of piss and fried food. No cops had come, the night manager assured me, and no one had seen the video. I could do what I needed to do, and no one would remember a damn thing.

The system recorded on videocassette, like a lot of them still did then. A cheap VCR in a cabinet in the manager's office, one tape in the VCR and a few extras on a shelf. Nothing labeled. They just rotated them through, recorded over the old ones. I took them all, put them in a duffel. Took the VCR, too. New story for management: the cameras were just for show, wires running down into an empty cabinet. Not that anyone was likely to ask, but in case someone from Force Investigation showed up, they'd buy it. In most of your low-rent motels, the security cameras ran to bare wires dead-ending in a dusty cabinet.

I poured coffee on the register page Bradley signed and smudged the whole page into illegibility. Did Bradley Farmington check in here? No one but me would ever get more than a shrug: *Who knows, boss? I just work here.* Half the names on the register were probably fake anyway.

I looked at the room Bradley had gone to—filthy, smelly, no phone. There was so much layered DNA in the place that you'd get a hundred hits in any sample you took. Not that anyone was ever going to come and look.

Which left me the parts of the story we were stuck with: Becker and MacAvoy had rousted Bradley at the bodega, tossed his car, and driven him away. And then an hour later a little old grandmother looking out her third-floor window at 141st and Frederick Douglass had called 911 to report a white man in pink pants running down the middle of the street yelling, "Help me!"

A unit from the 32nd Precinct responded and was on scene in four minutes. Regular patrol uniforms. I saw their report: when they pulled up, Becker and McAvoy had the suspect in custody. He was lying on his side, by the curb, hands cuffed behind his back. He was lying in a pool of blood, stemming from "apparent significant head trauma." He was moaning incoherently and was "unresponsive to verbal commands." The dispatcher called for an ambulance. The paramedics wrote a report, too. "Initial evaluation suggested trauma to the nose and orbital bones and possible skull fracture."

The last written report was from the emergency room doc at St. Vincent's. Nasal fracture; orbital bone fracture; dislocated tempero-mandibular joint, right side; basilar skull fracture, right side, causing otorrhea and periorbital ecchymosis. I looked those up: spinal fluid discharge from the ear and subcutaneous pooling of blood under the eyes.

Worse: linear facial lacerations to the patient's forehead and left cheek, with significant deposition of dirt and asphalt particles in the wounds. What you might get from having your face slammed into the pavement. Or falling off a motorcycle. But I wasn't going to be able to fit a motorcycle into Bradley's story.

Still worse: X-rays revealed a fractured scapula, with a radial fracture pattern emanating from a central impact point approximately five millimeters in diameter. The doctor didn't hazard a guess about how that one had happened. But I had a pretty good idea.

The scapula is the shoulder blade. It's a big, thick bone. Doesn't break easily. But you can fracture it at a point like that by cuffing a guy's hands behind his back, sitting him down, and torquing up on his arms while jabbing something sharp into his shoulder blade. Not a gentle jab, either. You have to really lean into it and put some muscle behind it. I'd never done it. But I'd seen it done, in Iraq. Say you've got some detainees, you cuff them and put them on the ground and tell them to stay put. And you really mean it, because you're in a dicey neighborhood with a small patrol and no backup. So if one guy doesn't want to lie still, you have to make the point. One time, and forcefully.

But Bradley wasn't in Iraq, anymore than he'd been on a motorcycle.

Two days in, and I took it to Settentio. We huddled in a corner of the break room. I laid out the facts that could disappear and the facts that couldn't. The little old lady had been quite descriptive in her 911 call, which was preserved for posterity in the databanks down at One Police Plaza where we couldn't touch it:

DISPATCH: Ma'am, can you see this person?
CALLER: Yes, I can. He's right outside my window. Just looked up at me.
DISPATCH: And is he injured?
CALLER: No, he's kind of jogging along and looking all around, and he keeps yelling, "Help me!" Like someone's chasing him.
DISPATCH: He's not bleeding or anything?
CALLER: No, nothing. Just yelling like he's seen a ghost.

And one more fact we couldn't get around. Becker and MacAvoy had told the responding patrol from the 32nd that Bradley had attacked them. Said they'd seen him on the street, recognized him from earlier as "that guy we tried to help," and gotten out to talk to him. At which point Bradley, in his Nantucket Red slacks and his banker loafers, had raised his manicured hands, contorted his fingers into "lobster claws," and started taking swipes at them. He'd then lunged at Becker, forcing MacAvoy to take quick and forceful action "out of fear for my partner's life."

The story smelled so strongly of bullshit that it made the laugh-track rounds in a dozen precincts at roll call the next morning. "How many goons from the 30th does it take to beat up a banker in pink pants?" I'd seen a mock training video some guys in the 32nd made, demonstrating proper defensive techniques against a lobster-claw attack.

So that was that. Bradley Farmington robbed and beaten by unknown street thugs wasn't going to fly. We were going to have to sell the lobster claw attack. Which might have sold if he'd been a transient out of his mind on PCP or airplane glue. But Bradley Farmington had been clean. Not a damn thing in his system. And he was a thirty-four-year-old office worker in pink pants and penny loafers. If the lobster claw attack was the official version, every half-wit reporter in the city

267

would see right through it to "Dirty Cops Shake Down Banker, Beat Him Senseless When He Runs."

And that, Captain Settentio could not have. His little kingdom could not stand long against the kind of scrutiny such a headline would beget. He needed to turn the tables. He needed "Banker Runs Wild on Dangerous New Club Drug."

And he had the perfect drug in mind. "Okay," he said, "this guy must have been on bath salts."

"Bath salts" was a name for what the chemists called synthetic cathinones. I'd seen pictures in the street drug update the Department put together each year—your typical granular white powder, next to the diagram of hexagons and lines with lots of Cs and Os and the odd H and N that the chemists always threw in just to remind the street cops of how much they needed the lab guys.

Synthetic cathinones were the street cop's fuck-you to the lab guys, however, because they didn't show up on tox screens. Settentio told me to go plant some in Bradley's car and apartment. The car hadn't been inventoried yet, so it would be easy to stroll on down to the impound lot and pop in a couple packets. They were sold in little plastic pouches, like fast-food ketchup.

It was the sort of thing you did if your crime scene needed helping along, or the dealer you busted didn't happen to be carrying. But this time, I said no.

"No," I said, "I don't think so."

He didn't get it at first, that I was saying no to him. "What, then? You got a better idea?"

I nodded. "Yeah. Let the gorillas take the rap."

Now he got it. He leaned in: "What the fuck did you just say?"

"I said I'm not doing it. That fucking guy was clean. He was just a fucking civilian. Becker scared the shit out of him, took him to a junkie nest motel, and ordered him to get a room. What the fuck do you think he was doing, Captain? *Best* case, he was shaking him down for a few grand. Worst case? He was going in there to fucking rape him with a broom handle."

Settentio let me talk. I could see the anger rising in his face. "And?" he said.

"And I'm not covering for that shit. I chilled out the motel for you, but he's gotta eat the beatdown."

Then he hissed at me, the hiss turning to a shout, every cop in the place keeping his face averted: "That is not your goddamn decision! You do as you are fucking *or*dered!"

And he did something he'd never done. He put his hands on me. Grabbed me by the lapels and shoved me back against the wall. I hit the wall hard, and my shoulder shattered a framed photo of the previous year's Academy class. I straightened up and saw him coming at me, rage in his eyes and a snarl on his face.

The fight didn't last long. But it was long enough. When they pulled me off of him, my forehead was smeared with bright blood from his nose and mouth, where I'd head-butted him in the face. My fists were throbbing from connecting a dozen times with his head and body. Settentio lay in a heap, not moving.

I knew I was done. I turned and walked out onto the street, away from the violence, away from the job. I never set foot in the precinct again.

Neither did Settentio. He left in an ambulance and spent the next week in the hospital. He was indicted the day he was discharged. Turns out the state Attorney General had had an anti-corruption probe targeting the 30th for the past year. They let him turn himself in for booking, then made him do a perp walk in front of the cameras with his arm in a cast and his jaw wired shut.

My union rep got me a medical leave and stretched it to six months. I drank the time away, waiting for my turn to take the perp walk and face the music. But my turn never came. The AG brought a dozen indictments all told, but my name wasn't in any of them. I could never figure out why.

Then one day Jennifer Curtis called and offered me a job.

Forty-Three

I watched Johnson's statement to the press in the hospital cafeteria. There wasn't much to do; Frankie was still in surgery, so I went downstairs to get something to eat. Angelides's death was the lead story on the local news, and they were showing a live shot of the Hall of Justice. The crawl at the bottom of the screen said: "Major Crimes Chief Alex Johnson to Address the Media."

Johnson appeared, looking sombre. He gripped the sides of the lectern and leaned forward. "Good afternoon. I'll be brief. First, let me confirm what many of you have already reported. Silvio Angelides died this morning. It appears that his production company sent a security guard to check in on him at his house. When the security guard arrived, Angelides opened fire on him with a .45 caliber pistol, hitting him in the chest. The guard fired back in self-defense. Angelides died at the scene. The security guard survived the attack and is currently in surgery. His condition is currently listed as critical, and I would ask that your thoughts and prayers be with him."

Johnson stopped, looked down at lectern. "And now," he said, "I have a lot of work to do. This is a sad day for our city." And he turned as if to walk off. The reporters immediately began shouting questions. Johnson took a step away, then turned back, listening. The guy was good. The impetus was going to come from the press; he was just going to answer questions like a dutiful public servant. Yes, he had a bright future.

He looked out at the throng of reporters, concentrating as if to make out a question. Then he hesitated and stepped back to the lectern. He cleared his throat.

"Yes, I heard your question. The question is 'Why?' That's always the hardest question in my line of work. And yours. And not one that we can always fully answer."

Now all of the reporters were yelling variants on the "why" question, if they hadn't been before.

Johnson frowned out at them again. "'Why did he shoot the security guard?' Oh, I'm sorry... 'Why was the guard dispatched to the house?' That, I can answer. Our information is that Angelides had made some disturbing statements in a phone call with another director, a friend of his. Statements that caused his friend to have concerns regarding Angelides's mental state. The friend contacted the security agency employed by his production company and asked if they could send someone over."

Johnson stopped and was buried in a scrum of questions, all shouted at once. He peered out, put a finger to his ear, nodded, and leaned over the microphone. "No, I'm sorry, I don't have any further details for you on the nature of the statements." He paused, listened. "Or the name of the friend. In due course, yes."

In due course, I thought. In due course, when Tom Jarron tells it to Phil Geronian and strong-arms him into memorizing it.

On the screen, Johnson was listening again. He repeated the finger to the ear gesture, then leaned forward. "The question is why didn't this person call the police."

Beautiful, I thought. The guy was *good.* The way he set them up, it probably wasn't even a plant.

Johnson frowned, furrowed his brow, looked genuinely troubled by the question. He opened his mouth to speak, stopped, pursed his lips. "We will be releasing a full report when the investigation is complete," he said, "but at this point..." He trailed off, pursed his lips again. "Our information," he said slowly, "is that Angelides told his friend he had a gun and was going to shoot any damn cops that came near his place. It appears that he shot the security guard because he believed that he was a police officer. I'm sorry? 'Any damn cops that came near his place'? Yes, that is a quote, based on the information I have at this time. So his friend called the private security firm in the hopes that they could talk him down. This firm has been working with actors and directors for many years and has a lot of experience dealing with, ah, unstable personalities. They thought they could talk to him, assess his mental state, calm him down. Tragically, they underestimated the gravity of the situation."

Now the hook was baited. Every single reporter was shouting a variant of the same question: Why would Silvio Angelides, one of the greatest movie directors of the twentieth century, vow to shoot any cop who came near him?

Johnson's answer was perfect. "We have reason to believe Angelides considered his arrest imminent, and he didn't want to go to prison."

The chorus was deafening. Johnson held up a hand. "It appears that Angelides had learned that the District Attorney's office had re-opened the investigation into numerous allegations of sexual assault made against him over a period of many years. The investigation was reopened shortly after his return to the United States. Angelides apparently was in touch with someone with inside knowledge of the investigation."

He stopped again, listened, nodded. "Was he...what? Yes, I can answer that. The question is: Was Angelides in fact going to be arrested for sexual assault? The answer is yes. I approved the warrant application myself. And on behalf of this office, I...as a human being, as a man, I will carry with me for the rest of my days the responsibility, the *shame*, that I didn't do it sooner."

Johnson looked at his watch, pursed his lips, semaphored to the crowd the weight of the urgent matters calling for his attention off-stage, then held up a finger. "One more, two if we're quick."

Or if you get the one you're waiting for, I thought. And he did. He listened, nodded sharply, and leaned into the microphone.

"Question is whether there's any connection to the federal litigation over Mr. Angelides's extradition." He paused, nodded again. "I obviously cannot speak for any federal officials or agencies regarding their decision-making processes, because I am not privy to those deliberations. I am bewildered and profoundly disturbed by the decision to grant Mr. Angelides a visa. I don't know who made that decision, or when, or why, or who else knew about it. But I will say this: the federal government owes an explanation to the American people and, most importantly, to every single one of Angelides's victims, of why this man was allowed, no, welcomed, back into the United States by our federal government." He stopped, held up a hand. "Not just an explanation— an *investigation*. I know, I am just a local prosecutor, I may be in way over my head here, but the circumstances, the timing, it just smells fishy to me. If I had any say in the matter"—*yeah,* I thought, *like if I were a media-darling DA who everyone knows is headed for higher office, holding a live press conference in the second-biggest TV market in the county...someone like that?*—"then I would open an inquiry to determine exactly how that visa got approved, and why."

When the press conference was over I went over to the cafeteria to wait for someone to come and find me and tell me about Frankie. I found a table in the corner and pulled the rubber band off Johnson's Redweld.

It was several hundred pages of investigation notes, the sort of paper that accumulates when you're working on a thirty-year-old case. I flipped through them, then turned to the back, where a manila folder held a single sheet of paper in a plastic bag. The paper looked like a photocopy of a page of blocky handwritten letters that read: "You arrogant son of a bitch. I warned you to stay away. Now run or die."

I looked closely at the paper. The blocky letters looked like they had been drawn with a stencil. So no handwriting analysis, and no record of a document on anyone's computer. You could even make your own stencil with a pair of scissors, so there'd be no record of you buying one. And you'd photocopy the original so there'd be no ink analysis or latent fingerprints on the paper. And you'd photocopy it with a batch

273

of other documents, at some self-service coin photocopier in the back of a drugstore. Best the FBI would ever do with it would be a chemical analysis of the paper, which would maybe narrow down the location where the paper was made. Probably not even that. "Sir, it's mostly pine! With traces of spruce!"

I put the plastic bag back into the manila folder and then went back through the investigation notes, case by case. There were twenty-six cases, neatly tabbed, twenty-six sexual assaults committed by Angelides over the years. The victims were groupies, actresses, interns, take your pick. I recognized a couple names. The dates ran from 1975 to 1989. The MO was the same in every case: swanky Hollywood party, starstruck young women, involuntary ingestion of whatever date-rape drug was in fashion that year. The last case was the one Angelides had finally been charged in, the one he'd pled out to in Judge Wittenband's chambers with no court reporter and no paper record, while young Deputy DA Alex Johnson cooled his heels out in the courtroom.

I turned the page. There was one more file at the end. It was from April 1989, just a couple weeks before Angelides's arrest. There was no criminal complaint and no photos. The file was slim, but it told me enough to know why Johnson wanted me to have it. The victims were two college students visiting from New York. Their names were Eleanor and Jenny.

I found a house phone and called the ICU. Frankie would be in surgery at least three more hours. My concern was very much appreciated but there was nothing I could do until then; how about I go and get some rest? I went out to the front entrance and found a cab. I took it to the Beverly Hills Public Library and went in and found a public computer.

It would have taken Phillip Marlowe an afternoon in the County Law Library downtown. It took me half an hour on Google. All the documents were there. I didn't even have to log into the firm's Westlaw account, which was good because I wasn't anxious to leave a billing record of my searches.

Angelides had boarded his plane to Paris in June of 1989. The DA's office had gone to the Feds with an extradition request two months later, in August. The federal DOJ had moved with its usual deliberate speed and had made a formal extradition request to France in December. The French thought about it for another six months, and then Angelides's French lawyers had persuaded the French government to request "clarification" about Angelides's sentence in LA. The Feds then forwarded the request to the DA's office, whereupon Angelides's LA lawyers hustled into court and made a motion for a declaratory judgment that Angelides had been sentenced to sixty days of psych evaluation and had served his sentence. The DA requested its own judgment, that Angelides had fled pre-sentencing and was a fugitive. The case languished in the trial court for two years, while Judge Wittenband sat on it and then died of a heart attack.

The case was reassigned, and the judge who inherited it threw up his hands and issued a ruling saying that there was insufficient evidence to say one way or another, so there could be no declaratory judgment either way. The DA's office appealed to the state Court of Appeal. That took another year, during which now-retired Major Crimes DA Pete Duplessis also died. The Court of Appeal affirmed the trial court, in light of the absence of a record and the impossibility of creating one with new hearings, given the deaths of two of the three people in the room. The state Attorney General took over the case and petitioned the California Supreme Court for review. The California Supreme Court thought about it for another year, then declined to take the case.

By this point it was 1994. I remembered 1994. I was back from Operation Desert Storm in Iraq, working patrol in the 30th Precinct, and Jennifer Curtis was a young legal advisor in the New York City Mayor's office, working as a liaison to the police department. I met her that year when I broke down the door of a motel in Fort Lee, New Jersey, so my union rep could snap a photo of her in bed with Captain Mike Settentio. Good times.

A year later J.C. was in DC, in her first stint with the government, as an attorney in the Office of Legal Counsel in the DOJ. It was one of the most prestigious DOJ postings, because the office's function is to give advice to the administration about the legality of proposed executive actions. High-profile stuff, requiring serious constitutional cover-your-ass firepower. Things like bombing campaigns, waterboarding, extraterritorial rendition, drone strikes. Also extraditions.

The mid-nineties were good years for Angelides. He kept making movies, and audiences kept flocking to see them. His distinguished peers kept giving him awards, and he shuttled between French beach resorts and Swiss ski resorts, depending on the season.

J.C. worked in the office until 1998, when she came back to New York for her first stint with Montrose Bryant. And three things happened in 1998, three things you wouldn't have connected unless you knew to look. And who knew to look? Just me, as far as I could tell. And maybe John Scofield.

What were those three things? Thing one: Eleanor Hausman, trying to take her dad's real estate development firm national, gets a ten-million-dollar investment in a never-to-be-built San Fernando Valley strip mall from a one-use-only LLC called Antelope Palms. Thing two: the Justice Department announces that after careful deliberation, it's decided to initiate legal proceedings to extradite Silvio Angelides back from France to face sexual assault charges in LA. And thing three: Angelides hires the white-shoe law firm of Montrose Bryant to fight the extradition in court.

Forty-Four

I stayed with Frankie for a week. No detectives or Deputy District Attorneys came looking for me. Jarron came by every day. He brought copies of the incident reports filed by the police and paramedics. He didn't say how he got them so fast. I wasn't in them, anywhere. I had been erased from the narrative, replaced by passive voice and ambiguous pronouns.

I read the paper and watched the details trickle out one by one. The redacted summaries of the assault allegations Johnson released didn't have names or enough detail for the media to seek out victims, but there was enough that I could follow along in Johnson's notes. And there was one case that never made it into the public disclosures. It had never generated an official complaint or investigation either. It was the 1989 assault on the two college students visiting from New York: Eleanor and Jenny.

After a week, the doctors were pretty sure Frankie was going to live, so I flew back to New York. Johnson had closed his case, but I hadn't. I couldn't help noticing that I had happened to be at the scene of the violent deaths of two people J.C. had good reason to want dead. Real good reason—a lot more reason than she'd probably had for all those Yemenis and Pakistanis she'd authorized for drone targeting. You couldn't call in drone strikes in the U.S. But you could call in washed-up detectives.

J.C. picked me up at Newark at 6 a.m. in a limo. She said she'd send a car, but I hadn't expected her to be in it. The driver came around and opened the back door for me and there she was. I got in.

"Well, well, well," she said. "Nice trip?"

I leaned my head back and closed my eyes. The limo was huge, the seats soft leather like Hausman's briefcase. "How much do you know already?" I said.

"Some of it," she said, looking down at her Blackberry. "Most of it, maybe. But not all of it." She put the phone down and looked at me. "I had a talk with Tom Jarron. He thinks quite highly of you, you know."

"Does he?"

"Yes. In fact, he'd like to hire you. As he pointed out, your role at Montrose Bryant will be somewhat unsettled after my departure."

"Which is?" I said, knowing she wouldn't answer.

"In due time," she said, wagging a finger. "They plan very carefully, and they don't like surprises."

"Yeah, well, me neither," I said. "I guess we're talking about the same surprises?"

She shrugged. "More or less. A bit less than more, though, is what we're going for. Simple things first. Silvio Angelides. Not a surprise, because you weren't there."

I raised my eyebrows. "Yeah, I figured that when I saw the LAPD report. You think it'll stick? All those cops? The paramedics? They're going to write it up, too, you know. Probably already have."

"They have," she said. "Another studio security consultant responded shortly after Muller, heard the shots, called 911, and ran into the backyard, where he put pressure on the wound. They didn't catch the guy's name. Not their job, and they were focused on saving Muller's life."

"Okay," I said, "so who was the guy?"

"Who do you think?" she said. "Tom Jarron."

"What about the detectives?" I asked, already knowing the answer.

"The detectives?" She held up a hand, ticked off points. "They have a closed case, they have justice served against a serial predator who thumbed his nose at the law for decades, and they have the favor of Alex Johnson, who is a good guy to be friends with. It's a no-brainer for them."

I didn't argue. She was right. It was an obvious no-brainer.

"So." She looked at me like a math teacher waiting for the dumb kid to finish the last problem on the test. "Now that we've established that you *weren't* there, I'd like to know why you *were* there."

If I was going to end up at the bottom of the Hudson, this was the prelude. "How much do you know?" I said.

"I have a theory. But I'd like to hear it from you."

I nodded. "Okay. But I want you to answer a question first."

She looked at me for a long moment. "All right."

"Why did you want him dead?"

J.C. threw her head back and laughed. "That's all? My goodness, Marcus. If I wanted him dead, it would have been for the same reasons all the other women wanted him dead. Because he deserved to be dead. He was an unrepentant rapist who drugged young women. He could have gotten all the pussy he ever wanted just by asking, but he didn't like to ask. It didn't *excite* him. No tears for Silvio, Marcus."

I waited. That wasn't an answer, and she had agreed to give me an answer. "But *did* I want him dead? No. No, I didn't. I wanted him destroyed. I wanted him *ruined*. And I didn't need him dead for that. No, I needed him *alive* for that. Alive and in front of the cameras on his perp walk."

"Because of what he did to you and Eleanor in 1989? Or because he was going to testify against you?" I was talking myself into a trip to the bottom of the river, but I didn't care. I needed to know.

She looked at me appraisingly, then nodded slowly. "I saw something in you, Marcus. Going on twenty years now, since then, and I still see it. It's what makes you so valuable in the right job. In *this* job. You just can't leave any maybes on the table. You can't turn off the lights, close the office door, and go home to your life. You just keep pounding your fist against the wall until it breaks."

She paused. I had to fill the silence. "Until what breaks?" I said. "My fist or the wall?"

279

She considered that. Then she gave me the smile she gave me out in front of City Hall when I was twenty-two and too scared to talk to her. "The wall, Marcus. And let's keep it that way. Silvio wasn't going to testify against me. He just wanted his Oscar. You think Kyle Simpson wasn't easy to manipulate? Their pathetic October surprise was dead on arrival. But Silvio broke his word, Marcus. The man made a promise. He made a *deal*. And I delivered. And the one condition that was sacred and nonnegotiable was that he *never*, under *any* circumstances, for *any* reason would return to the United States."

"He funneled money to you and Hausman, didn't he?"

She smiled again, but it was a different smile this time, a smile with a predatory edge. She reached out and put her forefinger lightly against my lips. Her touch was so unexpected that every muscle in my body tensed, and I felt a sudden electric surge of arousal run from my lips down to my toes, like every neuron in my brain was racing back in time to that moment in the motel in Fort Lee when Andy Naeman and I had burst in on her and the captain. She had locked eyes with me then, held my gaze with the same smile she wore now.

"That's two questions, Marcus," she said softly. "You only get one."

She slid her finger down from my lips and took hold of my shirt. She undid the first button with one hand, then the second, then reached over with her other hand and ripped my shirt open. I was in too much shock to move. She leaned toward me, swung a leg over me and straddled me. She ran a hand through my hair, leaned in, and kissed me, hard.

I had never had sex in a limo, let alone with the soon-to-be most powerful woman in America. And I was just off a cross-country flight. And some part of my brain was reminding me that I was still facing decent odds of ending up buried in a hole out in the Pine Barrens before morning. So I wasn't at my best. But it didn't matter. It was pretty clearly not about me. And J.C. got what she wanted, as she always did.

She slid off me and adjusted her skirt. Then she reached forward and opened the little refrigerator compartment and pulled out a bottle of vodka and two glasses.

"No cigarettes, but this will do," she said, pouring two shots.

I took my glass and tipped it back.

"Why?" I said, my voice coming out as a croak.

She laughed. "Because you wanted it back then but you were too scared to ask. And Eleanor and I have an agreement about things like this. It's been a while now since either of us invoked it, but fair's fair. So it was my turn."

I poured another shot.

"And you want something else, too," she said, "that you're too scared to ask for. But you need it, to close out your case." She took a Kleenex from her purse, rolled it up to a point, and put it in her mouth and sucked on it, just as Eleanor Hausman had, a lifetime ago in her apartment looking out over Central Park. "I think this will do nicely." She took a business card from her purse, folded it around the Kleenex, and handed it to me.

"Go on," she said. "Finish the job."

Forty-Five

J.C. got out at the office, and the limo driver drove me the rest of the way to my apartment. I was tired but I did what I was told. I finished the job. I asked the driver to wait, and I went up and got all my samples out of my freezer, threw them in the briefcase, and rode out to Mo Faizalla's lab in Jersey City in the back of the limo. It was the first time I'd been there in person. I was impressed. It was basically just a warehouse space in an industrial park, but it was *his*.

Mo cleared his morning for me and I dumped it all out on his conference table. Cotton ball, Kleenex, Q-tip, bloody shirt, bloody shirt. Eleanor, J.C., Duane, Linda, Talley. Samples 1, 2, 3, 4, 5. I wrote down the numbers and the names on a sheet of yellow legal paper and put it in my pocket.

"Time's up on this," I said. "I've got what there is to get, and two of the principals are dead. I just need to know if any of these people are related to each other. Just cross-check them all."

Mo looked at me strangely. "Okay, Marcus, you got it. Genealogy, right? Someone in Salt Lake City going for posthumous conversion, or what?"

"Since when do Muslims make Mormon jokes?"

"All the time, brother. *We* invented the whole planet-and-virgin afterlife thing, and they totally macked it."

"Yeah, well, nobody's getting a planet in this case that I know of. Give me a call, okay?"

"Hey, I can do it now, man. You look frazzled, take a load off. We'll go run 'em, all right? You can wait."

I went out to the parking lot and got out my clarinet case. In the sun, it was warm enough to play. I put the horn together and leaned on the side of Mo's van and started in on "Blue Train."

An hour went by, and then Mo tapped me on the shoulder. I opened my eyes.

"Sounds good," he said.

"How long you been out here?"

"Couple choruses. Waiting for a pause, you know? You had some good lines going, didn't want to break in." Mo was always polite that way.

"So?"

"All done."

I nodded and we went back inside. I took the clarinet apart on his conference table and swabbed it out while he talked.

"Cross-matched all samples," he said. "Definitive results, as follows." And he drew me a diagram:

"There's your family," he said. "All here. Mother, father, daughter. 1 and 3? No relation to anyone."

I pulled out my paper and looked at it. Samples 4 and 5: Linda and Talley. Sample 2: J.C. Samples 1 and 3: Duane and Eleanor.

"You're sure?" I said, stupidly. Of course he was sure. "Samples 4 and 5 are—"

"Right, 4 and 5 are the two bloody shirts; 2 is the very fresh sample on the Kleenex. Yes, I'm sure. There's your happy family."

Forty-Six

Six a.m., and the sun was rising over Queens in J.C.'s window. I was sitting on the white leather couch watching it rise. J.C. was off to D.C. for another meeting. The new administration was a month old and the first few cabinet picks were still bogged down in the Senate. The President still hadn't announced his pick for Attorney General, but we all knew it was coming. J.C. wanted to wrap up the Hausman matter before she left. She was standing with her back to me, staring out the window watching the eastern horizon turn gold.

"They vet you *seriously* nowadays. These retired Bureau guys, it's all they do. Someone like me, obviously you've got skeletons. Which is fine. Skeletons mean you can get shit accomplished. But they don't want you to have *unknowns.* You can have shady prior associates, affairs, a little questionably begotten wealth, but what you cannot have, Marcus, is a big fucking question mark that's gonna jump up and Anita Hill you in Congress. The President has enemies. *I* have enemies. Mine know better than to fuck with me, but *his* don't.

"And then a week before the election, my old drone strike testimony was on the news again, and I got a call. An old lady from nowhere, Texas, with a story about how the state took her daughter. They'd lied to her for so long, she thought her little girl was dead, but then she saw me on TV and it just hit her—there she is, that's my daughter.

"I didn't believe her. Would you? Her story is that thirty-five years ago she loses custody of her daughter, and the daughter is taken to a state orphanage, where she dies. Then, thirty-five years later, out of the blue, her old friend the sheriff tells her her daughter's alive after all?"

She looked at me as if expecting an answer. I didn't have one to give.

"I knew they were up to something," she said. "God, did they *not* want to lose that election. They had all the usual dirty tricks going. I knew I was on their smear lists, so I assumed it was part of that. I mean, paying someone to pretend to be my birth mother? Come *on*, man.

"So I would have laughed it off. Except...this is not something *anyone* ever knew. When I was in college my parents told me I was adopted. One conversation, and we never talked about it again. They've been dead for ten years. And *I* never talked about it with *anyone*. And I have *memories,* Marcus. Not very clear, and I remember when I was young thinking they were just dreams, but they're *in there*. I was curious. I wanted to hear her story."

"So you talked to her?"

"Yes, I talked to her. And she told me the whole story. I don't know how it hit you when she told you, but me..." She trailed off as the first crescent of pure sun surged up over Long Island. I didn't say anything —like, for example, "Linda didn't tell me the whole story." I still wasn't sure whether I was going to bed that night under six feet of soil in the Pine Barrens.

J.C. turned back from the now-blinding window and stood behind her desk, arms folded. "It could not have come at a worse time, professionally, but I didn't care. If her story was true, then justice had to be done, and I was going to see to it. I've made enough things wrong in this world. I was going to make this one right. That woman had had everything taken from her and then spent decades answering the phone for the man who took it, watching him get rich on her land."

"Why did she stay?" I said. It was a question I had not asked Linda.

She spoke with more fury in her voice than I'd ever heard. "Where the hell was she going to go, Marcus? She was a homeless prostitute in East Texas. What Talley offered probably seemed like a great deal. The *only* deal. You have no *idea* how powerless she was."

285

She was quiet for a moment, then she said in a whisper, "That evil motherfucker had to die."

I didn't mention the DNA test that showed that the evil motherfucker was her father.

I just stared at her for a minute. Finally I said: "And I was supposed to take the rap for it?"

She laughed at me in the gentle way she's always laughed at me. The way she laughed when Andy Naeman and I busted in on her and Settentio in the motel in Fort Lee. The way you laugh at something cute and sweet and harmless. I was none of those things, to the rest of the world. But I was to her. And it scared me.

"Marcus," she said, "don't be stupid. That's a terrible outcome for me. What's the narrative if you killed Talley? Murder for hire. Right? You've never been down there in your life, you don't know the victim, you're a violent ex-cop private investigator. So murder for *hire*, maybe one wonders who you *work* for, wouldn't you say? I may as well indict myself."

"Maybe I was freelancing," I said, knowing it was a dumb theory before I'd finished the sentence. "Maybe Linda put the arm on me and I acquiesced, spur of the moment."

"Oh, even better. So I send my *mother* to the chair? Even if she wanted that, and I were willing to facilitate it, what kind of headline would that make? 'Cabinet Nominee Lends Hired Gun to Estranged Mother for Contract Killing.'"

I didn't say anything. She took a sip of grapefruit juice.

"People are tough to predict, Marcus. I didn't storyboard this out. I wanted factual confirmation, quietly. I thought, worst case, she'd want to cash in with some *TMZ* money, and I was going to have to deal with some tabloid publicity, that's all. A couple of weeks of stories about my white-trash roots. Some hillbilly tabloid disclosures and an embarrassing press conference in the middle of my hearings. Roger Clinton, Billy Carter, you know. Best case? Months of press about the heartwarming story of the AG reunited with the mother she never knew."

"But then she shot him between the eyes," I said.

"I misread her. I guess that was inevitable, because I never knew her.

She didn't want the money or the publicity. She only wanted to be sure. She wanted to know that it was really me, that I'm here, I'm alive, and I made it out. Once she had that, she didn't need anything anymore."

"Except to see him dead."

"Yes, except that."

I thought about the manila folder in my briefcase. The DNA tests. Linda. Duane. Talley. Eleanor. J.C. I kept my mouth shut. I wanted to believe her. I had always wanted to believe her. It used to be easy. This morning it wasn't. Maybe Talley and Angelides did deserve to die. That didn't change the fact that they both happened to die at a very convenient time for J.C.

I had to ask, even if I was digging the first shovelful of Pine Barrens dirt. "Do you know what's under Talley's land?"

At least she didn't patronize me and feign ignorance. "The Haynesville Shale. Billions of dollars of oil and gas. Recoverable now. Talley had thousands of acres right on top of it."

"Did he know?"

"Of course he knew," she said. "The surveys are pretty thorough nowadays. He wanted it, but he couldn't get at it. His wells weren't deep enough, and he didn't have the resources for hydraulic fracturing. He wouldn't sell, though. He wanted investors."

"And now?"

"And now someone's going to make a lot of money," she said.

"Who?"

"Well, I am told that Talley did not have a will." She laughed. "That would be in character, I suppose. A will is an admission of mortality, after all, is it not? Of weakness? Do *you* have a will, Marcus?"

"Nothing to put in one," I said, feeling stupid as I said it. And I wondered who had told her that Talley didn't have a will. But I had a pretty good idea, and I wasn't stupid enough to ask.

She nodded at me, in that lawyerly way that makes the client feel as though whatever idiotic, boneheaded thing he's just told his lawyer he did was actually reasonable, sensible, what *anyone* would have done.

"Yes. Well. When a person dies without a will, his property goes to his heirs. Which is, first and foremost, his children."

"Like, for example, his daughter?"

"Yes. For example."

She sat there and looked at me for a long moment. The sun cleared the skyline of Long Island City across the East River and punched like a laser in through the glass and onto the desk. I had the momentary sensation that the beam extended straight through the desk, through my briefcase and into the manila folder, and lit up the pages inside, so that J.C. could glance down and read them.

Or maybe she knew what they said already. I had the photos from the Waters farm in my jacket pocket, with the lock of hair. I patted the envelope once, and my brain flashed to an image of J.C. looking at the pictures, tears welling up in her eyes as her old memories flooded back, coming around the desk to me with her arms open. Then the image shifted to the backseat of J.C.'s limo, and I shut it down and hated myself for being weak enough to imagine that it had meant anything to her.

"Why not just tell me?" I said. "Why use Hausman?"

J.C. paused and took another sip of grapefruit juice before answering. "Eleanor always wished she was adopted," she said, finally. "She probably believed it, too. She wanted drama in her life so much. You know, *Anne of Green Gables*? It was a game we had—how picturesque could you make your life story and get away with it? How far could you go before someone called you on it? Not that she really had to make much up about Harlan. Harlan was a bad guy."

J.C. sat in her chair, reached into her desk, pulled out her own manila folder, and tapped it twice with her index finger. "You've done an outstanding job, Marcus," she said. "I asked you to find Eleanor Hausman's birth parents, and you've succeeded. Exemplary work."

I stared at her for a moment, opened my mouth. "But—"

"Eleanor is not Samantha's daughter, obviously," she said, ignoring me. "Samantha was infertile, Harlan wanted an heir, and he was fucking the maid anyway. Samantha played along and so did everyone else because in their world, that is what their kind of people *do*. It was just not spoken of. Eleanor suspected, of course. At some level she knew. But she wasn't *satisfied* with it, aesthetically. It wasn't picturesque enough, romantic enough. That's one of the most beautiful things about Eleanor. She's always dreamed of having a tragic, Faulkneresque history. All our lives, Eleanor was prettier than me, richer than me, more popular than me. She would never say it, but she was. She didn't *need* me. Not the way that I..."

Her voice trailed off, and she opened the folder. She pulled out a piece of paper and held it up to the sunlight. "I always wanted to give her something that no one else could give her. And now I can. My gift to her. Her tragic history."

She handed me the paper. I looked at it. It was the DNA test. My DNA test. The DNA test I had done so carefully, so discreetly. My bloody shirts, my cotton swabs.

I looked at the paper. It was on Mo Faizalla's letterhead, with his signature at the bottom. Except that there in the middle, in bold-faced type it said, **"Eleanor Hausman. Father: Joseph Andrew Talley. Mother: Linda Elizabeth Waters."**

I stood abruptly, looked down to make sure my briefcase hadn't magically vanished. "No," I said. "No... Someone could—"

"Someone *could* do a lot of things, Marcus. But someone won't. Pops Talley had no other children. I suppose some inbred cousins could come out of the woodwork and challenge the inheritance, but Eleanor's claim is very straightforward. And impeccably documented. Linda told half a dozen people that her baby girl grew up to be rich and famous in New York and was sending someone down to get her inheritance back from Talley. You showed up right on cue and told them who you were working for. Chief Tarwood confirmed the whole story. And Dr. Trask signed a declaration, too.

"Now, if someone wanted to tell a *different* story, well, they're welcome to try. Unless they're in a line of work that takes professional confidentiality very, very seriously. Such as my line of work and your line of work." She tapped the folder again. "And Mohammed Faizalla's line of work. You didn't tell him the names that went with the numbers on your samples, so I had to fill in the blanks for him." She paused. "Although now that I give it some more thought, I recall that you *did* give him those names when you were out there yesterday. You gave them to him in a sealed envelope, to look at after he ran the samples. Mo recalls it that way, too. In fact, he has the envelope. Mo is a very good friend."

"Goddamn it!" I said, standing abruptly and knocking over my chair. "Talley was your—"

"*No*," she said, raising her voice for the first time. "He was not. He was *nothing*."

She waited for me to pick up the chair and sit down again. "You know the expression? If you're going to take a shot at the king, you better hit him? The past is like that, Marcus. If you're going to dig, you'd better be ready to dig all the way down and keep digging, because the minute you stop, the hole's going to collapse on you and you'll be buried in shit up to your neck.

"When Linda first told me her story, I thought maybe we could unwind the whole thing. Invalidate the original transfer to Talley. Get the land back for her. We looked at it. Wouldn't fly. *Kirchberg v. Feenstra*, 1981. Louisiana law said the husband was the 'head and master' of marital property, even if the property was in the wife's name. If the wife was the title-holder then she had to consent to a sale, but the husband was free to *mortgage* it without her consent. Without even telling her, like that piece of shit Linda married. And the Supreme Court said no more head-and-master transfers, but we'll let all the existing ones stand."

"Yeah," I said, "Talley had a thing for that case too."

"I bet he did," said J.C. "That case let him steal Linda's life. But tell me, Marcus, what if you were on the Supreme Court? Would you have the guts to order two hundred years of land titles thrown up in the air? Retroactivity's a *bitch*. You want to try to trace the history of every piece of property in Louisiana? Shuffle the title deck? Maybe one of those cards turns out to be yours. You dig too deep, you don't know what you're going to find. Some of it you might not like. You can't rewrite the past, so you clean up what's in front of you. Write a better ending."

"You told Linda all that?"

"I gave her my considered legal opinion. I told her that she wasn't getting that land back. But that if Talley had a child, the child had a right to it. Will or no will, the child would get a share. And of course, *no* will and the child gets it all."

"But Linda wanted—"

She cut me off. "What Linda wanted," she said, "was to shoot Pops Talley in the head, knowing that his land—*her* land—would go to her daughter. And you know what? Linda got what she wanted."

J.C. did a quarter turn in her chair and gazed out at the sunrise again. "People want what they want," she said. "I inherited millions of dollars I'll never use. Eleanor inherited Harlan's empire, what was left of it, and she sold it all off. This little...project...is something else entirely."

Yeah, I thought, among other things, it hands the motive for Talley's murder off to Hausman, if anyone ever asked. But I kept my mouth shut.

"You've done well, Marcus," she said. "The firm has done well."

"*How* well? Are we on a contingency?"

She smiled. "You, my friend, have earned a bonus, let's put it that way."

I shook my head. "I don't think so." I didn't want to know the price of two deaths.

Her smile dimmed, just a touch. "You've already accepted it. Direct deposit last night. On the books and reported to the IRS." Which meant motive for Talley's murder was now tattooed on my back, too. If anyone ever asked.

"Now," J.C. said, "I have to get to D.C. And if you would leave me the report I believe you've brought me, I'll read it on the train."

I handed her the folder and kept the envelope with the pictures and the lock of hair safely in my pocket. I don't know why. They were her, even if she wanted to pretend otherwise. But now I was suddenly afraid to show them to her. Afraid to let her know they existed. I looked out the window, out over the forest of windows at the pink sky over Queens. We were 500 feet up. Way too high to land on my feet and walk away.

Forty-Seven

TRANSCRIPT EXCERPT, Sabine Parish Police Jury Budget Committee Meeting, December 15, 2008:

[Shouting, crosstalk, indecipherable.]

MR. GUILLANE: Order, order, please. Order in the chamber. We are a legislative body here, so let's everybody try and act like it.

[Shouting, crosstalk, indecipherable.]

MR. GUILLANE: Order!

MR. PAINTER: I said, "Can you repeat that number?"

MR. GUILLANE: You should all have a copy of the letter in your packets. I had Cynthia make copies for everyone.

MR. PAINTER: Where?

MR. GUILLANE: It should be after the agenda and last month's minutes, hang on... Cynthia?

PARISH ADMINISTRATOR CALDWELL: Last item in the packet. Just flip to the back.

[Shouting, crosstalk, indecipherable.]

MR. GUILLANE: Order! Now, as I was saying, this just came in, and Buddy wants to have a full meeting next week, but he asked me to convene the budget committee to maybe come up with a few ideas for, you know, what we might could spend some of this money on.

MR. BROWN: Jesus Christ.

MR. EBERLEY: Thirty-two million? Billy, what was our budget last year?

MR. GUILLANE: You mean, for the parish?

MR. EBERLEY: Yes, the entire budget for the entire parish, all twenty-five thousand of us.

MR. GUILLANE: Well, I think it might have been north of $15 million, maybe? Cynthia?

MS. CALDWELL: It was $15.8 million.

MR. BROWN: That was without pension funding?

MS. CALDWELL: Correct, pension funding is separate.

MR. PAINTER: How much more?

MS. CALDWELL: Pension contributions were another $2.5 million.

MR. EBERLEY: Okay, then, let's see. We're talking about, what, eighteen-something—

MR. BROWN: Eighteen-three, all in. Jesus.

MR. EBERLEY: ...And this is thirty-two, just for...what?

MR. GUILLANE: Parish permission for drilling. Permits, road usage, public-land easements, that's basically it.

MR. PAINTER: So this is a lump sum?

MR. GUILLANE: Well, as I understand it—and keep in mind it was Buddy talked to the company personally—this is a lump sum, and then the annual payments'll be like a percentage of what they produce in the parish.

MR. BROWN: Now, I know they are contacting individual property owners—

MR. EBERLEY: My neighbor got a letter.

MR. GUILLANE: We'll all be getting letters, like as not.

MR. PAINTER: All of us as has got land, anyway.

MR. BROWN: ...Just handing out money, I suppose.

[Crosstalk, indecipherable.]

MR. GUILLANE: ...Which is why we are having this meeting. I thought we'd sort of go through the budget and put together a list of all the things we could spend some of it on. I had Cynthia put together a handout for you. It should be right... Cynthia, did we...? Well, could you just read it for us?

MS. CALDWELL: Schools, K through 8: teachers, playground, new buses. Schools, high school: teachers, football stadium. Road maintenance: gravel levelling. Sanitation: new trucks, finish landfill levee. Public works: road paving? Health: hire full-time clinic doctor? You put question marks on those last two.

MR. GUILLANE: Thank you. Yes, I wasn't sure on the last ones.

MR. EBERLEY: Oh, I reckon we can start getting sure.

MR. BROWN: Thirty-two million. Jesus.

CLASSIFIED AD: *Shreveport Weekly Courier*

Seeking Landmen. Immediate Work. Oil exploration and extraction services company seeking land-title researchers for immediate hire. Identify, locate, and obtain land title and mineral rights documentation throughout Louisiana/Texas/Arkansas area. No experience necessary. Will train. Must have car and willingness to travel. Generous per diem + commission per parcel traced. Bonuses for extraction leases signed.

TRANSCRIPT EXCERPT, WKN-Shreveport Local Morning News Segment, January 7, 2009:

MALE ANCHOR: For our next story, we'll be going down to Mansfield— and then waaay down, Becky—thousands of feet down! Because we're talking about shales.

FEMALE ANCHOR: Yes, our country's energy future may be right there waiting to be tapped, right under our feet.

MALE ANCHOR: And WKN's Tabitha Johnson tracked down the whole story for us, and she's here now with her report. Good morning, Tabitha!

REPORTER: Good morning, Brett and Becky! That's right, it turns out there's a whole new gold rush underfoot right now—*literally* underfoot. Because the new gold is shale rock holding billions and billions of barrels of recoverable oil and natural gas, and the whole tristate area is sitting right on top of it. Geologists call this deposit the Haynesville Shale. I spoke with Dr. Ron Dominico of McNeese State in Lake Charles, and he explained what it is.

[*CUT TO VIDEO*]

REPORTER: I'm here with geology professor Ron Dominico, in a soy field about twenty miles outside of Shreveport. Professor, what are we looking at?

PROFESSOR: This is a shale-gas fracking rig, Tabitha. It's essentially a giant drill and pipe system that can drill a hole thousands of feet deep, into the shale deposits, and inject high-pressure water and sand into tiny cracks in the rock. Then the gas comes bubbling out and gets piped to the surface.

REPORTER: But I had always thought that the fields around here were tapped out.

PROFESSOR: They were—for traditional drilling technologies. But there's still plenty of natural gas down there. It's just not in liquid pools. It's more like a wet sponge. The shale is very porous, and over millions of years it's soaked up the gas, so all we needed was the technology to give it a little squeeze.

REPORTER: With the high-pressure water and sand?

PROFESSOR: Exactly.

REPORTER: So how much is down there exactly?

PROFESSOR: Well, if the saturation is basically uniform across the formation—and we have every reason to think it is because we've drilled a lot of test wells—there may be 250 trillion cubic feet of gas in the Haynesville. Maybe more.

REPORTER: That sounds like a lot.

PROFESSOR: I'd say so. That's as much as the entire country uses in a decade.

[*CUT TO STUDIO*]

MALE ANCHOR: So Tabitha, I understand that oil companies are paying a lot of money for exploration rights?

REPORTER: That's right, Brett. By law, whoever owns a piece of land owns the rights to drill for oil and gas under that land. But over the years, a lot of landowners sold off those rights separately. And sometimes it's hard to figure out exactly who owns what. So the companies are in a race to track down the mineral rights for every property they might want to drill under.

FEMALE ANCHOR: And how many properties is that?

REPORTER: Thousands! The Haynesville Shale covers all of Northwest Louisiana, Southwest Arkansas, and Northeast Texas. It's huge! And also, these modern drilling rigs drill *sideways* once they get underground, so a single well might cross a dozen different properties.

FEMALE ANCHOR: It all sounds very complicated, Tabitha. How are they managing to sort through it all?

REPORTER: That's a great question! So I went down to the Webster Parish courthouse to find out.

[CUT TO VIDEO]

REPORTER: I'm here in downtown Minden at the Webster Parish courthouse. This beautiful building used to be pretty quiet. But lately, it's been packed to the gills. Not with lawsuits—but with land-title research. Because the courthouse holds all the parish land records going back to 1871! And right about now, a whole lot of people want to get a look at those land records, because they just might hold the key to millions of dollars of natural gas drilling rights.

[PULL BACK AND PAN TO SHOW GUEST]

REPORTER: With me here is Darren Hurst, who's a land researcher for an oil exploration company, on a quick break from the records room.

GUEST: I'm a landman, that's right, ma'am.

REPORTER: So tell us, what does a landman do?

GUEST: Well ma'am, there's about ten thousand different parcels of land sittin' over the Haynesville Shale, and about fifty different jurisdictions sittin' on a hundred years worth of papers tellin' us who owns what. So our job is to figure it out, for every parcel the company might want to drill on, so they know who to write the royalty checks to.

REPORTER: And how difficult is that?

GUEST *[laughs]:* Plenty! In there, today? There's probably a dozen landmen, all stuffed into one room, and we each have a dozen properties we're supposed to research. And for each one of those, you might have to go back through a dozen different sales to make sure there's clean title to the mineral rights somewhere.

REPORTER: Sounds like a lot of dozens.

GUEST: Yes, ma'am! And then when we get a line on a target, a property owner, you know, then we need to go through a whole different set of records looking for addresses and phone numbers. 'Cause we only get our commissions if the company can make contact and get a signature on the dotted line.

REPORTER: Well, I'll let you get back to it, then. Tell me, how many courthouses have you visited?

GUEST: Oh, my... Well, Caddo, Bossier, Webster, Claiborne, this week. Bienville and Lincoln. DeSoto and Red River for sure. Spent a ton of time in Sabine a couple weeks ago. And then I'm supposed to do a week in Texas, I think. Haven't been up to Arkansas yet.

REPORTER: Thank you, Darren, and good luck!

[CUT TO STUDIO]

MALE ANCHOR: So Tabitha, final question: how much can Becky expect to get for her drilling rights?

FEMALE ANCHOR: Careful, buster, they're not for sale!

REPORTER: Well, Brett, I spoke to a couple of gentlemen in Benton who I think can answer that for you. And spoiler alert—it's a lot!

[CUT TO VIDEO]

REPORTER: I'm here at Caddo's Best Barbershop in Benton with...

[PAN TO GUESTS]

GUEST 1: Ruben Burrows.

GUEST 2: Sammy Fairbairn.

REPORTER: So Ruben, you've run this barbershop for how long?

GUEST 1: Forty years, thereabouts.

REPORTER: And what are your plans now?

GUEST 1: Just bought a Cadillac, next I'm buying a boat, going to hitch it to my Cadillac and tow it on down to the Gulf.

REPORTER: That's all with your royalty check.

GUEST 1: Two hundred grand!

REPORTER: And that's for how much land?

GUEST 1: Eight acres. Eight acres! Used to be the family farm, back in the day. Wasn't worth nothing to no one. Then one day, there they were. Twenty-five thousand an acre, just for the drilling rights!

REPORTER: And how about you, Mr. Fairbairn?

297

GUEST 2: Well, I ain't got no eight acres.... But I got three and a half, and they done give me a hundred thousand! Just came in the other day. Went and opened a bank account. Ain't never done that before.

REPORTER: And what are you going to do with it?

GUEST 2: Don't rightly know. Something, that's for sure. Going to do something.

GUEST 1: I'm going to pick out a boat for him too.

GUEST 2: You know what I was wondering? There's people, plenty of 'em, with *hundreds* of acres, *thousands* even...

Forty-Eight

I walked out onto Sixth Avenue and headed north. It was a beautiful morning. Busy executives were striding down the sidewalk, heads held high, ready for a big day at the office. I found a food truck and got a breakfast burrito and a coffee. It occurred to me that the team of Italian designers behind Hausman's briefcase had probably included a perfectly sized burrito pocket somewhere in its recesses. I opened it up and took a look. There were two good candidates. I zipped the burrito into one of them and then walked north toward the park.

I crossed Central Park South and went into the park past the big statue of Simon Bolivar on a horse. The horse looked down at me, but said nothing. I found a bench overlooking the Pond. I set the coffee and burrito down, took off my jacket, and did some pushups. Then I sat down and ate my breakfast.

I waited awhile. No one tried to kill me. No one paid any attention to me except a couple of pigeons who hopped around hoping for some crumbs. I stretched my arms out on the bench, leaned back and closed my eyes, and felt the sun on my face. It felt good. At eight I stood up and walked north, past the Pond, past the merry-go-round, past the Zoo, and out onto Fifth Avenue in the eighties.

There was another person left alive who probably knew some of this story, and probably had for the last thirty years. Dr. Llewellyn Trask's office was on 82nd off of Park. J.C. said he'd given her a declaration to back up the Hausman story. But he might still talk to me.

The lobby door of Trask's building was open. A custodian was polishing the floor. He nodded at me and I went down the hall to Trask's office door. I put my hand up to the buzzer, then hesitated, and looked down at the doorknob. The door was closed, but there were scratches where the latch met the jamb and a depression in the wood of the frame next to the latch. The scratches were fresh, and the door was old. Easy to force, with the right tool. And there were so many tools.

I looked back down the empty hall, then put my ear to the crack and listened. Nothing. Very gently, I tried the knob. Locked. So if it had been forced, whoever forced it had locked it again from the inside.

So many tools to open a door. But I hadn't brought any. Judging from the scratches and the depression in the wood, the tool of choice here had been a screwdriver. Delicately done, too: he hadn't snapped the wooden frame or taken a chunk out of the door. Just a few scratches, which you wouldn't notice if you didn't know what they were.

I looked at the latch and thought about my options. Two came to mind—my shoulder and a credit card. The credit card seemed like a subtler choice, so I pulled one out. A door latch is just a metal cylinder on a spring, set horizontally into the body of the door. The end of the cylinder is cut at an angle, so that as you close the door the angled face presses against the jamb and pushes the cylinder back on its spring. Then when the door is closed, the cylinder pops back on its springs into a hole set into the doorjamb.

A latch isn't as good security as a true deadbolt, which lacks the angled face and so has to be manually retracted in order to open or close the door. To get through a door with a good deadbolt you pretty much have to batter it down or drill a hole in the door big enough for your arm and reach through and slide the bolt from the inside. Which plenty of thieves do, though it takes time and tools and can be foiled by a metal door.

In theory, a properly fitting latch should present itself to the would-be thief just like a deadbolt, because—in theory—the cylinder should insert deep enough into the hole in the doorjamb that the thief can't reach the angled face from the outside through the crack between the door and the frame. But in practice the cylinder almost never goes in far enough, because the whole point of the mechanism is for the cylinder to retract fully with a single half turn of the doorknob. And you don't get much movement from that half turn, so most latches are installed with the angled face sitting just a couple millimeters into the hole on the doorjamb. Which is plenty when the door is new. But a couple millimeters is not enough of a cushion to overcome time, humidity, warping of the wood, or the gentle levering of a screwdriver. And once the door gets loose against the jamb, you can slide a jimmy into the crack, find the angled surface of the latch, and depress it. Credit cards are good for that.

Trask's door was old and wooden and didn't have a deadbolt. Latches are so much more convenient than deadbolts that a lot of doors, especially in older buildings with at least a nominal security presence in the lobby, don't have separate deadbolts at all. And a lot of people who have them don't bother to use them. Trask's door was loose to begin with, and had been loosened further by whoever had broken in before me. There was plenty of room.

I slid the credit card into the opening and pushed down until I felt the angled face of the latch. It gave smoothly and the door swung open. I pocketed the card and stepped inside, closing the door behind me as softly as I could. I set my briefcase by the door and looked around the waiting room. It was empty. The lights were off, but morning sunlight angled in from the windows at the far end of the room, behind the faded couches and the receptionist's desk. The windows gave onto an air shaft on the interior of the building. No escape that way.

I looked at the inner door that led to Trask's office. It was ajar. I couldn't see into the inner office. It had a window as well, I recalled. Was it another air shaft, or the service alley that led to the back of the building from 82nd Street? I wasn't sure of the layout. It was an important tactical question, though, because if there was no other exit besides the door I'd just come in, and if whoever had broken into the office was still inside, they'd have to come out through me. I'd done enough house clearances in Iraq to know that people behaved a lot differently when they were cornered.

I stood just inside the door and listened. I counted to sixty. Nothing. The office was silent. I could hear the ticking of the mechanical grandfather clock on the wall and the faint hum of traffic outside on Fifth Avenue. I took one step toward the inner door, then another. Still nothing. I went the rest of the way to the door and pushed it open, stepping back against the wall as the door swung open. Still nothing. I counted to ten, then dropped to a crouch and went through the door low and at an angle, in case anyone was aiming a head shot at the doorway from behind the desk.

No one was. Certainly not Dr. Llewellyn Trask, who was slouched in his massive brown armchair, leaning back with his head resting at a slight angle. He was in his customary white shirt and tie. His suit jacket was draped over the back of his chair, and his sleeves were rolled up, the French cuffs loose around his elbows. His eyes were closed, and his arms hung limply at his sides. I scanned the room. There was enough light slanting in through the venetian blinds to see into the corners. But no one was hiding there. I went around behind Trask and looked under the desk. No one down there either. Just a syringe, lying on the floor under Trask's left arm.

I straightened up. Keeping my eyes on the open doorway to the waiting room, I put two fingers to Trask's neck, found his Adam's apple, and slid my fingers up and to the side, feeling for a pulse from the jugular. Nothing. His skin was still warm to the touch. I moved my fingers up under his nose, feeling for a breath. Still nothing. There was a lot of nothing in this room. A lot of nothing and a dead man and me. Not a good combination.

I stood for about ten seconds, going over my options, none of which I liked. I stared out the open door into the waiting room. In the halflight, the doorway was like a picture frame, and the Mies van der Rohe furniture and the grandfather clock looked like a still life. Then I heard a sound from the waiting room. A soft scuffling, and a figure shot across my field of vision from right to left, moving from the window side of the waiting room toward the door to the hall. For an instant, the still life sprouted a human subject, in profile, a man in dark clothing with a thick head of white hair. Then the figure was gone, and I heard the door slam.

I was out of the inner door in two strides. Two more to the outer door, which was now shut. I pulled out my shirttail and put my hand inside it to grasp the knob. I opened the door and poked out my head quickly, looked down the hall, then pulled it back. The man in the dark clothes was running to my right, down the hallway further into the building. The hall turned to the right about thirty feet toward the back of the building. The man turned his face halfway back toward me as he took the corner to the right. I stepped out into the hall, closed the door, and rubbed down the outer knob with my shirttail. Then I took off running down the hall after him.

I rounded the corner heedlessly, without slowing. If he was waiting for me there with a knife or a gun he'd get one stab or one shot. That wouldn't be enough to kill me unless he was right on target and I was unlucky. That was a chance I'd take. Because I'd seen him and he'd seen me. It was ex-NYPD Captain Michael "Big Mike" Settentio. I hadn't even heard that he'd been released from prison. But there he was.

He wasn't waiting with a knife or gun. He was running for the service entrance onto the alley. The service entrance was a heavy metal door that opened inward. It opened, like they all did, onto a ramp leading up to the alley. At the top of the ramp would be a tall iron gate to cut off access from the alley. Settentio was twenty years older than me. He could still climb a fence, maybe, but not before I'd be on him.

Settentio reached the door, grabbed the handle, and pulled. The door was heavy, and it swung open slowly. I was on him before he got through it. I grabbed the back of his jacket. He flailed back at my head with an elbow, but I leaned back away from the blow, planted my feet, and swung him around like a figure skater swinging his partner, letting centrifugal force do the work. He came around 270 degrees and slammed into the cinder-block wall next to the door frame. I hit him with three quick punches to the gut, one after another. The years hadn't softened him much, but I was still as strong as I was the first time I hit him, and I felt the air go out of him.

303

I reached across and got his left wrist with my left hand and pulled him away from the wall. Then I did a half turn, twisted his arm behind him, put my right hand between his shoulder blades, and pushed him across the hall toward the opposite wall. He got his right arm partway up to catch the impact, but he still took it mostly on his face. I cocked my right and rabbit-punched him in the kidney. Then I slammed him against the wall again.

I bent my right arm and shoved my forearm against the back of his neck. "What'd you give him?" I said.

Settentio turned his face halfway around so he could look at me. He tried a laugh. I was impressed that he could draw a breath. "Heaton? What the fuck? How about a heads-up next time, huh? You should have said something. I didn't know it was you."

"What did you give him?" I repeated.

"His usual," he said. "Little fentanyl in there this time, though."

"He's dead."

"Yeah. He died happy. The fucker likes it at dawn. Locked the damn door on me before taking his ride, so I had to jimmy it for the cleanup." This time Settentio's laugh was genuine. "Heaton, relax! The scene's neat and tidy, we're good. I took care of it. You fucking scared me, I didn't know it was you."

"Why, goddamn it?" I looked around. The bend in the hallway shielded us from view from inside the building, and the service door out to the alley had swung closed. But it was morning on a workday, and someone would come this way soon.

"*Why?* Why the fuck do you think? Why do you get up in the morning, Marcus? Because she fucking *says* so."

I leaned in on my forearm. "You're not walking away from this, you son of a bitch."

He tried another laugh, but it came out as a croak under the pressure from my forearm. "Lighten up, son. So I beat you to it, so what? You already got your bonus, right? And you got the better job anyway. Don't fucking horn in on mine, because I'm not splitting it."

"What are you talking about?" I tightened my grip on his wrist and twisted it up further.

"I said lighten *up*. What, are you jealous? You think I get the better assignments? You fucking prima donna. She's had me as that geezer's fucking *dope* mule for the last six months, because for some reason she pays her own shrink in smack. I don't see *your* ass doing that shit. *I* would have gone to Texas and killed the fucking landowner, and I fucking hate Texas. And *I* sure as shit would have gone out to California and killed fucking Angelides. Would have been *happy* to."

"What are you talking about?" I said again. It was all I could say.

"Would have done it a lot cleaner, too," he continued. "Unless you had something against your old Academy buddy, in which case my hat's fucking *off* to you, partner."

"What..." I started in for the third time, but I couldn't get the whole sentence out. My grip loosened on Settentio's left arm, and my right arm slid down from his neck. I couldn't see straight. I felt the blood pounding in my head.

Settentio must have felt me relax. Quick as a rodeo bronc, he lashed out with his right heel, driving it up into my testicles. A bright flash of pain exploded in my gut and I dropped to the ground.

Settentio stood over me, shaking his head. "That's for putting your hands on me," he said. "And for fucking up perfectly good work. I hope you wiped the damn room, at least. Did you even wear gloves? Jesus, Marcus, be a professional."

I rolled to a sitting position. The bright flash of pain had subsided to a roar. The steel door slammed. I forced myself to my knees and then my feet and shouldered the door open, still bent over at the waist. Settentio was already up and over the iron fence and was walking down the alley toward 81st Street.

Forty-Nine

I walked back down the hall to Trask's door. I had to jimmy it with my credit card again to get my briefcase. Then I wiped both doorknobs with my shirttail. I was a sitting duck if anyone came down the hall, but no one did, and there were no cameras that I could see. I took a last look at the door. The door and the jamb were both old and pitted and discolored. No one would look twice at them. Not the receptionist or the janitor, anyway. Not after they found Dr. Trask in his armchair, still taking his last ride on the white horse. Cause of death would be obvious and easily confirmed by an autopsy. Maybe he got a bad batch or maybe he pushed the envelope with the fentanyl mix. Doctors have always been the most notorious opiate hounds. Every coroner would know that. There would be no suggestion of foul play.

I went out the front, the way I came in. I crossed Fifth Avenue and headed back into the park. I walked aimlessly. That's the best thing about Central Park: Olmsted designed it with so many hills and curves and corners, so many walkways doubling back on themselves, that you can walk aimlessly for hours and no one will ever know. I ended up at the foot of Belvedere Castle, but I didn't have the heart to take the clarinet out of the briefcase and walk up to my usual spot. I sat on a bench and thought about nothing at all.

After about five minutes, my phone rang. I picked up. It was Chief of Police Bobby Tarwood from Mandanoches, Texas.

It's generally a bad idea for a murder defendant to chat on the phone with the arresting officer, even after the charges are dismissed. No jeopardy until the jury's sworn, as young Larry Nguyen had diligently explained to me, and we hadn't gotten that far. So they could, in theory, recharge me.

But so what. They weren't going to. And I still wanted answers.

Tarwood wanted to talk. Said he was retiring. Getting an RV and heading out on the road.

"Where to?" I said.

"Dunno. Depends on the time of year, I guess."

"Well, it's March now. So not too far north yet."

"Yeah, I'm thinking Florida might be the place to start."

I thought of Duane Hempersett. Florida was a big place, and Bobby Tarwood and his RV were going to be sticking to the coast. They wouldn't be crossing paths, and I was pretty sure Tarwood wasn't looking to track Duane down. If he ever had been, Duane wouldn't have been there for me to find.

"Florida's nice," I said. "Then what, up the coast?"

"I reckon. Maybe come to New York."

"Really? You ever been to New York?"

"No, sir. But I…I'd like to see…I'd like to see her," he finished in a rush. "Before I die, I'd like to see her with my own eyes."

"You're not talking about the city, are you, Chief?"

"No," he said, "I am talking about Sue-Lynn. I want to see her happy and safe and alive. Do you think you could arrange that?"

"Arrange what?"

"Arrange for me to see her."

"To see her, like stand across the street and watch her get out of a limo? Sure. To see her, like, have dinner with you? I dunno. Why do you think she'd want to talk to you?"

"Because I'm the only one left," he said. "I knew her as a baby. I was more of a father to her than that goddamn drunk Linda married. Also I promised Linda. I swore to her—"

"When?"

"Tell you what," said Tarwood, "we'll talk when I see you. I am concluding a forty-year career in law enforcement this morning, and then I am picking up my new vehicle and heading in your direction. Think about it. You may be quite interested in hearing the story."

He was right. I was.

Fifty

The swearing-in ceremony was a week later. March was a little late to still be filling the Cabinet, but things had bogged down when two of the early nominations got contentious in the Senate. J.C. invited me to the White House for the swearing-in. Maybe "invited" isn't the right word when you're there with the security detail, but close enough. I called Bobby Tarwood and told him I'd be in DC for a few days, if he'd gotten that far up the coast by then. I put him on the guest list for the swearing-in, just in case. I thought maybe I could introduce him to J.C., or at least get him within shouting distance. He'd sworn to Linda, after all. Not that it would matter to him. As far as he knew, little Sue-Lynn was Eleanor Hausman, living large in New York. And I wasn't going to open my big mouth. J.C.'s warning had been plenty clear. And if Tarwood was the conduit for Linda's wish to see her lost daughter, then there was some justice in at least putting them in the same city for a couple hours.

As it turned out, there never were any confirmation hearings for J.C. The President tapped her for National Security Advisor, not Attorney General, and the Senate doesn't confirm the National Security Advisor. On the TV screens in Penn Station, some talking heads were spouting expert opinions about the decision. The general consensus appeared to be that J.C. was a "solid choice to head the new national security team." I listened to Abby Huntsman ask some think-tank guy whether he was "surprised that Jennifer Curtis wasn't picked for AG." He smiled, politely and expertly, and said, "Well, I guess it shows that the pundits don't always get their fantasy-cabinet brackets right." The other heads arrayed around the screen laughed, politely and expertly. "Look," he continued, getting the ass-kissing tone just right—just in case J.C. was watching, I imagined him thinking—"Jennifer Curtis would have been...may well still be...a great Attorney General. But when we're talking about the national security of the nation, well, the President wants the very best advisors as close to him as possible, and there is simply no position closer to the President, than National Security Advisor."

The other guests agreed. They talked about her "controversial role" in approving drone-strike targets and her memos on Guantanamo and intervention in Libya and Syria. Nobody mentioned that the Attorney General has to be confirmed by the Senate, but the National Security Advisor does not.

It was one of those perfect spring mornings we get sometimes on the East Coast. Just a touch of winter in the air still, but the mid-morning sun brought warmth again, not just light. The snow was all melted and the grass on the White House lawn was as green as the grass by the beach in Santa Monica, except you appreciate it more on the East Coast after a winter.

The ceremony was at noon, but we were supposed to go check in at ten. My presence was not required; J.C. had had a Secret Service detail already for a week before the announcement. My job was to "liaise" with them in case they needed help with the transition. They didn't.

J.C. immediately disappeared with the President, and everyone else ignored me. I stood around for awhile in some great hall or other that probably had an official name. No one asked for my help with anything, so I decided my liaising had been a success. I wandered out into the Rose Garden, where the ceremony was going to be, sat down in the back row of white wooden chairs, and soaked up the sun and waited for someone to tell me to leave. No one did, so I just sat there. Me and about a dozen Secret Service guys, standing around the perimeter looking serious. I had Frankie's remaining Cuban cigars in my suit pocket. I took one out and put it in my mouth. I thought about lighting it, but I didn't want to push my luck on the White House lawn. I had been getting along so well with the Secret Service. So I stood up and walked across the lawn to the east gate.

Outside on 15th Street, I lit the cigar and turned right, down to the Mall. I walked along the path in front of the Natural History Museum. I vaguely remembered going there on a school trip as a kid. I looked at the triceratops statue out front and wondered if every guy nearing forty who looked at the thing had to fend off a herd of dinosaur metaphors stampeding his subconscious.

"Not me, pal," I said around the cigar. "Alive and kicking, motherfucker."

I turned and followed the path east toward the Capitol. Past the Natural History Museum was the National Gallery of Art Sculpture Garden, with its ice skating rink in the middle. Skating season had come to an end. The rink was drained, and workers were taking down the boards. I walked through the Sculpture Garden and sat down on a bench across from something big and abstract. I had the bench to myself. I sat back and pulled on the cigar, holding the smoke in my mouth and letting it out in a slow thick cloud that hovered in the still air. It was quiet. I could hear birds in the trees and the laughter of kids from somewhere along the paths. I closed my eyes.

"Good morning, Mr. Heaton." I opened my eyes and John Scofield was sitting on the bench beside me.

"Goddamnit," I said. "Give a guy a moment's fucking peace, will you?"

He laughed. "Nice day, isn't it?"

I looked around for his goons. "Let me finish this, at least, okay? Hate to waste the Cubans. They'll be hard to come by in prison."

He waved his hand. "Oh, by all means," he said. "In fact, I'd smoke one with you if you have another."

I turned to look at him. "Is this some sort of embargo sting? Did they kick you out of frauds?"

He shook his head. "Cuba's gonna be our friend soon, right? Anyway, it smells Dominican."

"Bullshit it does," I said, "but if you would like it to be Dominican, then I'm sure that's what it is." I reached into my pocket, pulled out the last cigar, and handed it to Scofield.

He put it in his mouth and chewed on it for a moment. "Can we take a walk around the Mall a little? Let me show you the Lincoln Memorial."

"What are you, a fucking spy?" I said.

"It's a nice day," he replied, "and I feel like walking. And yes, open spaces are always good conversational venues."

We walked west, along the wide, tan, dirt-and-gravel path bordering the Mall. It was early enough in the day that the grass expanse was mostly empty. No soccer games yet, just joggers and walkers and the early tourists heading for the Smithsonian or the Capitol.

"You jog out here on your lunch hour?" I said. "Run by the memorials, get all inspired to serve your country?"

"Affirmative on both counts," he said.

I laughed. "You know, John," I said, "I actually believe you are saying that without irony."

"None whatsoever," he said. "How about you?"

I puffed on my cigar. Scofield still hadn't lit his. "Without irony?" I said. "Here? The Vietnam Wall. Beyond that it's all irony as far as I'm concerned. But I was enlisted, remember? We like our irony down in the ranks."

"Are you relocating here now?" he asked.

"You mean am I now in the employ of the National Security Advisor?" I said. "No. I don't even know if I'm still in the employ of Montrose Bryant."

He raised his eyebrows. "Really?"

"Oh, like that should surprise you? You think I would want to be a government suit?"

"No, I think you're loyal," he said.

I considered that. "Loyal to the fucking grave," I said. "Does that end our conversation?"

He smiled. "No. No, it does not." He pulled the cigar out of his mouth, inspected it, and bit the cap off with a precise snap of his incisors. Didn't even ask for my cutter. I was impressed. I handed him the box of matches and he lit the cigar and puffed on it, getting it going. "Those Dominicans sure know what they're doing," he said.

We walked for a few minutes in silence. The Mall stretched in front of us, a green and beige carpet rolling up the hill to the Washington Monument.

"I want to tell you a story," he said, finally. "Don't know if you've heard it. Either way, good story."

I shrugged. It was a nice day, I was walking on the Mall, I wasn't in a wagon getting hauled off to federal prison. All in all, a good time for a story. "Okay," I said.

"March 2004," he said. "You and I were both in Iraq."

"I was, anyway," I said. "You were playing golf in the Green Zone. Or was it the putting green on a carrier?"

He smiled indulgently. "Racquetball," he said. "We played in the hangar. I was never much into golf. But the story's here." He pointed to the right, up 12th Street, where the main Justice Department building was. "Right up there, actually.

"March 2004. The Attorney General is John Ashcroft. White House Chief of Staff is a guy named Andrew Card. Auto industry lobbyist, friend of the President's family. White House counsel is Alberto Gonzales. The President's former attorney in Texas. And the Deputy AG is a guy named James Comey. AUSA, like me. Career prosecutor.

"So nowadays, we've all heard of the National Security Administration, right? Out there on its Army base in Maryland, running our spy satellites, siphoning up our Google searches? But back then, it was a little more obscure. And no one outside the government had much of a clue what it actually did. But after 9/11, it started mopping up phone data—"

"Yeah, yeah," I said. "I know."

"Well, we all know *now*," he said, "but in 2004? No one knew dick. And the government had a secret arrangement with the phone companies. Came up with a name for it: 'Stellar Wind.' Whatever the fuck that means. In practice? Give us all your data. No warrants, no subpoenas, no limits. Just give."

"You don't sound like a fan," I said.

"Doesn't matter," he said. "Doesn't matter what I think. This is a story." He puffed on his cigar. "So the phone companies, they want some assurance that they aren't opening themselves up to some serious civil liability. Lotta good lawyers, working for big companies like that. Lotta good advice. Cover-your-ass advice, the kind you make good money for giving.

"So the government, they come up with a plan: we'll have the Attorney General certify that all this is legal. And we'll reauthorize it every couple months, get you a nice signed letter. Cover your deep-pocketed asses.

"Things go okay for the first couple years. Ashcroft signs off. The companies are covered, which is all they care about. But Ashcroft has a lot of lawyers, too. A whole office called the Office of Legal Counsel, to give him advice on this sort of thing. And they start waving red flags. Saying this is looking pretty darned unconstitutional. So we get to March 2004, and Ashcroft says, enough. We have a Fourth Amendment, right? He tells the White House that DOJ has decided Stellar Wind goes too far. He's not going to sign off anymore.

"But then? Right after he makes that call, he gets sick. Serious, about-to-die sick. Pancreas. Sudden, unexplained failure of a major organ. The sort of thing that, if we're talking the fucking Soviet Union, we'd say was pretty suspicious timing, right? Like, check-his-martini-for-radioactive-isotopes kind of timing? But we're not in the fucking Soviet Union, Marcus, which is the point of this story.

"So Ashcroft, he's rushed in for emergency surgery at George Washington Hospital, down over there." He gestured vaguely west, past the Washington Monument and Lincoln Memorial. "And James Comey, his deputy, becomes acting AG while he's in the hospital. So Ashcroft's up there, just out of surgery, and Stellar Wind needs a reauthorization or the phone companies are going to stop ponying up with the data.

"There's no one in the hospital with Ashcroft but his wife. And she gets a call, late at night, from Andy Card. He says, wake up your husband, we're coming over. She thinks, what the hell? And she calls Comey. Comey calls the head of the Office of Legal Counsel, a Harvard Law professor named Jack Goldsmith. And Robert Mueller, the FBI director. Another former AUSA. And Comey and Goldsmith and

Mueller hustle their asses over there. Comey and Mueller have drivers with lights and sirens. Goldsmith takes his own car.

"They run up to the room, and there's the fucking White House Chief of Staff and the White House counsel, and Gonzales has his briefcase out and a pen in his hand, and they've got a fucking reauthorization letter on the bed, on Ashcroft's chest. On the fucking AG's *chest*. And Ashcroft's like an hour out of surgery, he's got a dozen tubes in him and he's barely conscious. And his wife's sitting there thinking her husband could die any second.

"And you know what happens then, Marcus? I forgot to mention one thing about Comey. He's 6'8". And not a pencil-neck, either. Like LeBron James big. Kind of guy that fills a room, you know? He walks in and backs Card and Gonzales off. Says I'm acting AG, and Mr. Ashcroft there, he gave me very clear instructions. So no one is signing that damn paper tonight. And if you don't like that, get the President on the phone. Because all three of us—the acting AG, the head of OLC, and the Director of the goddamn FBI—will offer him our resignations tonight. But no one's signing that paper.

"And then? Best part of the story, right here. Ashcroft sits up in the bed. Just had his fucking abdomen opened up, he can barely raise his arm, but he sits up and tells them his oath is to the Constitution, and he's not signing off on this program anymore.

"And Gonzales and Card slink off back to the White House. Comey sits there the rest of the night. Makes sure they don't come back."

We were heading up the hill toward the Washington Monument now. The White House was off to the right, past the green expanse of the Ellipse. Off to the left was the Jefferson Memorial, on the bank of the Tidal Basin.

"Every AUSA in the Department knows that story," said Scofield. "And it has a little motto attached at the end. They tell it to us in orientation: 'Say yes when you can, say no when you must.'"

He fell silent and puffed on his cigar.

"Metaphor?" I said. "Life lesson? What?"

"Ain't no metaphor, my friend," said Scofield. "It's history. History to provide an explanatory context for the pending termination of our relationship. Sometimes, you have to stand up and say no. I'm saying no."

"Meaning she won and you're scared of her?"

He rounded on me. "Meaning it was a political hatchet job from the start and my oath is to the fucking Constitution!" He looked sincere. I gave it better than even odds that he was.

"You have evidence of that?" I asked.

"I—" he stopped himself, paused. "I have a solid basis for saying no."

"Yeah? Such as?"

"I had reason to believe that the investigation was a political hatchet job on Jennifer Curtis."

"But you weren't sure?"

He shook his head.

"Or you were too scared to call bullshit to their faces?"

He shook his head again.

"Fuck it," I said. "Who cares. You sent me after Angelides because you couldn't do it yourself. You thought I might throw a scare into him and smoke him out."

He shook his head. "No," he said.

"You didn't know, did you?" I said. "You didn't know it was Angelides."

"No," he said. "I did not."

"And you decided granting immunity to a serial rapist was a little too much?"

He didn't answer. I didn't expect him to. We walked a minute in silence. I asked my last question: "You said you had some evidence the investigation was a hatchet job on J.C. What was it?"

This time he answered. "Sorry, Heaton, no dice."

"Well, do you *want* some? I mean, if you're planning to stake your career on this."

"What do you mean?"

I took out my wallet and found Alex Johnson's card. I handed it to Scofield. "Consider it a gift," I said. "A little something to cover your ass, just in case. Give him a call. Tell him I sent you. I think you guys might have a lot to talk about."

Vietnam Veterans Memorial, Washington, DC

Fifty-One

watched Scofield walk off back in the direction of the Justice Department building, and then I turned and followed the path to the left toward the Vietnam Wall. I had suggested it to Tarwood as a meeting place. He had never been there, and he had been in the damn war. I hadn't even been born then, but I've been to the Wall a dozen times. I'll keep coming, even if they make a memorial to my war. This one's plenty for me.

Tarwood was standing by the 1968 panels, holding a rose. He saw me and nodded.

"Found someone?" I said, though it was pretty obvious.

"Yeah, I looked in the damn book," he said. "Had to go back to get the flower." There was a phone-book-sized index on a stand at the top of the path leading down to the Wall, where you could look up names and find their location on the panels.

I didn't ask him for details. He'd tell me if he wanted to, and, if he didn't want to, it was none of my damn business. And Tarwood hadn't come to see me to talk about his war. He'd come to see me to keep a promise he'd made to Linda. Or so he said. I walked the rest of the Wall and then sat down on a bench to wait for him. He followed a few minutes later. I stood up and we walked back down the Mall, heading east, toward the Capitol.

"You still want to meet Eleanor?" I said.

He nodded. "Yes, sir, I want to meet her. I want to meet the little girl I carried on my shoulders and sang to at night. She won't remember me. That doesn't matter. I was a father to her and her mother was the love of my life."

I stopped and turned to look at him. "That comes as a bit of a surprise, Chief. The way I understood it, you and Talley ruined her life. You took her daughter, you took her farm, and you took her dignity." I was quoting J.C., but I could let Tarwood think the eloquence was mine.

He pursed his lips. "Yep. That is all true. We did that. And I know you talked to Linda and I will not dispute a word that she may have said, God rest her soul."

"But?" I said.

"*But,* it was a long time ago. People remember things differently, sometimes."

"Differently how? You busted her husband, and Talley showed up at the jail and talked him into mortgaging Linda's farm for his legal fees. Then walked him into prison, and foreclosed. It was robbery, and you were the muscle."

Tarwood pursed his lips and nodded. "I suppose that's mostly true," he said. "Thing is, you're leaving out the part where *I raised that girl.* Duane was a worthless piece of shit. He had a wife and daughter, and he left them to starve. Hardly saw his own daughter. Far as Sue-Lynn knew, *I* was her daddy. *I* took care of that family while goddamn Duane Hempersett was out drinking through Linda's inheritance. Such as it was."

"So you helped her get rid of Duane," I said. "I get that. But why'd you take her farm?"

"I didn't," he said. "That was Talley. Duane made a promise—"

"Yeah, I've heard that one. 'You always have to pay,' right?"

"It's true, ain't it? All Linda wanted was to get Duane gone. She was young. She didn't know what was going to happen. She didn't know Talley would make him sign a note on the farm—"

I rounded on him. "You're saying Linda didn't know Talley was going to represent Duane?"

"How could she? I mean, she'd never met him—"

"*Bull*shit," I said, with more force than I intended.

He stopped and looked at me, and I closed my mouth. Tarwood didn't know that Talley was Sue-Lynn's father. Tarwood might even think *he* was.

"She knew him," was all I said. "Don't lie to me."

He closed his eyes for a moment. "She was...she was the best thing that ever happened to me," he finished. "Raising a child, Heaton, that's what makes you a man. And I got four years of it. Goddamn, I wish I had it back."

"Duane didn't molest the girl, did he?"

He avoided my gaze. "Duane was a worthless piece of shit, like I said. Who knows if—"

"No," I said. "Your little girl, that you raised, that you carried on your shoulders? If he'd hurt her, you would have beat him to death."

He shook his head weakly. "Maybe I should have."

"No," I said again. "You didn't do it because you knew he didn't do it."

"I was young," he said. "I thought...I thought I could help her. She thought if..." Tarwood stopped. He wanted to talk. He'd driven a thousand miles to talk. But he couldn't make himself do it. I'd seen that look a hundred times.

I pulled Duane's yellowed 1973 oil-company letter from my jacket pocket, held it out in front of Tarwood, let him read it. The letter made more sense to me now, as I pictured a twenty-three-year-old Linda Waters reading her own letter at the kitchen table of her farmhouse, terrified that her drunken husband would sell the land out from under her.

Mr. Hempersett,

As you know, it is in the vital national interest to expand domestic production of petroleum resources. Over the past six months, our firm has been conducting subsurface reserve surveys on behalf of a major oil company. Our geological analyses suggest that the strata under your property may contain a substantial reservoir of recoverable oil. We wish to begin immediate discussions with you regarding further exploration and more definitive testing. If our projections are borne out, we will be prepared to offer you very substantial royalties for drilling rights. As head and master of the property, you have the authority to conduct these transactions.

We wrote to you and your wife in September. Unfortunately, we did not receive a response. Time is of the essence on this project, and your present incarceration may have interfered with your receipt of mail, so we are contacting you directly to invite you to phone us at our offices, at our expense, to discuss terms on a mineral-rights lease.

Tarwood's eyes widened and he exhaled slowly. "Where the hell did you get that from?"

"You've seen one of these before, haven't you?" I said. "Linda got the first one, didn't she?"

"Yes," he said. "She got two of 'em."

"And she came to you?"

He nodded. "She knew if Duane got a whiff of it he'd sign whatever they put in front of him. They'd lowball him and he'd roll over to get a little cash in his pocket. They'd get the rights, he'd get a few weeks of whiskey and cards. And then the money would be gone, and the oil rights would be gone forever."

"That's why you had to bust him for something and send him away?"

He kept his eyes on the letter. "They sent the first one to Linda because she was the title-holder. Then the second one came addressed to Duane. Linda got scared. Wasn't like Duane read the mail, but sooner or later they'd send someone in person. And once they found him it wouldn't take them long to get his signature on the dotted line. I reckon those oil companies knew all about that head-and-master stuff."

"Yeah," I said.

"Linda wanted to know what she could do. She was panicked. She asked me, was it true, could Duane really sign away all the oil rights? Me, I was just a baby cop with a high-school education. I didn't know shit. But Linda said she knew someone we could talk to."

"Talley."

"Yessir," he said. "That's how I met him. I'd heard of him, back in high

321

school. He was from Mandanoches, but he transferred to Marshall 'cause they had the better program. Two-way player. Tough as nails. They kicked our butts every year, them and Tyler. Damn good programs. Anyway, Pops had graduated by the time I got into high school, but I heard about him. Mean son of a bitch. Laid some poor kid out just about every game. He was runner-up for state 'Mr. Football' his senior year, which in Texas as you may imagine is something people remember in small towns. I don't know how Linda knew him. I mean, I knew, I guess, but I never asked her about any of that. Linda had it real hard there for a while. She was... Anyway, she knew him, and he was a lawyer, and me and Linda we didn't neither of us have any other ideas about who to talk to.

"So there we were, me sweatin' out patrols up in Longstreet for next to nothing, which was what cops got paid back then, and him trying to get a law practice going in Mandanoches. And neither one of us makin' much of a go of it, really. I mean, I knew *I* wasn't. Ain't much lower than a backwoods sheriff's deputy, and I knew I wasn't goin' much higher, and him... Well, I guess he wasn't doing much better, but I sure thought he was. A guy like me, I didn't know people like him. People who had gotten out, made something of themselves, you know? He'd gone to college, gone up to Fayetteville for law school, worked in a law firm up there, rubbed elbows with bigwigs, all that. Now here he was back in town with his own office and everything. You just kinda followed his lead. He was like that. Anyway, we walked in and showed him the letter and Linda said she wanted to get rid of Duane. I guess it just looked like the golden ticket to him."

"May I ask why you didn't just shoot Duane and leave him in a ditch?"

"I couldn't kill him. He was blood to Sue-Lynn, and I wasn't going to kill my Sue-Lynn's daddy, scum that he was. Linda wouldn't hear of it neither. She wasn't no killer. Duane drank and gambled and wasn't no provider, but beyond that there wasn't any call to kill him. I expect you understand the distinction."

I did, and I was glad that Tarwood expected me to.

"Talley said divorce was kinda a problem in Louisiana. You basically had two choices. You could go to court and get a judgment that he'd abandoned the family and left them destitute. 'Separation from bed and board.' But then you had to wait six months and go back and ask for the divorce. And we knew what would happen during that six months. Them oil guys aren't stupid. They'd get Duane's signature on a piece of paper, and them oil rights would be gone."

"What was the other choice?"

"Immediate divorce. And there were only two ways to get it. Prove adultery, or get him a felony conviction."

"And you decided the conviction was the cleaner option?" I had done my share of matrimonial work—every PI does, if you're not Philip Marlowe—and I knew that things get real complicated real quick when you get into court battles over who's the cheatingest cheater.

"Well, maybe if I tailed Duane long enough, I might've caught him with a whore, but as far as I knew, that wasn't really his chosen vice," said Tarwood. "Could set him up, sure, but then you've got one more person in the loop."

I knew that complication too. One more person to cut in, and one more person to blackmail you for more later.

"So a nice clean felony conviction. Moment the ink is dry, you got your divorce. Done deal. Had to be something serious, Talley said. And quick. It had to be quick. Nothing that would drag out for a year before trial. Had to get him to plead guilty."

He stopped. I waited for him to continue. He didn't. Finally I asked: "Whose idea was it to accuse him of molesting the girl?"

Tarwood pursed his lips again, hard. He looked down at the gravel and dug in it with his toe. "Talley's," he said. "Said that was the best way to get him to take a quick plea."

"And Linda went along with it?"

"We just did what he said. He was the lawyer."

I stood up and looked for something to hit. There wasn't anything. I took three quick steps down the path and waited for my fists to unclench. They did, slowly. I stood and waited for Tarwood. I was ready to walk again.

Tarwood got up and we began our slow procession toward the Capitol. I said: "I found Duane. I talked to him."

Tarwood didn't look surprised. He just nodded. "For what it's worth? Back then? When I arrested him? I went easy. Didn't hurt the boy anymore'n he had coming. But he had something coming. We both know he did."

"I don't care about that," I said. "I want to know what part of your little plan had Linda losing custody of her daughter."

Tarwood was a tough guy, but tough guys can cry. His eyes welled up, but he kept walking.

"That's why I'm here, Heaton. That's why I came to see you. That's why I've got to see her."

"Why?"

"That *wasn't* our plan, damn it! We didn't know."

"Didn't know what?"

"We didn't know, I'm telling you. The plan was to get Duane out of the way, then take our time and negotiate a good deal with the oil company. Get a good payment up front, then some long-term royalties. Talley'd take his fee out of the first payment."

"But you know what happened instead?"

"Of *course* I know what happened instead. I've spent thirty-five *years* living with what happened instead."

"And not doing a damn thing," I growled.

He turned on me and I glared at him.

"Thirty-five years," he repeated. "And I did a *lot* of damn things."

"You're saying Talley double-crossed you? That you didn't know that when you popped Duane, he was going to go in there and take the mortgage on the land for himself?"

"No, goddamnit!"

"And you didn't know that he was going to tell Duane to tell the judge that Linda was a prostitute and get the kid shipped off to the state orphanage?"

"No! I'm telling you, no! We didn't have any idea. We were going to get *married*, for Christ's sake. That girl was going to grow up with Linda and me as her mama and daddy. Just like it goddamned *was*. *That* was the goddamned plan."

"Then what happened?"

"Talley didn't want 10 percent of Linda's royalties, that's what happened. Talley did his research, figured out what that oil was actually worth. You remember 1973, right?"

I did not. But I knew what he was talking about. "We basically ran out of oil, right? Energy crisis? Iran? Jimmy Carter?"

"Yeah. Crisis up here, I guess. In East Texas, North Louisiana? It was goddamned manna from heaven. We'd been thinking them fields was tapped out, but turns out 'tapped out' is not really a measure of oil. It's more like a measure of how much it costs to *get* the oil. And so when the price of a barrel of oil *triples* over five years? Well, turns out them fields ain't tapped out after all."

"And Talley figured this out?"

"Course he did. He was a smart ol' boy. He figured it out, probably, before he was finished reading that letter."

"So he figured out a way to get the land for himself."

"Yes, he did."

"But what does this have to do with Linda's daughter?"

Tarwood nodded. "That's a puzzler, ain't it. Puzzled me for a lot of years. I mean, I wouldn't of put it past Duane to just blurt out that 'whore' comment to the judge. The man had no sense for the consequences of his actions, and he would surely have been feeling uncharitably toward Linda. I can see that. But him doing that, *and* Talley happening to be his lawyer? Well, it gets a body to thinking."

"Thinking what?"

"Thinking, Talley didn't have no money to start an oil business. And a patch of land on top of an oil reservoir ain't worth shit unless you can build the drills and pipes and whatnot and get the oil out."

I nodded. I wondered how much Tarwood knew.

He went on. "Now, all your banks and investment funds and such, they know a profitable thing when they see it. But they ain't just going to hand over a million dollars to a small-town lawyer who wants to be an oil baron." He paused, looked at me for confirmation. "Are they?"

I shook my head. "No, I don't think so."

"But someone *did*."

"Yes," I said, "someone did."

"And it wasn't no bank or investment fund, was it?"

"No," I said, "it wasn't."

"Now, I was a dumb kid, and I wouldn't have known what questions to ask or how to ask 'em," said Tarwood. "And I wasn't about to, either, because you know what Talley did with his first year's profits?"

I hazarded a guess. "Did it have something to do with you becoming the Mandanoches police chief?"

Tarwood nodded. "It wasn't quite as crude as that," he said. "Talley told me we'd have to take it a little bit slow. First thing he did, he put some money in the right pockets on the City Council. Got me hired on the force. Next thing, he bankrolls his own campaign, gets himself on the Council, keeps me movin' up through the ranks. Eventually the chief retires, he spreads the money around again, gets me appointed."

"What about Linda?"

"Oh, he took care of her. He let her stay in the house long as she wanted, hired her on at his company, paid her real well. Then he bought her a place in Mandanoches. He always told people he was taking special care of her, on account of the tragedy that had befallen her because of her drunken lout of a husband. Linda just...well, she sort of faded, you know? Just kind of disappeared into herself. I imagine it was a hundred times worse for her than it was for me. And for me? I almost didn't make it. I know I went entire years more or less in a blur. Stayed drunk most of the time, you know? Didn't matter none, long as the money came in. We hired folks to run the department for me."

"For twenty years?" I said.

"Oh, eventually I came out of it. I'd say the past fifteen years, I was a model small-town police chief. Talley's been off the council since 2000, and those fields haven't produced much since a few years before that. Tapped out again now, I reckon."

Maybe you reckon, I thought, but you reckon wrong. The Haynesville Shale held enough natural gas to mint millionaires for the next fifty years. It was 1973 all over again.

"Thing is," Tarwood said, "eventually I stopped being a dumb hick kid who couldn't think to ask questions. Eventually, I became quite proficient at asking questions. Asking them discreetly, too, if you understand my meaning."

"And?"

"And I kept coming back to the same question. What did Talley have to offer that would persuade some big unnamed East Coast *industrialist* to bankroll him in the oil business?"

He looked at me. I looked back at him.

"What could there be," he said, "what could there be in this world that he had to offer that a big unnamed East Coast industrialist might want, that he could not *buy?*"

I held his gaze. The story was true, so true. The husband and wife, the infertility, the yearning for a child, the need for secrecy—all true, all true, but true of a different family. Yes, the blue-blood Brideshead family had given Talley the money. That was true. But Harlan Brideshead was just passing it on from another blue-blood family. The blue-blood *Curtis* family, over on Fifth Avenue, on the other side of Central Park.

I said nothing.

Tarwood spat in the dust. "I'll tell you what Pops had to offer. He had a beautiful, healthy little girl, that's what he had. He had my Sue-Lynn. May his soul burn in hell."

He turned away from me, and I saw tears in his eyes again. "My little girl," he said. "Goddamn him. He told us she was *dead*."

"She's not dead," I said.

Tarwood grabbed the back of a bench and leaned over it, breathing heavily. I could hear him sobbing. I stood and waited. After a minute I said: "She's alive and well and she grew up just fine. She runs her own life and no one pushes her around."

Tarwood turned and nodded, thought that over. "I know," he said. "Least I thought so, anyway. Been reading about her for years, now. Five years or thereabouts, been checkin' up on her."

He looked at me, watching my face for a response, like a child holding up the watercolor she painted at school. I returned his gaze, thinking about the implications.

Finally I said, "You figured it out five years ago?"

Tarwood nodded and started walking again. "Some of it, anyway. Found out Talley's first seed money came from Harlan Brideshead. Found out the Bridesheads had a daughter, same age as Sue-Lynn. Found out the death certificate from the state hospital was bogus, or leastwise couldn't be verified no ways. Couldn't be sure of nothing, though. Not enough to tell Linda."

"So you never told her?"

"No, and I wasn't going to. She was...she was never the same person, quite, and I didn't know that it would do any good to stir up false hope. I also frankly was concerned that if I told her, she would shoot Pops between the eyes."

A reasonable fear, I thought, in hindsight.

"But then," said Tarwood, "last fall I had a little incident. A little scare, you might say. Minor heart attack. Made me think, you know. I had been watching Eleanor Hausman like she was a TV show. Easier now, you can just go on the internet and there she is. Your little girl, all grown up. It was sort of my own little fantasy world, 'cept it was *real*, you know? I mean, *she* was real—the fantasy part was imagining that she was my little Sue-Lynn. And it was like I knew just enough to believe halfway, but I didn't want to know any more, because I might find out it was all a dream."

He glanced sideways at me, as if to see if I understood what he meant. "But then?" I said.

"But then I'm lyin' there flat on my back in intensive care, in a paper robe with an IV in my arm, and I just think *fuck* it—if I'm going to die I want to die knowing it's her. And if it ain't her, why, then, I might as well just die anyway."

"So what did you do?"

"I called her. I mean, I didn't get through to her or nothing. I didn't expect to, and I don't believe I entirely wanted to, if you follow me. Half of me, I think, liked it better leaving it all as a maybe. You get my drift?"

"Yeah," I said. I got his drift. I knew how he felt because I'd heard people talk about feeling that way. But I never had. I'd never left anything as a maybe. Maybe I should have.

"Anyway, I called her company, and I got whoever I got, and I talked my way as far up the chain as I could and I left my message saying who I was and where I was from and that I thought maybe it was just possible that Ms. Hausman might be the girl that I was once a daddy to, long ago." He stopped, shook his head. "I reckon it sounded crazy, but I made them write it down and then I went back to wondering whether my heart was going to give out."

"I take it your heart's fine?" I said. Tarwood had had plenty of juice when he took me down with his shotgun butt.

"Oh, I reckon," he said. "Medicine, retirement, you know, I'll probably hit eighty. Point is I made my call and tried to forget it. But then I got a call from her lawyer."

"From Jennifer Curtis?"

"Yes, indeed. And she was quite interested in my story. Spent an hour on the phone with me. Asked a lot of questions. A lot of details. Made sense, I suppose. Woman like Eleanor Hausman's got to be careful. People probably try to scam her, that sort of thing. Anyway, the lawyer must have figured I was legit, because she told me to have Linda call her office if she wanted to talk."

"Did you?"

"I did. It was not an easy conversation. Linda and I had not been on the best of terms, these last few years. I thought when the time was right, you know, when she was ready, she'd talk to me. But then..."

"But then I showed up, and Linda put a bullet in Talley's head."

He nodded. "I suppose I bear some of the blame for that, making such a show of running you out of town. Too much of a show, I guess. I imagine Linda must have figured she'd have to do the job herself."

I took him roughly by the shoulder, spun him around. "I am not a goddamned contract killer. I shouldn't have to tell people that, like I told..." I stopped, felt my hand fall limply to my side. "Like I told her."

"Told her what?"

"Told her I wasn't a contract killer. At the coffee shop. Because the way she was talking, it sounded like...and so I told her, just like I told you. And she *laughed*."

Tarwood shook his head. "You couldn't have stopped her. It was too late by then. She'd already shot him. She wanted it to be her. No one but her."

"Well, why the hell didn't you say something on the damn car ride?"

Tarwood shrugged. "Could have been wrong. Not the sort of thing you just bring up with a new acquaintance, is it?"

"Well, you *are* wrong," I said.

"I'm retired," he said. "I don't care about how it happened. I was just trying to keep Linda clear of it. But Talley got what he deserved and Linda did what she had to do, and God rest her soul. My conscience is clear, Heaton. I didn't plant anything on you, I didn't falsify any reports, and I didn't bury any evidence."

No, I thought, you didn't bury any evidence. Except the fact that you gave the hit man's boss's number to the woman who wanted the victim dead. A jury might have found that a relevant fact.

I couldn't blame Tarwood. The pieces fit together easily enough. "You told her about Eleanor. You put her in touch with Eleanor's lawyer Jennifer Curtis, who just happened to be best known as the public face of a government assassination program—"

"Now hang on," he said. "Sure, I'd heard of Curtis. We watch the news, same as you. I knew who she was. I mean, I told Linda about her, I hoped it would make Linda believe me. Linda thought I was just crazy after the heart attack. So I said, 'No, this lawyer's the real deal, you can turn on CNN and see her for yourself.' It wasn't like I thought she was going to order a goddamn Predator drone strike or something."

No, no drone strikes. But death, one way or another. "And then I show up, and you assume—"

"I did what needed to be done," he said. "I knew Linda's mind would be set on revenge, and I could not let her spend the rest of her life in prison. If Sue-Lynn was alive, Linda needed to go to her, be a mother again. I told her that. I begged her. She said she couldn't let Pops walk away from this. And I told her—and I meant it—that if it came to it, I would do it myself. I wanted her nowhere near it. I'd make it clean and accidental, or a land dispute. Pops had plenty of those. It was easy enough to blow some rigs, cut some well lines, set the stage. I swore to her I would do what needed to be done. Keep her clear of it."

He trailed off, and we walked for half a block in silence.

I was pretty sure I knew the next part, too. "It wasn't enough, though, was it?" I said. "She didn't want to be clear of it. She didn't want it to be an accident or a land dispute. She needed it to be *her*."

He nodded, sadly.

"We forced her hand, didn't we?" I said, knowing it was true. "I showed up, and she thought I was going to kill Talley that night, and she'd lose her chance forever."

Tarwood didn't answer. He didn't need to.

He stopped walking and turned toward me. "Is she happy?" he asked.

"I think she is," I said, knowing he meant little Sue-Lynn, now grown up to be whoever she'd become. I realized with a jolt that it was a question I couldn't answer. About anyone. No one in this case was happy. Not Tarwood, for sure. Not Linda. Not Talley. Not Duane Hempersett. Not Silvio Angelides. And not Big Mike Settentio. Maybe Hausman was happy. But Tarwood's question wasn't about Hausman, though he thought it was. It was about J.C., who had actually been that little girl so long ago. Was she happy now? She was too much a force of nature to have emotions, as far as I could tell. But if she was going to show some happiness, she might show some on the day of her swearing-in as National Security Advisor. And Tarwood might see it and channel some of it to Linda, wherever she was.

"Tell you what," I said, "there's someone I'd like you to meet, while you're here. Special treat. I got us two tickets to the White House."

Fifty-Two

The swearing-in ceremony was held in the Rose Garden. Tarwood and I sat in the back and listened to the President praising J.C.'s dedication to public service, her work ethic, her courage, and her "unflinching commitment to accountability, transparency, and the rule of law."

His speechwriters were good, and the networks played the money shot at the end uncut:

For better or worse, as we work to forge a better world to bequeath to our children, we must face today's world with clear eyes and without fear. And there is violence in this world. There are those in this world who would attack us without a moment's hesitation, who would trample anyone and everyone standing in the way of their political ideology, their religious extremism, their military ambition. I pray that my children and grandchildren will inherit a world without these threats, but I am not foolish enough to imagine that that day will be tomorrow. And so tomorrow, and every day, as long as I am President, it is my duty to do everything in my power to protect my children and yours, from violence, from fear, and, yes, from evil. We must not turn our eyes away from what we see because we fear what we must do. It is a hard burden and sometimes a lonely burden. But I do not carry it alone. I carry it with a team of extraordinary and dedicated men and women who have devoted their careers to shouldering that burden. Today I turn to Jennifer Curtis to shoulder the burden once again, with me and with you. I am proud to say to the nation, to my children and yours, that in Jennifer Curtis you have a guardian, a guardian who does not turn her eyes away.

Later, Rachel Maddow gave a left-wing CliffsNotes summary: "Look, we kill people in secret, and we're by God going to keep doing it. But you're going to suck it up and go along with it because you can trust Jennifer Curtis to pick the targets. So stop carping at me, because the alternative would be a hell of a lot worse."

When the speeches were over, everyone stood up and began drifting away in different directions. The President smiled and waved and disappeared inside the White House. The reporters headed inside for the press office, or out front to where the networks had their cameras set up. The invited White House and Pentagon staff hustled back to whatever world crisis they were urgently monitoring. J.C. stood to one side of the lectern, with some new assistant I'd never seen before. A little receiving line formed in front of her, twenty or so people wanting to get in a moment's face time. J.C. stood, smiled, nodded, patted arms. I maneuvered Tarwood to the back of the line.

"I'm sure she'll want to thank you for reaching out," I said. "Eleanor means a lot to her."

The line moved slowly, but we were in no hurry. We were standing in the Rose Garden on a beautiful clear spring day. Tarwood kept his head on a swivel the whole time. I wondered if he'd voted for Hope and Change. Demographics and geography suggested no. But you never knew. And either way, he looked pretty damn thrilled to be there.

We finally made it up to J.C. The Rose Garden was mostly cleared out, and J.C.'s new assistant was scrolling through messages on her phone.

J.C. smiled warmly at me. "Marcus," she said, "thank you for everything. I'm so glad you could be here today."

"I'd like to introduce Chief Bobby Tarwood, of Mandanoches, Texas," I said.

Tarwood extended a hand. J.C. clasped it in both of hers. I looked down at their hands, hands that hadn't touched in thirty-five years. I wondered if tactile memory lingered after all that time, buried in the muscles and nerves and bones. I wondered what memories J.C. had of her first four years, and whether Tarwood was in them.

"Chief Tarwood was very close to Linda Waters," I said. "He was like a father to Sue-Lynn Hempersett. He's on his way to New York, to see Eleanor."

"That will be a joyous moment for you both," said J.C., still holding Tarwood's hand in both of hers.

"Yes, ma'am, it will," said Tarwood. "It'll be the best moment of my life. I feel like time stopped the day I lost her, and it's just about to start up again."

J.C. nodded. "I wish you all the happiness in the world. Eleanor is very dear to me."

"That little girl was my whole life," Tarwood said, beginning to tear up again. "My whole life, and they took her away from me. Now..." He stopped, looked down, wiped his eyes.

"Let us be thankful you've found her again," said J.C. She reached out and wrapped Tarwood in a hug, which he returned awkwardly. She held the hug, then lifted her head and whispered in his ear for a few moments. Then she pulled back. "Next time you're in DC, please get in touch," she said. She gestured to her hovering assistant. "Ashley will give you my number. I would love to hear all about the young Sue-Lynn." And with a final smile she was gone.

Fifty-Three

I found a garage for Tarwood's RV and put him on the Acela to New York, where Eleanor Hausman was waiting to play long-lost daughter. Not even playing, if I could believe J.C.: Hausman really believed that she was Sue-Lynn Hempersett. That was J.C.'s gift to Eleanor—the tragic, romantic life story she'd always wanted. That and a hundred million dollars of recoverable shale gas.

Bobby Tarwood would believe, too, because he wanted to believe. He shook my hand at Union Station with the beatific smile of a pilgrim rounding the bend on the last hill up to Our Lady of Lourdes. What was behind that smile I'll never know. I just knew I'd never seen it in the mirror. I thought about reaching into my pocket and handing him the envelope with the photos and the lock of hair. But I didn't. They would only plant seeds of doubt in Tarwood's dream of redemption. And who was I to do that? His dream was beautiful and pure, and even partly true.

I'll never know what J.C. whispered in Tarwood's ear in the Rose Garden. I'll never know what she said to Linda Waters, those late nights on the phone. Linda died knowing her daughter had grown up to be rich, powerful, and beautiful. But whether she thought little Sue-Lynn had grown up to be Eleanor Hausman or Jennifer Curtis, I'll never know. And I don't want to know, either. For the first time in my professional life, I'm leaving some maybes on the table. And I'm okay with that.

In the end what I did know was plenty. I knew that Eleanor Hausman was going to make a lot of money on Talley's gas fields. I knew that a long time ago, on some nowhere farm in some nowhere corner of Louisiana, some people made some bad choices, and they all paid for it. And I knew that J.C. got what she wanted. She cleaned up the loose ends that could have derailed her cabinet appointment, and she brought Talley and Angelides to justice. If gods stood up for bastards maybe she wouldn't have needed to. But she waited thirty years and no gods stood up. Maybe the only justice for bastards is when they figure that out. No gods are going to stand up for them, so they had better stand up for their damn selves.

And me? I walked back out onto the Mall and looked north along the Ellipse, up the wide expanse of green to the White House. J.C.'s new office would be in there somewhere, stocked with a new crew of Bright Young Things, and as many tough guys on her speed dial as she'll ever need. She won't need broken ex-cops like Marcus Heaton and Mike Settentio anymore. We'll fade away with our own forgotten secrets.

I never told J.C. I'd found Duane Hempersett in Florida. Maybe she knew. Maybe she guessed who "Sample 3" in Mo Faizalla's lab was. Or maybe she'd found him long before.

Maybe the fact that he was still alive was all the answer I needed. Maybe she felt sorry for him. Or maybe she liked the thought of him sitting there in the red dirt by his trailer in a single lawn chair, reliving his weakness and wondering why he had never stood up for himself. Maybe she didn't care one way or another.

I'll probably never find out. I don't work for her anymore. But she has my number.

AFTERWORD

Stand Up For Bastards is a work of fiction. I made up the characters and the plot. I'm not Marcus Heaton or John Scofield. But the characters and events in the book are the *kind* of people and the *kind* of events that exist, and happen, in the professional world where I work. The real things that real people do in real cases are as crazy, disturbing, depressing, and inspiring as anything a writer can invent.

If you're someone who cares about whether the novels you read are bullshit or not, I want you to know that this book is inspired by my own career doing a lot of the things you just read about. I've investigated, prosecuted and defended all manner of cases—violent crimes, frauds, drug crimes, gun crimes, property crimes, sex crimes, civil disputes over contracts, money, property, inheritances, you name it. I spend my time with people on all sides of the business: cops and agents, judges, prosecutors and defense counsel, defendants and victims.

What I and thousands of other people like me do for a living every day is try to get justice for our clients in court, one case at a time. That client might be the United States of America, as it was for me when I was a federal prosecutor; it might be a company or a union, as it is in most of my civil cases; or in criminal defense, which is the majority of my practice, it's an individual facing the loss of all he or she has in the world—liberty, job, money, reputation—an individual suddenly up against the full might of the government.

I spend my time trying to help people with problems. Usually the problem people come to me with is that they've been charged with a serious crime, and usually that's the biggest problem they've ever had. I have a lot of conversations with people on the worst day of their life.

This past year, I defended a 74-year old corporate charter pilot who was charged in a big multi-defendant drug trafficking and money-laundering case when it turned out that one of his charter clients—who presented himself to the world as a cocky tech entrepreneur and night-club investor—was actually making his money smuggling cocaine in his luggage on his private jet flights around the country.

My client, the pilot, was a Navy veteran who built his house with his own two hands and was raising his great-granddaughter there with his wife of 50 years. The government was threatening a ten-year mandatory prison term. That'd be a death sentence. And he wasn't a drug smuggler. So we went to trial. For eight weeks, in Kentucky, during the spring of 2020. It was the only federal trial that didn't stop for the coronavirus shutdown. At the end of the trial we stood up and listened to the jury say "Not guilty," and my client went home to his family.

A case like that takes about a year from start to finish. Every case is a story worth telling. At any given time, I am working on ten to twenty cases. I also sit as a Commissioner on the civilian oversight commission for the police department in the city where I live, and as you can imagine, 2020 has been an interesting year to be in the civilian oversight business. And I'm a Judge Pro Tempore on the Los Angeles County Superior Court. Every couple weeks, I go in, put on the robe, and hear cases. Mostly traffic trials and other minor infractions. I start every sitting by thanking everyone in the courtroom for respecting our legal system, coming to court and exercising their rights. And I mean it every time. Then they tell me their stories, and I try to do justice in their cases.

I believe in the ideal of justice and the possibility of realizing that ideal through the legal system. When Scofield tells Heaton he jogs around the National Mall and gazes at the monuments without irony and comes back with renewed belief in the ideals of justice and the Constitution, that's me. My trial-team supervisor at the U.S. Attorney's Office would tell us, when we went to her with some conundrum or other in a case, "Go in there and do justice." By which she meant: sometimes the law and the evidence and the Department policies and the Sentencing Guidelines and whatever other legal authorities you're looking at for guidance don't give you a clear answer. That's why *you're* here. That's why we run our justice system with human beings and empower them to make choices. We pick those people carefully and instill in them a belief in justice, fairness, and constitutional norms. And right now that person is *you*, and you have a tough choice to make. No one else is going to make it for you, and these books and papers can't make it for you. So go in there and do justice in your case.

She really meant it, and I really believed it. The criminal justice system is full of rules and guidelines and policies that limit discretion, but in every case there are choices that have to be made by people, and those people need to believe in the ideal of justice and fairness, if we're going to give them the power to prosecute criminal offenses and seek to deprive people of their liberty. And we do: the prosecutors and public defenders and hundreds of other people I've worked with over the years in the cops-and-robbers business do this work day in and day out because we believe that it's necessary if we want to live in a just and decent country.

But the legal system is far from perfect, and the best detective fiction—I'm thinking about Raymond Chandler, Ross Macdonald, James Ellroy, or Walter Mosely—explores its failures, blind spots, and cracks. You see those every day in this line of work, in your own cases, and in the cases you read about in reported decisions. One of the cases that inspired this book is the *Kirchberg v. Feenstra* case that Talley and J.C. tell Marcus about. It's a real case. Type "450 U.S. 455" into Google and you can read it yourself. It's a heartbreaking story: In Louisiana, in the early 1970s, a woman named Joan Feenstra owned a house as joint community property with her husband Harold. But according to state law Harold was the "head and master" of the house, because he was the man. Being "head and master" meant that Harold was allowed to "encumber" the property without Joan's consent or knowledge. "Encumber" means "use as collateral for a loan." "Collateral" is the thing the lender gets to take if you don't pay your loan back.

In 1974, Joan accused Harold of molesting their daughter. Harold went to see a local defense attorney, Karl Kirchberg. Kirchberg said sure, I'll defend you, for $3000. Harold didn't have the money, but Kirchberg took a note with a lien on the Feenstra house as collateral. Neither one of them told Joan. A few months later, Joan dropped her complaint against Harold, and the criminal charges were dismissed.

Harold left the state and disappeared, without paying Kirchberg's bill. So Kirchberg called up Joan: pay me three grand, or I'm taking your house.

You can read more of my thoughts about that case—and a bunch of other cases that inspired scenes and characters in the book—on the *Stand Up For Bastards* website, standupforbastards.com. Here's what I'll say about *Kirchberg* here: As you know, since you just read the book, the Supreme Court held that the Louisiana "head-and-master" encumbrance rule was unconstitutional, but that there would be no retroactive application of the holding, and thus no remedy for anyone other than Joan Feenstra.

The Louisiana state legislature got rid of the rule in 1980, so there were no more head-and-master liens after that. But there were plenty of prior ones, and the Supreme Court left all those untouched. I remember reading that case and wondering what it would have been like to be one of those *other* victims of the head-and-master rule, those other foreclosures that the Court left in place—being told that you had been wronged, but that the justice system was not going to stand up for you. How would it feel to be the last victim of a nonconsensual head-and-master mortgage, hearing from the highest court in the land that what was done to you was totally wrong, immoral, and unconstitutional—but that *you* are out of luck?

That was a long time ago. I worked on the book a little at a time over more than a decade, and it reflects my work and experiences and observations over the years. I wrote most of it by hand, in spiral notebooks and legal pads, at night in hotel rooms when I was travelling or on the train commuting to work in LA. By the time I finished it, I was a different guy from who I was when I started it. My experiences and perspective on the law grew over time, and I had to go back and rewrite most of it. I did that four or five times, and it wasn't until 2020 that I finally sold the manuscript.

Here's the guy I am now: I am grateful every day that I get to go into court and try to do justice for people, one case at a time. I mean that, no irony whatsoever. In a hundred other ways I am more cynical and jaded than I was when I got into this business. But on that one point—

that in this country, you can get up in the morning and go into court and seek justice, and get up the next day and do it again when you get knocked down—I am a no-bullshit true believer. If you're a law student or young lawyer wondering whether to try to get into litigation, give me a call—you read my book, so the least I can do is talk with you about your career. And if you're in LA, I'll buy you a drink. My office is across the street from the Standard.

One more thing: yes, I have indeed brought my clarinet to crime scenes; and walked into the Federal Building with the clarinet in its case and had the security guys ask whether I'd just bought a fancy new handgun; and played it late at night in empty marble courthouses and on the Santa Monica Pier and in the Sculpture Garden on the Mall in DC and a hundred other places around the country. And I'm still waiting for the perfect briefcase.   —*Los Angeles, CA, December 2020*

The author, as a young federal prosecutor, at a gig after work.

Read on for an excerpt from the upcoming novel

WARM AMONG ICE

When I got there, the body was still lying where it fell. I wasn't surprised. The client called his lawyer first thing. His lawyer called my boss, who called me. I was rolling within five minutes of the body hitting the pavement, and I was close. Marina del Rey to Malibu's a breeze at 2 a.m.

My boss tapped me because I was close to the scene, I knew my way around a homicide, and I was likely to be up. I was. There was a perfect moon and the sea lions were having a party on the boat ramp over in the park across the channel. I was sitting on the deck of my boat, tipped back in a lawn chair, listening to the chorus. I never got tired of the sea lion parties. Or the moon, or the fog on the water.

I stubbed out my cigar, threw a salute across the channel to the sea lions, and walked down the dock and up the ramp to my motorcycle. One of the perks of having a bike—you always get the best spot in the lot.

The boat and the bike were mine, the most expensive things I'd ever owned. They'd belonged to my old NYPD buddy Frankie Muller, but he hadn't used them in years, and never would again. Frankie had taken a bullet at close range. He wanted me to have them because I had saved his life. I wanted to pay him, because he had saved mine. Both perspectives were true, making the final valuation kind of iffy, as an accounting matter.

I took the 405 up to the 10, and west to the Pacific Coast Highway. Traffic was light. I took the tunnel under the bluffs and came out at the Santa Monica Pier, then veered north up toward the big western curve that wraps around the last tongue of the mountains as they plunge down into the sea. I gunned it and leaned in past Will Rogers Beach. Around the bend the road turned north again and I saw the flashing lights up ahead.

The red and blue made a nice purple if you squinted a little, and the light bounced off the mountain wall on the east side of the road and out across the stone breakwater down into the Pacific. The water was lit up by the moon, a bright trail of white pointing west out toward Catalina. I didn't see any midnight surfers, but there were probably some out there, daring the nocturnal sharks to launch upward at their moonlit silhouettes.

I'd done it myself a few times over the years, during my on-again intervals with Heather Cusamano. Heather was a CPA, an ex-Fed, and a water-sports connoisseur. "You're an adrenaline junkie, Marcus, you'll love it," she said, the first time. I wasn't sure why she thought that. We hadn't known each other that well then, and I hadn't told her much about my past. Maybe she could smell it.

I'd never surfed in my life, but I paddled out with her under the moon and sat there with her on the swells out past the breakers, my feet dangling in the water like two delicious seal flippers, looking out into the endless Pacific with its westward trail of moonlight.

When Heather whirled and paddled to catch a wave, I stayed put. The wave washed past us, she disappeared, and I bobbed there feeling the silence descend on me and, with it, the primal dread of a prey animal in a hunting ground.

I felt the dread rise from my bait-dangling toes up to my brain, pulsing like a nicotine rush. I let it wash through my brain, taking over my senses, turning every dark ripple into a fin, every tug of current into the slipstream of a great gray body sliding under the board on reconnaissance.

I lay forward on the board and dangled all four limbs, a full seal now, floating on the surface, floodlit by the moon. I put my face an inch from

343

the water and stared down. I could see the dark shape emerge from the depths; I could see the mouth open beneath me, feel each second ticking by as my last one.

I felt the panic rise in the back corners of my brain, pushing out all other input until the world narrowed into the black cone of water under my board. My fists clenched; my right drew back, cocked, coiled, ready to strike. I counted to ten, focusing my eyes down into the blackness, feeling nothing but the pulse of blood in my temples, the rush of adrenaline—purer, older, infinitely more powerful than sex. Heather was right. I loved it. I wanted more.

I pulled over and sat on my bike and looked out at the water, remembering. It was a long time ago, now, that first night on the water. I waited for Heather to paddle back out, let her guide me onto a wave, rode it in on my belly—no shame in not popping up, at midnight with no audience—and stood dripping with her on the beach, looking out at the water.

She leaned into me. "I knew you'd feel it," she said. "That moment, right when the wave catches you, when you move into it, you feel it with your whole body..."

I didn't say anything. We'd almost shared the moment. Almost, but not quite. Heather had just made love to the sea god. I had just punched a shark.

I squeezed the clutch, popped it down into first, and rolled up PCH toward the lights. It must have been twenty minutes since the call went out, but the response had been slow. The only cops on scene were patrol guys, two solo cruisers parked about fifty yards on either side of the crash site, a CHP car on the south side and what looked like a Sheriff's vehicle up on the north end. They'd planted magnesium flares in the traffic lanes. The flares were glowing red-white and hissing like a bed of coals in a cold rain.

I saw the lone deputy up on the north side waving off traffic, turning cars back up toward Topanga. They'd have to go all the way up the canyon and back down on the 101. That would be a long detour into Santa Monica—probably some pissed-off southbound drivers up there. The deputy would be busy until some more units arrived. There was no northbound traffic. I pulled up on the shoulder by the CHP cruiser in the middle of the road. I didn't see the officer by the cruiser. I looked up the road and saw a flashlight beam over on the shoulder of the northbound lanes, where the mountain came down in a steep wall of dirt and scrub that rose straight up from the shoulder at sixty or seventy degrees.

I looked left. There, on the west side of the road, was the Pacific Lounge, on everyone's annual top-ten list for the fanciest restaurants in LA. It was set out on a nub of land that projected out into the ocean, a semicircle of rock fifty yards in diameter. You had ocean views on three sides in there. The bar was right in the center of the floor, so the bartenders had a better office view than the bigwigs who came there for late, boozy business dinners. A lot of deals closed at the Pacific Lounge. It was like the old Palm steakhouse back in the day. I liked the Palm. I'd even eaten there a couple times: steak, potatoes, martinis. I had not been to the Pacific Lounge—I didn't have an expense account for a thousand dollar dinner—but my new client was evidently a regular.

Tom Jarron, the president of CenterPoint Investigative Solutions, and my boss, had given me a few details on the phone. The client was Paul Mayo, a medium-grade A&R suit at one of the entertainment conglomerates. He'd been having a nice suit dinner at the Lounge, getting some suit business done. Business must have been good, because the dinner had stretched past midnight. Around 1:30, they'd all given each other firm executive handshakes and hit the valet desk by the front door. I scoped the layout: the customer would come out and wait under the big blue awning in front of the door, by a bamboo latticework overflowing with some kind of flowering vine.

Next to the valet desk was a bright blue couch upholstered in what looked like velvet. I wondered how it handled the fog. You'd come out after your dinner and sit there while the valet trotted off to your Tesla or your Range Rover out in the parking lot. The parking lot was a triangular gravel space on the south side of the restaurant, pressing up against the guardrail of the southbound lanes of the PCH.

The valet would pull your car around, and you'd get in and nose up to the ornate white entrance gate and look out into the traffic on the

PCH. You'd look left, right, left, and then you'd floor it and hope for the best. The PCH was notorious for its speeders, and the nearest stoplight was half a mile north, at the bottom of Topanga. You'd be okay if you were making a right to go back into Santa Monica, but if you were headed to Malibu or up Topanga Canyon to Mulholland or Calabasas or the Palisades, you'd be looking for an opening to make the left. A left turn onto the PCH across southbound traffic would be dicey—two lanes to get across before you reached the safety of the center turning lane that ran between the four traffic lanes, and the sight line north was less than a hundred yards, as the road curved back to the right, hugging the sheer face of the mountain.

The right turn was easier, but then you'd be stuck southbound all the way to Santa Monica before you could turn around and come back north to Topanga Canyon. At eight or nine, with the PCH humming, you'd just make the right and eat the extra fifteen minutes. But 1:30 a.m, with the road looking clear, the left turn beckoned. So Mayo had gone for it. There was his BMW, planted there in the middle of the turning lane like a center divider, facing northbound, lined up perfectly with the yellow stripes.

Mayo hadn't seen the motorcycle coming southbound, leaning hard into the turn around the mountain's shoulder and gunning it down the straightaway in front of the Pacific Lounge. I looked over at the flashlight beam on the northbound shoulder and saw the CHP officer. He was standing over a lumpy shape on the ground, talking into his radio. The beam was pointed at the ground. It didn't come up and point at me. I didn't see anyone else.

I crossed the gravel lot and walked up to the Lounge entrance. No one around. I hit the door and took in the scene. There in the anteroom by the maître d's desk, on another blue velvet couch, was my client, for sure: alone, and giving off the unmistakable vibe of a guy who just killed someone and isn't used to it. I tried to remember the feeling. It was buried in there somewhere, but it came through muffled, like your neighbor's radio heard faintly through the wall.

Mayo looked up when I walked in, read "cop," and visibly steeled himself. He blew out a breath, squared his shoulders, and straightened up on the bench. He was a good-looking middle-aged executive: expensive suit, big shiny watch, perfect hair, fit like a dutiful runner. LA suit culture mandated that you take care of yourself.

He cleared his throat. "Officer, I—"

I cut him off with a finger to my lips. "Hang on a sec."

I stepped past him, took a look inside the main dining room. Dark, empty. There was a hallway to the right, behind the bar, with light spilling out from a doorway partway down it. I turned back to Mayo and took out a card.

"Marcus Heaton, CenterPoint Solutions," I said. "I'm your guy. Dorsey called us." Brian Dorsey was Mayo's attorney, the guy who'd called Tom Jarron.

Mayo looked like I'd just written him a triple-weight bonus check. "Oh, thank God," he said. "They told me...they said...*hom*icide? He's dead... I...I *saw* him."

"Shh," I said. "Not so loud. Who else is in here?"

"I...I'm not sure. The manager, I guess. The bartender? The valets? I don't know."

"What about your friends? You were here with?"

"Left before me. I saw them off."

"You guys closed down the place?"

"Yeah. Is that bad?"

"Maybe good, maybe bad. Simplifies things, anyway. Did you speak to anyone?"

"You mean, after...?"

"I mean like those two officers out there on the PCH?"

"Two? I only saw one."

"CHP or Sheriff?"

"I'm not sure."

"You talk to him?"

"Yeah! I mean, I called 911, right? First thing. I was alone out there, then the valet came over, and—"

"The cop. What did you tell him?"

"That I just pulled out and 'Bam!' Out of nowhere. Just like a bright flash of light and this big thud—it shook the whole car."

"Did he ask if you'd been drinking?"

"No! I wasn't! I mean, like a glass of wine three hours ago, maybe, but—"

"Did he ask if you were on your phone?"

"No, and I wasn't. I—"

"Give me your phone."

He reached for his pocket, obeying instinctively, then hesitated. "Wait, are you sure? I mean, I need it..."

"Look," I said, "we have maybe five minutes if we're lucky, and I need to get to the scene outside. Now give me the damn phone."

He looked at me blankly. I wondered if he thought I was going to destroy it—grind it under my bootheel or wipe it with some James Bond portable electromagnet. It was a natural enough impulse on his part, I supposed. You get in trouble, you make a call, and then a big guy in a leather jacket shows up and makes it all go away. But it was idiotic to think I was going to destroy his phone. The usage data was already in the phone company servers. I just needed to know what I was dealing with.

"Relax," I said, holding up my hands—see, no electromagnets! "I'm not going to throw it in the ocean."

He handed me the phone, still looking uncertain.

"Unlock it."

He did, and I pulled up his text log. Nothing later than 1:05. That was good. I took out my camera and took a photo of the screen. Then the call log. I snapped another photo, looked down the log. There was the 911 call at 1:34. The last one before that was midnight. Also good. I held the screen out, pointed at the call.

"Who's that?"

He looked. "Uh...client, maybe?" I filed the answer away. A problem maybe, but not an immediate homicide problem.

"Email." I thumbed the Outlook icon, pulled up "sent," snapped a picture. Nothing since eight.

"Any other email? Personal?"

"Yeah, but..."

I ignored him, found a Gmail icon, pulled it up, and took a photo. Nothing since the afternoon.

"Mr. Mayo, no one cares about the what. Get it? Just the *when*. This is all good news for us here. Repeat after me: when you pulled out onto the road, you were not on your phone, you were not texting, you were not on email. You were not using your phone at all. It was in your jacket pocket. In about five minutes the police are going to seize your phone, and I needed to know whether what is in your phone is consistent with that statement."

He nodded weakly.

I gave him his phone. "Did you blow?"

"Did I what?"

"Did the officer administer a Breathalyzer? Make you blow into a tube?"

"No."

"They will."

"Should I refuse? I mean, I can, right?"

"Last drink?"

"Wine! Like I said! A glass, like 9, 9:30."

"Cocktail? After-dinner drink?"

"No! I mean, well, Corey ordered these horrible coffee things, for the table, but one sip, and I'm like, 'No, thank you.'"

"Did you tell this to Dorsey?"

"Yes."

"What'd he say?"

"He said take the Breathalyzer. He said if I refuse, they can use that against me in court, and they'll get a warrant for blood."

"Then do what he says. He's your lawyer."

"But he's not a *criminal* lawyer. I mean, I don't *have* a criminal lawyer."

"He's right anyway," I said. "Is he coming?"

"I think so. He said he'd try to get here, but he's coming from La Cañada." Which meant a long haul down the 101. But police response was looking slow this evening. Maybe it was a busy night.

"He called a bail bondsman, I think," said Mayo. "And he called you."

I thought for a moment. "Okay," I said. "Don't talk to anyone else. And come outside with me, and sit on the bench where I can see you." I didn't want to leave Mayo inside the restaurant with the manager. If the manager wanted to throw Mayo under the bus, he could have Mayo flapping his lips or tearfully confessing. Or running to the bathroom to vomit. Which wouldn't work anyway, but a lot of people thought it would. And I didn't know where the restaurant management would be on this. Or the bartender. Maybe Mayo and his pals had been assholes, or light tippers.

I also didn't know what the bill would show. "You have the check?"

"No, Corey paid. He—"

"He from your company?"

"No, he's at Paramount."

"Key?"

"It's, uh, here." He reached in his pocket, pulled out a black plastic rectangle with the Beamer logo on it. "It's proximity, you know? You push the starter, it senses if the key's in the car."

I held out a hand. He gave me the key. I wondered if he thought I was going to drive off with the car.

"All right, come on," I said. I opened the door and gestured Mayo out to the valet area.

"Sit," I said, pointing to the couch under the flower-covered trellis. He sat.

I turned and walked back across the gravel toward the entrance gate. The fog was rolling in now from the Pacific, dropping the air temperature ten degrees in an instant. I called Jarron.

"You got the reconstruction guy coming?" I asked.

"En route," he said. "Probably a couple minutes out. What's your status?"

"On scene," I said. "Client's good, hasn't blown yet, no interview. Slow response, looks like. Just two solo patrol guys, directing traffic."

"Is he sober?"

"Looks like it, says he is. I have him where I can keep an eye on him. Which way is our guy coming?"

"From Santa Monica."

"Can you call him, tell him to pull over south of the parked CHP car and walk up on the southbound shoulder? He could probably just waltz right up to the car. No one's near it, they haven't taped it off, nothing. Key'll be in the car, it should have power."

"Ten-four," said Jarron, and hung up.

Accident reconstruction was about as scientifically precise as forensics got. You looked at the aftermath of a collision between two objects and tried to run the clock backward and figure out who hit what where, at what speed and vector. Turns out that the laws of physics make that kind of calculation pretty reliable in a lot of crashes, if you document the scene before everything's moved or washed away. There were a lot of variables that a smart reconstructionist could measure and use: vehicle locations and orientation, magnitude of damage, length of skid marks, amount of moisture on the road surface, sight lines around curves and through fog, and, for motorcycle accidents, "vault distance"—the distance between the impact site and the resting place of the body. So our first priority in a crash case was to get someone out to the scene to make a record of everything. Maybe CHP would get around to it later, but the name of the game in defense investigation is to do the police's job faster and better than they do.

And accident reconstruction had taken a giant step forward in precision, the past few years. The reconstructionists hadn't gotten any smarter, but the cars had. Mayo had been driving a late-model, luxury European sedan. It had enough computing power in it to run the trading operations for a midsize brokerage. It knew, down to the millisecond and millimeter, where it was in the world; how fast it was moving; what its engine, tires, gears, and brakes were doing; and—most importantly—the precise amount of force imparted at the moment of impact onto the array of pressure sensors embedded all around its body, under its glistening black shell. It probably had forward-looking video and maybe radar, too, for the automatic-braking collision-avoidance system that came standard nowadays with the leather seats and walnut paneling.

Which meant that our accident reconstruction was going to be a lot less about tape measures and skid marks and coefficient-of-friction estimates, and a lot more about plugging into the car's brain and tapping into that mother lode of data. For a more-or-less head-on collision like this, if you knew the speed of the car at impact and the amount of force of the impact, then you just plug in the weight of the motorcycle and you'd know exactly how fast the motorcycle was going. You didn't have to *reconstruct* what happened to the car if the car fucking *remembered* it.

The car stored all that memory in a unit called an Event Data Recorder. Like a black box on a jetliner. Thing was, to get that EDR data you had to plug a special download box into the car's computer. You couldn't—for some reason known only to the car manufacturers—just use the USB port on your phone. And you couldn't access it remotely. You had to use a big box that cost ten grand and came in a bright-yellow, foam-lined plastic case the size of an ice chest.

The download only took a minute, but our reconstruction guy would have to get into the car and plug his unit into the access port under the steering column. Which he couldn't do if the cops taped off the scene and impounded the car. If they did that, then we'd have to wait until CHP got around to downloading it, a week or a month or a year later, and then wait some more while the DA got around to producing it in discovery in the manslaughter case.

If CHP dragged their heels, you could get a court order allowing you access. The Penal Code was strict about guaranteeing a defendant's access to evidence. But you couldn't get your order until your guy *was* a defendant: he had to be charged and arraigned, so you had a case number and a judge to hear your motion. That made for a nice Catch-22 if the download was going to prove that your guy was stone-cold innocent, going ten miles an hour, and hit by a bike going ninety. You had to get charged in order to prove that you shouldn't be charged. You couldn't get the evidence until all the real legal damage was already done: the homicide charge, the headlines, the corporate ass-covering, your client out of a job, and the personal-injury sharks circling for the civil suit.

But the car wasn't taped off yet, and Mayo hadn't been arrested. The car wasn't the People's evidence yet, and until it was—until a cop strung the yellow tape around the car and pushed my ass away from it, one hand on my chest and the other on his holster—until *then*, it was still Mayo's property. And there was no legal reason in the world why he couldn't plug into its mainframe and find out what it knew. And if we could find out what it knew now, we could maybe persuade the DA not to file charges at all and stop the evidentiary Catch-22 from ever getting started. Which meant that the next five minutes were make-or-break for Paul Mayo's career, and maybe his life.

I looked south. I saw distant headlights coming up the PCH, and somewhere behind them, faint and still unseen, I heard a siren. I turned and ran my eyes down the northbound shoulder. The CHP guy was still kneeling next to the body. The body was at least a hundred feet down the road from the BMW and all the way over on the cliff wall, and the fog was getting thicker. I walked out into the road and took a look at Mayo's car. Mayo had left the driver's door open. I tossed the key onto the front seat and walked around to the front of the car.

The front fender was bent into an obtuse angle, maybe 100, 120 degrees. The windshield was unscathed. The impact was dead center. The frame was bent all the way back into the engine block. The bike was there, too—what was left of it. It was on its side, a few feet to the right of the car, half in the center left-turn lane and half in the inner northbound lane. The front of the bike—wheel, forks, handlebars—was completely gone. CHP would bag the pieces, which would be stretched out in an expanding V down the road southbound, way past the body. Some of the pieces would probably never be found.

The rear half, the half lying there on the pavement, was mostly intact. It was a Harley, a big one. It would have had metal saddlebags, but they were completely sheared off, probably fifty feet down the road somewhere in the dark. It was pretty clear what had happened. The biker was going fast, flying down the PCH in the moonlight the way bikers had been doing for the last half century. He was leaning in, cutting the curves inside using the center turning lane. He'd come around the bend past Topanga, seen the straight stretch opening up down toward Will Rogers Beach and Santa Monica, and gunned it. One more curve now, lean left into it, feel the centripetal forces pulling you out, out, out toward the stone breakwater and the ocean, resist the pull, lean harder, cut it in just a little more, to that sweet spot in the center turning lane, feel the bike making it, staying balanced, and then... And then there's a car there, and you're dead.

353

It would have been an eyeblink, at any decent speed, and judging from the shape the bike was in, its speed had been more than decent. The guy had gunned it around the curve with a sight line way less than his reaction time. He'd probably done it a hundred times before. Stupid every time. Lucky until this time.

I walked over toward the CHP officer and the body on the northbound shoulder. I walked up deliberately loud, my bootheels crunching the plastic debris strewn on the pavement between us. I counted my steps from the car to the body: forty-three. I was no expert, but 130 feet from the impact point was a long way to fly.

"You call the ME?" I said, loud and cop-voiced.

The officer turned and half straightened, reflexively deferential to authority. He kept his flashlight pointed down and didn't beam me in the face. That was a good sign.

"Yeah, and they're taking their damn time too." He gestured down at the man's chest. "I tried CPR, but it's like every bone in there is broken. Heard 'em snapping, first compression."

"DOA?" I said.

He shrugged. It was pretty obvious.

"You got your light?" I said.

He shone his flashlight on the body. No doubt. The man's head was at a sharp angle from his shoulders, and his limbs were splayed in an unnatural way that would have triggered a wave of nausea in someone who hadn't seen it before. The man's face was ghostly white. He'd probably severed an artery internally. And there was a glistening, dark-red pool of blood extending out in a semicircle from the back of his head.

We stood together and looked for a few seconds. He pointed at the tiny, beanie-like helmet the man was wearing.

"Skid lid," he said.

"Yeah."

"Don't do shit."

"Yeah." Skid lids were thin helmets of sheet metal with no padding. They were not approved by the state Department of Transportation, with good reason: they provided no protection in a crash. I'd seen the training videos—you put a watermelon in a standard, full-face helmet and drop it from ten feet. Nothing. Undented, no mess. Then you put the melon in a skid lid, same drop. It shatters like you hit it with a base-ball bat.

A DOT-approved helmet is full of a compressible foam that absorbs impact. A piece of sheet metal, on the other hand, transfers all the im-pact force straight through into your head.

The guy was wearing jeans, boots, gloves, and a flannel shirt under a leather vest—a "cut." No patches or lettering that I could see, which was good for Paul Mayo. You didn't want to be on the other side of a crash that killed a Hell's Angel or a Mongol, or one of the many lesser motorcycle-club tribes that prowled SoCal.

"Got an ID?" I asked.

"Not yet."

"Well, why don't we check his pockets. At least get a name for the ME." *And for me.*

He nodded, squatted down at the guy's waist, and fished in the front jeans pocket, where you could see the wallet outline. I squatted down behind him, next to the head. While he was fumbling for the wallet, I reached in my pocket, pulled out a Kleenex in a plastic baggie, soaked the Kleenex in the freshly pooled blood, and bagged and pocketed it.

The cop straightened up holding a brown leather wallet, opened it, and extracted a driver's license.

"Walter Jeffrey Manziel," he said. "DOB 6/20/85."

I pulled my notebook and jotted it down while he finished his sur-vey of the wallet.

"Couple hundred cash," he reported, "no credit cards." He put the wallet in a clear plastic bag, with the license on the outside of the wal-let so the medical examiners would see it. Then he set the bag on the dead man's chest and straightened up.

"You County or what?" he asked, sizing up our respective rungs on the ladder. As a uniformed CHP guy, he'd be below pretty much any-one who rolled in plainclothes.

"Retired," I said. "I'm private now. CenterPoint Solutions. This one could be a touch high profile."

I could have gotten the bum's rush off the street right there, with some choice words about contaminating the scene. I didn't. Every cop with twenty years in is thinking about his retirement, and this guy was probably older than me. He knew all about CenterPoint. Gateway to the post-retirement promised land. I could see the realization hit him like a fist to the jaw. Did he want to land $50-an-hour gigs escorting starlets up and down Topanga on shoots? Or get time-and-a-half sitting out all night at craft services drinking coffee with the rig drivers, while the director kept everyone waiting for that perfect dawn light?

You bet he did. And here I was, the guy with the golden ticket, just strolling up and introducing myself. He wasn't about to push me off the street.

"Yeah," he said, "yeah, CenterPoint. The perp—the, uh, the other driver—he's a client?"

"He is," I said. "He's also stone sober and totally broken up about this. He's not used to death." *Not,* the implied flattery went, *like you and me.*

I pulled a card. "Marcus Heaton," I said. "Nice to meet you."

He took the card and admired it. It was a nice card. Heavy stock, glossy finish, embossed logo. I let my gaze drift down the road toward the flashing lights of his cruiser. I saw a figure walking up along the far shoulder, carrying a large briefcase. Five minutes tops for the download, usually closer to one, Jarron had said.

The cop pulled out his wallet and gently inserted my card, then fished lamely in his pockets, as if looking for a card of his own. He didn't find one.

"Peter Larisse," he said finally, extending a hand.

I noted his name solemnly in my notebook as he spelled it for me. "How many years you got in, Peter?"

"Ten here. Seven other-agency credit. Used to be Border Patrol."

"No shit? Where at?"

"San Diego sector. East of the city mostly. Otay Mesa, Tecate. All the way out to Yuma."

"Any fun?"

He shrugged. "Sometimes. Action came and went, you know? You could go 100 bodies on a shift, then nothing for a week."

"Bodies" meaning live people, I knew, migrants crossing the border heading north. Jailers talked that way too—"Friggin' transport this morning? Twenty bodies and the goddamn holding cell's full. Had to chain 'em in the fucking hallway." I'd never picked up the habit, probably because I'd made detective early on and had never had to work in a lockup. To a homicide detective, "body" meant a dead body, like the one in the road in front of us.

"Not as violent as this, though, huh?" I gestured at the plastic debris scattered around us, glinting in the harsh magnesium flare light.

He laughed. "Fuckin' A. This has got to be the deadliest fucking stretch of highway this side of fucking Kuwait."

"Desert Storm?" I asked. The "Highway of Death" reference was two decades out of date, unless you'd been there. In which case it was the touchstone for all the carnage you'd see for the rest of your life.

He snorted. "Desert *Shield*, mostly." He tapped his chest. "Mechanic. Stayed on base. We just came through and picked up some of the pieces afterward. You?"

"Infantry," I said. "Same story, pretty much. Most of them were either dead or surrendering."

We were just two buddies chatting on the roadside, a little friendly conversation with nothing better to do. The siren was audible now, coming up from Santa Monica. He pointed down at the dead man on the pavement.

"*This* shit, though? Bike versus car? High speed? It's fucking *brutal*. Couple weeks ago? I get a call, first on scene, trying to take stock. I check out the car, fender's smashed to hell, except there's this big piece of like white plastic or something sticking straight out of the grille. Looked like one of those whales, you know? The ones with the horn? Motorcycle's twenty feet away, all in pieces, and I'm thinking, what is that, like some sort of fairing or something? So I go and look at it, man, it's a fucking *femur*." He held out his hands, a yard apart. "Clean and white, man, like the fucker had been *washed*, you know?"

The sirens were getting louder. Larisse turned and looked southbound toward the sound. I risked a glance back northbound at the BMW. There was no one visible on the street. The car's dome light wasn't on. I didn't know if the car had to be powered up to get the download. If so, I assumed our guy would be smart enough to dim the dome light.

Larisse wanted to finish his story before the paramedics arrived. "So I look for the rider, right? And he's, like, a hundred feet down the road, DOA, and his leg's just gone. I mean just *gone*. And the MEs say they want the femur, so I go to pull it out. And it's in there so tight I couldn't budge it. We had to cut the grille off to get it out. Snapped off to a point, man, like a fucking *spear*."

He shook his head. "I told my wife about that one, she made me promise to stop riding."

I smiled. "Did you?"

"Hell, yeah. I got four years, maybe five left. Take the sergeant's exam next year, get out at 80 percent? Shit, I sold my bike that *week*."

"Sorry," I said.

He shrugged. "Nah, it's all right. I got things I want to do. Might as well be alive to do 'em, right?"

I nodded. Thirty seconds more, maybe.

"I was NYPD for a while, after the service," I said. "We have a stretch of road like this. The West Side Highway. Runs up along the Hudson, all the way up the West Side. Guys went crazy out there on bikes. The little rice rockets, you know? Ninjas? Hit 12,000 rpm like nothing, guys out there pulling wheelies at 90. When I was on patrol, we used to pick up body parts off the shoulder seems like every couple shifts."

That was mostly true. Except that I hadn't done much of it myself. I got pulled off patrol two years in, when my captain figured out that I had a talent for the informal side of law enforcement. The off-the-books side. And after that, I put more bodies on the pavement than I picked up. That was a long time ago. But my fists still ached to punch a shark.

The ambulance came into view now, slowing to clear Larisse's cruiser. He held up his flashlight and waved it over. I decided to get out of the way.

"Hey, so give me a call," I said. "I assume they let you guys do outside work? Film set escorts, that sort of thing?"

We both knew the answer. They did and he wanted in. And he knew the right response.

"I believe they do," he said, "and, you know, give me a call if you need anything." He gave me his cell number, and I wrote it in my book. We shook hands and I turned back through the fog toward the Pacific Lounge. I didn't look at the BMW until I was back at the parking lot entrance gate. Then I turned and didn't see anyone. I heard more sirens, coming from the north this time.

I pulled out my phone and called Jarron.

"Is our guy all done?"

"He's clear," said Jarron. "Anything happening yet?"

"Slow response," I said. "Ambulance just got here. No CHP or Sheriff's backup yet. Victim's DOA." I gave him the dead man's info. "Looks to be a wannabe, maybe. Not a one-percenter"—the term meaning for bikers pretty much what it meant in politics, but with wealth measured in bad behavior rather than dollars.

"Check," said Jarron. If the biker had a record, we'd know it before the police would.

"Got a blood sample, too," I said. "Wager on the results?"

Jarron thought about it. "One bottle, whiskey or scotch, honor code as to quality, within reason?"

"Deal."

"Okay, call it."

"Easy," I said. "White male, thirtyish, skid lid, cut, and Harley. High speed, late hour. No credit cards. Meth."

"Yeah, too easy," he said. "Tats?"

"None visible."

"Okay. Tell you what, I still want my bottle. I'll go with meth plus cannabinoids."

The sirens from the north were loud now, and more were coming up from Santa Monica. I looked up at the moon, barely visible now through the thickening fog. Then I turned and walked back across the gravel toward Paul Mayo, sitting shivering on the velvet valet bench, stone sober, and sobering up more with each passing minute.

www.ingramcontent.com/pod-product-compliance
Lightning Source LLC
Chambersburg PA
CBHW071511260626
47170CB00002B/334